SYDNEY ASHCROFT
DANI NICHOLS

IMMORTAL
SECRETS

IMMORTAL SECRETS

SYDNEY ASHCROFT
DANI NICHOLS

CITY OWL
PRESS

IMMORTAL SECRETS

CITY OWL PRESS
www.cityowlpress.com

Cover Design by MiblArt. All stock photos licensed appropriately.

Edited by Danielle DeVor.

For information on subsidiary rights, please contact the publisher at info@cityowlpress.com.

Print Edition ISBN: 978-1-64898-440-2

Digital Edition ISBN: 978-1-64898-439-6

Printed in the United States of America

To all the curious people out there.

CHAPTER ONE

JOANNA SHEPARD STOOD IN THE LIVING ROOM OF HER childhood home and looked around. Her stomach twisted into knots at the sight of the various boxes sitting around the otherwise empty room. She hadn't been here since her parents' funeral a few months ago and at the time never thought about what would happen to the house. While she would never live here again, it was still supposed to be home.

She had been living in Boulder, Colorado, since starting undergrad at the University of Colorado Boulder over four years ago. Once she graduated, she decided to stay in Boulder. If she could have avoided coming home to Maine, she would have moved heaven and hell. She told herself that if she didn't, somehow her life would reset, and she would find her parents alive. Now she had no more excuses. As executor of her parents' estate, Alex had handled the legal issues regarding life insurance, readying the house for sale, and guardianship of her younger brother, Ben. They would have been lost without her.

Alex Thorne, their family friend and honorary aunt, kept in contact with her and her twin brother, Mike, about every step and decision she made, but she wouldn't go through their rooms.

Somehow Jo hoped no one would want the house, but then a buyer was lined up and ready to pay a fair price. Now they had to come home and get the remainder of their possessions, and anything else they wanted before the final renovations were made. Then the sale.

Ben, in the last few weeks of high school, had already taken care of his room. Alex and Ben had packed and stored most of their parents' things, with the idea that the three of them would go through them when they felt ready. Furniture and housewares were in storage, along with most of their possessions. There were a few boxes of personal things Alex would put in her attic for safekeeping once they'd gotten them all. She told Jo she didn't like the idea of irreplaceable photo albums, letters, and jewelry in a place where anything could happen. They could replace a couch or a set of dishes. They would feel the loss of pictures and journals.

Jo thanked the heavens for Alex. She couldn't imagine doing all that needed to be done while dealing with the overwhelming grief of losing her parents. She had spoken to her mother that fateful morning, never expecting it to be the last conversation she would have with her.

Ben seemed the most stable of the three when it came to dealing with the accident and aftermath, even though Jo had witnessed his sudden silences and furtive wiping of tears from his eyes. He'd lived with Alex for the last three months. His support system had been a physical presence. For Jo and Mike, it had been long distance.

Tears welled up in her eyes, and she furiously wiped them away. Three months later, it still hurt as it had the night Alex called her, informing Jo of her parents' deaths. The memory still made her sick.

She rubbed the bridge of her nose and took a deep breath. She tried not to see the room as she had known it. Tried not to mentally place all the pictures her mother had of the family hanging on the walls. Grief cut deeper into her heart. It had been a good life, a wonderful life to grow up in. She never imagined she would have to live without her parents at the age of twenty-three.

"Jo." Ben entered the living room with a box in his arms. "I think this is all Mom's pictures. She had so many, I don't think we've found them all. Do you want to go through it with me later?"

The word "No" wouldn't form on her lips or get past the lump in her throat. She shook her head and looked at Ben through tear-filled eyes.

She'd swear he was taller than the last time she had been home, which had been for the funeral. His hair was longer and hanging down into his eyes. Apparently he had been hitting the gym too. If she remembered correctly, he was going to the University of Maine on a football scholarship. Right now, it was hard to think about anything.

He set it on top of a stack of boxes near the door. "I'll go through it first. You and Mike can do it later. I think I saw Mike heading into your room."

Jo offered her younger brother a weak smile. Leave it to him to give her the nudge she needed to move. Otherwise, she would have been rooted in place forever. Ben smiled back. He looked so much like their dad.

Jo took a step, her feet feeling like lead, and then another. Ben gave her a small push to get her momentum going. She snorted a bit, sounding dreadful through the tears. She turned her head to say something, but Ben had moved off again.

She somehow made it to the doorway of her old room. Mike wasn't in there, but she could hear him moving about in the room next to hers. She took a deep breath and stepped inside.

Memories rushed back, and she struggled not to be swept under the wave. She put a hand on her old desk to steady herself. Footsteps behind her forced her to straighten up and regain her composure. She didn't want Mike to see her break. She turned to see Alex standing in the doorway.

Alex wasn't family by blood, but she was family in every other sense. She had been a constant in their lives, knowing Jo's parents since college, or so they had said. The woman was godmother and aunt to all three of them and had been there for every major milestone. Jo, Mike, and Ben would have never gotten through the past few months without Alex. Alex called Jo daily to check on her since Jo returned to Boulder after the funeral. She probably did the same for Mike. Some days Jo dreaded the daily call. Some days she feared Alex would forget.

As always, Alex's long, dark hair was perfect, and the makeup she wore was subtle. Alex wore jeans and a T-shirt instead of the flowing dresses she usually favored. She looked at Jo, and it seemed like those gray eyes felt everything Jo did in her soul.

"Need some help?" Alex asked.

At first Jo shook her head, but then she nodded. Alex stepped into the room and wrapped her arms around Jo. Jo clung to Alex and buried her face in Alex's shoulder. Tears weren't far behind. All she needed was a little help to keep moving. How was Alex so strong? She could use some of that strength.

At some point, the tears stopped, but the strength of Alex's embrace never lessened. Alex's heart beat in her ear, and in a way, it helped comfort Jo. She dropped her arms, and only then did Alex release her.

Jo wiped her eyes, and Alex brushed a lock of Jo's hair out of Jo's face. No words were exchanged. The need didn't exist. Instead, Alex kissed Jo's forehead and picked up a box from the floor next to her. She placed it on the bed and began removing books, most of which Alex had given Jo, from the bookshelves and placing them in the box.

Jo took a few deep breaths to orient herself. Once some of her composure came back, she opened a dresser drawer. She removed a stack of clothes and placed them on the bed. The two women worked in silence while they emptied shelves and drawers. Alex carried filled boxes out to the living room and returned with empty ones.

"Hey, Ms. Thorne." Jo turned to see Greg Sullivan standing in the doorway. She forced a small smile.

"Hello, Greg. I'm glad you could make it."

"I'm sorry I'm late." Greg smiled at her. "Hey, Jo."

"That's fine, Greg," Alex said. "I appreciate your offer to help."

Jo vaguely remembered seeing Greg at the funeral, but she had gone through most of the day in a haze and couldn't remember who she saw or spoke to. Greg had to have been there. He and Mike had been best friends since junior year of high school when Greg and his family moved to Good Harbor and opened a restaurant. Mike returned to Good Harbor for summer breaks, but Joanna had always remained in Boulder. It was another regret she carried with her. All that time she could have spent with her family.

"Hey, Greg," she croaked. Great, she sounded like a frog. She cleared her throat. "Hi."

Greg had changed since she first met him. He'd been cute then. He now had to be around six foot three and filled out to match the height. His dark hair was long enough to have some curls and was kind of tousled. She rather liked it.

"Did I hear Greg?" Mike's voice floated from the room next door. The next moment, Mike materialized in the doorway next to Greg. Jo realized how much taller Greg had become as he hugged her brother. Mike and Greg had always been around the same height, but now Greg had about five inches, maybe six, on Mike.

Mike's dirty blond hair was a mess, and it looked like he found the oldest shirt and jeans he owned to work around the house. His pale skin, the product of hours spent gaming and avoiding sunlight, showed the red splotches where he'd continually wiped his "I'm not crying, you're crying" eyes. Mike's coloring echoed their mother, while Jo's and Ben's dark hair and high cheekbones favored their father in looks.

"Hey, man." Mike released Greg. "Good to see you. What are you doing here?"

"Good to see you, Mike. Ms. Thorne said you might need an extra hand to move boxes. I said yes because she may have mentioned you and Jo would be here, and it's been a while since we got together. Seemed like a great time to talk while being useful."

"Well, she didn't tell us." Jo glanced over at Alex, and the woman had a slightly self-satisfied look on her face. Surprises and Jo never went well together, but she was glad Mike had a good friend to help with the task.

"All we need now is Carrie."

"She will be joining us for dinner at the house," Alex said. "Greg, you are more than welcome to join us, provided you do not have to work."

"Thanks, Ms. Thorne. I'd really like that. Dad gave me the night off as long as I show up in the morning to start the bread dough."

The thought of seeing Carrie helped lift some of the ever-present grief and help unwind Jo's stomach a bit. The two had a lot to catch up on, and it would help Jo not think about emptying out her childhood home for a few hours. Opportunities to think about something else were far and few in between.

"Why isn't Carrie here?" she asked. "It's not like her to miss out."

"She's minding the store. Work needs to be done here first. Then you can all catch up over dinner." Alex handed a box of books to Greg. "You can even have a house party if you like."

"Of course, Ms. Thorne." Greg stepped inside the room and accepted the box.

"The boxes in the living room can go in the back of my truck. The rest of the boxes will go into the rental truck."

"Yes, Ms. Thorne." Greg turned and slipped past Mike and out into the hallway. But not before Jo had a second to notice Greg's backside. Some men were meant to wear denim. She had definitely missed out on visits over her college years.

"Mike, your room," Alex said, reminding him of the task at hand.

Mike nodded and disappeared out of the doorway.

Jo scanned her old room. The bare walls looked strange. Jo couldn't remember a time before when they had been bare. She used to have posters all over the room, along with pictures she had taken. Alex had probably removed them and packed them safely away.

Her room and Mike's room were the only rooms that had remained the colors Jo remembered. She remembered when she had asked her parents if she could have her room painted. She must have been around ten or so. Mike heard her ask and wanted his room painted too. He picked a dark gray while Jo had picked a jewel-toned purple.

The other parts of the house Alex had cleaned out had been repainted, all the same light shade of gray. Some of the carpets had been cleaned, while the others had been replaced. Alex had taken care of it all. She imagined Alex already arranged for the remaining work. At least Jo didn't have to deal with those things.

"I'm going to go help Greg with those boxes and see what Ben has gotten into. Do you need any help now?"

"I don't think so." Jo sat on the edge of the bare mattress and savored the relative silence when Alex left the room. The sounds of Mike moving around in his room drifted through the wall. Jo didn't envy her brother. Mike shared the habit of never throwing anything out with their mother. Jo took after their father and had always been organized and didn't like clutter. They kept the things that were important and managed to let go of anything that wasn't. Ben landed somewhere in the middle of keeping things and letting things go.

Now it was time to let go of one of the major things tying the three of them to their past. They would never physically return to the house, but their memories would always take them back when they wanted to be here. Jo took a deep breath and slowly let it out. Inside, a part of her wanted to refuse and hang on, but logically she knew neither she, Mike, nor Ben could afford to keep the house at this point in their lives. Their parents wouldn't have wanted them to be stubborn about keeping it. She sighed and continued packing up her belongings.

Jo felt a million times better when Carrie walked in the back door of Alex's old Victorian and wrapped Jo in a bear hug. Jo held on to her best friend for what seemed like ages. Carrie held on just as tightly. Eventually they released each other.

"Hi!" Carrie grinned the biggest grin Jo had seen. Carrie's reddish-brown hair was a little longer than it had been at the funeral. Carrie wore the same style of black-rimmed glasses as she had worn in high school, her brown eyes sparkling with excitement. "I'm so happy to see you! When Ms. Thorne told me you were coming back for a few days, she was nice enough to invite me over for dinner. Thankfully I have a really short way to go."

"What do you mean?" Joanna tilted her head.

"I'm renting the apartment above the store. Makes getting to work so much easier."

"Really? That's incredible. She never rented it before."

"Yes! She took pity on me and rented it out to me at a really reasonable rate." Carrie danced a happy shuffle. "I think she did it because she was tired of hearing me complaining about still living with my parents and the kids still at home, or how I didn't have space or quiet to study. Or me moaning that I had to keep asking Mom for rides to work. I'm working in the store until I can find a full-time position at one of the nearby schools, and she lets me borrow her truck sometimes."

Jo was thankful she only had Mike and Ben to deal with, even if they were annoying. Carrie had three sisters and a brother, all of whom were younger. The second oldest after

Carrie was Ben's age. Jo sympathized a lot with Carrie's situation.

After high school, Carrie stayed in the state and went to U Maine at Orono and completed an education degree with the hope of teaching history. Last Christmas Carrie mentioned the idea of going for her master's. Jo surprised herself by remembering that much.

Carrie wanted her master's. Greg worked for his parents at their restaurant and had earned a business degree at the local community college. Mike had a degree in computer science and learned about video game design. He had a job waiting for him as soon as he was ready. Ben was bound for UMaine in Orono in the fall. Jo completed a degree in journalism but had no idea what she would do now. She didn't have a plan the way the others did. It made her feel a little disconnected and unsure, but she'd figure out what she wanted to do with her life sooner or later.

Jo had forgotten all about the apartment over the carriage house shop until Carrie mentioned it. It would have been the perfect place to stay while they were handling all the details necessary to get the house sold. Still, it was ideal for Carrie, and that made her happy, if somewhat a little envious.

"I'm glad. You're in the right place."

Carrie smacked her own forehead. "What's wrong with me? You could stay there with me if you want. It has two bedrooms. Plenty of privacy unless Munchkin wants in, and he doesn't talk about what he sees."

Jo smiled through the threat of more tears. The people in her life were so good to her, and she didn't feel that she lived up to that standard as often as she should. "That'd be great, if you're really okay with it and Alex doesn't mind. I don't know how long Ben and Mike would live if I had to stay in the house with them."

"Hey now, we're not that bad," Mike called from the kitchen.

"Yes, you are!" Jo yelled back. "C'mon." She hooked an arm through Carrie's. "We have pizza, and we're planning on watching some movies. Alex bought dinner tonight instead of cooking. It's been a long day."

"I bet. That's another perk of living so close. She takes pity on me and lets me raid her fridge. She even brought meals to me when I was deep in studying for finals. She always says she cooked too much, but she's just nice enough to not let me starve."

Jo chuckled. That sounded like Alex. There had been many times Alex brought meals for her family over to the house. Usually Jo, Mike, and Ben's favorites. Alex's homemade bread was to die for.

They entered the kitchen where Mike and Greg sat eating pizza from a local place. Local in the sense that it was in the town of Good Harbor, still twenty minutes away from the house. Delivery wasn't even an option. She often thought a delivery service in Good Harbor during the tourist season would make a lot of money in the summer months alone. It was another reason Jo loved Boulder with its delivery options and availability of all kinds of ethnic foods.

The kitchen was a cook's dream. The house might have been built in the 1800s, but the kitchen was as modern as any house recently built. Alex had spared no expense in renovating the space, including black stainless-steel appliances, while still managing to make it feel warm and cozy. The countertops were dark granite and set off the white cabinets. The island in the middle of the kitchen had an eating bar and space for food preparation. The breakfast nook was large enough to seat an unruly family of six, yet cozy enough for one or two people to enjoy a meal. Like the rest of the house, the kitchen was spotless.

The antique table in the formal dining room could expand to seat eighteen people, but it was seldom used. Alex wasn't the hostess with the mostess when it came to entertaining groups, but small gatherings of friends and family were always well fed and entertained. Jo had always wondered why she didn't have more people in her life.

"We have meat lovers, pepperoni, and sausage and peppers," Greg announced. "Provided Mike hasn't eaten all the meat lovers by now."

Her brothers could eat an entire large pizza each, and it caused Jo's stomach to hurt just watching them. She always wondered where they put all the food. When she asked, they always replied that they were growing boys and needed as much food as they could get. Mike had five inches on Jo, standing at five foot ten to her petite five foot five. Ben was a different story. Ben had cleared six feet two years ago and had managed to grow another two inches.

"I didn't eat it all," Mike vowed. "But now I will."

"Like hell you will." Jo snatched a slice of meat lovers from the box.

"Hey!" he protested.

A bang at the back door halted what might have been the first cross words they exchanged in an emotional day. Mike's protest turned to a lopsided smile as he disappeared from the room. A moment later, a huge dog entered the kitchen and stopped all talk. Each one of them had to greet Munchkin as he made his way around the room to sniff everyone's shoes and get their adoring ear scratches and pets. To call the giant Caucasian Shepherd Munchkin had to have been a joke at one point, but Alex never told them how she'd come by the dog or why she named him something so tongue-in-cheek.

He settled down at Mike's feet and rested a huge paw on his foot. It was his subtle reminder that he, too, wanted his dinner.

Carrie selected a slice of sausage and peppers and sat in one of the empty chairs at the breakfast nook.

"Drink?" Jo asked Carrie.

"Water, please. Thank you."

"Certainly." Jo took glasses from the cabinet and filled them from the water dispenser in the fridge. She placed one in front of Carrie and one in front of her own plate.

"Are we going to do anything tonight?" Mike covered his mouth between bites so he could talk without spitting food at them. "Besides the movies."

"I just want to take it easy," Jo said. "I'm wiped after today."

"A movie night upstairs?" Greg smiled at her, and she swore her knees went a little weak. He had definitely gotten cuter in the last four years. "That brings back memories."

Alex's Victorian had three floors, and one of the bedrooms on the top floor had been turned into a gaming room for Ben. He slept in the bedroom next to it. It gave him the privacy a teenage boy needed. With him at a friend's house tonight, the giant—and only—television in the house was available for use.

"That sounds like fun," Carrie said.

"Yeah, we can do that."

"We are taking turns picking movies," Jo warned. She knew her brother. If left to his own devices, they would be watching movies with explosions and bullets all night. While Jo didn't mind them, she accepted the fact that other types of movies existed.

"Fine." Mike shot her a death glare with no heat or force behind it.

Jo laughed. Thwarting one's brother was never a bad thing in her book, and it had been some time since she had the opportunity to do it.

"When was the last time we were all together like this?" Carrie asked. "It feels like it's been ages."

"I'd say winter break. When Jo came home for a week, but Greg missed all those because he had to work."

"Oh yeah," Carrie said. "It still feels like forever."

Jo's chest tightened up. It had been the last time she had seen her parents alive. She swallowed past the lump in her throat and tried to force her stomach to unwind.

"Jo, you okay?" Carrie put a hand on her arm.

"I'm fine," she automatically answered. It was the same answer she gave whenever anyone asked her how she was doing. More so lately. She'd reached her limit of having folks ask about her current state.

Carrie lowered her chin and looked over the rim of her glasses. Of course Carrie didn't believe Jo; she knew Jo too well. The best friends curse. Other people would accept Jo's answer, but not Carrie.

Jo waved her hand. She would. Eventually. With a lot of time.

"You know I'm always here to talk if you want to, right?"

Jo leaned over and squeezed Carrie's arm. "Yeah, I know, and I appreciate it."

Carrie smiled in return. "Good."

"Let's go watch some movies," Mike suggested.

"We need to clean up first." Greg picked up Mike's plate and his own. "How about Jo and I clean up while Mike, you and Carrie gather some snacks and drinks and take them up?"

"Sounds like a plan." Carrie went to the fridge for canned drinks. Munchkin hurried to follow the food when Mike left the room with the pizza.

Greg stacked the plates while Jo gathered the dirty napkins. She stuffed them in the compost bin and then collected the glasses. Greg had already started washing the plates.

Jo set the glasses on the counter next to the sink, and Greg turned and offered her a smile. "Thanks."

"Welcome. Thanks for washing. I hate washing dishes."

"I remember. I'm used to it. I wash dishes at the restaurant when we're running short staffed. Can't believe Ms. Thorne still doesn't use the dishwasher."

"I thought you'd be expediting by now. Like a polite Gordon Ramsay," Jo said.

"You honestly think Dad would let me polite him into hurrying a dish to a table? I like cleaning more than cooking. I can cook and do when we're that busy. I just prefer not to. Especially during tourist season."

"I can imagine." Jo grabbed a dish towel to start drying the dishes. Even though Alex had a dishwasher, four plates and four glasses weren't enough to run it. If she'd had paper plates in the house, they would have used those instead.

"It gets brutal," Greg continued. "We get a few customers from hell every week, and I can stay out of the line of fire. Not to mention cleaning means I don't have to remake dishes."

"Your dad is too nice. He doesn't have to put up with that crap. No way is a bad review from a jerk customer going to affect his business. He's too good, and Good Harbor adores him."

"It's better that he doesn't snap back. He can get hairy when he loses his temper. I'm better at the behind-the-scenes work. I like getting up at 3:00 a.m. to start the dough and get the sauces going for the day. I even made the bread dough for tonight's service before I left to help out at your house."

"I'll have to stop there for lunch one day."

"The family would love to see you. How's Boulder?" he asked, handing a plate to Jo.

"Still awesome." She accepted the plate. "Great food, always something going on, and the people are nice. I love the mountain air, but I miss the ocean, though."

Greg nodded. "Sounds like it really agrees with you. All but the no ocean part, of course. I understand missing it. I've only been in Good Harbor for six years, but the ocean draws you in, and Good Harbor makes you a part of it."

"Yeah," Jo agreed.

"How long are you going to be in town?"

It was a curious question for sure. Jo wondered why he asked it. He had never asked before during her visits.

"A week or two, I think. Mike, Ben, and I are going to start sorting through the boxes we packed today and the stuff in storage. See who wants what, and what can be sold or donated. Alex has offered to handle any sales for us."

Greg nodded and handed her another washed plate. He looked around for a second to see if the other two were paying attention and turned back to her. "Would you be interested in grabbing some ice cream with me?" he asked in a low voice.

Jo paused in the act of taking the plate. Did Greg just ask her out? It sure sounded that way. Her mind raced for an answer. An acceptable answer. He was her brother's best friend, and that alone could make it uncomfortable. But Greg was seriously one of the nicest guys she had ever met. He never said anything disparaging about anyone and always helped when he could. Not to mention he had grown hotter as he had gotten older. When Jo first met him, he had been tall and skinny. But in the past few years he had muscled out, and Jo rather liked it. An ice cream date would be just the thing to take her mind off her troubles for a while.

The plate slipped a bit. How old was she anyway? He was not the first guy to ask her out. She grabbed at it before it could crash to the floor.

"It's okay to say no." Greg chuckled, and Jo felt a shiver down her back. "I mean, it could be weird seeing how I'm Mike's best friend."

"No, it's fine. What I should have said immediately was I'd love to get some ice cream with you."

Greg smiled, and Jo loved the dimples that came along with the smile. "Great. I'll let you know when. Sometimes it can be hard getting some time away from the restaurant."

"I understand. Like I said, I should be around for a week or two, and you have my number. You do have my number, right?"

"Unless it's changed from high school, I still have your number. It's a plan then."

"It's a plan," she repeated.

They both froze when they heard a knock from the front door. Munchkin's bark from above carried through the house, followed by the thunder of four paws down the stairs. "I wonder who that could be. Alex usually doesn't get a lot of visitors." Or maybe she now did. Jo hadn't been around much in the past four years. Maybe she was dating, and it hadn't come up yet.

Greg shrugged. "Don't look at me. I don't know."

Jo dried and put away the last glass. She tossed the towel aside. "Come on. There are movies to be watched. After we see who's at the door."

CHAPTER TWO

ALEX YAWNED AND RUBBED HER EYES. THE NUMBERS ON her computer screen blurred together. Maybe it was time for a break. Today had been a long day of packing boxes and carrying them out of Thomas and Claire's house. Then they had to carry those boxes into her house. Some went directly to the storage unit she'd rented specifically for the purpose. It wasn't just the physical activities today. The emotional ones were tiring as well.

After all that, Carrie arrived, and the four friends converged on the kitchen to eat pizza and catch up. Even Munchkin, her Caucasian Shepard, elected to stay in the kitchen near the four in anticipation of being fed crusts. The dog enjoyed having other people he loved in the house. Greater opportunity to beg for food existed with others. Alex retreated to her office to give the four young adults some space.

Alex didn't mind in the least. Jo and Mike needed a break from dealing with the grief of losing their parents. Ben opted to go to a friend's house for the night. She didn't worry about him as much as she worried about Mike and Jo. The twins came home for the funeral, but then returned to school. While still a difficult time, they weren't in Good Harbor and so close to the memories of their parents. Now that they were here, the sharp edge of memories reopened the wounds caused by the deaths of their parents.

Alex's chest tightened at the thought of Thomas and Claire. The two had been dear friends for almost thirty years, and they knew what Alex really was. She didn't have to pretend around them, and they became family. Something that had been missing in her life for a long time.

She couldn't die by normal means, but she had to watch others around her die. Some lived to die of natural causes, and others like Thomas and Claire—were ripped from her in the blink of an eye. Anger coursed through her, and a moment later grief took take its place. She had lost so many loved ones in her long life, and she should have had a few more decades with Thomas and Claire.

She leaned back in the executive-style leather office chair and struggled to get her wild emotions under control. Alex looked around the office, letting the space calm her. The dark wood bookshelves were lined with books, some centuries old, and heavy, dark drapes covered the windows. The calm, quiet environment spoke to her soul and love of learning, calming her turbulent emotions.

Her personal cell phone beeped, signaling she had a text message. She eyed the infernal device warily where it lay on the large mahogany desk. Not many possessed her personal number, and she immediately went from tired to on guard in the span of a few heartbeats. Alex took a deep breath and picked up the cell. She looked at the display. A text from Bob Wharton had arrived.

She unlocked the phone and read the full text. One of her agents sent a text saying he thought he was being followed. This didn't bode well at all. Bob Wharton was an academic, a researcher with little care for drama. He gathered information for her and passed it along. Many of her agents were in academia, which was useful in her line of work. They were not espionage agents, and they should have been beneath anyone's notice.

If Bob thought something was off enough to text her about it, it was cause for concern. Anyone that knew the man worked for her might gamble on her coming to his aid if necessary. She always took care of her agents. That care was generally in the form of monetary compensation and academic items of their field of study. Occasionally a pension of sorts from a special trust was provided.

She opened the list of contacts and selected Bob's name, initiating a call. She pressed the phone to her ear and waited for Bob to pick up. After six rings, his voice came through the line and Alex frowned. Voice mail.

"Bob, it's me. Please contact me as soon as possible." She didn't elaborate or say anything else before hanging up. Alex distrusted phones and had since they were invented. She always remained mindful when using them.

She stared at the computer screen with her cell phone clutched in her hands, mulling over what his non answer could mean moments after his text.

She frowned and brought up her contacts again. She selected another number. It picked up on the first ring.

"Hello," a male voice answered the line. It was calm and even, and some of the tension in her neck and shoulders lessened a bit.

"Paladin, I'm glad I caught you."

Paladin, otherwise known as Jack Kirby, was another of Alex's employees and had become the most reliable agent for her for the past five years. Others worked for her, but he knew what she was and didn't care. More importantly, he didn't talk. Jack had taken the additional step of training at the Supernatural Police Department academy after his early retirement from the Philadelphia police force. He collected information from her other agents, filtered it, and sent it along to her. He also acted as a courier on occasion, bringing rare and valuable items to Alex. His father, Michael, had been one of her agents before Jack.

His tone lightened. "Hey, Boss Lady."

She smiled. "I'm sorry to bother you, but I would like you to check on Bob Wharton for me."

"Is something wrong? Is he in trouble?"

"I don't know," Alex admitted. She hated not knowing, especially when it came to the personal safety of her employees. "That's what concerns me. He texted me that he thought someone was following him, but I haven't been able to reach him. Would you please check on him?"

Silence echoed through the line for a few long seconds. "Sure. Where is he again?"

"Seattle. I'll text you his address and take care of the plane ticket. It'll be waiting for you at check-in."

"Boss, what's going on? What am I looking for?"

Alex paused, not sure how much she should say. Hell, she didn't know what she could say. A gut feeling wasn't a lot to go on, but her instincts had guided her well over her long life. She didn't have a good reason to start ignoring them now. "Call it a precaution. It may be nothing, but I want to be sure."

"I understand."

"Thank you, Jack."

Another moment of silence, and Alex guessed he was surprised she called him by his real name. It eased some of the apprehension developing inside her. "You're welcome, Alex."

Jack calling her Alex was almost as strange as her calling him Jack. She smiled. "Take care and stay safe. Victoria would never forgive me if something happened to you. You know how long she can hold a grudge."

A light chuckle echoed through the connection. "I will. Are you okay?"

"I'm holding my own."

"Dare I ask?"

Alex could hear in the concern in Jack's voice. He might have been her employee, but over the years, they had become friends and genuinely cared about each other. Not to mention he was involved with one of her closest friends.

"The kids are here, and we're dealing with cleaning out their house. It's a trying time for all, and it's the reason I can't check on Bob myself." Without Mike and Jo in town, she would have parked Ben with a school friend and already been on her way out the door to the airport. She had to keep her cover story in place. Giving three grieving people desperate for anything else to focus on another story to think about was not the best idea.

"I bet. If there's anything you need, call me."

"I will. Jack, be careful."

"I will, Boss."

- "Cheeky kid." Alex disconnected the line. Voices of the four in the kitchen drifted into the office, and Alex smiled. Relief washed over her when she heard laughter. It was muted and reluctant, but it was there. Life would move on for them, but she knew from experience that the deep wounds of losing someone would never go away. She still mourned friends and loved ones she lost centuries ago.

She closed the laptop and turned in the chair to look at the shelves under the window. Photo albums beckoned her. She stood and lovingly ran her fingers along the leather spines of the thick albums. Photos going back half a century filled ten albums. Older photos were safely stored elsewhere. Alex removed a red leather one, the last in the line.

She lowered herself into the desk chair and placed the album on the desk. She flipped it open. All the photos contained within were taken in the mid-nineties when she returned to this house on the Maine coast. Had it really been twenty-five years already? It seemed like yesterday when she reunited with Thomas Shepard and met Claire Smith.

The three became fast friends, and nothing made Alex happier than when Thomas and Claire married. Alex helped Claire plan the wedding and even stood as maid of honor. Alex had been there when all three kids had been born and helped Claire adjust to motherhood. Alex remembered how tired and stressed she had been after childbirth and did everything she could to help them through the rough days of having twin infants in the house, and again when Ben was born.

As the kids grew, Aunt Alex was frequently around and was the go-to babysitter. Holidays were always shared and alternated between the two houses. Thomas and Claire's family was her family, and now her family had been ripped apart by a car accident.

Thomas and Claire both knew her secret and had never broken the trust Alex placed in them. The kids didn't know Alex was immortal. Thomas and Claire had been the first mortals in a long time to know what she was, and they had taken her secret to an early grave.

Her stomach twisted when she thought about the fateful telephone call informing her of their deaths. Alex slowly paged through the album and smiled at the photos. Time flowed unnoticed as she lost herself in memories.

A knock at the door dragged her out of the past and back into the present. She glanced at her watch. Who would stop by at nine in the evening without calling first? Another knock came, this one sounding more insistent. Munchkin barked from upstairs, and Alex rose from her chair. She met the dog at the library door and looked down at him. All four of the young people were waiting behind him. Lovely, an audience.

"What do you think?"

Munchkin sniffed at the crack between the door and the frame, and a low growl slipped from him.

The locals visited frequently, but they always texted or called on her business cell phone before coming over. Customers sometimes showed up unexpectedly at her house instead of the store and annoyed the hell out of her by doing so, but never in the evening. With Bob's strange text still fresh, she didn't have a good feeling about the visitor. Munchkin didn't seem to either. She fondly patted the large head. Alex wasn't armed to deal with any threat, but the dog was all the protection she needed. She trusted him and his instincts. He had been a faithful companion for the past seven hundred years and had protected her well.

Munchkin growled again when another knock rang out. Alex sighed and opened the door.

Son of a bitch.

"Gods be damned." Alex straightened up to meet the threat standing outside the door. "What are you doing here?" Alex asked as she stared at the man standing on her front porch. She wanted to slam the door in his face and pretend she never saw him. Or better yet, wipe that smirk off his face and then slam the door in it. Next to her, Munchkin growled.

Seven billion people on this planet, and Damianos had to be the one to show up. Of course he was. The universe enjoyed playing jokes on her, and Alex never found any of them funny. Ever. Especially when they involved Damianos. She wondered what deity she managed to piss off to deserve this.

Yet at the same time her heart skipped a beat at the sight of him. His dark hair was longer than the usual military cut he favored, and his dark eyes looked into her soul. The breath stayed in her chest as her eyes traveled the length of his body. His broad chest and arms were more defined than they had been the last time she saw him.

"Alex, do you know him?" Mike stood behind her. She could almost smell the protective male instinct.

"Unfortunately, yes," she answered, still glaring at the man who'd caused her so much trouble and heartache through her long life.

"Hello to you too." Damianos's smile grew to encompass the small group. "Always a pleasure...Alex."

"I wish I could say the same," Alex snapped and instantly regretted doing so. Damn him. He was a complication she didn't want, and she certainly didn't need the kids to get curious about him. Damianos practiced weaponized honesty when it suited him, and he was maliciously honest when someone was too persistent with their questions. She placed a hand on Munchkin's head, quieting the dog's growls. Her first reaction would be enough to make anyone curious.

"Are you going to invite me in?" he asked, the smirk still on his face.

"No."

He laughed, and the urge to hit him grew. "I have missed you more than you'll ever know."

"I haven't missed you," she shot back. "Not even a bit."

He laughed again, irritating the last nerve she had left.

"What do you want?"

"We need to talk."

"No, we don't."

"Yes, we do. Now. It's important."

His forceful tone caused her to bite back the words waiting to be unleashed She looked him in the eyes, and the smirk she hated so much vanished. Dammit. Something was going on, and she knew she wouldn't like it. Damianos wouldn't show up out of nowhere to annoy her. Well, he would, but based on his stern expression, she knew this was something more than a social call.

Shit.

She sighed heavily and stepped back out of the doorway and into Mike's solid presence behind her. Greg was just to her right, already exuding an unaccustomed menace. Trust young men to react to her attitude and come to her aid when she needed none. She turned to catch their eyes and nodded to let them know it was all right. Not that there was no danger. Damianos would always be dangerous. She didn't need him facing off with the two young men. Munchkin wouldn't be able to stop himself from attacking if that happened. Someone could die, and it wouldn't be Damianos.

She turned back to her unwelcome visitor. "You can enter if you can behave yourself."

He brushed past her and stopped just inside the door. He eyed Munchkin, and the dog stared menacingly up at him. The thought of letting Munchkin bite Damianos crossed her mind for the briefest of moments. Maybe later if he annoyed her enough.

She closed the door. "What are you doing here?"

He ignored her question in true Damianos fashion. "Who are your guests?"

Alex sighed. He'd answer questions when he wanted to, not before. She hated that about him. "This is Joanna and Mike Shepard, Carrie Reynolds, and Greg Sullivan. This is—"

"Stavros Nicademos," he finished for her and extended a hand. He shook each of their hands. "Nice to meet you all."

"Nice to meet you," Carrie said with a bright smile.

Jo, Mike, and Greg echoed her words, albeit with less enthusiasm.

"Is there someplace we can talk?"

Alex looked up at him and motioned to her office door. "In here. If the rest of you will excuse us?"

"Of course," Jo said. "We're going to head upstairs and watch a movie."

"We could hang around," Mike stared at Damianos. "If you need a witness."

Damianos grinned again. "I'm flattered, boy, but she can handle me."

That sounded even worse to Alex's own ears. She closed her eyes and sighed. "Stavros, in my library. You four." She opened her eyes and looked to the stairs. "Go watch your movie, and we'll talk later." She waited until all four moved toward the stairs. Munchkin hesitated before she gestured to him to follow. He went, more for the snacks and the suckers who would fall for his sad look and feed him.

She followed Damianos into the library and closed the door. She wished she could join them and enjoy a movie, but she didn't have a choice.

CHAPTER THREE

"WHAT ARE YOU DOING HERE, DAMIANOS?" ALEX DIDN'T have the energy or the patience to deal with the man. Seventy-one years wasn't enough time. She could have gone another century or two without seeing him.

"Pleasant as always, Akantha. I see you still have that dog."

"Yes, I have that dog." She should have let Munchkin bite him. "What are you doing here, Damianos?" She tried not to put too much of an edge in her voice but failed.

"I missed your beautiful face and sharp tongue." He took a step toward her. She instinctively stepped backward.

"Why are you here?" Energy drained out of her as adrenaline evaporated and exhaustion flooded in its wake.

"I thought we could exchange pleasantries first. You know, like civilized people."

"It's been a long day, and I'm exhausted. This is not a civilized time in my life, and I don't want to go multiple verbal rounds with you. Tell me why you're here, and then I can tell you that I don't need or want you here." Damn him. He used her irritation at his lack of manners to point out her rude greeting.

The bastard laughed, and Alex looked at a point past his

shoulder, not daring to look him in the eye. She hadn't fallen in love with him just once. She fell in love with him every time she saw him, and she hated herself for it. She couldn't afford the distraction of him while she had other responsibilities.

"All business, and it only makes me want you more. Which is why it pains me to tell you that someone is after you, Akantha."

"Who did you hear it from? And it's Alex now." She believed him to a point. She knew he loved her and wouldn't do anything to intentionally harm her, but it was just like him to use something like this as an excuse to be back in her life.

"A source." He stepped toward her again, and she took another step away from him.

"Who is this source? I don't need your protection or your help." He was too close for comfort, and she was running out of space.

"I can't say."

"Then it can't be a reliable one."

"Just because it's not yours doesn't mean it's not reliable. Someone is after you. I would never joke when dealing with your safety or the safety of your children. Had I known you had more children, I would have been here sooner to keep you all safe."

It was such a Damianos thing to say. If there really was danger, which she doubted, she wouldn't hesitate to trust the safety of all in her care to him. In all the centuries they'd both walked the earth, he had never taken her well-being lightly. One would think he cared if he hadn't been such an all-around bastard and more concerned with his own skin. Damianos was a legendary fighter. The young adults in her care were a weakness now if what he said proved to be true.

"They're not my children. Their younger brother is my ward, and he is not here now." Ben had turned eighteen a month ago. Her legal obligations as of his birth date and graduation were now solely focused on the estate. Her heart would always consider the three of them her family. "Their parents were dear friends. They died in a car accident some months ago. This is their home until they decide where to go from here."

"I'm sorry."

Damn him again, he did look apologetic. "I don't want or need your sympathies. I explained so you would know why I have young people in my house, and you are not to disturb them with your tales." The chances of him leaving dwindled away—she saw it in his face. There was something else lingering behind his eyes. She wanted to be left alone, and it was not going to happen if he could force his will upon her. "Tell me who is after me so I can hunt them down. I will even enjoy the distraction."

He shook his head. Son of a bitch. Just once she wanted him to make things easier. One time would be a nice change of pace. "Normally I would, but the kids here change everything. You need to go. Change all your names and start over someplace else. I'll help."

Gods damn this man. "I can't do that. They don't know about me, and I'm not going to tell them." She gave him a hard look. "And don't you tell them either. They have lost enough with their parents' death. I'm not uprooting the youngest. He'll be leaving for college at the end of summer. The other two will leave in a week or so."

"Gods dammit, Akantha! Stop being so damn stubborn. They're going to bring in major players to go after you this time. You have grown too complacent here."

"Like you?" She had to ask, even though she really didn't believe it. The man had been a mercenary for longer than she could remember. He fought in countless wars throughout the centuries and had no qualms about taking a life when necessary.

Damianos laughed. "Do you seriously believe I could be paid enough to harm one hair on your lovely head?" He reached out and took a lock of her dark hair between his fingers.

She smacked his hand away and thought about wiping that smirk off his face with a fist. Knowing him, he'd take her hitting him as foreplay, and that was absolutely the last thing she needed. "I believe if it's something you also wanted, you would accept payment for almost anything."

"You do believe that someone is after you."

"You're twisting my meaning, but that's to be expected. Go back to whatever you were doing, Damianos. I'm busy."

The pleasant expression on his face didn't change as he took a last step closer. Alex stood her ground without flinching as he leaned in.

"It's Stavros now. You're in danger, and whether you choose to believe it or not, I'm here to make sure nothing happens to you."

]"Go away and leave me alone." The clean cedar scent of his soap and the warmth he radiated were addicting. Despite how much she couldn't stand him, her knees trembled a little, and the breath she took felt thick and heavy. Her heart pounded. Her blood rushed as if it were the first time they'd touched. A part of her wanted to rush into his arms and lose herself in his embrace. She shook her head, slaughtering such traitorous thoughts.

"You do." He leaned in a little closer.

"No, I don't."

"Akantha." His voice, barely a whisper, sent a familiar shiver down her spine. "Let me help you."

"Leave. Now."

"I'm not leaving. No matter what has happened between us in the past, I do care for you. I worry about you."

Her resistance melted under those dark eyes and the heat radiating from him. She hated herself for it. Her reaction to him being so close told her it had been some time since she had taken someone to her bed. She needed to rectify that soon, just not with him.

"I don't want you here." It was weak, and they both knew it.

He smiled, and she scowled. "You need me here. The kids are a liability, and you can use the help. I'll stay by your side until this threat is dealt with. It's a real threat, Akantha."

She narrowed her eyes and glared at him. "What aren't you telling me?"

"I'm telling you all I know."

Alex growled. She knew him, and she knew he held something back. Something that could get other people hurt. It was just like the bastard to do this. "Fine, you warned me. Now, leave."

"I'm not leaving. I want to make sure you're safe."

"I can take care of myself."

"I know you can, but even you need help on occasion." He reached out and took her hands, engulfing them with his own. "Your hands are cold."

Alex's first thought was to yank her hands away, but something kept them in place. His were so warm, and she wanted to soak up the heat. Electricity coursed through her. She shook her head and pulled her hands away. His touch meant trouble, and it never hurt to keep some space between them. Alex knew best how much trouble he could be. Though she had to admit she could use his help.

"Fine. You can stay at the motel in town."

"How long has it been since we've seen each other?"

"Not long enough," she grumbled. He laughed, and she wanted to hit him. She took a step away from him. More space was good. She'd rather have it be a thousand miles than a few feet.

"I think it was after the war. Hunting down those bastards in South America, if my memory doesn't fail me. We have unfinished business."

"No, we don't." She knew full well what he wanted to talk about, and she was not in a mental space to have that conversation.

"When this is all over, we're going to have a serious talk. Where's Paladin? He should be here with you."

Her eyes narrowed. That son of a bitch. "How do you know about Paladin?" She tried to keep her employees anonymous, especially from him. She didn't need him interfering with her personal business. That smirk she hated so much appeared on his face.

"Who do you think trained him? I worked with him while he was at the SPD academy. We're friendly acquaintances who like to spar and drink together."

"I hate you."

He laughed. "No, you don't."

"Was that your idea or Morrow's?" She hated to think that he had been interfering in her life, and she didn't know about it.

"It was Auggie's, but I agreed so I could vet Paladin for myself. I knew he'd be working for you, and he's involved with Marie. Two birds, one me. It was a neat solution that covered a few of my debts."

"He's an investigator, not a bodyguard. He's investigating something for me." She liked to think she didn't need a bodyguard, but there were times when she needed help. Like now. She just didn't want it from Damianos.

"He's an instrument, and you should use him when you need a guard."

"So if I get him here, you'll leave?"

"I didn't say that."

Her mouth thinned as she pressed her lips together. "You never stop being a bastard, do you?" She didn't expect him to answer her question. He never did when it suited him. He would never change. "Fine. Sleep in your car."

He smiled and pulled her in against his body, snaking his arm around her to keep her from escaping his embrace. The feel of his hard body pressing up against hers made her head swim. She wanted to sink into the warmth he offered and stay there. "There's that thorny part I love so much. A couch is fine. Or better yet, your bed."

Alex opened her mouth to protest, but he covered it with his in a deep kiss. Her toes curled up inside her boots. She leaned against him, and his arms were steel, keeping her on her feet. The searing kiss rekindled a desire for the touch of another human.

Alex groaned and pulled her mouth away from his. Breathless, she tried to push away from him, but he kept her in place.

"I have missed you more than you will ever know," he whispered.

"Are you done?" Feigned indifference was her best option. Otherwise, he would take her to her bed right now if given the chance, and she couldn't afford that.

He laughed and released his hold on her. "For now. I won't let you off so easy later."

Alex sighed. He meant what he said, and she had to try her damnedest to keep him away.

"Where can I put my bag?"

"In your room at the local motel."

"Did we already decide I would stay here? A couch, or I can warm your bed." The smirk returned.

The gods help her get through this. He was the last thing she needed in her life right now and certainly the last person she needed in her bed. She shook her head. "No."

"Don't worry, I know the way. But I need a beer or two first." He released her and left the office, leaving her standing there.

CHAPTER FOUR

"I'D NEVER PICK YOU AS A VANILLA TYPE OF PERSON."
Greg peered into the bowl Jo held as they walked away from the
window of a local ice cream stand. Good Harbor had several ice
cream stands, and all of them made their own ice cream. They had
their choice, but they picked the one Jo and Mike had both worked
at during high school. The owner called her by name and gave
them the employee discount.

"Sometimes I want simple and uncomplicated." Actually, most
of the time she preferred simple and uncomplicated. Life,
unfortunately, didn't.

"Good to know."

"Is it now?"

Greg smiled. "Well, I now know not to plan anything complex
for a second date."

Jo smiled. A second date sounded good. She hadn't even been
sure this was a first date, but she supposed it was if he talked
about planning a second one.

"You do realize that I'm going back to Boulder soon, right?"

"Yes, but why can't we enjoy each other's company while
you're here?"

Jo shoved a spoonful of ice cream in her mouth. Nothing beat homemade ice cream. Most of the ice cream stands in Maine made their own, and it was far superior to other ice cream. Maine even had an ice cream trail, which she and her family followed one year. She remembered how full of ice cream she had been at the end of the day.

His idea sounded good to her. "We can. I'd like that."

Greg returned her smile. "Me too."

"What about Mike?" Jo took another bite. Sweet vanilla and the warm scent of Greg sitting close was intoxicating. She wanted to reach over and tuck a lock of brown hair behind his ear.

"He's not my type."

"Well, you're his best friend, so it might get weird. He'll want to spend time doing things with you."

"We're not in high school or even college now. He's my friend, but we don't spend all our free time together. Besides, he said he'll be in town until the beginning of August. I can hang out with him after you go back to Boulder. You and I can have some fun."

"True." The idea of fun with Greg sounded, well, fun. "I'm sure he'll object to us going out together."

"I'm sure, but you can handle it."

"Yes, I can. With a bat, if I have to." Jo scooped up more ice cream.

Greg had gone with a mix called Wookie Dough. It was a chocolate lover's dream with chocolate and brownie batter ice creams with chunks of fudge brownies and chocolate chip cookie dough.

"Have you ever thought of getting out of Good Harbor?" Jo asked after a few quiet minutes of eating their ice cream.

"A few times. But I've never given it serious consideration."

"Why not?"

Greg shrugged. "Mostly because my family's here. The family business is here."

Jo could understand it. Carrie said almost the exact same thing when Jo asked her. Greg had six brothers and sisters, and they all lived on a farm in a large, old farmhouse. Jo had only visited it a handful of times in high school. Each time, it overflowed with kids and chaos. She couldn't imagine living with so many family members under one roof. She had barely survived growing up with Mike and Ben.

"That's cool. I'm sure your parents appreciate you helping with the restaurant."

"All seven of us work there. Even the runt clears tables and empties the dishwasher. I don't mind, though. It does well, and I've learned a lot about the business side of things at school. I'm using what I learned to help the family. We might be able to expand into a second location in a year or so."

Jo envied him and others who had figured out what they wanted to do for the rest of their lives, or at least for the immediate future. Jo held her bachelor's in journalism but still wasn't sure what she wanted to do. She could always blog until she landed a paying gig, or she could try to find an online news outlet to write for. At some point, she had to get a job that paid real money. She couldn't live off the trust her parents' estate created for each of them for too long. Her parents had been well off and didn't have too many financial concerns that were ever mentioned, and they each had a decent amount for their futures.

"That's great. Maybe one night I'll come for dinner. It's been a while since I've eaten there. I miss it."

"Time it right, and I can have dinner with you."

Jo smiled. "I'd like that." If she could get away for dinner without Mike and Ben. She loved her brothers, but they would be gleeful third wheels, intent on ruining the experience.

Jo scooped the last of her ice cream out of the bowl and ate it. She'd miss the little things like homemade ice cream on a summer evening with the smell of the ocean in the air when she returned home to Boulder.

Greg finished off the last of his ice cream. "All set?"

"Yeah. Thanks."

"You're welcome. Thanks for coming with me." He held out a hand for her empty bowl.

"Entirely my pleasure," she said, placing the bowl in his outstretched hand. Greg walked the trash over to the closest barrel, and Jo admired the view. Greg had a nice ass. Nice body too, but his butt was particularly watchable when in motion.

"Shall we?" He held out a hand.

She took it. It was too good an offer to refuse.

He didn't release her hand as they walked to his car. Jo didn't mind in the least. Warmth spread from his hand into hers, and she soaked it up. Early June temperatures on the coast of Maine weren't exactly the warmest. To Jo, it was quite chilly at night, and eating ice cream didn't help. They could've come out earlier, but Greg had to help with the dinner service at the restaurant for a bit. And 8:30 p.m. wasn't late, and they were both adults, not kids with a curfew.

"Thanks for asking me out for ice cream." Jo ran her free hand along the side of his car. It was an older model, and Jo recalled his father driving this car during their last two years of high school. Greg must have inherited it. Probably so he could get back and forth to school.

"Thanks for saying yes."

The crunch of gravel very close to them prevented Joanna from speaking. She turned to see a man, dressed in all black with a shaved head, approaching them. Joanna didn't recognize him, but she hadn't really lived in Good Harbor for four years.

"Can we—" Greg stopped in midsentence.

Joanna screamed, seeing a knife, and Greg put up his arm to block the blow. The knife sliced across Greg's forearm, and he released Jo's hand. He used his free arm to shove Jo backward, out of the man's reach.

A scream died in Jo's throat as the knife cut into Greg's skin. What the hell was happening?

"Help!" Joanna screamed, hoping that someone at the ice cream stand heard. "Someone help!" She frantically looked around for someone to help. She didn't see anyone near them at the far end of the parking lot. It had been full of cars when they had arrived, so they had to park at the end. They'd lingered over their ice cream, and it had been enough time for the parking lot to clear out.

Her heart pounded in her chest, and blood thundered in her ears as the man swiped the knife at Greg once more. The knife blurred, but Greg managed to block the attack by slamming his forearm into the man's, sending the blade wide.

The thought of calling for help slowly filtered in past the panic. She fumbled to remove her phone from her pocket. It took two tries to get it unlocked, and she dialed 9-1-1. She pressed the button to connect the call a second before Greg bumped into her. The phone slipped from her grasp, hitting the pavement of the parking lot with a loud crack. "Dammit!"

She looked away from the phone to see the man make a lunge for Greg, the knife leading the way. Greg dived to the side to avoid the lunge, the knife slicing across his upper arm. He yelled out from the sharp pain. More blood stained his shirt. Joanna scrambled to find anything to help Greg but came up empty in her search.

The attacker paused for a moment as if he were seeing her for the first time and needed to reassess the situation. He moved toward Jo, and she flinched backward until she backed up against the car.

Any courage she possessed drained away, leaving fear in its wake. "Leave us alone!"

"Walk away, and you won't be hurt." His voice was deep and calm, disturbing her more than if it had been menacing or threatening.

"What do you want?"

Greg's pain-filled voice came from beside her. "Jo, you need to leave."

Jo spared a glance at Greg. Leave? Why would he tell her to go? The man was trying to kill him. She wasn't about to go anywhere and let this man hurt Greg.

"Listen to him, girl." The man gestured with his knife. "This doesn't concern you. Walk away, and I swear by all that is holy, you won't be hurt."

Greg stepped in front of Jo and held out his arms, shielding her from the man. His white shirt glowed in the moonlight, making the blood staining it look obscene. "Leave us alone," he growled. His voice was deeper than normal, hitting a nerve in her that made her want to cringe back, but she was rooted to the spot.

"I'm not here for the girl. I'm here for you, demon spawn."

"Jo, run!"

His words sank into her brain, and moving seemed like a good idea. Jo could run to the ice cream counter and use a phone to call the police. Only her feet refused to move.

"Go!" The man in black moved in for another attack, and Greg lifted an arm and brought it back. His elbow connected with her face, and pain blurred her vision. She lunged to the right, but her feet caught on something. She tripped and fell, her head striking the hard pavement of the parking lot.

White spots danced in front of her eyes as gravel bit into the side of her face. The taste of blood filled her mouth, and the world spun around her. Blackness gathered on the edges of her vision. She heard a deep animal growl just before the blackness overwhelmed her.

CHAPTER FIVE

ALEX HELD ONTO JOANNA'S HAND IN THE HOSPITAL room. Alex's stomach bottomed out when she received the call. Mike and Ben had been out of the house, so Alex texted them and told them she'd meet them at the hospital.

That was two hours ago.

Jo had yet to regain consciousness. Alex would only be able to relax a little once Jo opened her eyes. Until then, she kept a vigil next to the bed. Damianos sat in a chair not far from her.

"She'll be okay, Akantha." His voice seemed loud in the quiet room. "It's only a concussion."

"She's not one of us. I'll feel better once her eyes are open."

"Who do you think did this?"

"Not here, Damianos. Later."

He shook his head. "She's still unconscious, and no one else is here."

"Could you please listen, just once?" An exasperated sigh left Alex. He had never listened and never would. No matter how much time passed.

He put his hands up. "Fine. Is Durendal safe?"

That got her attention. "Why would you ask about Durendal?"

Jo moaned, and Alex turned back to her immediately. Jo's eyes fluttered open. "Where am I?"

Alex squeezed Jo's hand and leaned in. "You're in the hospital."

Jo looked around. "Where's Greg?"

"He's fine. How are you feeling?" Her stomach unwound a bit, and her heart started to move back down to her chest.

"My head hurts." Jo put her hand to her temple.

"It will for a bit." Alex gently squeezed Jo's other hand, attempting to be as comforting as possible. It didn't come easy to her. "Is your vision clear?"

"Yeah."

"Good."

"Glad to see you're awake." Damianos stood and moved toward the door. "I'll let the nurse know and get your brothers. They left a while ago to go find some food. I think they got lost."

Jo and Alex both chuckled as Damianos left the room.

Jo groaned as the motion made her head hurt. "Greg's okay?"

"Yes, he's fine. I talked to his mother when I ran into her in the ER. Do you remember what happened? Do you remember how you hit your head?"

"A little. It's all fuzzy. Everything happened so fast. One moment Greg was opening the car door and the next, a creepy man attacked us." Jo put her hand back to her temple again. "I remember Greg's elbow hit me in the face. I went to move out of the way, and I tripped on something. I fell and hit my head."

"The doctors say it's a mild concussion. Nothing too serious. It could have been much worse."

"I think Greg got cut with a knife." She scrunched her eyes shut. "I don't remember a lot."

"Don't strain yourself. I'll call his mother in a bit and double-check."

"Why are you so calm about this? I was attacked!"

Sometimes Alex forgot how young Jo was, but then again

everyone was young compared to Alex. Jo usually acted more mature than her twenty-three years, but that was under normal circumstances and the moment was far from normal.

"Yes, you were, but you are going to be fine. While it was an unfortunate incident, overreacting won't do anyone any good. The police are investigating." She didn't know if she was assuring Jo or herself. With this attack coming so soon after Damianos's warning, Alex had to wonder if Jo and Greg had been attacked because of her.

"Did they say when I could leave?"

"The doctors said they're going to keep you overnight for observation. Is there anything I can get you?" Alex squeezed Jo's hand again.

The gesture was small, a maternal one. It was the same one Alex had used when she had been nursing a loved one. Jo was another daughter to her. Mike and Ben were sons. They had filled the past two decades with laughter and love. It had been so long since Alex had any children of her own.

"I think I'm good. Or I will be when the pain goes away."

Alex smiled. "The miracle of modern medicine will keep the pain to a minimum. You know, a hundred years or so ago, you would have been given cocaine or even heroin for the pain. Did he have any other weapons?"

"I only saw a knife."

"What did he look like?" She hated to do it, but she'd ask Damianos to hunt the bastard down.

"He was tall, about as tall as Greg. Bald. He wore all black, and it looked like the type of military uniform you see on TV."

Alex leaned in. "Are you sure it was a military uniform?"

"No, I don't think so. But I'm not sure. It looked like one, but it could have been all-black clothes."

"Do you remember anything else?" Alex's mind raced with different scenarios, none of them good.

"I screamed for help, and no one answered. I thought small

towns were supposed to be safer with everybody minding everybody else's business. One wardrobe malfunction and it's in the paper. Somebody attacks us, and it's crickets."

"Generally, they are, but bad things can happen no matter where you live. Tourist season is starting, so that means more strangers in town. Is there anything else you can remember?"

"I thought I heard an animal growl."

"Like Munchkin?"

"I don't know. Maybe? It was a deep growl like something really big, but I didn't see anything."

Alex wasn't sure what to make of that. It was bad enough Jo was attacked. If something else was skulking about Good Harbor, that made it worse. She lived in Good Harbor because it wasn't a supernatural haven. If something supernatural was in play, the situation was much worse than she thought. A mundane creature was her only hope. Otherwise, Damianos would get involved as an SPD officer. He would never leave if that happened. It was one of her worst nightmares.

"As far as I can make out from what Mrs. Sullivan said, sirens chased the guy away, and the police called for an ambulance when they arrived. The hospital called me, and we came right away."

"Did they catch the guy?"

Alex hesitated a moment. She hated telling Jo the man was still out there. It wouldn't help put the girl at ease. "They didn't. Greg gave the police a description of the man. They're looking for him."

"Good. I hope they find him and put his fucking ass in jail." She tightened her hands around the thin blanket.

Alex smiled and patted Jo's forearm just above the wrist. "That makes two of us. The police want to talk to you later."

"Sure, but I don't know how much help I'll be."

"You never know. With some rest and a little time, you'll remember more."

The door opened and Ben poked his head in. A moment later, he was pushed aside as Mike's face appeared in the doorway. "Jo?"

"You both can come in." Alex stood and smoothed her shirt. "I'm going to find a decent cup of tea. If there's one to be found here, though I doubt it."

Mike and Ben entered the room and waited for the door to close behind Alex before speaking. "Are you okay?" Mike asked as he fell into the chair Alex had vacated. Ben sat in the chair on the other side of the bed. His gangly frame made it look uncomfortable.

"Yeah, for the most part. My head is killing me, though."

"What the hell happened? Alex texted us saying you were in the ER," Ben said. "It was pretty scary."

"I don't know for sure. We were at Greg's car, and this guy carrying a knife came out of nowhere and attacked us. Greg accidentally hit me with his elbow, and I tripped and fell, and I whacked my head on the ground. I blacked out. That's all I can tell you."

"I was worried." Mike frowned.

"We were worried." Ben reached over and put a hand on Jo's arm. "But we were looking for a more exciting story. Can you add an alien with two heads and seven legs?"

She wouldn't call out Ben or Mike about being worried or tease them about it. She knew if their positions were reversed, she'd be at their sides, holding their hand and wondering if they were okay. It brought back a flash of what they'd gone through with their parents' sudden death. The important thing was that both of her brothers were here now.

Instead, she put her hand over Ben's and patted it. "I'm fine. All I can add is a deep growl."

"Are you sure?" Ben asked. "About being fine?"

"I'll have a headache for a while," she said. Mike drew closer and stopped a few inches in front of her face. Jo narrowed her eyes but clutched the edge of the blanket a little tighter. "I'll give you a matching headache if you try to hug me," she warned.

"I'm not going to hug you. I'd rather hug a snake. A poisonous snake. If you want a hug, Ben can hug you."

Jo laughed. He wasn't as worried he appeared if he was cracking jokes. The jokes made her feel like the world was normal. She loosened her hold on the blanket. "Venomous. Snakes are venomous, not poisonous."

"Whatever." Mike shrugged and pulled away. "Did you get a look at the guy?"

"Alex asked me the same thing. Everything happened so fast, and it was dark. She said the police will ask, so I need to think about it."

"They'll find him. Strangers have to stand out here," Ben said.

"Alex said the busy season is starting, so there will be more people in town. I'd sleep better knowing he's caught, but…"

"We'll all sleep better when that happens." Mike peered into her eyes, and Jo recognized the old trick their parents used to use to see if they were telling the truth. It usually worked. That parental trick always made them cough up the truth quick. She almost rolled her eyes at her twin. "You really okay?" he asked in all seriousness.

"I am." She stared straight into his eyes without blinking. Anything less and he wouldn't believe her. She didn't want him acting all protective-like.

Mike sighed. "Good." He slouched in the chair. His face smoothed out, the worry disappearing. "I guess that's a date you'll never forget."

"You can say that again. Greg won't want to go out with me anymore."

"I don't know about that."

Jo perked up. "Did he say something?" She hoped the attack didn't ruin the chance of another date.

"Maybe. I'm sure he'll ask you out for a second date. That's if I allow it."

"What do you mean, if you allow it? Who made you my social dictator?"

"As your big brother, it's my job to look after you. And Greg. Somebody has to look out for him. Dating you might get him hurt."

Four lousy minutes, and Mike played the big brother card whenever he could. "You're a jerk."

He grinned. "No, I'm just awesome and the best brother in the world. No. In the universe!" He laughed in his best maniacal overlord manner. The loudness made her head hurt more, and she winced. "Four minutes still makes me the big brother."

"No, I'm the best brother in the universe, dork," Ben said. "Do you need me to bring you anything? Magazines? Books?"

"If you happen to see my phone anywhere—"

Mike pulled Jo's phone from a pocket and offered it to her. "Here. I knew you'd want it first. Alex got all your stuff from the emergency room people. It still turns on, barely. Alex decided to order you a new one instead of getting it fixed."

Jo snatched the phone from his hand. The crack ran down the screen and into the casing. So much for the protective outer shell. There must have been some force behind the landing.

Jo tried to turn on her phone and winced at the slow response. "Oh hell. Thanks anyway."

"Your new one should be here in a day or two," Ben said. "Mine got busted, and a new phone came pretty fast. Alex either doesn't mind paying for expedited shipping, or she's that good of a customer and they throw it in for free."

"Good to know." A small town in Maine sometimes meant that things took a little longer to get there. Jo had no such problems in Boulder. She could even order stuff from Amazon and have it delivered the same day. "Have either of you talked to Greg?"

They both shook their heads.

"Mike, can you call him and ask him how he is? Alex talked to his mom, but she said he's okay. I remember him getting cut by the psycho's knife."

"I will."

CHAPTER SIX

"Not one lead. It's like the guy vanished into thin air."

The morning after her release from the hospital, Jo sat in the chair behind the counter in the antiques shop, using a cotton swab to clean the nooks and crannies of what looked like a Victorian dust catcher in the form of a statuette. Where Alex got it, she had no idea, but after insisting on helping Carrie dust the shelves, she found it easier on the lingering headache to just sit.

Except she couldn't just sit. Carrie found her something to do that Jo clearly knew was make-work so she would stay out of the way. It didn't matter. She didn't want to stay in her room upstairs, and she didn't want to sort through her parents' boxes yet.

"It's that time of year." Carrie wore two old socks on her hands as she wiped down shelves and larger pieces of furniture. Every so often, she would change them out for cleaner old socks. "Summer people are starting to arrive. If the closed sign wasn't up now, we'd get people coming in here all day."

"Why isn't Alex open now?" Jo wondered aloud. "She's missing business."

"She does a lot more business online. She hardly makes enough here to justify my pay, but she doesn't seem to mind."

Did she ever wonder about Alex's finances before now? Jo couldn't recall a time where Alex seemed worried about making a car payment or paying the winter heating oil delivery.

"Want to hear something weird?"

"Of course."

Jo chuckled. Of course Carrie wanted to hear something weird. "When I was in the hospital, Alex and Stavros were in my room. I was just waking up, and I swear he called Alex Akantha and she called him Damianos."

"Are you sure you heard them and weren't dreaming you heard it? You do have a concussion."

"I heard it." Her head started to throb a little harder, and she took a deep breath to calm herself.

"Maybe they're nicknames. Not as cute as 'pooky' and 'sweetie,' but nicknames."

Time for a subject change. "This is ugly." Jo made a face at the statuette. The little face grinned evilly back at her. "What kind of person would like this in their living room?"

"Don't say that around Ms. Thorne. She'll tell you more than you ever wanted to know about Victorian art. Have you heard from Greg?"

"Sort of. He texted a few times, but I'm sure he's busy."

The words sounded like pouting to her own ears. Carrie's sidelong glance told her that her friend thought so as well.

"With the tourist season starting, the restaurant is busy." Jo fixed her eyes on the evil little face she cleaned. It would win if she blinked. "It was one date. Maybe it wasn't even a date. Who knows anymore?"

"If it wasn't a date, Mike would have been there."

That was a horrifying thought. "Okay, one date. An ice cream date. A half date."

"In Maine, that counts as courtship. If you have ice cream and a lobster roll, you're automatically engaged. Did you have a good time? What did you talk about?" Carrie swapped out dusty sock mittens for clean ones.

"It was date talk. The usual stuff."

"The usual stuff for me was about my class notes and if I'd share them. Group study dates. I didn't date. I enabled lazy researching on their part."

Jo opened her mouth to downplay that but thought better of it. "We talked about his job at the restaurant, my life in Boulder, and why I like vanilla ice cream. Then the attack and our ice cream date ended up in the hospital. We're supposed to do something tomorrow night. So if I don't see him today, I'll see him tomorrow." She shrugged as if it wasn't a big deal. But it did feel like a big deal to a small part of her.

"I heard about it the next morning when I came down to open the store. Mr. Nicademos was walking the grounds and stopped in to tell me. He said your head was hard enough to take it."

"The way he's been agitating Alex, he should have been the one in the hospital."

"He's a little scary."

"He's been nice enough, I suppose, but he's really riled Alex up. I keep expecting her to shoot him, and I never thought of her as a violent person."

"It must be love then." Carrie sighed in unrequited longing for their new will they–won't they couple. "She's attractive and smart, and there's no reason why she shouldn't have a boyfriend."

"I wouldn't call him a boy." Jo stood and knocked the container of swabs onto the floor. She reached down to pick them up and felt a bump under the small rug. "Munchkin hates him. I wish I knew why. That dog never even snapped at us when we pulled his tail as kids, or when Mike tried to ride him when we were eight years old. Stavros sitting quietly in the same room makes him growl."

"He's very handsome. He adores her. You can see it when he

looks at her and her attention is elsewhere." The sigh that accompanied the words held a touch of envy. "Are you okay? Do you need help?"

Jo glanced up to see Carrie's concerned expression. She supposed the way she was bent over might appear like she was sick. "There's something under the rug."

Jo moved the chair off to the side while Carrie came around the desk. Together, they folded the rug back and found a metal handle in the floor. The only reason Jo had noticed it was because one end hadn't settled into the slot.

"Does that look like what I think it looks like?"

"A trapdoor." Carrie toed the edge of the line cut across the boards. "Maybe that's where she hides the valuables. Who would think to search there?"

"Other than us? Someone who cleans the store might if they're thorough about it."

"Ms. Thorne does the cleaning. She said she doesn't like anyone else but her doing the heavy work. I dust and sweep every week, and she knocks a little off the rent. I want to do more because the rent's so cheap, but she says she's happy with the arrangement."

Jo grabbed the handle and hauled it open. The black maw gaped at them as they peered down. How did Jo, Mike, and Ben never find this? They spent as much time at Alex's as they did at their own house. Although, to be honest, she and Mike never spent much time in the store. Maybe Ben knew about it. Ben kept secrets with a vengeance.

"That's dark. Like there's no bottom dark. Got a flashlight handy?"

Jo tried her cell phone flashlight, but the tiny illumination was nearly useless. "I need a real light. Where does she keep a flashlight?"

Carrie pulled a desk drawer open. "She keeps one here."

Jo snatched it up. Once she flicked the button, she angled the light into the hole. Both women peered down.

"That's a ladder," Jo said.

"I can't disagree. It's a ladder. Under the shop."

"Under Alex's desk where she can keep an eye on it. Is the door locked?"

Carrie ran over to look. She turned the lock. "It is now."

"I'm going to down to take a look."

"You can't go down there by yourself. What if you get dizzy? We don't even know what's there."

The headache was gone, washed away in the rush of anticipation of a mystery. "Then come with me."

Carrie hesitated. "If we get caught, she'll evict me. I just know it."

"She won't. She might get mad, but she's always been fair. And I don't recall her ever yelling. Even when we accidentally broke things when we were kids."

"I'm going with you because you can't be alone with your head injury and if something happens to you, it would be worse." Carrie patted her pockets to show she had her cell phone and straightened her shoulders. "She'd get mad if you were alone and fainted."

Jo handed over the flashlight. "Hold this so I can see what I'm doing. Give me your phone so I can use the light when I get to the bottom." She slid her legs over the edge and stood on the ladder. Carrie moved to her knees and angled the light at the rungs. "Wish me luck."

"I wish you weren't doing this."

"When did saying that ever work?"

Jo took each rung as carefully as she could while moving as fast as possible. The second she'd uncovered the trapdoor, she knew she was on a timer. Alex would come out to the store sooner or later, or a shopper would try knocking on the locked door instead of reading the Closed sign. She didn't know how far down she was until the light grew dimmer and the dark felt like a physical shadow wrapping around her.

She finally touched bottom and stepped away. She aimed the phone light into the darkness, but it was barely enough for her to see relatively smooth rock walls and floor. The light vanished down a tunnel, swallowed up by the blackness.

"Jo?"

"It's fine. It's actually pretty interesting. You have to see this."

"Did I ever tell you I'm afraid of heights?"

Jo pointed her light at the ladder. It had seemed like a bottomless hole from the other side. Now she could see it was about ten feet. Carrie's face was pale and worried from above.

"I'll be okay. You stay."

"I'm more afraid of Ms. Thorne than heights. Wait for me."

Carrie's trip down the ladder was one careful step at a time, with Jo trying to hide her impatience. She tapped her hand against a thigh as she waited for Carrie. When Carrie reached the ground, Jo grabbed her arm and began pulling her down the tunnel.

Carrie pulled the flashlight from her pocket. Jo wished she were as prepared as Carrie always seemed. "The floor is clean like she keeps it swept. How weird, but good for us."

They found their way through the dark with their lights moving from side to side as they did their best to avoid walking into walls. Jo hooked her arm around Carrie's and kept it there. While it was relatively straight, the utterly black atmosphere threatened to swallow them.

"This would be the place to have a Halloween party. I'm not convinced it isn't haunted," Carrie whispered.

"I would come back to Good Harbor just for that party." Jo pulled Carrie against her side for a long moment to reassure Carrie and herself. A solid metal door loomed out of the dark right in front of them. Her light played over the metal rivets and old-fashioned lock.

"Look at this! Why in the world would this be underground?"

Carrie shined her light on the lock. "It's old. Maybe it was here before the house was built."

"That doesn't explain why there's a trapdoor under her office chair. It had to be in the building plans." Jo unhooked her arm from Carrie's and ran her fingertips over the lock.

"Or the plans were made because of the tunnel and door. I can think of at least two reasons why it's here." Carrie leaned in to take a closer look at the lock. "It could have been a stop on the Underground Railroad."

"Then Alex would have mentioned it to us. She loves history and loves teaching it to us. If it was a stop on the Underground Railroad, why hasn't she ever shown us?"

"If you knew it was here, would you have tried to get into it?" Carrie looked over at Jo.

Her friend had a point. Forget the town troublemakers—it would have been Mike trying to get inside of it. And herself, if she was going to be honest.

"Of course. I'd want to look inside. Can it be opened?"

Carrie yanked on the large lever handle. It didn't budge. "Locked."

"We should have expected it to be locked." Jo's hopes of seeing behind the door dashed. She frowned, but this was only a temporary setback. She would find a way.

Carrie played the light around the ring. "How about 'Open Sesame?'" The light glinted over a lock. "Or a key?"

"Hold the light on the lock." Jo leaned in to examine it. She considered the size and shape of the keyhole. The lock was the same as the vintage ones in the house, only the keyhole was twice as large. Using the skeleton keys from the doors in the house wouldn't work. "I don't think I've seen a key that fits this. It has to be somewhere, though. Maybe in her office."

"Or in her bedroom. You're seriously not going to search her things, are you?"

"No, of course not. But if I happen to see one serving as a paperweight or hanging from a hook—"

"There's a reason why this is all locked. Why don't you ask her? Maybe she doesn't know it's here."

Carrie made sense, but Jo doubted she'd ever be brave enough to ask Alex. "She knows it's here. The floor is swept, and the door hinges are oiled. That's maintenance."

"Okay, fine, she knows it's here. But maybe it was here when she inherited the property, and she can't get into it either."

"Maybe." Jo considered and discarded that excuse immediately. She couldn't imagine Alex not getting into a locked room on her own property. Even if there wasn't a key, Alex was a determined person. Jo had watched her negotiate with other antiques sellers and in the end, Alex always got what she wanted. The woman could be ruthless and utterly in control. "But why else would she be maintaining all of this?"

"Let's go before we're caught."

The fact that Carrie didn't answer the question didn't get past Jo, but she let it drop. "Wait." She grabbed the cell phone from Carrie and took a picture of the lock. "Send me the picture when I get my new phone tomorrow. Just in case I see a key somewhere."

"Can we go now? I don't want her to catch us down here."

Jo didn't want that either.

"Okay, I'm done. Let's go." She hooked her arm around Carrie's again, and they headed down the black tunnel. They reached the ladder, and Jo allowed Carrie to climb the ladder first. Once they were out, they closed the trapdoor and made sure it looked like it hadn't been disturbed.

"I'll look for the key." Discovering what was behind that door was now Jo's number one priority. She had to know what Alex kept locked up, and it would provide a good distraction from the attack. She had been waking up in the middle of the night in a cold sweat. Maybe her subconscious would give her a break if she focused on something else. "As soon as I find it, we can see what's behind that door."

"It sounds like a plan. What do you think is behind there?"

Jo shrugged. "Could be anything, but probably more antiques. What else would she have?"

"I don't know. I think it's a storeroom from the old days when smugglers ran off the coast. One of her ancestors might have been in the black market. That makes it interesting all by itself. It would have worked just as well as a stop on the Underground Railroad. It would make a great field trip for some history class."

If that were the case, then why hadn't Alex brought any classes here? It would have been a natural thing to bring one of her history classes here if this had historical significance. Something more was going on here, and Jo was determined to get the bottom of it.

CHAPTER SEVEN

ALEX SET HER CUP DOWN ON THE SAUCER AND LEANED
back in the chair. Customers filled the only café in downtown
Good Harbor, and Alex and Jo had been lucky to get a table. It was
a little too crowded for Alex's taste, but coming here had gotten
her out of the house and away from Damianos for a while. She
could put up with people and noise for that alone.

Except, why had he asked about Durendal? That was the
question she couldn't get out of her mind.

"How are you doing?" she asked Jo.

Jo looked up from her cup of coffee at Alex. "I'm okay."

Alex noticed the pause before Jo answered. "Are you sure?"
Alex pulled a small piece off her croissant and ate it. A section of
her brain wondered if she could reproduce the recipe. Her
croissants were never this flaky.

Jo traced the rim of her coffee cup with an index finger. "I am."

"Really?" Alex leaned forward in her chair. She folded her arms
in front of her on the table and looked at her goddaughter. Her
too-good-at-deflecting goddaughter. Their eyes met, and Jo looked
away first.

"Yeah."

Alex picked up her cup and took a sip of her tea, letting the fact that Jo lied go. Thousands of years of experience taught Alex when to fight battles. This was not a battle she wanted to fight. She tried another way. "How are your headaches?"

Jo shrugged as she picked at the chocolate croissant on the small plate in front of her. "Still there. Painkillers are helping a little."

"Good. If you need anything in addition to the painkillers, please let me know." Alex believed in modern medicine, but she also knew that certain herbs and plants could also be used to alleviate some ailments.

Jo nodded and picked up her cup of coffee. "I know."

Alex took a sip of her tea. "Are you having any nightmares?" Alex assumed Jo was having nightmares but needed to confirm it. Anyone would be experiencing nightmares after being attacked.

"Some."

"That's to be expected. Would you like to talk to a professional about it and the attack? There are some resources in Brunswick."

Jo shrugged. "I dunno."

Alex refrained from sighing in frustration at Jo's short answers. She wanted to get Jo to talk more about any lingering effects of the attack, but she knew how stubborn Jo could be. "Fair enough. If you decide you do want to see someone to talk to, please let me know."

"I will. Promise."

"Good." Alex took another sip. "What are your short-term plans? When do you plan on returning to Boulder?" Maybe a change of topic would get her to open up a little more.

Jo took a long drink from her cup. She set the cup down on the table and sighed heavily. Alex looked at Jo a little closer, trying to discern the cause of the sigh. "I don't know yet. I don't know if I want to go through any of the boxes before I go back or go back and worry about that stuff later."

"The boxes will stay in storage until you're ready to go

through them. You know you can stay here as long as you like. I doubt Carrie would mind sharing the apartment for any length of time."

Jo smiled a little. "She wouldn't."

"And Greg?" The attraction between the two didn't go unnoticed. Jo was family, and Alex had gotten to know Greg and his family through the years.

"What about him?" Jo shot back. The look in her brown eyes turned hard, and Alex saw a small part of the old Jo show its face. It gave her some hope that Jo would get through this intact.

"Just curious. You seemed to have taken an interest in him and he in you."

"So?" Jo challenged.

Alex put both hands up. "I was just curious. I don't want to see either of you get hurt."

"I won't get hurt. And I won't hurt Greg."

"Good." Alex put her hands down and picked up her cup. "I want you to be happy, and if that means a fling with Greg before you go back to Boulder, then so be it."

Jo looked at Alex in surprise. Alex loved knowing that she could keep Jo on her toes.

She watched Jo try to formulate a response. Twenty-three was a fun age to observe..

Alex sipped her tea. "Sex is nothing to be embarrassed about." She smiled when Jo's cheeks change to pink. The corners of her mouth turned up in a slight smile, and she set her cup down.

"I know."

"Good. You know what we need?"

"What?"

Alex smiled. "A girl's shopping day. Like we used to do." Alex, Jo, and Claire would declare a girl's shopping day once a month and take off to one of the cities and shop on Alex's dime. They'd buy clothes and shoes and anything else that struck their fancies.

Sometimes they took a whole weekend and spent the nights in the nicest hotel in the city.

Jo smiled for a moment, and the smile faded. Alex's heart ached for the young woman. "Yeah, that'd be great."

"We don't have to," Alex said. She reached across the table and took Jo's hand. She gave it an affectionate squeeze. Alex wished she could take the pain away. The hardest lesson to learn in life was dealing with the loss of loved ones, and it never got easier, no matter how many years passed. Alex still mourned the loss of people she lost so long ago. "I know it was a thing we did with your mom. We can do something different. We could establish a new tradition."

Jo remained quiet for a moment, and Alex wanted to hug her, but she stayed seated. Jo was no longer the little girl who would run for comfort when something bothered her. Jo and Mike had both grown and matured in the four short years they had been away for college. Alex was still adjusting to them being adults, and she had to remember to treat them as such.

"No, we can go."

"Let's invite Carrie." Alex made the suggestion, but she wanted Jo to be sure. "I'm sure we can tempt her with a bookstore visit."

"Carrie would love that."

Alex nodded. "She would. Where should we go? Portland? Bangor? Boston?" Jo lit up the moment Alex mentioned Boston. Alex didn't blame Jo. Boston was a wonderful city for shopping and museums. Alex remembered Boston not long after it was founded. "If we go to Boston, we could make a weekend of it. We could go to some museums while we're there."

"What about the store?"

Alex waved her hand. "It can be closed for a weekend. It's still early in the season." She looked around the café. Despite being early in the season, the café was crowded. In a week or two, they wouldn't have been able to find an empty table during the day.

The hairs on the back of her neck stood on end, and centuries of training kicked in. Alex scanned the café carefully, looking for the person or thing who'd tripped her senses.

"Only if you're sure."

Alex blinked and looked back at Jo. "I'm sure. It'll be fun. It's been some time since I've been to Boston."

"Me too."

Alex forced a smile. She was relieved Jo had agreed to go. The uneasiness didn't abate. Something was off, but she couldn't let Jo catch on. There was no reason to add to her trauma. "It's a plan then. The boys will have to fend for themselves for the weekend."

"Are you sure you want to leave them unsupervised for a weekend?" Jo joked.

"There's a risk involved, of course, but they can't do too much damage." Or so she hoped. Damianos wouldn't allow permanent damage to the house or property, but she expected things to get out of hand with him and two young men. There would most likely be cosmetic damage done to the house and a few broken items. Nothing worse than Mike, Jo, and Ben did when they were much younger.

"I'll ask Carrie if she's interested."

"I think she'll say yes as soon as you mention a bookstore."

Jo laughed a little. Alex wanted to laugh with her, but the nagging sensation of something wrong wouldn't leave her. She scanned the café again, not seeing the source of her uneasiness.

"You're right." Jo leaned toward her. "Everything okay?"

Did the girl sense the unknown danger? No, she couldn't have. Jo lacked the training and experience to recognize danger. "We should probably get going," she suggested. The last thing she wanted or needed was a public scene. Immortals lived among mortals and interacted with them, but they kept low profiles out of necessity. She picked up her cup and drained the remainder of her tea. Standing, she looked around again. What was going on?

She still didn't see anything or anyone that could be a source of danger.

Jo finished her coffee and stood. "Alex, is something wrong?"

Alex shook her head. "No, of course not. I have things I need to get done today. That's all."

Jo nodded, and Alex followed her out of the café. They stepped out of the café, and Alex blinked against the bright sunshine, giving her eyes a few seconds to adjust to the brightness. She scanned the surrounding area. Still nothing. She fell into step next to Jo as they headed toward the Jeep.

They reached the Jeep, and Alex climbed into the driver's seat. She slammed the door shut and started the motor. Damn Damianos for making her paranoid. Good Harbor was home and the one place where she was supposed to be safe. Double damn him. He had her jumping at nothing. She wouldn't put it past him to warn of a threat just so he had a reason to stick around. She'd kill him if she could.

Jo closed her door, and Alex pulled the Jeep out of the parking spot.

CHAPTER EIGHT

FROM THE BACK OF THE OLD TRUCK, JO STARED UP AT the endless black night sky. One of the nicer things that could be said for Good Harbor over Boulder, it was much better for stargazing and watching the Bootid meteor shower.

Greg invited her over to hang out and watch the summer meteor shower. She had been looking forward to seeing him, as she hadn't seen him since the attack. They did keep in contact over text messages, but it wasn't the same as actually spending time with him. Relief washed over her the second she saw him. He was okay and didn't have any serious injuries from the attack, but she would have sworn he had been cut with a knife. She must have imagined it since Greg didn't have any bandages on his arms or even the slightest trace of a wound.

Stargazing took her back to high school and being with her friends on summer nights. At their age, hanging out should include wine and some more sophisticated activity. Yet there was little in the world so perfect as stargazing. As they parked the truck in a dark corner of the Sullivan land and spread a blanket in the truck bed, Jo felt all her acquired sophisticated expectations disappear with the anticipation of watching the night sky with a handsome guy, and the memories of doing this very thing as a child.

Back then, it was her, Ben, and Mike with their dad every time there was an astronomical event. Sometimes they just watched the stars and talked about things. Sometimes Alex joined them and told the Greek myths of how the constellations came to be, even though Jo knew them all by heart. It was better when Alex told them; her storytelling made it seem as if she'd been there and had known the people in her tales. It was no secret what made Alex a popular substitute history teacher.

"Thanks for inviting me over." Jo watched as a meteor left a trail of light behind it. Thankfully it was a clear night and cool enough to have an excuse to lie up against the length of Greg's body. He radiated warmth, and Jo wanted to sink down into it.

"It's totally my pleasure. Thank Ms. Thorne for letting you use the truck when you go back. It's much better than lying on the ground."

"I will. My days of a blanket on the ground are long over."

"Did Mike say anything about you coming over here?"

Jo looked over at him, their faces mere inches apart. "Nope. I didn't tell him. I just asked Alex to borrow the truck. He and Ben were too interested in inhaling their dinner so they could go play video games to ask where I was going. Mike seems to be having a last fling at childhood before he starts his job and tries adulting."

Greg chuckled. "Well, I'm sure we're going to be interrupted by my family at some point, and they'll make up for the lack of Mike."

Jo figured his brothers and sisters interrupting would eventually happen. The next one after Greg was Ben's age, but the youngest of the seven just turned ten years old. Joanna couldn't imagine growing up with six of them and not leave at the earliest opportunity. She didn't know how Greg did it and remained sane.

Jo looked up at the sky, not wanting to miss the natural light show. "When you talk about six people making up for the annoyance capability of one person, that says something."

"They recognize boundaries. They just don't care."

"You're a saint for dealing with so many brothers and sisters. I thought dealing with two was hard."

Greg shrugged. "I'm used to it and the chaos. I think it's weird when the house is quiet."

"I bet." Another meteor streaked across the sky, this one with a greenish light. "I've grown to like quiet since living in an apartment. My roommate doesn't have people over, and our work schedules are opposite each other."

"That sounds nice. I was going to ask Ms. Thorne if I could rent out the apartment above the store, but Carrie beat me to it. I took too long saving up a deposit."

"You know it has two bedrooms, right? I'm sure Alex wouldn't ask for a deposit, either. Carrie probably wouldn't mind a roommate if you don't leave the toilet seat up. She asked me to stay with her while I'm in town. It'll be available when I leave."

"It's a thought. Speaking of being in town, how long are you staying?"

"Not sure. Right now, two weeks."

"Any chance it may be longer?"

Jo stared straight into the night sky. "Possibly. Depends on the reason. The house doesn't need us to stay for a sale, and now that it's cleaned out, there's nothing else to do for Mom and Dad."

He pushed up and leaned over. He kissed her, lightly brushing his lips across hers. Jo held her breath and savored the feeling of his warm lips on hers. The kiss ended, and he pulled away.

"I'm sorry," he said.

Jo looked at him, puzzled. "For what?"

"For kissing you without asking if I could do it. I should have asked for consent first."

Jo melted a little inside at his thoughtfulness and consideration. "Thank you. And for the record, you may kiss me."

Greg smiled and kissed her again. Jo returned the kiss, her stomach fluttering and her heart beating faster. It ended much too soon.

She cuddled into his side. "That was nice."

"It was."

"It was gross," a voice said. Jo jumped and saw Greg's younger brother Jake crouched on the tailgate of the truck, looking down at them. Jo never heard him approach or climb up.

Greg sat up. Jo missed his warmth immediately. "Get!"

"No." Jake glared back defiantly.

Greg sighed. It was clear to Jo how this would play out. She put a hand over her mouth to keep from laughing out loud.

At ten years old, Jake was the youngest and apparently the most fearless. Not even intimidated by his older brother in the least. He had his big brother's number and knew it. When it came to the younger kids, Greg was a softy.

"Will you please leave us alone?" Jo could hear the exasperation in Greg's voice, and she patted his arm.

"What will you give me?" Jake's mischievous smile was pretty adorable.

"I'll give you five dollars to go away."

"Fine. Hand it over."

Greg shook his head. "I don't have my wallet on me, pup. I'll give it to you later."

The smile disappeared from Jake's face, and his eyes narrowed. Jo stifled a small laugh. Jake reminded her of Ben when he was younger. "I'm not falling for that."

"I'll give it to you later," Greg said. "But for now, I'll let you use my laptop."

Jake perked up, and the smile returned to his face. "Deal!"

"My pass—"

"I already know it." Jake tilted his head back, howled, and then leaped off the tailgate. He ran toward the house. The skinny little guy was fast.

"Sorry about that." Greg turned back to face Jo.

"It's okay," she assured him, giving his arm an affectionate squeeze. Now that her hand was on a part of him, she wasn't going to remove it. "My brothers would have interrupted us as well. Mike wouldn't have left, no matter what bribe I offered. In fact, he would've sat down between us and asked for the popcorn. It's the price we pay for family. I hope there's nothing embarrassing on it."

Greg lowered himself down to lie next to her. "I've been an older brother long enough to know I don't do anything on a laptop that can't be read out loud at the dinner table. Jake's proof of that. He's actually pretty good at respecting some boundaries. In this house, the offender and the tattler both get into trouble."

"Good to know."

Jo shifted over and snuggled up next to him again. She smiled when he slipped an arm under her and hugged her against his side.

"Want to hear something weird?" Jo watched another meteor streak across the sky.

"I'm always interested in something weird."

"Carrie and I found a trapdoor in the store office. We opened it, of course, and there was a tunnel. We followed it and found a heavy metal door. Locked, of course. We have no idea what's down there."

"That is weird. Did you ask Ms. Thorne about it?"

"Hell no." Jo laughed at her strong denial. "I didn't mean that as... Well, yes, I meant it."

"Why not?"

"Because I doubt she wants people knowing about it."

"Why do you think that?"

"I've known her all my life, and she has never once mentioned it or showed us. Carrie had a thought that it could have been a stop on the Underground Railroad, or for smugglers, but either of those seem like something Alex would have told us about. She loves telling us stuff like that."

"She does, and yeah, it seems like if it had some historical importance, she would mention it. Unless she wanted to keep curious people out of it. Jake would have made himself a den in there if he knew it existed."

"She's keeping something from us."

"Why does that bother you?"

"Because I don't want us mixed up in something dangerous. Locks are keeping people out or keeping something in. You and I were already attacked, and what if our parents' accident really wasn't an accident?"

Jo had considered it before, and each time she did, her chest tightened with panic. She didn't want to think her parents died because of Alex. Alex was family. Family wouldn't allow others to get hurt. Right?

"That's a pretty big leap." He held her a little closer against his side. "You think the attack on us was because of Ms. Thorne?"

Jo shrugged. "I'm not sure, but it could be. I don't like people keeping secrets when those secrets could get people hurt."

Greg looked away for a long moment. "Understandable," he finally said. "You could just ask her about it. Might be your best bet."

Jo wasn't sure it if was. How did one ask someone about all of this? She'd have to admit being in the underground tunnel, and she didn't want to do that. At least right now.

"Maybe," she said.

"People keep secrets for a reason," he said. "But you should ask her about the tunnel and the other stuff. The longer you wait, the more suspicious it will look that you knew about it and you were somewhere you weren't supposed to be."

"Well, that makes me sound like I'm twelve again. I get your point." Jo sighed. She heard her high school self in that sigh and didn't like it. "I just don't like people lying and keeping secrets that could get someone hurt."

Greg nodded. "I get it. No one wants to see their families hurt."

"Enough about all that stuff. Let's focus on the meteor shower and the kissing. Especially the kissing." Jo grinned, and Greg smiled.

"Especially the kissing," he echoed and kissed her.

Jo inhaled and held her breath, kissing him in return. His kiss was firm, not wet or sloppy. It was perfect. Jo's head spun, and blood thundered in her ears. Greg cupped her cheek with a hand, and Jo groaned against his mouth.

The kiss ended, and Greg pulled back. Jo didn't know if this was just a fling while she was here, or if it could turn into something more, but now, she didn't care either way. She was just thankful she was single and with Greg.

She put her head on his chest and closed her eyes for a long moment, listening to his heartbeat. It drained away thoughts of the attack, of Alex keeping secrets, and everything else.

CHAPTER NINE

ALEX AND STAVROS LEFT THE HOUSE MIDMORNING THE next day to spend the afternoon in Portland, giving Jo the perfect opportunity to search Alex's office in the house. Provided her brothers didn't find her. Those two would let it slip to Alex that Jo had been in there, or they'd ask why she was searching Alex's desk. She loved her brothers, but they were pains in the ass most of the time.

A half hour after the two left, and making sure the boys were out, Jo slipped into the office. The thirty minutes she waited were the longest in her life. She waited just in case Alex and Stavros forgot something and returned. Better to be safe than sorry.

Jo closed the door behind her, reached for the light switch, and looked around the room. She had rarely entered the room. It was Alex's personal space. Her presence was overwhelmingly there. Bookshelves made of dark wood lined the walls, and they were filled with worn leather-covered books. Jo wondered how old a book had to be to look like the ones on the shelves. Some even had titles in other languages. She knew Alex spoke other languages—Alex had even helped Jo, Mike, and Ben with their Spanish homework.

Small items lay scattered among the shelves, and they looked older than the books. They reminded Jo of museum artifacts.

A large Persian carpet covered most of the hardwood floor, and an imposing dark wood desk took center stage. Two oversize leather chairs sat in front of the desk, and a leather office chair sat behind it. She had to make her search quick.

A painting of a woman who looked eerily similar to Alex hung on the wall behind the desk and seemed to watch her. Jo had asked Alex about the painting in the past, and Alex had said it was an ancestor of hers. Jo would swear that it was Alex, just in old-fashioned clothes. The woman even wore the same silver star pendant Alex wore. The gray eyes even seemed to look at her the way Alex did. She heard once that if you thought the eyes of a painting were following you, it was done by a skilled artist. The artist had to have been amazing because Jo would swear the eyes recorded her every move. She shook off the feeling and crossed the room.

Heavy, dark curtains covered the three windows, blocking out the sunlight. The room was the only one in the house without sunlight pouring in. Jo wondered if the old books had something to do with it. Probably. Sunlight could destroy old books and paintings. The number of old things in the house greatly outnumbered the modern things.

Jo crossed the space and lowered herself into the leather office chair. A closed laptop sat in the middle of the desk, and a large red leather book sat to the right. Curious, Jo opened the book. A photo album. Jo picked it up and placed it on top of the laptop. Her heart leaped into her throat at the sight of her parents. The pain of their deaths cut right through her, and she resisted slamming the book shut.

She studied the pictures on the first few pages. They were of her parents and Alex, but in college before her parents were married. All three of them were so young, probably around Jo's age at the time. They were smiling and laughing in the pictures.

Jo peered closer at a picture of her mother and Alex. Alex looked exactly the same in the photo as she did now. The photo had to be over twenty-five years old, as Jo and Mike were not in the picture. Alex hadn't aged a day in all that time. Not even one wrinkle or a single gray hair. The woman must have the most amazing skin care regimen or had plastic surgery and colored her gray hair. Something had to explain it. Right? Though she didn't think Alex was the type to have plastic surgery.

Jo had never realized how long Alex and her parents had known each other. She had always assumed they met in more recent years since Alex seemed so young compared to her parents. These photos proved her wrong. She paged through the album and reached a few photos of her parents' wedding. Alex stood as her mother's maid of honor.

She continued to flip through the book, looking at the pictures and remembering her parents. Birth announcements for her and Mike and then for Ben were protected by plastic. Baby pictures followed each announcement, along with pictures of Alex holding each of them. More pictures of the three of them followed, including their school pictures. Pictures of Alex with Jo's family during the holidays also were contained in the book.

She snapped out of her reverie and remembered why she was sitting in Alex's office. She shut the photo album and returned it to the desk. She pulled open the top drawer on her left and peered inside. Office supplies and a few other items. Curious, Jo opened a small box. A silver baby rattle. She gave it a little shake and smiled at the tinkling sound it made. Was this something from Alex's own childhood? It had to be since Alex didn't have children. Or maybe it was an antique item she had picked up and intended to sell or give away at some point. Joanna returned the rattle to the box and put it back and searched for the mystery key, to no avail. She pushed the drawer shut and opened the middle one.

File folders and papers in this drawer. Most people kept their files electronically on a computer, but apparently not Alex. Jo lifted the stack and felt around the bottom of the drawer for the key. No such luck, so she shoved it closed and opened the large one at the bottom.

This drawer held a mix of cloth-bound notebooks, each with a ribbon bookmark curling over the cover, and some leather-bound books. She lifted out one of the leather books, expecting it to be one of the books Alex was always reading, but Jo realized it wasn't a book. It was a journal. The one in her hand didn't show signs of wear or use. Jo opened the cover and discovered blank pages.

Her new phone beeped, and she jumped. Her heart raced, and the sudden noise seemed twice as loud as normal in the quiet room. *Mental note, turn off the sound when snooping.* She grabbed it out of her pocket and looked at it. A text message from Carrie. She typed out a quick reply and shoved the phone back in her pocket.

She looked down at the drawer. The other journals showed signs of wear, but Jo didn't remove them. Even Alex deserved privacy. For now. Later could be a different matter. She felt around the drawer for the key, but again found nothing. With a sigh, Jo put everything back in the drawer and slid it shut.

Dammit. All of this had been for nothing. Knowing her luck, Alex kept the key to the mysterious door in her desk in the store office. Alex kept that desk locked and the key on her person. Jo wouldn't be able to search it unless Alex unlocked it and forgot to lock it before leaving. She didn't think that would happen any time soon.

The only other place the key could be was Alex's bedroom. Jo wasn't going in there unless it was the absolute last place left to search.

The door opened, and she practically jumped out of the chair. She held her breath until she realized it was Greg.

"You scared me!"

"What are you doing in here?" he asked, stepping into the room.

Her heart raced, but only part of it was caused by being startled. "Me? What about you? What are *you* doing here?"

"Making sure you're not getting into trouble."

Jo stood and walked around from behind the desk. "I was looking for the key to that door I told you about."

Greg frowned, and Jo took it as a sign of disapproval. Right now, finding the key and learning what lay beyond the door was worth a little disapproval from Greg. "I don't think Ms. Thorne would appreciate you going through her desk and office."

"I want to know what's in that room."

"Ms. Thorne probably has that room locked for a reason. There may be something dangerous in there. I think you should just ask her about it."

"I don't know. I'd rather find out what's in there myself."

"I don't think that's a good idea. She may have a good reason for not telling you. People keep secrets for a reason."

"I know, I know. Enough about her and her secret. What are you doing here?"

Greg smiled, and Jo swore her knees turned to jelly. Why had she never realized how charming he was when they were in high school? "Wanted to surprise you, maybe grab some lunch? My folks gave me the afternoon off."

"Remind me to thank your folks."

"You can do that yourself if you'd like to go to the restaurant. Or we can go somewhere else. Any place you want."

"I'd love to go there. We better go before Mike and Ben come home. They'll want to come along." Even if they had just eaten. One of them would claim they were still hungry, and Greg would invite them to go because he was just that nice.

"Let's go then." He took her hand and tugged her toward the hall. Jo followed him out, thoughts of the locked door and key pushed to the back of her mind.

CHAPTER TEN

"ARE WE IN THE INDY 500?" JO ASKED AS SHE LEANED forward between the two front seats to look at the speedometer. "You're going fifty-five in a thirty-five."

"Somebody's following us." Mike glanced in the rearview mirror.

She shook her head. Mike had to be imagining things. She turned around in her seat and shifted a little so she could see the car behind them. Beside her in the back seat, Carrie looked around as well. A silver SUV was indeed behind them, but it didn't mean it was following them. Mike's imagination was running away with him again.

It was after 7:00 p.m., and the twins, along with Greg and Carrie, were on their way home from Freeport, Maine, about an hour away from Good Harbor. Jo had insisted on going down for the day so she could go to the flagship L.L. Bean store. Three solid rainy days had made her crave being somewhere else. Mike was happy to go since it was a rare day Greg and Carrie were both off work at the same time. It didn't come as a surprise that Carrie came along. Ben had wanted to join them, but the Jeep Wrangler only sat four comfortably. Jo had felt a little guilty, but not as much as she might have a few months ago. Ben had friends to hang out with, and the four of them had their day out. It had been a nice drive until now.

This would be the part in a movie where someone said they had a bad feeling about this. Jo wasn't going to say it out loud, but she did have a bad feeling about this.

"The silver SUV behind us," Mike said.

Jo looked behind again. The SUV drew closer to the Jeep.

"Are you sure it's following us? Like how you think Alex is some vampire or something else long-lived when you saw her old pictures?"

"It's been following us since we left the highway," Mike said. "I'd like to see you come up with something to explain why Alex looks no different from old photos."

"What's this about Ms. Thorne?" Greg asked.

"I'll tell you later," Jo said. She should have never told Mike about seeing the old photos and her observation of how Alex looked like she hadn't aged in over twenty-five years. She glanced out the rear window again. Maybe this wasn't all in Mike's head. The SUV was close. A broken clock was right twice a day. Mike could be right. Maybe.

"What should we do?" Carrie's voice sounded a little panicked. Jo felt it too.

"Hold on." Mike slowed down just enough to safely take the next turn. Once around the turn, Mike stomped on the gas and increased their speed.

At least the roads were dry, Jo thought. She turned around again, and the silver SUV reappeared around the corner, sped up, and once again drew closer to the Jeep.

"He's definitely following us," Mike said.

Her stomach twisted as her heart pounded in her chest. Images of the night attack flashed in her mind. She took a deliberate breath to settle the panic trying to rise.

"Jo, call Alex. Now."

Jo yanked her phone out of her pocket. She should have thought of it sooner. Her hands shook as she hunted for Alex's contact information. "Greg or Carrie, one of you call 9-1-1."

"Faster, Mike," Greg urged.

Mike increased the Jeep's speed.

Alex picked up after one ring, and Jo frantically told Alex what was happening and where they were. She glanced back to see the SUV pick up speed. She urged Alex to hurry as she gripped the handle above the window, her knuckles turning white from the effort. The SUV drew even closer, and then a hard bump rocked the Jeep. Carrie screamed, and her phone fell from Jo's hand..

The SUV hit them again, harder this time, and Mike wrestled the steering wheel to keep the Jeep in the right lane. Trees lined the side of the road, and Jo knew hitting one at this speed would be disastrous. The SUV hit them a third time. Mike nearly lost his battle with the wheel.

Fear coiled inside Jo and sent chills throughout her body. Her breath came in ragged gasps, and blood thundered in her ears.

The SUV came up alongside and turned into the Jeep, causing Jo and Carrie to scream once more. Mike spun the wheel toward it, trying to keep the Jeep on the road. It worked, somewhat. Mike pushed the pedal all the way to the floor, and the Jeep shot ahead of the SUV, all four tires returning to the pavement.

The SUV sped up and smashed again into the rear of the Jeep, sending the Jeep off the road. It bounced over the uneven ground, and tree branches scraped against the side. Mike jerked the wheel and brought the Jeep back on the road once more. The SUV swerved and hit them again.

"Hold on!" Mike yelled as the Jeep veered off the road and went down a small embankment. The right corner smashed into a tree, and the quarter panel crumpled. The engine sputtered and died. The front airbags deployed. Mike and Greg each got a face full of nylon and powder. In the back, Jo and Carrie were jerked around, held in place by their seat belts.

It was a moment before anyone could speak.

"Everyone okay?" Mike asked.

"Sort of," Carrie said weakly as she tried to sit up straight. "I'll know in a minute."

"I think so," Greg said. He held his left arm against his body. "That didn't feel good."

"Now that I'm not dead, I'm going to kill someone," Jo said as she struggled with the seat belt and tried to push away the icy tendrils of fear. Anger was easier, and she focused on that.

"You may get your chance," Mike said as the silver SUV came to a stop ahead of them. A moment later, a man emerged from around the other side. He walked purposely toward the Jeep.

"Everyone out!" Mike yelled.

For a long moment, they all were still, and then the world stuttered into motion as they scrambled to release seat belts. They climbed out as fast as they could. Instead of running as Mike had ordered them to do, they stood transfixed as the man stalked toward them.

"That's the same guy." Surprise overtook Jo's anger. Her feet refused to move.

"What guy?" Mike asked.

"The man who attacked us," Greg said.

He stood nearly six feet tall and wore a black military type of uniform. Sweat glistened on the dark skin of his bald head. Dark eyes stared at them. Gravel crunched with every step, and the closer he got, the more threatening it sounded. A gun holster was strapped to his left side, and what looked like a knife handle adorned his right.

Jo knew they should run, but she was frozen to the spot.

Carrie grabbed Mike's arm.

"Guys." Jo swallowed past the lump in her throat. "We really need to run." Her brain was working, but her feet refused to follow orders.

None of them moved as the man walked toward them.

"You can't escape me, monster." The man drew the pistol from the holster on his hip.

Confusion trickled through the fear, and Jo wondered which one of them the man was talking to. "There aren't any monsters here," Jo said as she backed against the Jeep and pressed her side against Carrie's. Her voice cracked from the fear that squeezed her insides.

"Leave them alone." Greg stepped out and stood in front of the huddled girls.

Not to be left out, Mike also stepped in front of the girls to shield them from the man's line of fire.

"I'm not here for them," the man spat. "Just you."

"Fine. I'll come with you if you let them go," Greg said.

Jo's outrage drowned her fear. "What are you doing?"

"Protecting you all. You three need to run."

"We're not running or leaving you. He can try this with witnesses."

"Yeah, what Jo said," Mike added. "We're not leaving."

"The three of you can leave, and you won't get hurt," the man told them. He kept aim on Greg, but he didn't advance toward them.

A black truck pulled up behind the silver SUV, and Alex and Stavros climbed out. They approached the man pointing a gun at them without pause.

Alex had such a look of determination on her face that Jo almost felt sorry for the guy. "Leave them alone!"

The man glanced over at his shoulder to look at the newcomers. "This is none of your business."

"It is my business. They're my family."

"Claver, isn't it? Peter Claver. I know you," Stavros said.

"So glad you remember." Claver didn't seem glad of it, though. He looked back at the group, then to Alex and Stavros. He appeared to be weighing his options. "I know you as well."

"It's best to leave. Right now. You know what you're dealing with, and you know you can't possibly come out of this alive." The two stopped about three feet away from the man. Stavros called to Claver, "If you're going to do something, you better make it count. You only have one chance."

Claver stared at Alex and Stavros, appearing to forget about Greg. The strange part was that Claver held a gun, and Alex and Stavros were unarmed. Claver seemed wary of them.

Jo's jaw dropped open as Claver lowered his weapon and returned it to a holster. He gave Alex and Stavros a long look and then walked toward his vehicle. Alex and Stavros watched his every step. After Claver pulled away, they turned back to them.

Jo let out a sigh of relief once Claver's SUV disappeared out of sight and sagged against Carrie. Alex reached them quickly. She pulled Jo in for a tight hug. She hugged Alex just as tightly. The incident had shaken her more than she realized.

"Are you okay? Did he hurt any of you? Tell me now before he gets too far away."

"Yeah. Just shaken up." Jo pushed back from Alex to shake out her fear. "That was unreal."

Alex moved on to Mike. "How are you?"

"Just banged up a little. Who was that?"

"Answers later. Carrie, are you all right?"

"Like Mike and Jo. Shaken and banged up." Alex wrapped her arms around Carrie and pulled her in for a hug every bit as fierce as the one she'd given Jo. Carrie's eyes widened at the gesture, but she clung to Alex as well.

Alex released Carrie and looked at Greg. "How are you?"

Greg stared at her with an expression that said he was on the verge of understanding something important. She had to ask again before he answered. "I'll be fine. Arm's bruised with Mike's evasive maneuvering. You might want to get him some driving lessons."

Mike scowled but said nothing under Stavros's amused gaze.

"I need to get home," Greg said urgently. "My parents need to know what's happening."

"They're on the way."

THE ARRIVAL OF THE GOOD HARBOR POLICE AND AN ambulance interrupted the reunion and gave Alex time to regain her composure. Her stomach had been tied up into a knot since she received Jo's call. Seeing them all relatively okay helped unwind it a bit. She thanked the gods she had thought to track Joanna's phone with GPS as she had with Ben's. They wouldn't have reached the kids in time if she hadn't. There were times infernal technology was useful to have.

Carrie's mom and Greg's mom arrived moments after the police. Damianos talked to the officers while the EMTs checked injuries. The four gave statements to the officers once medical attention had been given. Alex explained to the mothers what had happened, leaving out the part of knowing the instigator's name.

Alex watched Damianos talking to the local police. She wondered what story he was telling them. He probably told them a story close to what happened, but not the whole truth. They could never tell mortals the whole truth about most things in their lives.

"Who was that man?" Jo asked.

Alex sighed. How did she explain this without telling them her secret? The two halves of her world were colliding, and she didn't know how she would deal with it. Now she understood why she had felt uneasy the other day at the café. Claver had probably been nearby watching.

What did the Catholic Church want with the kids? None of this made sense. Mike, Jo, and Ben, like their parents, were human and wouldn't attract the notice of the Catholic Church. Well, this sect of the Church. Their operatives weren't dumb enough to use the kids to get to Alex. They had tried to kill her in the mid-fourteenth century, and the incident ended with dead operatives. Three to be exact, if she remembered correctly.

There might have been another incident in the 1600s, but Alex wasn't exactly sure. Her memory had a nasty habit of mixing the centuries at times. If the Inquisitors were after her for some unknown reason, maybe it was time to remind them why it was a bad idea. Maybe Damianos had been right, and a big name was hiding in the tall grass, waiting for a chance to grab her. Perhaps that big name just happened to be the Catholic Church.

"Why was he after us?"

Mike's question dragged Alex back to the here and now. She wanted to tell them the truth, but they were better off not knowing. The kids could be used by people like Claver against Alex. If she didn't tell them, they couldn't offer up any information they didn't have. Telling them she was immortal and over twenty-four hundred years old was a last option.

"I don't know. I've only heard his name. This is the first time I've actually met him. His name is Peter Claver."

"He seemed to be after Greg." Jo watched Greg and his mother talk with Damianos.

"Did he say why?" The mystery surrounding the Sullivan boy grew. Alex needed answers, and the one person who could get them wasn't talking.

"When he got near us, he said, 'You can't escape me, monster.' Then Greg got in front of us like he could make Crazy Guy listen to reason and told him to leave us alone. Why did Greg think the man was talking to him?" The tone of Jo's voice was more demanding than questioning.

That was a question to which Alex wanted an answer. She was

missing something important. It could be the piece of information to make sense of the situation.

"I don't know. I'm as baffled as you are."

She glanced over to see an EMT putting a splint on Greg's arm. Alex turned her head to listen. She overheard the EMT telling Greg he should let them take him in for an X-ray. Greg declined with a sharp jerk of his head. Mrs. Sullivan told the EMT she would take him to their own doctor.

Something was definitely going on with the Sullivans. What was it? Why would they be the target of the Church operative? Maybe having Damianos around would be helpful. The man had many more connections than Alex did. Plus, it would give him something to do and keep him out of her business and away from the kids.

"Something weird is going on," Mike said.

"On that we agree. Did Greg say anything to why Claver was after him?"

Jo thought about it for a half second before shaking her head. "No. I would have remembered."

There was nothing more to be learned by standing here and everything to lose by letting the local authorities listen to their conversation. "Let's go. The police will have the Jeep towed. I'll call the insurance agent." There were no arguments from Mike or Jo. They climbed into the extended cab truck and waited for Stavros. She hadn't realized Carrie and her mother had gone. She wanted to give them both reassurances that everything would be fine, and any injuries Carrie might have to be covered by Alex personally, but that would have to be done by phone later.

"Are you two sure you're okay?" she asked again.

"Yeah," Mike said. "I'll be sure to let you know if I spontaneously gush blood from any gaping wounds."

Jo raised a fist to punch his shoulder, but adulthood and sheer relief they were okay only let her swat at him. "Why didn't

Stavros arrest that man? He's in law enforcement, right? He knew the guy. What good is a badge if he can't arrest the bad guy?"

Alex refrained from sighing in frustration. Jo would not let things go unanswered. She had been like this her whole life. To think she used to admire that sort of tenacity when it wasn't directed at her personally. "I would imagine jurisdictional issues. I really can't say."

"Couldn't he detain him until the local police arrived?" Mike chimed in.

"I don't know," Alex said. "You'd have to ask Stavros. Though, the man probably won't answer you. He never gives a straight answer if he doesn't want to talk about it."

"It was the same man who attacked Greg and I the other night."

Alex turned in her seat to look at Jo. "What?"

Jo nodded. "Yeah. That's him."

"Did you just realize that now?"

"It took me a bit, but the whole monster thing was the dead giveaway."

"I had hoped the attacker had left town."

"Me too. Now that I know what to look for, I'll be looking over my shoulder."

"I think for a short time, all of you should stay near the house." Claver didn't dare come there if he knew what was good for him. Even Church officials were fatally mortal. She wouldn't hesitate to kill a few more as a reminder. She'd use Damianos to kill if she had to. She'd do anything to protect those she considered family. The weight of protecting the whole world didn't rest on her shoulders, but the weight of protecting her world did, and it was proving to be the heavier of the two.

"It's going to suck not having a car we can use."

"Let's worry about that a little later, Mike. It's not the important thing right now."

"I guess it doesn't matter too much. Jo and I are only going to be here for a short time. Ben's the one that'll suffer."

Alex managed a tiny smile. Despite the circumstances, Mike couldn't avoid taking a jab at his younger brother. Mike resilience was always impressive, and the three's antics toward each other while they had been growing up had always amused Alex.

"We'll deal with the suffering tomorrow. Tonight, we're going to go back to the house, have some dinner, and try to relax."

"Easier said than done," Jo grumbled.

"I know. Stavros will figure out what's going on."

"Is he going to be around from now on?" Mike asked.

"I hope not too long." Alex didn't want him around, but she saw the necessity of the man's presence. She just hoped it didn't end in heartbreak for her like it always did.

It took a while, but Damianos eventually climbed into the passenger's seat.

"All set?" Alex asked.

"For now."

"Jo, will you please call Ben and ask him to come home tonight? I'll feel better with all of you at the house."

"Yeah, sure."

"Thanks," Alex said as she started the engine. "I'll pick him up."

"What are we doing for dinner tonight?" Mike asked.

Alex smiled as she pulled the truck onto the road. Leave it to Mike to make things seem normal when they clearly weren't. "I was thinking takeout tonight. Pizza if that's good. I know we just had it the other night."

"You can never have too much pizza."

Alex chuckled. Ben and Mike thought the same. Though when she and Ben had pizza, most of the time she made it at the house. "We can get Chinese. I'm fine with either."

"Pizza," Mike said. "I get hungry after eating Chinese."

"Fair enough."

They reached the house and climbed out of the truck. Ben texted Alex that he was ready whenever she was.

"Mike, place an order for dinner. I'll pick it up after I get Ben."

"Yeah, sure. You'll need him to carry everything I'm going to order."

"Within reason," Alex reminded him. "Think of the space I don't have in the refrigerator."

"I promise you that won't be a problem," Mike vowed.

CHAPTER ELEVEN

"Earth to Jo." Greg tapped her on the shoulder.

Jo pushed herself off Greg and sat up. She turned and looked at him. "What?"

Greg smiled. "Wondering where you zoned off to. I asked you a question, and you didn't answer. What's going on inside your head?"

Jo and Greg were spending the evening in the apartment. Carrie was spending the night at her parents' house, leaving Jo alone. Her parents decreed that their adult daughter was required to spend some time at the family home on occasion. It was a thinly veiled demand for a sitter when they wanted to have date night.

The last thing Jo wanted was to be alone, so she invited Greg over to watch a movie. His company was preferred over her brothers hanging out in here with her.

The movie they were watching couldn't keep her attention. The privacy they were finally enjoying in her living room didn't compete with the loop of events of two days ago playing in her mind. She enjoyed cuddling on the sofa with Greg, and it was as perfect a night as she could ask for if her brain would slow down.

"I was just thinking. The man, Peter Claver, called you a monster. Do you know him?" The man bugged her. Why had it seemed so personal? If someone was after Alex, then Jo, Mike, and Ben would be the logical targets too. It was well-known in Good Harbor how close their families were.

Greg shook his head. "No. Never saw him before he attacked us. I don't have a clue why he would say those things."

"He seemed to know you. It just all seems weird. Especially how he backed down in front of Stavros and Alex."

"Now that part was weird. He was armed. He had all the advantage."

"Too many strange things happening lately. I thought small towns were boring and I needed the fast pace of big city life."

"We get our share of fast pace. It just happens every other decade."

Greg settled her closer against his chest. She dropped a light kiss on his mouth but couldn't let the subject go. "With Stavros staying here, Alex looks like she's chewing on nails." That wasn't all true. There were the moments when a softer expression appeared on Alex's face. She knew Stavros was worming his way back into whatever good graces Alex might have left for him.

"So lots of entertainment then?"

Jo smiled. "Something like that. What I want to know is what police department he's with. His badge said SPD on it."

Greg shrugged. "Dunno. There are a lot of towns in Maine that start with S. Scarborough, Skowhegan, Sanford, Saco. Could be any or none of them."

"And that's just Maine. I can ask Carrie to look into it. Maybe she can find out."

"I've never seen anyone like looking stuff up as much as she does, not even any librarian I've ever met. She helped me find research articles in high school when I first moved here and had to catch up on my graduation requirements. She helped a lot of people in high school and college. Some of them didn't seem to appreciate it."

"Mike and I did, so did you." Jo kissed him again. "You are one of the nicest guys around."

"You exaggerate my awesomeness."

"I didn't say awesomeness, but I don't exaggerate one bit."

"I think you may be a little biased," Greg teased. He kissed her.

It was a great kiss, but her brain wouldn't stop and let her enjoy the moment. "What do you think Alex may be hiding?"

She almost missed the resigned expression. She could see he really didn't care about it.

"I honestly don't know. I really don't know Ms. Thorne like you do. I had her a few times as a substitute teacher in school, but I don't know anything about her personal life. She comes into the restaurant occasionally for dinner, but mostly talks to my parents. She must believe that whatever it is, it's about your own safety."

"I don't get it. She's keeping a secret, but it's supposed to be for our safety? What could be threatening us?" She paused for a moment. "Except for that guy who keeps showing up, but it sounded more like he was after you."

"I don't know why. My life is boring. I work for my parents and like this really hot girl."

As distractions went, that one worked. "I want to know her name," Jo mock growled. "So I can kick her ass for poaching this hot guy I like."

Greg laughed and pulled her in for a thorough kiss. Jo was breathless when it ended. She smiled and rubbed his nose with her own. Now he had her full attention.

"Everyone keeps secrets," he said quietly. "Big ones and little ones. I don't think Ms. Thorne would do anything to harm the three of you. It's easy to see she cares a lot. That's not nothing."

"I don't like it."

"You don't like it because you don't know what it is. You're not entitled to know her business."

Greg was right, but Jo still had issues with it. She wanted to know Alex's secret before it ended up getting someone hurt. "What about you?"

"What about me?"

"Do you have secrets?"

"Do you?"

Of course she did. She assumed he did since he didn't answer. The only question was, did she want to know his? Not right now, she decided. She didn't want to do anything to jeopardize their budding relationship. If this was a relationship. She was supposed to go back to Boulder in a week. She tried not to think about it much, figuring they would make a decision about their relationship when the time came.

"Stay tonight," she urged, following with a persuasive kiss. Jo never lacked boldness. They had seen each other almost every day in the past week and a half, and she felt comfortable enough around him. It wouldn't be the first time she had a sleepover. This one just had more potential to turn into something serious.

Greg pulled back. "What?"

"Stay tonight," she repeated. "I want you to spend the night."

Greg stared at her, and she wondered what was going through his mind. Silence slammed in between them. It shouldn't have taken him this long to answer.

"Greg?"

"I shouldn't," he finally said.

"Why not?"

"Because this is Ms. Thorne's house, and I don't want to offend her."

Jo sighed. "Yes, this is her house, but we are both adults. You won't offend her. She's pretty laid-back about sex. She asked Mike and I each if we were sexually active, and if we were using protection. She also said it was okay to have people stay over since we were adults. Ben complained it was unfair."

"Really?"

"Really."

"That's very open-minded of her. My parents wouldn't be so understanding. Fine, I'll stay as long as I can."

"Not all night?"

"Ms. Thorne might be okay with it, but my parents like me to be home before the sun comes up. They worry about me, and I don't like to make them worry. Especially with that crazy guy running around. Besides, if I'm not there to start the sauces at dawn, I'll lose out to one of the others and have to wait tables."

"That I can understand. At least you'll stay awhile." She smiled and kissed him hard. The movie was forgotten as she worked her hands under his shirt. He wrapped his arms around her.

The kiss deepened, and Jo moaned as Greg slid his hands down her back into the back of her jeans.

He groaned against her mouth and ended the kiss. He leaned back and looked at her. "Jo, I..." He scrunched up his face.

Jo had a sudden pang of alarm. "What is it? Whatever it is, you can tell me."

"I've never..."

"Never what?" she prompted when he didn't continue.

"I've never had sex."

That was definitely a secret. Greg was hot enough to have girls chasing him for it, and he was in college. She found herself in a quandary. It didn't matter to her or in the grand scheme of things if he had never had sex. She wanted him, but finding herself on the other side of the issue was a surprise. He seemed so uncomfortable, and she wanted to put him at ease.

"It's okay. We can just watch the movie. We can watch movies all night."

His sigh of relief told her that was the right thing to say. "No, I want to. I really do. I just wanted you to know in case I really suck and you're disappointed."

Jo kissed him and climbed to her feet. She held out her hand. "I could never be disappointed in spending time with you, no matter what we're doing." Greg put his hand in hers and stood. Jo tugged on his hand and led him to her bedroom. She closed the door. She locked it, just to be sure. Her luck wasn't so great lately. She didn't need a brother barging in on them.

Jo wrapped her arms around Greg's neck and pressed her body against his. She kissed him and a sudden rush of heat flooded her. The heat settled below her stomach as desire filled her. She deepened the kiss, and he shifted against her.

She broke the kiss. "Do what I do." She pulled her T-shirt over her head. She dropped it to the floor. His appreciative look was an ego boost.

He hastily removed his shirt, and it was her turn to admire the view. He was a treat to see. Defined muscles and a dusting of chest hair beckoned her to touch.

Seeing if he would continue to follow her lead, she unfastened her jeans and slid them down. She stepped out of them and left them in a heap on the floor. She stood in a bra and panties, exposing as much skin as she would wearing a swimsuit. Greg smiled and unfastened his pants. The denim fell to the floor around his ankles and left him in his boxer briefs.

Jo removed her bra and panties, her eyes never leaving his.

Greg maintained eye contact as he slipped his underwear off.

"Still with me?"

For an answer, he closed the distance between them and wrapped her in his arms. The feel of skin on skin was better than anything else. With his kiss, Jo lost a little bit of herself in the sensation.

She released him and walked to the bed. She stretched out in the middle and crooked a finger at him.

He laughed. "You look so cute doing that."

"Cute and all by myself," she mock pouted.

He crawled into bed next to her and pulled her to him. Lying side by side, feeling her skin touching Greg's from chest to toes, was unexpectedly erotic. Jo's past encounters had been hurried on one level or another. Roommates, early morning classes, late night studies, even the lack of real interest in her partner all conspired to keep sexual activities quick and infrequent. Greg holding her, his face in her neck breathing in the scent of skin, was the hottest thing she'd experienced in a long time. Maybe ever.

"You smell good," he muttered into her hair. The snuffling noises around her ear tickled. It reminded her of Munchkin sniffing around the table for dropped food. Probably not a sexy thing to think at the moment, but it was cute.

She took his hand and cupped it around her breast. He grasped the soft mound with a gentleness that made her fall a little bit in love with him. She moaned into his kiss.

He broke the kiss. "Too rough? Say something."

"It's okay to touch," she assured him. "It feels good. Touch anywhere you want."

She closed her eyes as he stroked her side and cupped her hip to press her closer to what felt like a pretty impressive erection.

"Might be a little late to say this, but I don't have anything."

"I think you have a lot," she teased and moved against him.

It was his turn to moan. "I mean, I didn't come here intending to have sex."

Joanna couldn't stop shifting against the erection pressed to her stomach. "What are you talking about?"

"Uh, protection?"

Oh crap, she remembered now. Why hadn't she thought of it before they got naked? It broke the mood. She had to get the mood back fast. "Right, protection. Let me go. There's some in the bathroom."

Greg rolled away to lie on his back, and she scrambled to her feet. He was such a mouthwatering sight that she didn't want to leave him. For someone so inexperienced, he looked comfortable in his nudity. She liked that. She'd like it even more if she was on top of him.

She ran for the bathroom and grabbed a handful of foil-wrapped packets. She was grateful now that Alex had made a point of providing condoms. At the time, it was embarrassing to speak of it with another person, especially a family member.

Hurrying back, she practically leaped onto the bed next to him and was immediately enfolded in his arms again. He ran his hands over her breasts, brushing his fingertips over hard nipples. Jo sucked in a breath and felt a low ache begin.

He kissed her chin and then her neck. Nipping the tender flesh, he moved downward to lick the sweat sheen between her breasts. He caressed a nipple with his tongue. Flames leapt to the surface. She arched and pressed against his mouth.

Greg moaned and playfully nipped at the hard nipple. She gasped, tunneling her fingers into his hair to urge him on. He worked his way down toward her stomach and slid his hand down between her legs.

Her moan stopped him. It was a moment before she realized he had stilled. "What?" she asked breathlessly.

"Are you okay? Is this okay?"

"*Yes!*" She was trying to whisper, but her voice echoed in a loud demand. "I mean…" She covered his hand with hers and guided him on. Under her instructions, he parted her with his fingers, and she pushed against his touch. "Right here. Touch me…here."

He did as she directed, moving his fingers in hard and soft touches, rubbing the sensitive nub as she writhed against him. He lifted his head to kiss her as he did, breathing in her gasps. She came, stiffening against his body, waves of pleasure washing over her body as he worked her, her cries swallowed by his mouth.

When she opened her eyes, she found him staring down at her. "We're not done," she assured him. "I didn't expect that."

"I didn't either," he said, the half-smile oddly tender.

Joanna surged up and rolled with Greg, ending up on top of him. She rose to sit over him. She looked down into his eyes and smiled. "Are you sure about this? We can stop."

"I'm sure."

She reached for a foil packet and opened it. Now that she was actually face-to-face with his erection, so to speak, she had to admire it. She removed the latex circle and slipped it on him, rolling it down with ease. He pushed against her touch, and Jo smiled.

Jo positioned herself over him and slowly lowered herself down. Greg surged up, catching her off guard, and missed entering her. For a first moment, it failed spectacularly. She had to laugh.

"I'm sorry." The words fumbled past his lips.

"Don't be sorry. It happens. We get a do-over." She wrapped her hand around him and guided him inside her. Greg gasped, and Jo smiled. She relished the feel of him sliding into her, all hard strength and power.

Jo moved her hips slowly, getting comfortable with the seat. He placed his hands on her hips and urged her on.

"Oh God, Jo," he groaned.

She increased the speed of her hips, faster and harder against him. She leaned over and kissed him hard, her tongue entering his mouth. Tightness formed where their bodies were joined.

Jo straightened up, and her head fell back. She braced her hands against his shoulders as she rode him. She didn't think. She couldn't think. All she could do was chase the pleasure spiraling through her again.

Greg pushed up with his hips against her, and she responded with a deep moan. The pressure inside her continued to build, tightening like a rubber band about ready to snap.

She increased her speed, aching to release again and take him with her. She tensed for a long moment and broke apart, her climax washing over her. Every nerve in her body was stimulated, every sensation enhanced. A small scream slipped past her lips.

He pulled her down and rolled them over. She held on as he moved, thrusting hard and fast inside her. She wound her arms around his chest and dug her fingers into his back. She tried to move with him, but he was too fast for her. She tightened her legs around his hips and held on.

Greg groaned, and his whole body tensed. His face scrunched up, and after a few moments, he collapsed on her. Wet with perspiration, sated, and for the moment, exhausted, they rested together.

"That was amazing," he said, kissing her. "You're amazing."

Jo smiled tiredly up at him. "I'd like to think we're both amazing."

Greg grinned. "I'll agree with that."

CHAPTER TWELVE

ALEX LOOKED UP FROM HER PHONE WHEN THE OFFICE door opened. She expected to see one of the kids standing there, but Damianos filled the doorway. She pressed her lips together and sighed. She had managed to get through the day without seeing him and had hoped to get through the evening as well. No such luck.

"Problem?"

"It's currently standing in the doorway."

Damianos laughed, the sound louder than it should have been in the quiet office. He shut the door behind him. Alex suddenly wished Munchkin was in the room and not outside. "That look on your face tells me there's a problem."

"I haven't heard from an agent. I sent Paladin to check on him, and he can't find him."

Damianos slid his denim-covered butt onto the corner of the mahogany desk. He loomed over her. It was an old trick of his to gain the upper hand in a situation, but Alex was immune. He might come off as scary and intimidating to others, but not to her. Alex looked up at him and into his dark eyes. She immediately found something else to focus on. Stress and loneliness were a bad combination with a far too perceptive former lover in the house.

"Any idea what happened to him?"

Alex shook her head. "No. I got a text from my agent saying he thought he was being followed, then nothing. I sent Paladin to Seattle to follow up."

"Which agent? Have you pissed anyone off recently?"

"No." She glared at him. She wasn't about to give him the name of any of her employees. It was bad enough he knew about Paladin. She didn't make enemies left and right like he did, and how dare he think so.

He put his hands up. "Just asking. Do you know of anyone who could be out to get you? Anyone in your professional life mad at you for scoring a big find at the auctions?"

"No more than usual. It's been decades since I actively got into anyone's way. The last time I did anything worth making an enemy was with you in Argentina."

He smiled. "That was a fun time."

Alex couldn't help but smile at the memory. "It was." Together they had hunted Nazis in Argentina for a decade. It had been a relatively pleasant decade after the horrors of war they had witnessed in Europe. Killing Nazis never stopped being a good time.

"I can talk to Auggie and see if he'll lend some help," he suggested.

She didn't need August Morrow, head of the Supernatural Police Department, getting involved in her personal business if she could help it. While on occasion she and August, Auggie to most, collaborated, this wasn't something the SPD needed to be involved in. "No. I'd rather keep the SPD out of things."

"Okay. Your house guests are interesting."

She raised a brow in inquiry. "Which one?"

"All of them. But Mike and Jo grilled me the other night when you went to pick Ben and dinner up."

"Do I dare ask?"

"About you, about us, about the SPD, and they tried to get answers out of me about Claver."

"What did you tell them?" She narrowed her eyes and set her jaw. She prayed to whatever gods were listening that he had not told them something he shouldn't have. She doubted he told them about their immortality. The kids, especially Mike and Ben, would have grilled her the second she returned from picking up dinner and would have asked questions all night.

"I didn't tell them about what we are, if that's what you're concerned about."

"I know you didn't. They wouldn't believe you anyway."

"The older boy would. He seems like the type. I told them we used to date when we were younger."

"And?" Alex prompted. That couldn't be it. There had to be more. It was just like him to not give her the full story up front. Instead, he would make her ask and get it little by little.

"They talked about getting another vehicle, and I told them that you probably had one around that you've forgotten about at a property somewhere," he said nonchalantly.

"Why would you tell them that?" She didn't want the kids knowing too much about her. They were bound to ask, and she hated lying to them.

"Because it's true."

"Just because it's true doesn't mean you have to tell them."

"I had no reason to lie about it. It's a car, not a crown. Many people invest in property and dare to store things. I do myself."

"You mean you have safe houses. It's not the same thing."

"I should have said vaults?"

Alex sighed and stood. As soon as she moved, he grabbed one of her hands and pulled her toward him. She resisted, and he tugged again, pulling her against him. He stood and captured her lips in a fierce kiss. Alex put her hands on his chest and pushed to no avail. The kiss ended, and she could scarcely breathe. She wisely took two steps away from him.

"Don't do that!"

He chuckled. "I like doing that."

She liked it herself, but she had to think. "What did you learn about the Sullivans? Why is Claver after them?" He had spent the day out of the house, and she assumed he was investigating the Sullivans and why Claver appeared to be after them. Or at least she hoped that's what he had been doing.

He reached out to grasp her hand, and she took another step back. "They're fine."

"I didn't ask how they were," Alex grumbled. The man never answered questions when it suited him. "I asked what you learned about them."

"I spoke to George Sullivan. They're not sure how Claver found them. I have some agents keeping an eye out, but Claver appears to be gone. They're likely to be gone in the night themselves soon. I gave him my card in case there are problems."

She wanted to ask what supernatural type the Sullivans were, but she didn't. Everyone had a right to privacy, and Alex held firmly onto that belief. "Did he mention moving?"

The Sullivans were nice people, and Alex hated the idea of them having to uproot their lives again. If she remembered correctly, they had moved here about six years ago, and with what had recently happened, now she assumed their relocation had something to do with Church-sanctioned killers.

"No."

"I hope they don't."

"Why do you ask?"

"They're good people, and I enjoy eating at their restaurant. I think there's something happening between Jo and their son Greg."

With everything that had happened in the past week, she'd prefer Jo and Mike to stay in Good Harbor until Alex knew things had been resolved and they'd be safe. Greg might be the reason why Jo would stick around.

"How long has it been since you've had children in the house?"

A knot formed in her stomach, and her chest tightened. She swallowed past the lump in her throat. The single word barely made it past her lips. "Eleni."

Silence slammed in between them. The pain of Eleni's death honed to razor sharpness at the mere mention of her name. Time failed to heal the deep wound.

His face echoed the pain of her expression. "I'm sorry. I shouldn't have brought it up."

"It's okay," Alex assured him. It wasn't okay, but she wouldn't drag him across the coals for it. He still mourned the loss of their daughter just as much as she did. Even after more than two hundred years. "It's no one's fault, only the time she lived in."

He reached out and took her hands. "It still hurts like hell."

"It does. But I would rather feel the pain than ever forget her."

He released her hands and placed his hands on her cheeks. He tenderly kissed her forehead. She closed her eyes when his lips touched her skin.

He removed his hands from the sides of her face and wrapped his arms around her. Normally she'd resist, but Alex leaned into him and rested her head against his wide chest. He kissed the top of her head, and she breathed easier.

His heart beat steadily in her ear, and time slowed, the world slowly righting itself. Calm engulfed her, and his love gave her some solid ground to stand on amid the chaos of recent events. No matter how much of an asshole he usually was, he was always there when the bottom dropped out in her life.

"How are they?" he murmured into her hair.

He never needed to say who "they" were. Their daughter's line continued into the present day, some of them still living in Good Harbor. Alex watched from afar through two centuries. It was the most contact she allowed herself, except for the few who knew nothing of her but accepted her friendship.

"They're safe. Happy enough."

"Good."

She lifted her head and placed a light kiss on his mouth. He tightened his embrace, pressing Alex's body flush with his. The kiss deepened. Embers of desire flared to life and settled below her stomach. Danger grew with every second she touched him, and she'd be past the point of rescue in no time.

Alex ended the kiss and stepped back. She tried to. His arms kept her against his body. It was silly to think he would just let her go. She knew better, but still held onto hope.

She pulled at his hold on her. "Please release me."

He sighed, and to her surprise, he did. He crossed his arms over his chest. "Fine. Let's talk about our unfinished business then."

"We don't need to talk about that now. It can wait until this is over."

"Dammit, Akantha. We are going to talk about this. Now."

She didn't want to acknowledge their past and the lessons it had exquisitely crafted. She wanted to deal with one thing at a time, and right now, that was the threat to her and the kids. "Is it really necessary? I know what I said. There's nothing to talk about."

"You know there is." Exasperation laced his words. "You said you'd give us an honest chance. I want that chance. I've waited since 1945."

She'd keep him waiting another sixty or so years if she could. She loved him, that hadn't changed, but it wasn't the time to focus on anything but keeping the kids safe. Especially since he possessed the uncanny ability to turn her world upside down and put her off-balance. "We had Argentina."

He shook his head. "No. We spent ten years hunting and being hunted by ex-Nazis and worse. That wasn't a real chance."

He had a valid point, and she hated it. She had the scars and the occasional nightmare to prove it. His timing sucked, but that was normal for him. He always showed up at the worst possible moment.

"Fine, but only after this is over."

"Fine."

He smiled and closed the distance between them. He wrapped his arms around her and kissed her. Light at first, the kiss deepened, and Alex melted against him. A deep, buried hunger that had been ignored for untold years flared to life. She snaked her arms around his neck, pressing her body against his, molding it to his hard muscles. She was drawn tighter into the addiction of his touch. The distance created by time and location was erased with the greatest of ease. He released her and then scooped her up in his arms.

Damianos carried Alex through the old Victorian and into her bedroom, kissing her as he moved. The late hour prevented any of the kids from seeing them, and for that, Alex was grateful. The kids didn't need the two of them providing any more entertainment. His strong arms provided warmth and security, things she desperately needed now.

He pushed the bedroom door shut with a foot and carried Alex to the king-size bed.

He laid her on the bed and stretched out next to her. His dark eyes looked into the very depths of her soul. The cracks in her emotional armor widened. He wore away her defenses with his searing kisses and warm hands.

His hands were at once rough and familiar, roaming her body and removing her clothing as his mouth danced on hers. She let the world spin, let the old feelings catch and spark into flames. Her armor fell away, and her heart and soul were laid bare before him. In the lust-filled haze, she knew he would break her heart again, but right now, there was nothing she could do about it.

It was a good thing they weren't young and new to each other.

Foreplay was only in the mind. His knowledge of her body set every part of her on fire as she tried to get his clothing off just as quickly. She fumbled with buttons and the zipper in her rush to have him bare before her.

In little time, they were naked and pressed together on the bed, hands revisiting sensitive places, touching and licking in ways long remembered. Alex had had many relationships in the course of her long life, but none of the men, or women, affected her like Damianos. The man had ruined her for others ever since they first met. She hated him for it.

He trailed his hands down her back, coming to a stop on her backside. He squeezed, and Alex groaned against his mouth. He surged up and rolled both of them over, pinning Alex against the mattress.

The weight of him thrilled her, and she pushed her hips against him. He pushed back. She savored the sight of hard muscles moving under tanned skin, and he greedily claimed her as his, all in service to the addiction they shared. The wildness inside her grew, and blood thundered in her ears. This is what she wanted, what she couldn't deny herself, and what she needed. She ground her mouth on his, and he bit at her tongue. He ended the kiss and kissed along her jaw. He captured an earlobe and playfully bit it.

Heat shot through her. His warm breath against her ear sent a surge of energy through her. This wasn't about slow exploration as new lovers. This was about reigniting the fires of passion from embers burning for over two thousand years.

"Damianos!" It was an order, a plea. She needed release. She needed him.

Alex gasped as he entered her, and his mouth came down hard on hers, swallowing her reaction. He slid in and buried himself to the hilt. He moved even deeper inside her. Alex arched her hips up to meet the thrusts. She clenched her hands into his sides, urging him on.

He kissed her, swallowing her demands. He moved more fiercely against her, and she tightened around him. She put her arms around his neck and wrapped her legs around his waist. A deep groan escaped him as he thrust into her. Alex echoed his groan.

He settled into a powerful and fast rhythm, and Alex couldn't get enough of him. Deep enough and hard enough didn't exist. She wanted as much of him as she could get. She tore her mouth away from his and dropped hungry kisses along his jaw and down his neck. She kissed along his neck and toward a shoulder. A thrust harder than the others caught her off guard, and she bit him in response. That encouraged him, and his speed increased.

Tension coiled snakelike inside her, slowly ratcheting up to the inevitable conclusion she knew existed. Then it came. That blissful feeling of snapping and waves of ecstasy crashing down upon her. Every nerve inside her danced with the release. For the first time in six decades, she felt completely alive.

Her body gripped him even tighter, and his body stiffened as he followed her over the edge. He broke the kiss and groaned as he emptied himself into her. Her breathing came in ragged breaths, and she wrapped her arms around him as he lay atop her, spent. Her heart thudded against his, and blood pounded in her ears. He teased the corners of her mouth with light kisses as he threaded his fingers through her dark hair.

"Mmmmm," she purred, basking in the afterglow.

"I love you," he said, before kissing her forehead.

She looked into his dark eyes. Her chest tightened, and she could scarcely breathe. The dangerous words lingered on her tongue, ready to escape if she had the courage to utter them.

"I love you," she whispered, not daring to say it any louder. Loving him was never a question. Trusting him was something completely different.

He eased himself out of her and rolled to the side. Alex hissed at the sudden loss of him and the heat he generated. He gathered her in his arms and pulled her against him. She rested her head in the middle of his chest, as her breathing gradually returned to normal. A thin sheen of sweat covered both their bodies.

She closed her eyes and listened to the steady rhythm of his heart beating, swearing it beat in time with hers. The world slowed, and nothing else existed except the two of them. For the first time since their time together in Argentina, she felt complete. She sighed deeply, and he tightened his arms around her.

"Gods, I have missed you."

Alex lifted her head and lightly kissed his mouth. "And I you."

He gave her a quick kiss. "That was 'welcome home.' Wait till you see what I'm going to do for my 'stay forever' plan."

She smiled and pushed down thoughts of forever. Forever was the most dangerous word she knew. "You're incorrigible."

"We have sixty years of making up to do."

She shook her head, laughed, and kissed him. She'd worry about the fallout of tonight later. Right now, she was going to enjoy herself and bask in what only he could give her.

CHAPTER THIRTEEN

THE TWO ATTACKS AND GREAT SEX COULDN'T KEEP JO'S mind off the secret tunnel under the barn and what the metal door could be hiding. In fact, the tunnel and the door helped keep her mind off the two attacks. She searched high and low for the key in the house and store, but no luck. She wasn't about to give up though. She'd keep searching until she found it because she had to get that door unlocked and see what was on the other side. It could hold the answers to all the secrets Alex was hiding and maybe answers to all the recent mysteries.

A few days after the Jeep had been run off the road, she dusted items in the shop while Alex went over paperwork. The now normal routine was a little lonely without Carrie to help pass the time. The other woman was at home with her sisters and brother, playing sitter for her parents while they went away for a long weekend. It was quiet without Carrie's chatter.

With so much time in her own head, it made the accident seem unreal. Jo could have almost believed it hadn't happened if Stavros wasn't still around. Alex had been spending more time than usual in the shop. Munchkin was at her feet more, apparently guarding her from the house guest. Or was that house pest? The huge dog didn't seem to realize or care that he couldn't fit under the desk, but he tried.

The shop was slower in terms of customers since it was a weekday, and Jo understood why Alex substituted at the high school during the school year to supplement her income. She imagined it was even slower during the spring and fall, and Alex needed occupation as well as an income source.

It was late Tuesday afternoon, and the store was open, but so far not one customer had come in since Jo wandered down from the apartment after noon.

"I'll be right back." Alex entered the store from the office in the back. "I need a file from my office in the house."

"Okay. I can keep an eye on the place while you're gone, though I doubt anyone will come in."

"It's what happens this time of the year. We're not in the summer craziness yet. You remember what it's like when the tourists arrive. Do you want any tea or coffee? I'm going to make some coffee while I'm in there."

"No thanks." Jo wondered how Alex could drink so much coffee and tea. They seemed to be the only things she drank besides water. Though Jo knew Alex had wine on occasion since the basement of the house was a huge wine cellar. Alex had more than once opened the cellar to their parents to raid for special occasions. Some of the bottles looked really old. The dust on them was probably older than Jo, Mike, and Ben put together. That would mean Alex's ancestors had been wine collectors. Maybe the vault was full of family treasure.

When Alex moved toward the door, Munchkin lumbered to his feet to follow her. If she ever had a pet, Jo wanted a dog as loyal and faithful as Munchkin. He rarely let Alex leave his sight, except at night when the dog hunted for a place to sleep. He had beds designed for large pets in several rooms, but Ben reported the dog had begun sleeping with him when he moved in. Not just in his room on the third floor, but in his bed. The dog might be the reason why Ben had kept himself from drowning in grief.

She watched the door close behind the dog and realized that now was her chance to search the office desk for the mysterious key. Alex always kept it locked, but since she planned to return, there was a chance she didn't take the extra seconds to secure it. She waited until Alex had disappeared into the house before ducking into the office and hurrying to the desk. She opened the middle drawer and did a quick search. She carefully shuffled and pushed papers aside until her fingers brushed across something cool to the touch. Jo moved some of the papers and found a large, very old skeleton key. It looked the right size to fit the lock in the mysterious door.

"Bingo!" She quickly snatched the key out of the drawer and stuffed it into her pocket. She put the papers back the way she found them and hurried out from around the desk to get back to her dusting.

It was some time before Alex came in carrying a cup of coffee. Jo had rushed for nothing, but the important thing was that she had the key. Or what she hoped was the key.

"Thank you for watching the store. Did you get mobbed by a rush of customers while I was out?"

"Yeah. It was brutal."

Alex chuckled and sat down behind the desk. "I bet."

Jo did her best to finish dusting without looking like she was hurrying through it. The key burned a hole in her pocket, and she desperately wanted to see if it unlocked the door. It took an eternity to finish the dusting, but she put the duster away with a sense of accomplishment. She returned the cleaning supplies to the backroom cabinet and stepped into Alex's office.

"I'm done," she announced as she approached the desk. She played it as calm as she could. Getting caught at this stage would be disappointing. There would be nothing she could do if Alex threw her out for invading her privacy.

Alex looked up from the paperwork. "Thank you. Do you have plans for the rest of the day?"

"I'm going to go see when Carrie's coming back. It's been quiet without her."

"I would have thought you'd enjoy having the apartment to yourself while she's watching her sisters and brother."

"Why would you think that?"

"Privacy. I know you and Greg have a hard time finding any."

Jo opened to her mouth to retort that she was an adult, but before she could, she saw the Alex's mouth twitch at the corner. Alex was teasing her. It was hard to tell sometimes. Alex's wit was so dry it was a unicorn sighting of its own.

"That's what we get for having families."

"He knows you're leaving before the end of summer?"

This time Jo did let a little irritation into her words. "I have been clear about my future plans." What little she had of them. Plans that changed every other day. She really needed an exit strategy. Good Harbor was too small for her dreams of becoming a journalist.

"Good. I don't want to see you hurt."

That was more like the Aunt Alex they'd grown up with. Jo nodded. "I understand. Do you need anything before I hunt Carrie down?"

"I'm fine. I've neglected the books for too long. I'm hoping to catch up enough to get the business taxes filed. The accountant likes it when the paperwork's in order. She charges me extra if I hand her a shoebox of receipts."

"Do you really have a shoebox?"

Alex grinned. "Go find Carrie. Let me know if you'll both be here for dinner."

Jo nodded and left the office. She grabbed her phone out of a pocket as she mounted the stairs up to the apartment. She dialed Carrie's cell and waited for Carrie to pick up.

"Mom and Dad are here," Carrie said when Jo called. "They arrived an hour ago."

"An hour? Why didn't you leave then?"

"I was giving Mom the final report and packing my bag to come back. It was pretty fun to see the others silently begging me from the doorway to tell Mom everything was fine."

"Wasn't it fine?"

"Yes, but I like having that little bit of control over their heads. After everything they put me through, I like some payback on occasion."

Jo chuckled as she entered the apartment. "That's mean of you. I like it. Now get back over here."

"Something wrong? Did you forget to get groceries?"

"No, and yes. But that's not it. I found the key, but Alex is still in the shop office. Later tonight, we can find out if it opens the door."

"Okay, I'll be there soon. Did you want me to stop at the grocery store?"

"We can put it off until tomorrow. Tonight, we break into the tunnel door."

She didn't have to wait long for Carrie to arrive, but it was long enough to make her restless. Carrie had enough time to drop her overnight bag inside her room before Jo dragged her out for a walk to the stables.

Alex's property wasn't the only one in the area to have stables on the grounds as a holdover from the days of horses and buggies, but she was the only one in Good Harbor to keep horses rather than stabling them at a professional facility. Jo always thought that while they were beautiful, the care and upkeep would have been a lot of work, and who had the time? Alex didn't seem to mind, and she had part-time help. There was always some kid who didn't mind shoveling manure for good money. Alex always paid well.

"What did you find out?"

"Find out?" Carrie shot her a quizzical look.

"You've been making mental notes since Agent Hottie arrived. It's time to spill it all."

"He is handsome, but what makes you think I was trying to look him up?"

"Because I know you, Ms. Bookworm. You live to research. I don't know why you didn't study library science and become a librarian."

"There's not a lot of call for librarians in the area, and at the time, I wanted to stay close to home. Teachers have better luck getting jobs."

That made little sense to Jo, but she was never the homebody Carrie was. "Well?"

"Well, okay, I did look some things up. I was curious about the tunnel and thought I'd check into the history of the area. Being so close to the ocean, there are accounts of smugglers using the coves and sea caves. But nothing specifically about this property. Since her land ends at the shore"—she gestured toward the sliver of blue visible through the trees—"it makes sense that's what's underneath us now. She inherited a multimillion-dollar view with the house. If the beach were sand, it would be even more."

They reached the open barn doors and stepped inside out of the heat. The air inside was kept in motion by fans and vents set into the roof. The smell of manure was still obnoxiously present.

"What about Stavros?"

"Nothing I could find, other than a post office box in New Mexico and urban legend sites. A hundred years of a secret assassin stories really doesn't fit a man who doesn't look older than forty years old."

Jo walked down to where a curious horse put his head out to see who was coming. If she'd been thinking, she would have brought an apple or carrot for him. He was a big horse, and she wasn't fool enough to approach too quickly.

Carrie followed, still in her lecture mode. "Internet searches from a home computer aren't all that in-depth. You might think you're getting everything on a subject when it pulls up three hundred thousand hits, but there are layers to the web, and we're mostly in the fluffy topping. I logged into Mom's real estate network to see what I could find on the property, and something odd stuck out to me."

Jo carefully stroked the horse's forehead. "What's that?"

"The property has a clear line of ownership going back over three hundred years. No contested title, no lost deeds or heirs. It's passed from one woman to another woman for decades. There are times when it's been in the care of trust, but that hasn't been contested either. The taxes have always been paid, and insurance when that became a necessity. A woman takes possession of it for about twenty years, and then she leaves, or passes away, it goes into a trust, and then after twenty or thirty years, a new heir arrives. Ms. Thorne has been here about twenty years. If the pattern continues, she'll be gone soon."

"That can't be right."

"It's a possibility. The internet is garbage in, garbage out, so the information may be incomplete or just wrong, but something about this feels odd."

Jo frowned and moved on from patting the horse to the rear of the barn. The stable helper had been here this morning, although she didn't recall seeing them come or go. Most of the barn was swept, and the manure had been shoveled out. Except for the rear stall. It still had some straw scattered on the floor and old crates stacked in random piles. She walked in and circled around the space. "Alex doesn't have any family. There are no pictures, she's never mentioned any, and she doesn't even have an ex-husband or a dead one." She took a step and frowned.

"Okay, but I'm just telling you what's there."

"I get it. Do you hear that?"

"What?"

Jo walked back and forth across the small section between the crates. "That. The floor here sounds different than it does by the door."

Carrie walked over to hear it for herself. "Different how?"

"Like there's a crawl space underneath."

"Maybe there is?"

"The barn is dirt level, and there's no basement here." With a new idea taking hold of her brain, she knelt on the floor and knocked on it. "There's a space under here."

"It's an old barn."

"You were curious enough to do internet searches, but you're not curious now?"

"It's a floor. The internet is clean. Well, okay, it's not clean, but I don't have to leave my desk."

"Help me."

Carrie sighed and awkwardly got to her knees to look at the floor around Jo. She rapped on it with her knuckles in different spots. "Okay, I believe you."

They explored the floor, Jo enthusiastically, Carrie less so, until Jo found a seam between the planks just as she had in the shop office.

"Tell me how unbelievable it would be if there was another trapdoor here? Help me move the boxes."

Together they lifted several crates out of the way and uncovered what looked like a large door set into the floor. The one in the office was small with barely enough room for a single person to climb through. This one was big enough for boxes to be passed through.

Another ladder stretched from the edge into inky black. Now that Jo knew it what to expect, she climbed onto it and was halfway down before Carrie could get the flashlight app on her phone on and pointed down.

"Another tunnel," she called up after turning on her own phone's light app. "Come on. It's like the other one."

Once Carrie was standing next to her, they walked through

another well-kept tunnel. "Where does she find the time?" Jo said, moving her light from side to side. "Seriously, this is upkeep. She doesn't disappear that anyone notices. Munchkin follows her around, and no one has seen him standing guard over anything other than her house office."

"Maybe she has an entrance to the tunnel from the house. Look, another door! It's just like the other one. Maybe the key fits this one too."

Carrie held the light on the lock, and Joanna put the key in. "Here goes nothing." The breath stayed in her chest, and her hands felt a little clammy. She paused to wipe them on her jeans before she turned the key.

"I don't think—" Carrie began, but the distinctive click of a lock disengaging interrupted her.

"It worked!" Excitement flooded Jo. Now she could finally see what was behind the old door and uncover some of Alex's secrets.

For such an old door, it opened effortlessly and almost silently. The hinges had been kept well-oiled, and Jo knew Alex had to use the door on a regular basis. The theory that Alex didn't know about the door and tunnel was discarded. What was she hiding? It was time to find out. She cautiously took a step inside the room, and Carrie was right behind her.

Jo moved her flashlight around, and the beam of light cut through the blackness to shine on reflective surfaces all around them. There were quick flashes of polished copper, silver, and gold. Carrie rummaged behind her, and a moment later, there was a click. Overhead fluorescent shop lights came on. Their hum filled the room.

Room didn't accurately describe what they were standing in. It was a cavernous space filled with rows and rows of shelves. It had to stretch as far back as the house. The shelves themselves were high and stacked with objects from lamps, bowls, small statues, to things Jo couldn't even identify. The walls they could see were covered with weapons from swords and daggers to even more things Jo didn't recognize. On the far wall was another door. Jo wondered where that one led. Was it a second entrance? Another room stuffed with more things?

"I found the—" Carrie stopped in midsentence as she turned around and saw what Jo saw. "Wow."

"Yeah."

"That's a lot of stuff."

"Yeah. I thought she had a lot between the house and the store. This is…" Overwhelming. Extraordinary. Mind-boggling. Jo couldn't find the exact word to meet the situation. Who would have thought an antiques dealer had a secret lair filled with expensive things? She could imagine Mike's reaction. She'd bet money he'd go straight for a sword and end up hurting himself. Ben too.

"Amazing. I don't even recognize some of this stuff. My mom would think this is heaven."

"I don't either. Look at the weapons." Joanna pointed to the wall. "That could supply an army." Each weapon in the collection appeared to be in excellent condition, and light reflected off well-polished steel and other metals.

"They all look almost new."

"They do, but they're not. They're just well-kept." Jo's father had encouraged her love of history and taken them to museums in Boston. She felt the sharp twinge of pain at the thought of him and how he would have loved this. Maybe he had known. All of these could be museum pieces. Heck, some were in much better condition than what she had seen in museums. Maybe he had known more about Alex than they thought. "Some are bronze weapons. No one makes or uses bronze weapons unless it's a hobby."

"So where do you think she got them?"

"I have no idea. Your average antiques dealer doesn't have stuff like this. You and I both have visited all the other shops in the area over the years. None of them have stuff like this."

"She doesn't either, not when you think about it. You've seen her store inventory." Carrie cautiously touched the handle of a bejeweled dagger. "Even her online inventory doesn't hint at anything like this. Sure, she has a sword in the store, but that seems more like a conversation piece than an item for sale. It might not even be real. Antiques dealers specializing in weaponry make a lot of money selling to collectors, but there's nothing indicating that she's one of them. I've never seen anyone come in to buy a weapon, and I've never seen her ship one. Plus, it would be a messenger delivery, not through the local post office."

"You can't tell Mike about any of this. He can't keep a secret, and he'll think of something else she's supposed to be. He sees this, and he'll go full-on conspiracy nutcase."

"I won't tell him."

"I mean it. I know you've been crushing on him since high school."

Carrie's face reddened. "That was high school."

Jo knew why Carrie liked her brother. Mike was a nice guy. He was one of those guys who was friendly to everyone, from jocks and cheerleaders to the library mice like Carrie. It continued in college, and she knew that once he took the job he got after college, it would extend into the workplace. But she didn't want Carrie's crush on Mike to affect what she told him. If he even suspected there was a cave vault under the property, there would be no containing him and his imagination.

"Don't tell him about this. He'll bug me to come down here and probably cut himself on something sharp."

"I said I wouldn't tell him. Put the key back, and no one will know."

"Oh my god, is that real gold?" The golden glitter drew Jo in past a shelf of decorative objects.

"There's a set of gold-rimmed plates over here." Carrie made her way down another aisle. "We really should get out of here."

Jo stopped in front of a large chest. Black metal bands wrapped around the dark wood and the metal rivets were aged. The top curved into a hump, resembling a pirate's chest. Was this one full of gold? The chest alone would fetch a thousand or maybe even two on the antique market. Especially one in such good shape. She carefully lifted the lid, and the old hinges protested with a squeak. Old black-and-white photos covered in protective plastic filled the chest along with some sepia-colored ones. Fascinated, Jo lifted a few from the chest and inspected them.

The first one was of a woman sitting in a chair Jo would swear was in one of the downstairs rooms. She had seen enough of Downton Abbey to recognize the dress was from around the turn of the century. Something about the woman seemed familiar and reminded Jo of Alex. The woman had the same dark hair, and her facial features were similar. It had to be some ancestor of Alex's.

Jo held up the next photo. It was a sepia-colored photo, and this one was of a woman standing with a rifle over her shoulder and wearing pants. She couldn't tell what year it was, but it was before 1900. The clothes reminded her of the clothes in movies set in the Old West. The photo was taken at a distance, but the woman had dark hair and looked like she could be related to Alex. Jo and Mike had photos of their family, but very few of their family past their grandparents. She would swear she'd seen the same rifle in the shop.

Some were of men, very handsome men, and some were taken with an ancestor of Alex's. There was even one of a dog who was identical to Munchkin. The resemblance to the woman and the dog in the house was eerie.

"Carrie, come look at these photos," Jo called out.

Carrie materialized at Jo's side. "I love old photos. I wonder why they're not in albums." Carrie removed some from the chest and shuffled through them. "The family resemblance is uncanny. These could be Alex. That one man looks like Officer Nicademos."

"I know, but it can't be them," Joanna noted. She carefully set the photos back in the trunk. She could spend all day studying the images, but they didn't have much time. "These were taken over a hundred years ago. She has some in her office taken at my parents' wedding, and Alex hasn't aged a day in twenty years."

"Well, then either Alex is over two hundred years old, or she's identical her ancestors. Not to mention they all have the same taste in dogs." Carrie shrugged. "Maybe she has a great moisturizer."

"No skin care regimen is that good."

"Are those rolled-up canvases?"

Jo reached into the bottom of the chest and pulled out a thick roll tied shut with a leather thong. She untied it, and the two girls unrolled it between them. They looked at the five canvases. "Look at these painted portraits. They're incredible."

Up close, the top canvas was a collection of paint daubs and streaks, but she could picture it from a distance. The dark-haired woman would resemble Alex in a gown fashionable at least two hundred years ago. Maybe longer. And it wasn't protected by a glass frame. Why weren't these in some sort of protective case?

They needed to get moving, so they quickly rolled and retied it. Before they closed the chest, Carrie found a set of large cards in a box that looked like miniature portraits. They were incredibly detailed, down to the lace ruffles and almost everyone was a woman with dark hair who resembled Alex. There were a few that didn't, but the women were still beautiful. Each portrait wasn't much larger than a playing card.

"This one is really familiar." Carrie showed Joanna a portrait of a sweet-faced woman with dark-brown hair.

"How so?"

Carrie shrugged. "I don't know, but I think I've seen this woman before."

"Weird. Let's keep searching around." They returned everything to the chest and closed it.

Jo's gaze followed a shiny display along a particular wall. "Wait a minute. Look at that!" She pointed to the one part of the far wall covered with guns and knives. Some were old enough to be antiques, but quite a few were modern weapons.

"Who needs that many guns and knives besides militia groups?" Carrie shook her head. For once, her voice was firm. "No. Let's go. Take a picture if you must and look at it later, but we need to go."

"Why didn't I think of that? Maybe I can search for some of this stuff online." Jo pulled out her phone and started taking pictures. The air was filled with the electronic sound of a camera shutter.

"What are the two of you doing in here?"

Jo jumped at the voice and turned to see Alex standing behind them. Busted. So busted. Her stomach dropped to her feet like it did on roller coasters. Worse, she had dragged Carrie into this. She suddenly didn't feel so grown-up.

"We stumbled on the door and wondered what was behind it."

"Curiosity got the best of us," Carrie added helpfully.

"I see."

Jo straightened up to seem taller than she was. Despite being twenty-three and out of college, she felt like a kid being caught doing something wrong. Alex's unreadable expression did nothing to help that feeling.

"We didn't touch anything," she said, hoping to soften whatever punishment was coming. She dreaded hearing what it would be. "We found this place by accident. It was so old we thought it might be some sort of bomb shelter."

"Or a stop on the Underground Railroad," Carrie chimed in. "If it is, I have questions."

Jo tried again. "I'm sorry. I should have asked you about the tunnel and the door when we found it."

Alex nodded once. "Yes, you should have."

"What is all this stuff?" Carrie asked.

"Items my family has accumulated over time. One of my

ancestors had the natural caves turned into a vault made to keep it all safe."

That was entirely reasonable, and Jo wondered why it was such a secret. The feeling of being a nosy kid slowly dissipated. "Are you planning on selling any of it?"

"No. At least not right now. Once in a while something is sold if there's an emergency and cash is needed."

"Most of this stuff looks priceless." Carrie's tone encouraged Alex to go on.

"That's an astute observation, Carrie. And it is. I'm not upset that you're down here, but please ask next time. I would have told you what's in here."

Jo nodded. "We're sorry."

"Yeah, we're sorry. I would really like the chance to examine items more." Carrie cast a longing glance at the trunk with the pictures.

"Apology accepted. Now, please do not mention this vault or the contents to anyone." Alex looked at Jo. "Not even your brothers. I don't need them down here playing with things they shouldn't be playing with." She held out a hand.

Jo nodded. "I won't tell them." She placed the key in Alex's outstretched hand. No one would believe them anyway, even if they told someone about what they found.

"I won't either."

"Thank you both. Now, shall we?" Alex gestured toward the door with her hand.

Jo and Carrie walked to the door. Alex flipped the switch, turning the lights off. She closed the heavy door and locked it. Jo and Carrie walked down the tunnel and climbed the ladder.

Munchkin sat next to the entrance in the stall like a brooding idol over a tiny village. The dog stared at them as they exited the stall and left the barn.

"It's all weird," Carrie breathed with suppressed excitement as they walked toward the apartment they shared.

"It's not what I expected either. What was weird for you?"

"All those pictures. Think about it. The original house on the property was built before the town was founded. Sofia Poyer was the first owner and one of the town founders. She left the property to a distant relative and so on down to Ms. Thorne. A law firm in Boston has handled the wills and transference of the property title since the first house was built. Did you know that Maine was part of Massachusetts before it became Maine?"

"Nothing about a gigantic vault?"

Carrie shook her head. "Nothing. It must have been built a very long time ago. Otherwise, there would have been records and permits filed. The current house was built in the mid-1800s by Isabella Laganzo after a fire destroyed the first house. No mention of the vault anywhere. It could have been built during the first or second house construction. But think of the pictures. They all resembled each other more than distant relations can explain. One or two yes, but not all of them."

Jo stopped in her tracks. "So Alex is related to the first woman to own the house," she mused. "One of her ancestors must have built the vault and put those items there."

"Probably, but it's like every owner added more to the hoard. There's just too much for one to have done it all. What's really strange is that every single owner of the house was a woman who didn't have any other relatives outside of a distant relation, who happened to be a woman who didn't have any other relatives except a distant relation. It's like that for all of them."

"I take it that's not normal in real estate?"

Carrie stopped and looked at her with surprise. "It's not normal anywhere. There are usually kids or cousins or something. Not to mention a husband here and there with family that might make a claim to the estate."

"If there was, they're probably in the vault in a really dark corner."

A giggle escaped Carrie. "That's terrible."

"What do you think it means?"

"That there are too many places to hide bodies here?"

"I mean about Alex."

"It sounds like it means there were a lot of lonely women in her family. I did some research into the name Akantha." Carrie's words came faster, and her voice went up in pitch as she talked about her research results. Jo could hear how much she enjoyed it by the way she talked about her findings.

"What did you find?" she asked as she opened the door to their apartment. "Akantha sounded like one of those names mothers give their kids when they wanted something unique. Like in Unique with two Es and a K."

Carrie followed her in and flopped on the sofa. "It's Greek in origin and means thorny. The only other things I was able to find were related to some urban legends about a woman and a bunch of baby name sites."

"Her last name now is Thorne. I wonder if Thorne is a reference to her real name. What were the legends about?"

"One was about a woman who couldn't die. It mentioned she was shot, stabbed, strangled, all kinds of gruesome things, and she didn't die."

Joanna paused before taking the chair and looked at Carrie. "Huh. That's strange. Anything else?"

"I looked into the name Alex Thorne. Almost everything is related to the antiques shop. She has a reputation for finding very rare items, things no one else seems to have. I didn't find much on the personal side. Most of the searches came back with male Alex Thornes. There was one other female Alex Thorne, but she died in infancy in the seventies."

"Nothing about where she was born? Grew up? Went to high school?" When they found the answer to one question, many more popped up. Jo was beginning to see the advantage of carrying around a notepad.

Carrie shook her head. "Nope. Nothing. She appears in a

university archive in Europe as a graduate and a grad student at the University of Colorado in Boulder. She taught in Toronto for a bit before taking possession of the house. She would need a degree to substitute teach here."

"That's strange, but then again, she's not into social media or anything like that. The shop is, but that's it. Alex never told us anything about her life before she met our parents. I'll see if I can find out where she went to high school. I don't recall ever seeing any high school yearbooks in her library."

"I also I looked into Peter Claver."

"What did you find?"

"The only thing I've found is that it was the name of a Catholic saint, patron to slaves and seafarers. A bunch of Catholic high schools named Peter Claver, but that's it. Nothing that could be related to the psycho guy who attacked us."

"Isn't it normal to find at least something on a person on the internet these days? Nobody escapes social media," Joanna said.

Carrie nodded. "Yeah. Nothing on this guy though. I'll keep looking."

"Did you find anything on Durendal?" With all the things to research, Carrie must be in heaven. Jo would still have been still researching the list if she was writing an article about it. Which wasn't a bad idea. She needed to start a portfolio of work if she was going to try for a job in her degree field.

"Just legends. Durendal was the sword of Roland. It was indestructible, and it could destroy an invincible foe. The literary work called the Matter of France centers on Roland." The joy of the chase, in this case the research chase, showed on her face with her brown eyes twinkling. "When you think of a knight in shining armor, that was Roland."

"Do you really think Alex, of all people, has a sword that belonged to this famous knight?" Jo asked herself more than Carrie. Would the woman she knew have something like that hidden on her property?

"I don't know. Yesterday I might have said there was no chance she did. Durendal is only a legend. A romantic one, but it probably didn't exist, and if it did in some way, it couldn't still be around today. Charlemagne ruled in the 800s."

"But is it possible it could still be around and in that vault?"

"I highly doubt it, but I won't say no for sure. Not after what we just saw."

"Did you research the SPD?"

Carrie gave her a look that screamed *What do you think?* "I did. Found nothing except an urban legend about some supernatural police type group. They're supposed to be a men-in-black organization in the shadows. I found it on a conspiracy website."

Jo sighed. Way more questions and no answers. Something about all of this nagged at the back of her mind, but she couldn't say what it was. "Let's go grab some lunch. There may be some leftovers, but Ben and Mike probably already got to them."

"Miracles happen all the time." Carrie jumped up from her seat. "That could be one."

Joanna laughed. "If it happens, I'll believe in the rest."

CHAPTER FOURTEEN

ALEX STOOD AT THE KITCHEN SINK, WASHING THE dishes from dinner. Mike was out, probably at the Sullivan's restaurant flirting with the waitresses, and Jo, along with Carrie, seemed to be avoiding her. Probably for the best. She still had to decide what to do about the inquisitive young women. The look of surprise on their faces did make her smile. Like they didn't expect her to have security in place for any potential theft.

It left Ben to join her and Damianos, and his ability to read a room was far superior to his brother's. Ben wasn't the type to ask inconvenient questions, especially given that Damianos was the type to answer inconvenient questions without thinking.

"Need any help?" Damianos asked from behind her.

She ignored the shiver that ran down her spine from that deep voice. "I never decline help when it comes to dishes. The towels are in the second drawer down."

Damianos pulled it open and removed a towel. He slid it shut and picked up a plate from the dish strainer. "I remember when you had servants to do the menial work."

"Times change. I don't mind it when it's just a few dishes."

"You have a dishwasher right there." He motioned to toward the appliance with the plate in hand.

"The house has to be kept up to date. Doesn't mean I need or want it."

"Do you ever take a break from being so stubborn?"

She smiled and handed him the next dish. "Not if I can help it."

Damianos laughed, and she chuckled along with him. For a moment, it felt normal being with him. The man had caused her so much grief and heartache during her long life, but he had also brought her periods of happiness and contentment. Moments like this made a secret part of her hope things could be good between them. Maybe they could leave behind centuries of acrimony, but she knew he would do something to kill that hope. Or she would. It was just a matter of time.

"I can't remember the last time I've done something so... domestic." He put the plate in the cabinet and took the other from her.

"You're still living on takeout," she playfully accused, rinsing off the third plate and glancing over at him. She didn't have to ask if he was or wasn't—she knew. While he was no stranger to cooking, she knew he didn't do it if he had any other option. Yet she remembered the times when he cooked for her without being asked. He had never shirked from any chores. Some of her best memories were of him holding their daughter, trying to soothe Eleni's cries by singing long-forgotten war songs off-key.

Damianos shrugged. "I'm on the road a lot. It's the easiest way."

"August keeping you busy?" She handed him a glass. He dictated his own schedule, and she knew he could take time off whenever he wanted. But like her, he had to keep busy. It helped them both deal with the thousands of years weighing on their souls. One could go mad if they stopped to think about the passage of time and their long lives. Others had gone mad. It was a pitiful condition.

"You could say that."

"What are you handling for him now?"

"Stuff." He put the dried glass in another cabinet.

"Any interesting stuff?"

"Just stuff."

Alex let it go. There were certain aspects of their lives that were kept private for good reason, and they didn't discuss with each other. For her, it was her work with the Guardians. For him, it was his work with the SPD. She knew that whatever she told him would go no further, and he knew the same about her. Their tenuous relationship only worked for as long as it had because they didn't feel the need to share every single thing. She assumed he'd had other relationships in the decades since they'd last seen each other. She'd had her own during that time. They didn't speak of it. It was just another part of their immortal lives.

She glanced toward the breakfast nook to make sure Ben had a left. "Has Claver been sighted?"

"No. He either left town after our confrontation, or he's gone to ground well enough that I haven't found him yet."

"Maybe you're not looking hard enough," she teased, but she also knew he would use Claver as an excuse to stay.

"He'll show up if he's still around. As for whether or not I'm looking hard enough, I assure you I am."

"Uh-huh." She handed him the now cleaned serving dish.

"I might be a little distracted." He leaned in and kissed her temple. "But it doesn't interfere with my job."

She smiled when he pressed his lips against her temple. "Your focus is legendary, so I must accept your word."

He laughed, and her knees weakened. "It's always best when you follow my lead."

Alex shook her as she washed a sauté pan. As much as she denied it, she'd never stop loving him, and that was the problem.

Whatever it was that was happening now between them, it would eventually end up in heartbreak. Just like it had done so many times in the past. They were destined to keep hurting each other, and they couldn't escape the other, no matter how hard they tried.

Alex wrung out the dishcloth and shut the water off. She was disappointed there were no more dishes to clean. She enjoyed the moments of peace between them and wanted them to last longer. She glanced over at him. He hung the dried pan up with the other pots and pans. He turned and their eyes met.

"How about I raid your wine cellar for a bottle while you light a fire in the fireplace?" he suggested.

Alex slowly smiled. Maybe the peace between them didn't have to end with the dishes. "How about I get a bottle of wine, and we sit on the swing on the porch? It's too warm for a fire." Not to mention he wouldn't grab just one bottle of wine. He'd grab a few and take them with him when he left. He always did.

He chuckled. "Fine. I'll meet you on the porch. I'll do a quick walk around outside while you find a bottle of wine."

"Deal." Alex tossed the dishcloth in the sink, and Damianos draped the towel over the handle of the oven. She stood on tiptoe to give him a quick kiss on his mouth and left him standing there as she went to the cellar door.

Fifteen minutes later, she stepped out onto the porch with an open bottle of wine and two wineglasses in her hand. Damianos climbed the few steps and smiled. Alex poured wine into the two glasses and offered one to him. He accepted it with a smile and sat on one end of the porch swing. Alex placed the bottle on floor on the other side of Damianos and sat on the swing next to him. She leaned back into him, and he placed an arm around her. She sighed contently and enjoyed the lovely summer night.

A frog chorus filled the air, and occasionally a firefly blinked in the tall grass surrounding the house. The oranges and reds in the sky slowly faded to navy and eventually black. Alex sipped her wine and enjoyed the moment. Damianos kissed the top of her head, and she smiled.

"How long has it been since either of us slowed down to do something like this?"

"I've done this often in the past twenty years, but I imagine it's been too long for you."

"Especially together."

"The last time we were together we were hunting Nazis in Argentina and in the middle of a world war before that," she said. "We didn't exactly have time to do put our feet up and just breathe."

"Have you been back since then?"

"To Argentina? No. I know we missed a few, but they're probably dead already or on their way to dead. But like cockroaches, Nazis are hard to kill. Now the new ones are out in the open."

"You're not wrong. It's the organizations still in the shadows we're concerned about. Which reminds me, where are you hiding the carpet on four paws?"

"He's probably upstairs with Ben. They have a close relationship built on shared leftovers."

"So..." Damianos made a show of scanning the immediate surroundings.. "I have you all to myself."

Alex , smiled. . "It looks that way."

"If I carried you upstairs, you would be entirely in my power. I'm sure I could remind you of better times."

"I'm enjoying this moment now." Calm enveloped the two of them, and Alex wanted to enjoy every second. Tomorrow morning, the chaos would rush back in. "We can go upstairs in a bit."

His arm tightened around her. "I'm enjoying this too." He kissed the top of her head again, and she smiled once more. "Your wish is my command."

Alex's first instinct was to scoff at his remark, but she kept it in. It would lead to an argument, and she wouldn't let bickering shatter the peace between them and the peace of the evening. Selfish, yes, but she wanted these stolen moments.

"Have you heard from Paladin?"

"No," she answered with a sigh. "Not yet. And I'm concerned. He's usually good about checking in."

"I'm sure he'll check in soon."

"I hope you're right." She couldn't imagine something happening to Jack any more than she could imagine something happening to the kids.

"I can request a sight report on him if you want. If you tell me where he went, I'll give August a call."

"That's SPD encroaching too far into my territory."

"You were the one who requested SPD give him modified training to let him function as your agent."

"And that's as far as I wanted it to go. He would have been no use to me if he melted down at the sight of his first demon. But I'm sure you're right and he'll check in as soon as he can."

"I'm always right."

Alex laughed hard. He tightened his arms around her, causing her to laugh harder. A moment later, he started laughing with her. Their laughter faded away, and Alex sighed heavily. She needed that laugh more than she cared to admit.

"I love you." He kissed her forehead. "I will always love you."

The words lingered on her tongue, but she couldn't say them. They were dangerous words. Instead, she opted to remain silent and enjoy the feel of his arms around her and the peace of the evening.

CHAPTER FIFTEEN

"WE HAVE DRINKS AND SNACKS," JO ANNOUNCED AS SHE and Carrie entered Ben's game room on the third floor of the house. It was the only place on the property that had a television large enough to allow all of them to watch comfortably. Alex didn't seem to believe in them, and Carrie had a tiny one in the apartment.

"What took you so long?" Mike said in mock whining. "We're starving up here."

The way her brother talked, one would think Carrie and Jo grew the corn themselves. Jo rolled her eyes.

They had popcorn, drinks, and Netflix. It was the perfect way to pass a summer Saturday night in a small town in Maine. Not like there was anything else to do. Jo didn't want to go back to an ice cream stand at night anytime soon, at least while that madman was still loose. Nobody wanted to drive to a bigger place for entertainment. Since Ben was at a friend's house for the weekend, they made use of his space.

"Mike's speaking for himself," Greg said. "Thanks." He held out a hand to take one of the bowls from Jo.

Carrie set down the armful of cans of soda and a few water

bottles, and then rubbed her arms briskly. "If you were starving, you should have helped."

"I will next time," Mike promised.

"Thanks," Jo said to Greg as she passed him a bowl of popcorn. "Alex stopped us on the way up."

"What did she want?" Mike asked.

"Just asked what we were doing," Jo replied as she set down the remaining two bowls on a small table. She grabbed a handful of popcorn. She didn't blame Alex for asking. Given the terrible breach of privacy she and Carrie committed on her property, it could have been a lot more awkward. But Jo thought that maybe she understood Alex a little more. Like why she walked the perimeter on a nightly basis. "She was on her way out for her walk around the buildings. I think she's enjoying the quiet since Stavros went out this afternoon and isn't back yet."

"Thanks for making the run," Greg said.

"You're doing the next trip," Jo said. "This is our second and last for the night. We're not waitresses."

"It's not a problem. Sometimes I'm a waiter."

"What do we want to watch next?" Mike asked. "The girls picked the last one, so it's the guys' turn to pick. I say *Star Wars*."

Joanna groaned. She liked the movies, but not to the point where she had to watch them as many times as possible. "How many times are you going to see those stupid movies?"

Mike's jaw dropped, and he gasped dramatically. "They're not stupid. They're only the best movies ever made."

"Please." Jo dismissed his protest with a hand wave. "They're stupid and full of plot holes."

"They're good, but they're not the best movies ever made," Greg said. "We can watch something else."

"Suck-up," Mike said in mock accusation. Jo smiled, happy that Greg took her side. As he should.

"I don't mind them. My family watches them during the holidays," Carrie said. Mike smiled at Carrie.

"Can we find something that we all like?" Jo asked.

"You just made us watch *The Notebook*," Mike said. "It's our pick. I want to see something with explosions and blood."

Alternating movie picks between the guys and the girls became the standard after one night they argued for two hours about what to watch and then ended up not watching anything. Mike just had a habit of picking the same movies repeatedly. Joanna liked a variety in movies and wished her brother did too.

"How about *Pacific Rim*?" Greg suggested. "I think the girls will like it, and it has *kaiju* and mechs for us."

"Sounds good to me," Carrie and Joanna said in unison.

"Cool." Greg navigated the menu to find the movie.

"It's—" Mike stopped midsentence. He turned toward the window. "Did you guys hear that?"

"Hear what?" Jo asked hesitantly. Goodness knew what her brother was thinking.

"I hear Munchkin barking."

"So what? He barks. He's a dog. It's what they do." Jo rolled her eyes. Her brother's brain worked on a different level than everyone else's. She just wasn't sure what level it was.

There was a loud bang before Mike could say anything else. "That sounded like a gunshot." Mike went to the open window and peered out into the night. Jo rose and walked over to the window. She looked out into the blackness over his shoulder.

Of course Jo wouldn't let the moment get away without mocking him. "I think your imagination is running away with you."

"It was a gunshot."

"I think he might be right," Greg said, joining the twins at the window. "It's not hunting season. It could be fireworks."

"Are we playing 'Was that gunshots or fireworks?'" Carrie asked.

Jo had been in Colorado long enough to forget that gunshots

going off and fireworks exploding were frequent things in the summer in Maine. "I haven't played that in forever."

The four crowded around the window in time to hear more gunshots echo in the night. Judging by the loudness, the person shooting wasn't far from the house.

"Those are definitely gunshots," Greg said. "And they are way too close... Hey, was that a person crossing the driveway? I think they're heading for the front door."

"Come on!" Jo yelled before running for the door.

Mike bolted after her. They charged down the stairs, Carrie and Greg's footsteps following behind him. The front door opened with a crash, causing Jo to jump back into Mike. Mike caught her and kept his balance. Alex barged in and seemed surprised to see them run into each other at the foot of the stairs like a clown act.

Alex reached into her shirt collar and yanked a large metal key and chain from around her neck. She grabbed Jo's hand and pressed it into her palm.

"Listen to me. Joanna, take everyone into the store and into the tunnel. Follow it to the vault, and once you're inside, go to the far wall and the other door. Exit through the barn and run into the woods," she ordered. "Run until you reach the neighbor's."

"But what's—" Jo started.

"Just do it! Now! I will find you!"

A shiver ran down Jo's spine as Alex yelled. Alex hardly ever yelled. She was the type who could quiet a classroom with a look.

"Okay." Jo curled her fingers around the key. She grabbed Carrie's hand and pulled her through the house to the back door in the kitchen. Mike and Greg followed on their heels.

As Jo and Carrie burst through the back door, more gunfire shattered the quiet of the night. They ducked down. Somewhere nearby Munchkin barked furiously. It had a vicious edge that sent goose bumps over her arms. The dog sounded bigger with the ferocious barking. Jo froze, and Mike almost plowed into her. He gave her a shove, and she was in motion again.

They ran across the deck connecting the two buildings, and Jo fumbled with her key to the shop. Their run didn't escape the notice of whoever was shooting. Windows exploded as they ran to the shop office with their heads down. The glass rained down around them.

"Hurry!" Carrie yelled. "They're coming!"

Jo pushed the chair out of her way and into Mike. Mike caught the chair and moved it in front of the desk as she yanked the rug away. Greg reached for the handle of the trapdoor and yanked the door up. Carrie had her phone out and the flashlight app on. Jo grabbed her phone and turned on the flashlight. Mike and Greg did the same. She angled the beam down the yawning hole in the floor. The lights cut through the darkness of the tunnel, gleaming off the top rung of a ladder descending into the black.

"Go," Mike said, nodding toward the hole.

Jo lowered herself down the ladder, her heart pounding in her chest. Carrie went next, and Greg followed her. Mike stepped onto the ladder while the others held their phones up so he could see. The sound of the shop door banging open reached them, and Jo's heart raced faster.

"Hurry, Mike!" Jo said as loudly as she dared as her brother pulled the trapdoor shut. He descended the ladder. "This way." Jo started down the tunnel. Her mind raced. People attacking with guns wasn't something on the list of things she thought she'd experience when coming home to Maine. Seeing moose, smelling the ocean air, eating a lot of lobster and seafood—those were expected experiences. Getting run off the road by some psycho and an attack in the night, not so much. She'd rather have the lobster.

They reached the end of the tunnel, and the metal door. Sounds of boots on the metal rungs of the ladder echoed down the tunnel, and Jo struggled to keep the panic down. She shoved the key into the lock and turned it, sighing with relief when it clicked open.

She yanked the door opened and reached for the light switch and flicked it. The lights sprang to life, illuminating the room, and they blinked against the sudden brightness.

"Come on!" Jo urged in a loud whisper as the sound of boots thumping on the dirt floor grew louder. The four of them poured into the room. Greg pushed the door shut and locked it.

"Oh my God," Mike gasped as he looked around the vault.

"My thoughts exactly," Greg said.

"Come on! We don't have time to do any sightseeing." Jo pulled on Mike's arm to get him moving. This was not the time for her brother to go off on a tangent. Jo was thankful Ben wasn't here.

Mike grabbed a sword, and Jo didn't tease or chide him about it. If it made her brother feel safer, more power to him.

They ran along the end of the rows. She glanced over her shoulder as she ran, imagining the folks who had been running down the hall in the vault and chasing them. They reached the other door, and Carrie unlocked it.

Carrie pulled it open. The darkness greeted them.

"Do we know where this goes?" Mike asked.

"It comes out in the barn," Jo answered and stepped into the darkness, her phone flashlight barely cutting through the black.

"When this is over, we're going to talk about why you didn't tell me you've been down here," Mike told his sister.

"Yeah, yeah," Jo grumbled. A sound like a gong rang out, and she assumed it was the other door being slammed open.

"Turn off the light in there," Carrie ordered.

Jo reached back to flip the switch. They heard cursing from the far end of the vault and a crash as metallic things hit the floor.

Greg shut the vault door behind them. "You three go," he said. "I'll take care of them."

"What? Are you crazy?" Jo asked. "We all go. Where's the key? We'll lock the door."

"Ah, the key is in the other door," Carrie said in a tiny voice. "We forgot to take it.

"I was going to talk to you before you left, but now is as good a time as any," Greg said to Jo. "I want you to remember, no matter what you see, you're safe. I won't hurt you."

"Can't you two work this out later?" Mike asked. "There are guns out there with people attached to them. We have to get out of here!"

"You're safe," Greg repeated. He kissed Jo quickly and pushed her toward the others. "Stand back."

It had to be a trick of her brain. She had never seen anything like it outside Hollywood special effects. Even then, nothing in her life prepared her for what happened next.

The air around Greg blurred. In the weak light beams, they watched his body transform in ways that didn't seem possible. His limbs and torso lengthened with the audible sounds of cracking bones and cartilage while his body bulked with shifting muscle. Sharp teeth gleamed in the light. Most of his clothing ripped at the seams and dropped to the floor.

His face was the most terrifying change Jo had ever witnessed. It rippled as the mouth and nose stretched into what had to be a muzzle. Large, sharp teeth filled his mouth. He writhed as a thick layer of dark fur covered his body.

His eyes rolled and focused on the three people standing scant feet away.

"What the hell!" Mike exclaimed.

A deep growl echoed around them.

"Greg," Carrie said in a tiny voice that knew it was prey and still tried for brave. "Uh...can you open the vault door?"

The shock of Greg's secret and Carrie's logical observation in the face of nightmares come to life jolted Jo into action.

She took a cautious step toward the now nearly eight-foot creature. "I know what you're doing," she said as calmly as she could manage. "I'll let you into the vault and close the door behind you. Just...let me by."

For a moment, she didn't know if he understood her, but then he shuffled back to give her access. She looked up into the nightmare face and glimpsed his attempt to smile. It gave her courage.

She grabbed the handle and tugged the heavy door open. Greg bounded into the dark vault with a howl. Courage fled, and Jo pushed it shut.

"That was it," Jo squeaked out as panic rose. "That's what I heard when Claver attached. That's the howl. It was Greg!"

"He's a werewolf." Carrie gasped. "I can't believe it."

"It's not possible." The tremor down her spine said it couldn't be anything else.

"This is wild," Mike said. He sounded excited, and that only made it worse for Jo. She turned on him to let him have it, but a faint howl from inside the vault reached them, along with screams.

"Yeah, we aren't standing here another second," Mike said. "Go!"

Carrie grabbed Jo's wrist and pulled her along to the ladder leading into stables. Mike brought up the rear.

"Let me make sure it's clear," he said when they reached the ladder. He climbed up and opened the trapdoor. When that happened, they heard faint pops from a distance.

"Gunshots," Carrie and Mike muttered at the same time.

"I'm going to check around and make sure it's okay for us to go out there," he told the girls. "Stay here. Don't go back."

Joanna barely heard him. Her mind was still on replay. She peered down the tunnel, scanning for signs of Greg or the people pursuing them. Only the black silence looked back.

"Jo!" Carrie snapped harshly, getting her attention. Carrie never spoke in that tone of voice. In a way, it was just as disturbing as Greg's reveal.

"What?" she snapped back.

Carrie didn't answer. She climbed the first few ladder rungs and looked back. Jo put her hand on the ladder to show she was going to follow. Her stomach twisted up, thinking about what might be happening in the vault. The terrible fear of something happening to Greg outweighed the terror of seeing him as a nightmare creature.

Mike reached down to pull her up when she was a few rungs from the top. He closed the trapdoor quietly. The horses were agitated by the muted gunfire, neighing and stamping their hooves.

Joanna's focus shifted to the horses. They couldn't break down their stall doors, could they? A stampede, if three horses could be called a stampede, was one thing they didn't need. The gunfire continued, but not as rapidly as before. It sounded farther away now.

"Alex said to run for the woods and keep running until we reached the neighbor's," Mike said.

"Shouldn't we take the horses?" Carrie asked. "What if they get hurt?"

"I don't know, but we have to do what Alex said." Jo looked out of the barn door toward the house. Flashes of light still appeared, but it didn't seem as noisy as it had at the beginning.

"There's no time to saddle them, so they stay here," Mike said. "I think whoever is shooting is near the house, but if we run and don't make too much noise, we should be okay." He looked back at Jo and Carrie. They both nodded. "Run, but stay as close to the ground as you can."

Jo blinked. Mike's words made sense, and he remained calm. Maybe her brother had grown up, and she hadn't realized it until now.

Mike opened the door a little wider, taking care to not make any noise. "Keep moving, stay low, and keep quiet." He took one more look outside. "Go," he whispered.

Carrie and Jo bolted from the barn with Mike on their heels. They ran as fast as they could, yet it didn't seem fast enough. Jo heard a man shout, and panic tightened its grip around her heart. Breathing became difficult. They had been spotted.

"Get them!" a man's voice yelled, and Jo tried to run faster. Carrie and she ran straight for the dark shapes of the trees. She dared a glance around as they ran. She caught a glimpse of faces, but she couldn't tell who they belonged to. A gun fired, and while Jo knew the bullet went nowhere near her, she'd swear it buzzed by her head. She did a quick check to make sure Mike and Carrie weren't hit. A snarling filled the air, cutting off a yell. *Go, Munchkin!* All they had to do was make it to the woods. It sounded simple enough.

They heard Alex yelling, and Jo turned to see her charging toward the man now fending off Munchkin. Alex shot at the man, and the dark shape fell to the ground. Someone else fired, and Alex jerked backward as if she'd been hit.

"No!" Jo screamed and stopped. That got the attention of everyone who hadn't seen them yet.

Mike grabbed her hand, yanking her forward. "Run!" he yelled at her and tugged on her hand. He pulled her along toward the trees.

The short distance to the tree line seemed like miles. She ran headfirst into the woods, Carrie on her heels. As they crashed through the undergrowth, a bullet slammed into a tree a few feet from them. With the weak moonlight filtering through the trees, they had just enough light to keep from running face-first into a tree, but not enough to avoid all the ground cover. Jo didn't want to slow down, but the tree roots, bushes, and brambles forced her slow her pace. The last thing she wanted to do was trip, or sprain an ankle, or lose the others. Bad things happened in the woods, just ask every horror movie ever. She put her hand out in front to keep from running into anything.

Fear kept Jo running as fast as she dared and she knew the

men would catch them if they stopped. Her chest hurt, and her lungs burned. Her legs started to feel like they were made out of rubber. She glanced over her shoulder to see Carrie leaning against a tree.

"I can't run anymore," Carrie gasped. "My lungs are on fire."

"Mine too," Jo huffed as she leaned against a tree out of breath. "My muscles are jelly."

"They shot Alex," Mike said, his breath ragged. "I saw her go down."

"I did too," Jo said.

"Me too." Carrie's voice bordered on a sob.

"Do you think she's dead?"

"I don't know." Jo's gut twisted at the thought of losing the last person connected to their parents. She might have just died for them.

"People survive things all the time," Carrie said in her most hopeful, breathless voice. "You see it on the news every week."

She hoped Carrie's words would prove to be true, but she could feel the emptiness inside her growing. First her parents and now Alex. She looked at Mike. She knew she'd get through anything if her twin was there. The saving grace was that Ben wasn't here. He was safe.

"Now what do we do?" Carrie asked. "She said to run and she would find us. I don't think she'll be able to do that now."

"I don't know," Mike said.

"She said to run to the neighbor's and that's what we'll do."

"Shouldn't we call the police now? I still have my cell phone." Carrie pulled it out of her pocket and held it up.

"And tell them what? The house was attacked and we're sitting in the middle of the woods?" Jo asked. "We don't even know exactly where we are, and there may not even be service. They'll think we're cranks."

"Jo is right." Mike straightened up. "If we call, our small-town cops are going run right into whatever that was. We'd be better off with the Marines."

"Okay, you have a point. As soon as we can, we'll find a house and call the police. I'm getting a signal, so we can't be that far."

"We should keep moving." Mike tried to peer through the trees. The moon added some light to the area but not enough to get a clear view. "Put as much distance between us and them as we can. If we get lucky, we'll come across a neighbor's house." He looked at the sword he'd taken and let it drop. "This is only going to hold us back."

"Oh no, that can't happen." Carrie picked it up. The weight dragged on her arm. "Do you know how old this might be? We're not leaving it in the middle of the woods."

"Just come on!" Jo grabbed Carrie's other hand and pulled her long. Mike followed.

ALEX WALKED SURELY AROUND THE BORDER OF THE cleared area of her property with Munchkin beside her. It was a nightly ritual to walk the perimeter. She couldn't sleep unless she did it. Funny thing was she couldn't remember when she first started doing it. She knew it started when she moved to the New World, but she couldn't remember the exact date or even the general year. Now it was so ingrained, she couldn't imagine not doing it.

The late June evening was perfect and a little on the cool side. The day had been sunny and warm. She'd swear June and September were the best months in New England, where the weather could be temperamental at best. Damianos always said she and the New England weather were well suited to each other.

Alex inhaled deeply and smiled at the scent of lilac filling the air. The tree frogs provided a chorus during the evenings, and even a few fireflies appeared as points of light in the cleared land. Alex loved the rebirth of spring and the warmth of summer after long New England winters. She had other properties around the country as well as in Canada and Mexico, but her Maine house would always be her favorite. She longed for it when she lived elsewhere and never wanted to leave when it was time to move on.

Munchkin froze in place, and a deep growl rumbled from him. Alex stopped next to the dog and looked around. She listened, knowing she would not be able to see anyone moving in the woods. Whatever lurked in the woods wasn't an animal. Munchkin would either ignore those or bound after them. This was something more, something dangerous.

Alex looked down at the dog. "Find them," she whispered. Munchkin didn't hesitate. He ran off into the trees. Alex ran after the dog. She wasn't going to sit back and wait for the danger to show its face.

Her mind raced to form a plan as she weaved through trees, trying to keep up with Munchkin. She assumed whoever was in the woods was armed and coming for her. Maybe it was the people Damianos warned her about. Her being outside should keep them away from the house and away from the kids. Munchkin kept a lot of people away just from his sheer size and loud bark that excelled at finding the ingrained behavior of avoiding big, scary-looking animals.

Munchkin disappeared out of her line of sight, and a moment later, he barked. A scream followed his ferocious bark, and she knew Munchkin had found someone. She never doubted her loyal companion.

Alex rushed ahead as fast as she dared toward the screaming, and then it suddenly stopped. She found Munchkin standing on top of a man lying on the ground. The man didn't move or make a sound. Alex cautiously approached. She was unarmed, but Munchkin would protect her if the man made a sudden move. The dog nudged her hand with his snout when she drew close enough.

She pulled her hand away and looked at it. Even in the almost no light, she could see dark liquid coated the skin where the dog's mouth made contact. Blood. She bent over and checked for a pulse. There was none. Munchkin had ripped out the man's throat. She couldn't ask for a better protector.

Alex searched around the corpse and found the man's weapon. It appeared to be a Sig Sauer pistol, but the darkness made it difficult to be certain. She felt around the man's waist and chest and found two clips for it. She smiled as she removed them and tucked them into her pockets.

She looked at Munchkin. "Take me to the next one," she whispered. This man couldn't be the only one. Alex would bet money on it. Hopefully the next man wasn't too far away. Alex stood and followed Munchkin.

They reached the second man in little time. Munchkin led the charge. The man managed to fire a few shots, all missing, before the dog got him. All hope of quiet was gone. The man screamed as Munchkin went for his throat. Alex aimed and fired a few shots, taking care not to hit the dog. The man collapsed in a heap. Voices yelled out in the night.

She checked for a pulse, and once satisfied there wasn't one, she straightened. Leaves rustled behind her, and a hand covered her mouth before she could turn around. Munchkin growled but did not attack. Alex struggled to break free, but arms like steel bands wrapped around her.

"Stop," a voice whispered. Alex knew that voice, and she went still.

The hand slipped away from her mouth. She spun on the balls of her feet to find herself face to chest with Damianos. She looked up into his shadowed face. Munchkin not attacking now made sense.

"Are you okay?"

Alex nodded, not daring to speak. She put her hands on his upper arms and held on. She needed a moment of using him to center herself. Damianos dropped a quick kiss on her forehead. She wanted to ask him where he had been and how he had found her, but she didn't. There would be time for that later when all of this was over.

"You and the dog keep going this way. I'll circle around the house the other way."

"Okay. But I have to get the kids out of the house."

Damianos nodded. "Send the dog ahead of you, and I will distract them while you do that." He gave her a hard kiss. "Go. Be safe."

She nodded, sent Munchkin to patrol ahead, and ran for the house. She wouldn't die if she was shot, but it would still hurt like hell. She took the front porch steps two at a time and threw open the door.

She skidded to a stop in the hall when she saw the kids racing down the stairs toward her. She reached into her shirt and yanked the leather lanyard. She grabbed Joanna's hand and pressed a metal key on a chain into it.

"All of you, go into the store. Joanna, take everyone into the store and into the tunnel. Follow it to the vault, and once you're inside, go to the far wall and the other door. Exit through the barn and run into the woods," she ordered. "Run until you can't run anymore. Run to the neighbors." She would have told them to stay in the vault, but she wasn't sure whoever was attacking wouldn't find it.

"But what's—" Jo started.

"Just do it! Now! I will find you!" She hated snapping at them, but this was not the time for group discussion. She left them for her home office and grabbed a book off the shelf. She opened it and removed the Glock and ammunition clip. She tossed the book onto the desk. She then reached above on a high shelf for a hunting knife between two more books and ran out of the office. It was all she had time to retrieve. She heard the kids in the kitchen going out the back door as she raced out the front door.

Several men in dark clothing approached the house from the lawn. Alex aimed and fired at the closest one. He jerked back but stayed on his feet. Dammit. They were wearing body armor. This was going to be harder than she originally thought. Alex fired again, this time aiming for a leg. Headshots were much more difficult, despite what Hollywood portrayed. The man fell to the ground clutching his wound.

They circled around, clearly thinking they had the advantage over one female. She waited. When they were close enough, she aimed for the unprotected space between vest and helmet. Rage and anger went with every shot. It felt good to defend what was hers.

Gunshots echoing in the darkness told her Damianos was dealing with the attackers on the other side of the house. A voice in the dark yelled, "Get them!" Alex knew the kids had been spotted.

"Gods be damned," she growled and frantically searched for movement in the darkness.

A vicious growl came from behind her. She whipped around to see Munchkin attack another person trying to sneak behind her. They were still a good distance away, but they could have shot Alex before she knew what was happening. She took off running toward the man fending off Munchkin.

Someone fired, the sound adding to the hail of gunshots. Pain slammed through her shoulder. She stumbled backward and intentionally fell to the ground. Maybe the shooter would approach to see if she were dead. Bastard! She winced and remained still. More gunfire rang out, closer this time, and she knew Damianos had to have made his way around the house.

Moments ticked by, but footsteps eventually approached. Alex held her breath, waiting. She slowed her breathing and remained still. The night had gone silent except for the blood pounding in her ears.

The footsteps stopped next to her. Alex brought her pistol up, aiming at the person looming over her.

"I'd prefer not to be shot this evening," Damianos said. "Although I like the idea of us treating each other's wounds."

Alex relaxed and sighed. The movement caused pain to lance through her shoulder. She swore and pushed herself up to a sitting position.

She extended her right hand for help up. Pain spiked as she moved, and she grunted. "Anyone left alive?"

"No. They've all been taken care of. Do you need a doctor?" He reached out and took her hand. He pulled, and Alex climbed to her feet.

Alex looked at herself as best she could. White-hot pain seared her shoulder, but she had movement. Blood soaked the shirt and cardigan she wore. It wasn't the worst she'd ever taken, but it wasn't the best, either. "I'm okay."

"Let's get you inside, and I'll dig that bullet out."

"I have to go find the kids. I told them to run into the woods. I have to make sure they're okay first."

"You know what will happen if—"

Alex cut him off with a glare. "They are more important right now than a little pain from reopening the wound."

Damianos grimaced, and it pleased Alex to know she frustrated him. "Fine. I'll call this in and get a crew out here to clean up."

"I don't like strangers on my land."

"Do you have a cleaning crew to call when you carelessly leave dead bodies lying around?"

"Bastard," she muttered. "Fine, call them." She couldn't imagine having to explain this one to the local police. She wouldn't know where to begin, and she didn't need to get on any mundane law enforcement radar. The SPD handling cleanup was better and quieter. Thankfully gunshots weren't uncommon in Maine and wouldn't draw attention.

"I'm glad you see it my way."

"I'll be back," she warmed and whistled for Munchkin. The dog appeared out of the dark and bounded over to Alex's side. He didn't growl at Damianos as usual. The dog, at least, could be counted on to act professionally in a crisis. "Find them," she told Munchkin. "Get the kids back."

The dog trotted off toward the forest. Alex followed.

CHAPTER SIXTEEN

Jo stopped and leaned over, putting her hands on the top of her knees, struggling to catch her breath. Her legs barely supported her, feeling more like rubber than muscle and bone. Her lungs burned with every breath. Sweat ran down her face and soaked the T-shirt she wore. Nearby, Carrie and Mike panted, trying to catch their breaths. Carrie slumped against a tree. Mike seemed to be breathing easier than Jo and Carrie. Joanna took a moment to glare at him for it.

"Where are we going?" Carrie asked. She looked like she was ready to collapse. She had barely kept pace with the twins. "We should have reached a neighbor's by now. Right?"

"No." Jo swallowed and sucked in another breath. "The Youngs' house should be just past the woods."

"It never seemed this far before."

"That's because you were probably driving on the road." Mike looked around. "Not running for your life. I don't know if we're even on the right way to the Youngs'."

"You have a point."

The sound of leaves rustling and a snap of a branch seemed ten times louder in the darkness.

"We should run," Jo whispered loudly. "It could be one of those men with guns."

"I can't run anymore," Carrie nearly sobbed. "I can barely stand. You go on. I'll hide under the brush or something. I'm small. They'll go right past me."

"No one is left behind," Mike whispered back. "We'll do this together."

Jo never thought she'd be making a last stand, let alone making that last stand in the Maine woods at night. It didn't seem right. The horror movie just kept on going.

"That's as stupid as hiding behind the chainsaws." Carrie limped around the tree. "They'll follow you if you make enough noise."

Jo joined her. Weird that they could reference a stupid commercial at a time like this. "Then we'll hide behind the chainsaws. Come on, Mike. We can't run anymore."

They waited, crouched together under the branches of a big tree. The blood pounded in Jo's ears, and her heart threatened to burst out of her chest. Her breath stayed in her chest as another branch broke underfoot. Carrie grabbed her hand, and Jo tightly squeezed it. The meager moonlight was just enough to make out a dark figure walking toward them.

"Jo? Mike? Carrie?"

Jo sighed with relief when she heard Greg's voice. He stepped out of the darkness.

Even in the dim light, She could see what remained of his shirt hung loosely on him and his ripped pants barely stayed on.

"Greg!" Jo rushed toward him. She stopped suddenly, remembering what she saw in the vault. The image of Greg turning into a hulking beast with teeth was one that wouldn't leave her anytime soon.

Greg closed the distance and wrapped his arms around her. Jo stood stiffly for a moment and then relaxed, hugging him.

"I'm glad you're all right," he said, holding her tightly.

"I'm glad to see you're all right too." Jo squeezed him just as hard.

"We're okay too, if anyone was interested," Mike said.

"I'm glad you're okay too." Greg's smile seemed toothy in the moonlight.

"We're glad to see you," Carrie said. "Although I have a lot of questions."

"That goes double for me," Mike said. "How did you find us?"

"I can imagine you have questions. But here's not the place or time. It'll have to wait for when we're not in the middle of the woods at night. As for how I found you, I followed Mike's sweat smell."

"Any other time I'd say that's creepy, but I'm happy you did, buddy."

"Now what?" Carrie asked. "We still don't know where we are or what's happening at the house."

"We keep heading toward the neighbor's," Jo said. "We can't go back to the house, even if we could find it. Do you know where we are?"

"I know," Greg assured them. "We're not that far from the road."

"Did you see Ms. Thorne?" Carrie asked Greg. "We saw her get shot."

Greg shook his head. "I didn't. I followed your trail. You were making a circle. If you kept going, you'd hit the road and end up about a mile from the house."

"What about you? Did you get hurt?" The stress knot in Jo's stomach twisted more. On one hand, Greg terrified her, him being a werewolf and all, and on the other, she really liked him. It was a weird dichotomy.

"I'm fine. I was shot twice, but they used regular bullets. It hardly slowed me down."

Jo and Carrie both gasped. "You got shot? Do you need your

wounds bandaged? We have to get you to a doctor," Carrie exclaimed.

"No. The wounds are already healed. I'm a little sore, but fine."

"What happened to the guys in the tunnel?"

"Not the time," Greg said shortly. "Do we know anything about what's going on?"

"Nothing," Mike said. "Do you think we should head back?"

"No. It's safer out here."

"Especially with you," Mike said cheerfully. "Glad you're on our side."

"Yeah, I'm glad the werewolf is on our side," Carrie agreed. "We should keep moving. We don't know if someone is still following us or not."

"Good idea," Jo said. Her legs felt like legs again, and her breathing had somewhat returned to normal. She could make it, provided they didn't have to do too much more running.

"If you don't know where you are, you shouldn't be wandering in the dark."

"Only if we don't want to get found. The people looking for us will be moving, too," Mike said. "Besides, Greg knows where we are."

"Stop making sense," Jo groused.

After a brief discussion on who would take point, Greg winning by saying anyone coming after them would be behind them, Mike led, with Carrie and Jo following. Greg brought up the rear. They hadn't gotten too far when she noticed Greg had stopped walking. She turned around.

"Greg?"

He held up a hand, and Jo remained quiet. Did he sense something or someone out there? She assumed that he could probably see and hear better than the three of them. She glanced back to see that Mike and Carrie had also halted.

"Keep going," Greg growled and ran off to the right.

"Wait! Greg!" Joanna called after him. "Keep going," She told Carrie and Mike. She turned and started after Greg.

"Where are you going?!" Mike called after her.

"Just keep going!" Jo yelled and ran after Greg. They lost Alex tonight. She wasn't losing Greg.

JO LOST SIGHT OF GREG, BUT SHE FOLLOWED THE NOISE he made moving through the underbrush. He wasn't trying to be quiet. Was he trying to be a hero? She didn't need him to save her —she needed him to not get hurt. With Alex dead and the four of them in the dark running around the woods, another death was not helpful. Horror movies started like this and ended horribly for those involved.

Then her mind stopped racing for a minute, and she remembered he was a werewolf. She was chasing a werewolf through the woods, in the dark, and she was worried about him getting hurt. Apparently, she possessed no sense of self-preservation since she was the one most likely to get hurt if they ran into one of the bad guys.

She ran as fast as she could, but tree roots sticking out of the ground slowed her down. Her foot caught on one, and she fell hard. When she lifted her head, she saw Greg standing a short distance away. Silver light from a half-moon illuminated the small clearing, allowing her to see him and a dark figure poised across from him.

"There's no one here to save you now," the dark figure growled. "This ends tonight."

Jo recognized the voice. It was Peter Claver. He was behind the attack on the house? But why? Was it to draw Greg out? If so, it had worked. They all played right into his hands.

Greg stepped back from Claver. She almost yelled for him to run, but her mouth wouldn't form the words. He started to change again, and this time Jo wasn't so shocked or so terrified. Terror swirled inside her, but curiosity took over.

Greg shifted from human to werewolf, and from the looks of it, Claver didn't seem surprised. Greg threw his head back and howled. A shiver raced down her spine.

Greg snarled and insanely large, sharp teeth almost gleamed in the dim light. He charged Claver, swiping sharp claws at the man, but Claver deftly moved out of the way. Claver brought his knife around to strike at Greg. The knife sliced through the thick pelt and into flesh, Greg howling in pain. The howl cut through Jo's initial shock and pushed back the fear. She had to do something to help.

"Claver!" she yelled and climbed to her feet. He turned to look. Jo swallowed past the lump in her throat. What did she do now? She was unarmed and scared out of her mind.

Greg took advantage of Claver's hesitation and struck at him with razor-sharp claws. They raked across Claver's chest and biceps, causing the man to cry out in pain. Claver recovered and brought the knife up for another slash, cutting across Greg's belly. The werewolf seemed more frenzied and leaped at Claver, this time clawing at his legs. The force knocked Claver to the ground. He went into a roll, and when he stopped, he pulled something out of his jacket.

Jo realized it was a gun. "No!" she yelled as he fired and Greg stumbled backward, snarling.

The sound of something big crashing through the brush made Jo shrink back and huddle against the tree trunk again. What else could be possibly coming out of the surrounding darkness? A werewolf and a madman were enough. Her mind tripped over the thought and still insisted werewolves didn't exist. Munchkin appeared from the night like an avenging guardian bear and immediately lunged for Claver. Alex charged into the clearing behind her dog.

"Claver!" Alex yelled and aimed her gun at Claver.

Jo's heart dropped back down into her chest. Alex's arrival caused both Claver and Greg to freeze. Greg seemed folded into himself, clutching his midsection and breathing hard. This time, Claver made use of the distraction by turning his gun on Alex. For a long moment, they stared at each other with guns drawn and pointed.

"You get one shot before I kill you," Alex said to Claver, her voice low and holding a deadly edge to it. "Make it count."

Jo couldn't comprehend what Alex said. Did she hear the woman tell Claver to shoot her? Who in their right mind bluffed like that? Wasn't she supposed to be dead?

Munchkin was a much better guardian for his mistress than Jo had been for Greg. He didn't give Claver time to take the one shot as his powerful jaws clamped onto the arm holding the gun. They all heard the snap. Claver screamed in pain and tried to shake off the dog. Alex continued to aim the gun she held at Claver, but she didn't fire. Jo didn't blame her. The idea of Munchkin getting shot was worse. He had more worth to them than Claver.

A deep growl came from Greg. He unfolded himself and attacked Claver while the dog had him distracted. Munchkin backed out of the way as claws ripped out the man's throat and came away in a spray of blood. In the moonlight, Claver's eyes widened with shock a second before he collapsed into a heap on the ground. Greg threw his head back, and another long, deep howl filled the night air. The satisfied howl sent another hard tremor down Jo's spine.

Her world had gone totally insane.

Alex, who should be dead, wasn't, and her boyfriend was something that didn't exist. She watched Alex look down at Claver's body for a long moment. The woman nodded once in resignation and did a quick check for a pulse. Munchkin didn't seem interested in the creature retreating from the body, which was a good sign the werewolf wasn't a threat to them.

Jo stared at Greg. He swung his massive head slowly her way, golden eyes glowing in the dark. They were the eyes of a predator. Her skin turned clammy with sweat, and her mouth went dry. Icy cold fear wrapped around her core and squeezed. She wanted to run. Her feet wouldn't move an inch.

Alex watched the werewolf and didn't look to be scared. Her gun was still up and pointed at him, but her face was a mask of calm. Jo knew Alex wouldn't hesitate to shoot Greg. "Let's go, you two," Alex said. "Greg, it's time to let the wolf retreat. We still have a lot to do tonight."

The situation was too weird for Jo to listen to Alex, and her feet didn't move. "What the hell just happened?" she demanded. "Why aren't you dead? We saw you get shot! You went down!" She swung around to Greg to see the monster in mid-change and abruptly spun back to Alex.

"Down isn't dead. This isn't the time to explain," Alex said. "Or the place." Her voice was calm, and she looked too composed.

Was she even human? Or was she something else from a nightmare?

"Come back to the house and I'll tell you what I can." She turned to Greg, now in his human form. "So will he." Alex patted her leg, and Munchkin trotted over. The fierce defender was once again a loving pet. He licked Alex's hand before she ran her hand over his head and scratched behind his ears. "Munchkin, find Carrie and Mike. Bring them home." The dog woofed and bounded off through the trees.

Jo turned back to Greg.

Greg wiped his bloody hands on the remnants of his jeans. She noticed the wound in his side, slashes from the knife on his arms and legs, and the dark blood smeared over his body. A body that was mostly naked. He turned around to see her reaction and what was left of his pants fell to the ground, leaving him in a pair of ragged boxers. Her gaze was transfixed on his body. A moment ago, he was a walking nightmare with sharp claws that had turned a breathing human being into a pile of dead flesh and bone.

"This is so embarrassing," he said in a low voice. "I hate it when this happens, and I don't have any fresh clothes."

"You have a lot of explaining to do," she said tightly, pinning each one with a fierce look. "Both of you. No more secrets."

"First, we go back to the house," Alex said.

"Back to the house? But what about the men with guns?"

"Dead."

Jo blinked. She was surprised how calm Alex said the word.

Alex looked at Greg and eyed the wounds he sported. "Are you going to be okay until we get back to the house?"

"I think so." He flexed the arm that had been shot and winced. "I think the knife and bullets were silver. It went through but will take a long time to heal." He bent over and picked up his torn shirt. He ripped a long strip of fabric from it and offered it to Alex. She took the piece of cloth and tied it around his stomach wound.

How could the two of them be so casual about this? Alex had been shot. Greg had been shot and cut. There was a dead man a few feet from them. "Who were they, and what did they want?"

"We'll talk about this at the house." The edge in Alex's voice wasn't hard to miss. The woman didn't wait for an answer. She strode off between the trees, a clear sign there would be no more discussion.

"Did they attack us because of you?" Jo asked after her. She refused to move until she got an answer.

Alex stopped walking and turned around. Even in the dim light, Jo could see the irritation on Alex's face. Quite frankly, Jo didn't care if the woman wasn't happy with her. Jo wanted answers, and she would get them.

"I don't know. We'll discuss this once we've doctored everyone's wounds. I need to make sure your brother and Carrie are okay before anything else."

As effective as a slap in the face, Alex's words pushed the anger and fear away. Guilt rushed in to fill the void. Jo knew she should have been thinking about her brother and her best friend before demanding answers. Mike and Carrie were out in the woods in the dark with no idea what was going on. They had wounded people to care for, and here she was, acting like a spoiled little girl. She took a deep breath. "You're right. I'm sorry.

Greg fell into step with Jo. "Are you okay?"

"You could have said something."

"Yeah, that would have been a great conversation starter. I'm a werewolf. Want to get some ice cream and see a movie?"

"Anything would have been better than this," Jo snapped.

"Maybe, but who could have predicted this? Maybe this was the only way. You're mad, not scared. I can deal with mad. Fear is a whole different story."

He might be right. Now that the immediate danger was over, she was too angry to be scared, especially with him in boxers and makeshift bandages. But she had been scared down to her bones. Getting over that wouldn't be easy.

The little clues had been there all along, but she just hadn't seen them as part of the bigger picture. She now understood why Greg didn't go to the ER after the accident and why she had heard the howl during the first attack. She was angry with all of them and at herself for not picking up on the hints. Claver had also called Stavros a monster. What type of creature did that make the man? What was Alex? Alex had said that Claver knew better than to go after people like her and Stavros.

"What do you think Alex is?" Jo asked in a low voice so Alex wouldn't hear.

"I have no idea," he answered just as quietly. "A lot of supernatural types can survive a bullet wound. I wouldn't have even suspected she was one if she hadn't been shot. There are always clues to their true identity, but not this time."

"Clues such as?"

"Scent is a big give away. Usually, supernatural types have a distinctive scent, and I can tell with a sniff. Ms. Thorne doesn't smell any different from you."

"What if she's something you've never heard of?"

Greg shrugged. It looked painful. "I guess we'll find out. She may not even be one of us. She could be a plain human who happened to survive being shot."

"I guess we'll soon find out." She paused. "I hope."

"I'm sure we will."

Jo would get answers before the night was done, no matter what it took.

CHAPTER SEVENTEEN

ALEX, JO, AND GREG EMERGED FROM THE TREES NOT too far from the house. An ambulance sat in the drive with its lights on but not flashing. Men in black uniforms picked up filled body bags and laid them out in a row. Several dark SUVs with headlights on were parked in a row behind the ambulance. It looked like the SPD arrived rather quickly.

An armed guard stepped out in front of the little group, causing Jo and Greg to jump. Alex stopped and glared up at the man. He took a step backward.

"Are you going to let us pass, or do I have to go through you?" Alex asked. She was not in the mood to deal with some agent trying to act tough or tell her what to do. Sure, he was bigger than she was, but right now she had anger on her side.

The man hesitated and didn't answer.

"They're with me," Damianos said, interrupting his conversation with another agent nearby.

The man in front of Alex nodded and stepped to the side.

"Thank you," Alex said. She turned to Jo and Greg. "Please go inside. Jo, there's a medical kit under the sink in the downstairs bath. Use it to clean and bandage any wounds the two of you have. I'll be inside in a minute."

"Um, Ms. Thorne, I killed a few of them in the vault," Greg confessed a little sheepishly. He seemed embarrassed by the admission. "They followed us down there, and I dealt with them while the others got away."

Alex's stomach dropped to her feet at the mention of men in the vault. She put her hands on the side of her thighs to keep her hands from shaking. She prayed to whatever god was listening that they didn't remove anything from the vault.

"Thank you for telling me, Greg," she said carefully. She heard her own voice threaten to crack. "It's all right. I'll deal with it. Go inside. I'll be in soon."

"Come on." Greg took hold of Jo's arm and steered her toward the house before Jo could say something.

To Alex, the girl looked to be winding up to give them both an earful, and right now, Alex didn't want to deal with it. It had always been Jo's way of dealing with unpleasant things. Jo let Greg lead her away while Alex turned her attention to the line of body bags. Ten in all. It reminded her how dangerous a man Damianos was. He'd killed many more than the three she and Munchkin had killed.

She walked over to the bags, squatted down, and unzipped the first one in the line. She searched the corpse's pockets for any sign of identification or clues as to who he might have worked for. Movement in her peripheral vision caught her attention, and she turned to see Damianos standing next to her..

"They've all been searched. Look at his left wrist," Damianos suggested.

Alex did as he instructed. The tattoo wasn't hard to miss. "Is this what I think it is?" She looked up at Damianos, not really wanting to hear him confirm her suspicions.

He nodded. "Yes."

"Fuck." She had a wide vocabulary of swear words in many languages, but that was the only one to come to mind right now.

"Precisely."

Alex stood. "Any idea who they are working for?"

Damianos shook his head. "You know what they're after."

It wasn't a question, and it didn't need an answer. She answered anyway. "Yes." Her stomach flipped and her hands shook. "Greg said he killed some in the vault." Blood had already been spilled over that sword, and she didn't want more added to it.

"Do you think they found it and took it?"

"I don't know. I need to go check." Durendal, sword of Roland, in the hands of the Dragon Knights frightened her on a level she didn't want to admit. It was almost as bad the thought as the Spear of Destiny in the hands of the Nazis. "We ran into Claver in the woods. Any chance they're working with him?"

"I don't know. It's unusual for them to work with anyone, let alone a team. Where's Claver now?"

"Dead."

"How?"

"Greg Sullivan. You could have told me the Sullivans are werewolves." Just like him to keep important information to himself. Had she known about the Sullivans, she would have been better prepared in case Greg lost control inside the house. She didn't think he would, but it never hurt to be prepared.

"Aren't you the one always saying that an individual's state of being is a private matter and it's for them to disclose?"

"Yes, but Greg is a possible danger to everyone around him. Including those whose safety I'm responsible for."

"Speaking of those kids, shouldn't you be in there with them?"

Alex narrowed her eyes at him. He had a point, and she didn't like it. "I need to check the vault first. Don't you dare think this conversation is over. We will continue this later."

"I assumed as much. You bring the wine, and I'll bring the handcuffs."

Alex glared and turned to go into the house, but a bark cut through the low conversations of the SPD agents. "Munchkin!" she called out. A bark answered her, and a moment later, the dog with Mike and Carrie following emerged from the trees. Munchkin raced across the clearing to her and bumped against her legs. "Good boy," she praised as she scratched behind his ears.

"Alex!" Mike yelled, as he and Carrie hurried over to them. He wrapped Alex in a bear hug and lifted her off the ground. Pain from her wounded shoulder streaked through her. "You're alive! We thought you were dead!"

"Obviously I'm not. Please put me down," she pleaded. She wouldn't fault him for his emotional display of relief, but it hurt so much. He sat her back down on her feet and released her.

"We're so glad you're alive," Carrie breathed. "We were so scared."

Alex pulled Carrie in for a hug, taking care not to aggravate her own wound. "I'm glad I'm alive too. Are either of you hurt?"

"Just some scrapes and bruises," Mike said. He looked around. "Did Jo and Greg make it back?"

"They're in the house." Alex released Carrie and looked her over. "Are you hurt?"

"I'm okay. I just have a few scrapes and scratches from tree branches."

Alex hugged her again and then noticed Carrie dragged a sword. Carefully, Alex tried to take it from her hand, but the girl's fingers were locked around the hilt.

"Release the sword," Alex told her in a gentle voice. "My antiques are not toys."

Carrie gasped and dropped the sword. Damianos caught it before it reached the ground.

Damianos put a hand on Carrie's shoulder. She looked up at

him, wide-eyed with apprehension. The big, bad shadow government agent imperceptibly softened.

"No harm, no foul," he said in a voice that tried for reassurance.

"Thanks," Carrie squeaked out.

"I think we should head inside to continue this conversation," Damianos suggested.

"What happened? Why were we attacked?" Mike asked.

"Alex will answer questions inside."

Alex would admit she wasn't looking forward to it. Telling the kids about her would complicate their lives, but they should know the truth after this evening's events. She wished they could have gone on with their lives not knowing.

"I'll be right in." She gave Mike a slight push toward the house. "I have to check something first."

CHAPTER EIGHTEEN

MIKE AND CARRIE ENTERED THE KITCHEN JUST AS JO finished fastening the bandage on Greg's arm. As soon as her brother saw her, he rushed over and pulled her in for a tight hug. Jo returned the hug just as tightly. Relief washed through her. She held onto her brother for a few moments longer than sisterly affection demanded.

"I'm so glad you're okay," Mike said. "You are okay, right?" He pulled back to look her over.

"I am," Jo assured him. She wouldn't even tease him about caring. Not now. Maybe tomorrow.

"Good." He released her and looked at Greg. His eyes went wide at the bandaged wounds on the other man's chest. "What happened? Are you okay? Shouldn't you go to a hospital?"

Greg shook his head. "No hospital. I'll heal. It wasn't that bad."

Jo gave him a flat look. "Not that bad" were two deep gashes and a bullet wound. She didn't want to ever see what he considered bad. At least he had found a pair of Mike's sweatpants in the clean basket in the laundry room, so he wasn't sitting there nearly naked.

Munchkin flopped on the floor in front of the refrigerator.

"What happened to you two?" Carrie asked. "Where'd you go?"

"I smelled Claver and went after him," Greg said. "I didn't want him to get near you all. I didn't count on Jo following me."

"I didn't want you running off on your own," Jo said. Looking back, there wasn't much she could have done for Greg when he faced Claver, but she liked to think that she helped distract Claver enough to give Greg a little advantage.

"You could have gotten seriously hurt," Greg told her.

"You did get hurt."

"Both of you shouldn't have run off like that," Carrie admonished. "Don't do it again."

"Yes, ma'am," Greg said.

"I'll make some tea to help calm nerves." Carrie grabbed the kettle from the stove and filled it at the sink. She returned it to the burner. Flames flared to life when she turned it on.

"What happens now?" Mike asked.

Jo shrugged. "I guess Officer Nicademos is seeing to the cleanup judging by the body bags out there. After the bodies have been removed, I have no idea."

"Do we know who did this?" Carrie asked.

"No, but we can ask Alex when she comes in."

"Where is Alex?" Joanna asked. "I thought she would be in here doctoring her wound."

"She said she had to check something," Mike answered.

"Probably the vault," Greg said. "I left a mess in there."

"She's probably worried something was stolen," Carrie said. "It's the most logical reason why she'd go there before seeking medical attention."

"I'm fine." Alex entered the kitchen. Everyone but Greg jumped in surprise.

Jo turned to look. Alex must have come in the front door and had done it without any of them hearing. After the night they'd had, it disturbed her to not to have heard the woman approach.

"How are you even alive? It should have at least hit a lung," Mike pointed out.

"You find her alive and wonder why she's not dead of a sucking chest wound?" Jo asked sarcastically. Only her twin. At least Ben had some sense. One thing to be thankful for was Ben not being here right now. "You sound like my brother, all right."

"Sit, have some tea, and I'll explain. We'll address your understanding of human anatomy later."

Carrie removed mugs from a cabinet and a teapot. She put some loose-leaf tea in the basket and placed it in the teapot.

Stavros entered the kitchen and set a pair of needle-nose pliers, a bottle of whiskey, a needle, a spool of thread, and some bandages on the counter. "Let me dig the bullet out."

"Not now," Alex said. "I have to talk to them first."

Stavros shook his head. "You can talk to them while I work. You know what will happen if it's in there too long."

Jo watched Alex glare at Stavros, and the battle of wills commenced. Alex backed down, and Jo flinched, surprised.

"Fine," Alex grumbled.

"Mike, let me have your seat," Stavros said.

"Uh, sure." Mike pushed the stool toward the man.

Stavros slid the stool over to the other side of the counter near the sink and patted it. Alex glared at him, but she sat down anyway. Stavros handed her a bottle of whiskey. She opened it and took a long drink. Mike watched with fascination. She had another long drink.

"I'd rather have that than the tea," he said hopefully.

Stavros took the bottle from her and handed it to Mike. "Help yourself."

Her brother seemed defiant as he lifted it to his mouth. A second later, he was coughing and wheezing for air. Jo chuckled at her brother's misfortune.

Alex grabbed the bottle back for a third drink. "You had to grab my best bottle of whiskey, didn't you?"

"It was the closest one."

"That was a gift from Jefferson and hidden in the back of the liquor cabinet. You always seem to purloin my best liquor and wine."

"You have more, and it can't be that good if the boy isn't breathing."

"He's not used to whiskey, and you were warned not to use children as food tasters centuries ago."

"I'm not Rufus." He grinned, and Jo thought him quite handsome when he smiled. "I won't drink your whole liquor cabinet. Just select bottles."

"Thank the gods for small favors."

"Who's Rufus?" Mike asked.

"How are you not dead?" Jo demanded, interrupting Alex and Stavros. She couldn't remain quiet any longer. The anger building inside her couldn't be contained. She wanted answers, and she wanted them now. They all deserved to know what the hell was going on and why they had been attacked.

Alex didn't answer right away. Instead, she took another pull from the bottle and nodded to Stavros. He used scissors to cut her shirt over her shoulder, baring enough skin to expose the wound. He grabbed the bottle and poured some over the wound and over the pliers. Now Alex reacted with a hiss from between clenched teeth. After a few deep breaths, she nodded to indicate her readiness.

"My name is not Alex Thorne," Alex started as Stavros probed the wound with a competency indicating this wasn't his first bullet removal.

Jo leaned in to listen.

"The name I was given is Akantha, and I was born in Ephesus. On today's world map, it is in modern-day Turkey."

"Her real name means thorny," Stavros added. "Not so different from her disposition."

Alex glared at him but continued her story. "I was born in the year 420 BCE. I am two thousand four hundred and thirty-three years old, give or take a few years." She paused for a long moment, letting the information sink in.

Mike shook his head. "That's impossible."

"It's not impossible," Alex said flatly. "There are people in this world who are immortal, or as close to immortal as one can be. It's a fine line."

"Ephesus? Did you see the temple of Artemis?" Carrie asked, her eyes wide with awe.

Jo smiled; she couldn't help it. Of course Carrie asking a historical question instead of the issue at hand, Alex's immortality, was completely in character. Jo glanced at her brother and Greg. Greg was the only one without a look of surprise on his face.

"Okay, so how is it even possible?" Jo asked. Alex couldn't be thousands of years old as she claimed. If there were immortals in the world, wouldn't people know about it? On the other hand, Greg existed. And there were a lot of family photos with Alex in them, and she looked the same in those as she did today.

"It's unbelievable," Carrie said. "Think of all that history."

"I thought immortals were a myth. You hear stories about them, but I never thought they actually existed," Greg said as he pulled one of Mike's shirts over his head. Mike and Carrie whipped their heads around to give Greg a look. He looked back and shrugged. "I didn't."

Alex shook her head and answered the easiest question. "I was born a mortal human."

"Then how did you, you know, become immortal?" Mike asked. "Can you be killed if someone cuts off your head with a sword?"

Jo did the only thing she could. She hit her brother in the arm.

Hard. "Idiot. You watch too many movies." There were days where she found it hard to believe they came from the same parents. Carrie giggled softly.

With the giggle, the tension in the air evaporated. They all seemed to breathe easier.

Alex smiled. "I don't know if I can be killed if someone were to cut off my head. I really haven't had the chance to test out the theory, not that I'd ever want to. It's best to just forget those movies for my sanity's sake."

"So how did you become immortal?" Jo asked. If Mike would just shut up, they might hear the story. The thought of stuffing one of the tea towels draped over the oven handle in his mouth flashed through her mind. She'd do it the next time Mike made another movie reference.

"My parents were very poor and couldn't afford to feed us all. They had four surviving children, and I was the oldest and a girl. Girls... Well, the view on female children back then was a lot different than it is today. Children in general were a commodity that was wasted if not used. I was six when they handed me over to the temple of Artemis. So, yes, Carrie, I did see it, and I lived there."

Carrie's eyes shone with excitement. "Wow. I have questions."

Mike's jaw dropped. "Wait, they just gave you to a church?"

"It wasn't a bad thing," Alex said. To Jo, it sounded like Alex was trying to reassure them. "They really did try their best, and giving me to the temple was a good option for me. Unwanted children were sold into slavery by their parents on a regular basis. Girls and boys were sold to much older men as house slaves or worse. Instead, I would have shelter and food, and be raised to serve the temple. It was an honor to be chosen."

"I guess you got a better deal than most," Carrie said.

"So you became a member of the temple," Jo prompted, anxious to get back to the story. "Then what happened?"

"When I was about seventeen, I was in the market running

errands for the priestesses and I met a man. We saw each other in secret, and eventually he convinced me to run away with him. And I did."

"That's so romantic." Carrie sighed dreamily with a smile on her face.

"I thought so too," Stavros commented. He had the bullet out by now and plopped the bloody slug down on the counter. It looked small compared to the ones on television and movies. He threaded the needle with a proficiency that told Jo this wasn't his first time stitching a wound.

"You were the man?" Carrie asked. "But that means—"

"I'm also immortal," Stavros answered.

"That's incredible," Mike said.

Ever-practical Jo normally would have scoffed at doing something stupid as that, but she was too caught up in the story and said guy was in the room and really hot. "It still doesn't explain how you became immortal," she pointed out. "If it did, lots of seventeen-year-old girls would be immortal. It also doesn't explain why you've been lying to us all this time."

Alex sighed. "I have my reasons for not explaining." She flinched as Stavros started stitching her wound.

"You mean like how you're both using fake names?" Jo snarled. "And why someone keeps attacking us?"

"How do you know about that?" Alex asked. They had managed to surprise Alex. A first.

"I overheard you and Stavros talking in the hospital," Joanna replied. "Or should I say Damianos?"

"Call me Damianos," he said with a grin. "It's my given name, and Stavros never did fit as well," he said as he stitched up Alex's wound. The conversation amused him, and his amusement annoyed Jo.

"I tried to keep all of you out of this," Alex said. "It just happened. I don't know why yet."

"You mean like psycho man all in black?" Carrie asked.

"Actually, he was after me," Greg said. "Ms. Thorne had nothing to do with him."

"What?" Mike exclaimed.

"Why you?" Carrie asked.

"There are people out there who hunt down people like me."

The teakettle whistled, startling Carrie. She slid off her stool and lifted the kettle off the burner.

"Carrie, please turn the gas off," Damianos said, his attention still focused on his doctoring.

"Oh, right." Carrie twisted the knob to off. She filled the teapot and returned the kettle to the stove.

"His name was Peter Claver," Damianos said as he put another stitch in Alex's skin. "He was an Inquisitor. He would not have hurt you, Joanna, had you walked away. I'm guessing you didn't. He only wanted Greg."

"Of course I didn't walk away," Jo said, insulted by the idea. "Who would do that?"

"Many people," he said quietly as he worked. "The unknown is terrifying. Few would stand up for it. The smart ones run away."

Carrie's eyes reached epic proportions as she sat down, and her glasses made them look even bigger. Jo could see the gears turning inside her mind. "Inquisitor, as in the Inquisition? But that ended centuries ago."

"Officially, it ended centuries ago. Unofficially, it's still in existence. Inquisitors are Church-sanctioned killers," Alex explained. "The Church has an excellent public relations department."

"They hunt down beings the Church classifies as evil. Which is everything not human," Damianos added. "Their idea of human is very narrow."

"So that includes immortals and werewolves," Mike stated rather than asked.

"Yes," Alex said. "Though they generally stay away from

immortals since they can't easily kill us, and they're far too human. It ends badly for them."

"It ended badly tonight," Greg muttered. "My parents are going to have kittens."

"Don't you mean puppies?" Mike asked.

Jo rolled her eyes, and Greg reluctantly laughed. The world could be ending, and Mike would find a way to joke about it. "Yeah, I guess."

"So who were the men with the guns?" Carrie asked. She put her elbows on the counter and leaned forward.

"They weren't with Claver. Inquisitors usually don't rely on others due to secrecy issues. I think the assault team's attack happened to coincide with Claver's attack on Greg. I thought Claver was after Jo to force me out into the open, but that's not the case. I should have known better. They usually go out of their way to avoid killing humans. It was a mistake and a costly one."

"What happened to him?" Mike asked.

"He's dead," Alex said. Jo watched Alex glance over at Greg. It didn't appear she was going to tell the others Greg killed the Inquisitor. She was thankful for that.

"Oh," Carrie said. She slid off the stool and went over to the teapot. She poured tea in each of the mugs and passed them out.

"What about the police? Are they going to take our statements?" Mike asked.

"No," Damianos answered. "I've already spoken to them. SPD took jurisdiction and provided a statement. We're cleaning up now."

"Speaking of SPD, what is it?" Jo asked.

"Supernatural Police Department, and I'm a senior agent."

"So it's not just an urban myth," Carrie said more to herself.

"That sounds awesome," Mike said. "Except for the name. It's kind of corny. What does the SPD do?"

"Just what the name says. We police the supernatural world. Keep things from getting out of hand. We also try to keep the mundane world safe from supernatural threats and keep the supernatural world safe from the mundane threats."

"I think my brain is going to explode from all of this," Carrie said, not at all unhappy with the idea. "I have to write this down."

"No, you don't," Alex said sternly.

"Supernatural threats? Such as?" Jo prompted.

Damianos shrugged. "Anything classified as supernatural. Which is anything not human. There's a whole world out there most people don't know exists, and they're happier not knowing."

"Are you saying things that go bump in the night are real?" Mike asked.

Jo shook her head to clear it. Her eyes were open after a lifetime of being half asleep, and she wasn't sure she liked it. Her plans for her life had been on track until her parents died. The detour so far had been a bumpy ride.

"As one of those things that goes bump in the night, yes, he's saying that," Greg added dryly.

Mike blinked. "Oh. Right. Sorry. Still processing you're a werewolf."

"It's okay. Sometimes, those supernatural threats are werewolf sightings."

"How do people not notice?" Jo asked.

"Everyone has seen those things, but they just don't remember and don't want to remember. People are the best at lying to themselves," Alex said. "It hardly takes any effort, but we don't have all night to go into it."

"What happens now?" Carrie asked.

"We go to bed and get some sleep. It's late. We'll be okay here until tomorrow. They'd be stupid to try again tonight."

Jo caught Alex and Damianos exchanging looks, and she knew they would be talking about what next steps to take. She assumed there were things they didn't want to talk about in front of others. Plus, they probably still saw the four of them as children, and likely saw almost everyone as children, considering how old the two of them confessed to being. And were there more like them out there in the world?

"You expect us to sleep after all that?" Mike said.

Alex looked at Mike. "I do. It's late, and tomorrow is another day to face."

"I'm not even remotely tired. There's no way I could possibly sleep," Mike said.

Jo wouldn't argue with Alex and Damianos, but adrenaline was still pumping through her veins, and sleep was the last thing she wanted to do.

"Me either," Carrie said.

"What are we going to do tomorrow?" Jo asked.

"We'll cross that bridge in the morning," Alex answered.

"But we have more questions," Mike said.

"We'll have more answers tomorrow," Alex said. "Immortals can't die, but we do need to sleep. Carrie and Jo, I would like the two of you to stay in the second-floor guest room tonight."

"Sure, Ms. Thorne," Carrie said. "May I ask one question first?"

"What is it, Carrie?"

"When Jo and I were wondering about the vault, I did some research into the house and property, and, well, have you always owned it?"

Alex stared at Carrie long enough to make the young woman shift uncomfortably. "That was very resourceful of you," Alex finally replied with a frown. "I came to this area in 1590 from the Roanoke Colony. Every few decades I leave the area, the owner dies somewhere else, and the house and property are willed to a distant relative. After enough time has passed and the generation of locals die away, I come back to stay for a time."

Carrie's jaw dropped. "You were in the Roanoke Colony? What happened to it? Why did the colonists abandon the settlement?"

Jo unwillingly smiled. While her brain was overloaded with information and close to bursting, Carrie's mind raced ahead and wanted to know more. Jo wanted Carrie to let it go so they could leave the room without the fear of missing something important.

"Those are questions for another time. Right now, it's time to go to bed." Irritation laced Alex's words, and Joanna suspected the immortal's patience was played out.

"You never answered the question about how you became immortal," Jo pointed out.

"I was cursed by a priestess of the temple. Not a very interesting story."

"Why?" the ever-curious Carrie asked.

"I stole something belonging to the temple."

"And that was..." Mike prompted.

"I think it's time to get some sleep," Damianos said. "Tomorrow's going to be a long day."

"Ms. Thorne, Agent Nicademos, my family—" Greg began.

"I've already called for a team to watch your house," Damianos said. "In case Claver wasn't the only Inquisitor in the area. There's no evidence he traveled with a partner. They've also been notified you're all right and still here at the house."

"Thanks."

"Now bed," Alex said again. "We have all day tomorrow to talk."

They got the hint and rose from their seats. One last glance at Alex and Damianos, and they headed out of the kitchen.

ALEX RUBBED HER EYES AND YAWNED. THE LONG DAY and night caught up to her, and now that the adrenaline was wearing off, she just wanted to fall into her bed. She didn't even care if Damianos was there or not.

She opened her eyes, and Jo stood there, glaring at her. Alex was too tired and too sore for this, but she knew Jo would not give up until she had her say. She was so much like her mother it hurt.

A weary sigh escaped Alex. "You've been glaring daggers at me since we got in the house. Out with it."

"How could you lie to us all this time? Why didn't you tell us the truth?" Jo demanded.

A little energy returned in the form of anger. "If you think I was going to put my life in the hands of someone grieving for their parents, you're not as smart as I thought. Especially when it wasn't necessary. The attack forced my hand just as effectively as Claver forced Greg to tell his secret. People keep secrets for a reason."

"Your secret could have gotten us all killed!"

"And now I'm handling it. I'm doing my best to keep you safe. I promised your parents I would." Alex struggled to keep her anger in check. She didn't want to yell and escalate the situation.

"How can you call any of this keeping us safe? I've been attacked. We were driven off the road. To top it off, a small army of men showed up in the middle of the night and started shooting. How is that keeping us safe?"

"What would you like me to say? The only thing I can tell you is I'm doing all I can to keep the three of you safe as your parents wanted."

"Are you? Are you even human anymore? Or are you some cold, unfeeling, unconcerned shell of a human being too old to remember what it was like to be one?" Jo demanded.

Each word hurt more than the needle going into her skin as Damianos continued to stitch up her wound.

"She is," Damianos answered for Alex. His deep voice seemed louder in the now quiet house. He snipped the last thread and put a bandage over the stitches. "She is good at what she does. I suggest you moderate your words, girl, before you can't take them back."

Alex shot him a look that said she could handle this alone. She didn't need him adding any unnecessary fuel to Jo's anger. "Yes. I have people trying to find out who is after me. Outside of that, the only thing I can do is pack up and move to another place with the three of you. We can assume new identities and hope it's enough to hide our tracks. I've gotten pretty good at that in the past two thousand years."

Jo opened her mouth to say something, but no words came out. She stared at Alex. Alex gave her a few moments to process the options.

"Well? You keep telling me you're an adult, and you can make your own decisions. Now it's time to be an adult, make a decision, and accept the consequences. These consequences will be long-term. Do you want to stay here, or do you want to move and take on a new name? We can go tonight. The Sullivans will be protected by the SPD, and I don't know if Carrie was identified or if she'll be safe, but I can guarantee you, Ben, and Mike will live another day."

Jo didn't reply right away. It wasn't playing fair to make the girl decide the fate of her brothers, but Alex didn't care about fair now. Fair would be Thomas and Claire still alive and the family together. Alex had had a long time to learn that there was no such thing as fair.

"I...I want to stay here."

"Then you'll have to trust me a little. I know, you don't think I deserve it, but you will have to believe I know what I'm doing. I've lived a very long time, and I know how to fight and protect someone. Do as I tell you, and you'll be safe."

Jo stared at her. If the girl wanted a battle of wills, Alex was willing to play. The girl would lose. Eventually, Jo nodded. "Fine," she said, the word coming out harsh. "What are you going to tell Ben and when?"

"I will tell him what I've told you when he comes home tomorrow. Now go get some sleep. Morning will come soon enough," Alex instructed.

Jo gave Alex another hard look and left the kitchen. Alex sighed with relief. Damianos went after Jo. Alex debated calling him back but decided against it. She knew he would have words for Jo. Maybe the girl needed a little fear instilled in her.

Alex looked at the teakettle on the stove and pondered another cup of tea. It would calm her, but the caffeine would keep her awake. Munchkin still needed to be cleaned up after his own attack spree. She opted for the whiskey. Damianos left the bottle on the counter, and she painfully reached for a glass from a nearby cabinet. She grabbed the bottle and sat heavily on a stool to pour a healthy amount. She drank half in one gulp.

The whiskey burned a trail to her stomach, allowing some of the stress to flow away with it. She took another drink, this one going down easier than the last. She would love to drink herself unconscious, but not tonight. Not with a possible danger lurking in the shadows.

Damianos returned and fetched a glass from the cabinet. He took the bottle, and Alex didn't even bother to give him a look. It had been a long night for them. He poured himself a glass and took the stool next to her.

"The girl has spirit," he said before taking a drink.

"Yes," Alex agreed. "She reminds me a lot of her mother."

"You must have been close to them."

Alex nodded. "I was." She grabbed the bottle and poured more. "I knew them over twenty years. The three kids were over here almost as much as they were in their own home."

"They knew about you?" He took a drink from his glass.

"They did. The kids didn't until tonight."

He nodded and reached for the bottle. "Have you decided what you're going to do?" He filled his glass and set the bottle down on the counter.

"I'm not leaving here," she forcibly said. "Tomorrow, I start hunting down those Dragon Knight bastards who stole Durendal."

"Durendal was stolen?"

"Yes," she said. She pinched the bridge of her nose and yawned. Exhaustion settled over her and into her bones. She would start the hunt for Durendal right now if she weren't so tired.

"You're going after it," he said, rather than asked.

"I just said I am. I cannot let that remain out in the world."

"Akantha, you should consider changing identities and moving."

She turned and pinned a look on him. "What aren't you telling me? I must go after Durendal before I do anything else. You know I must."

"I'm not keeping anything from you."

"You always do," she accused. "No matter the situation, you always keep important information to yourself. Save us the argument and me getting angry and tell me now."

"I'm not keeping anything from you. How they connected you with Durendal from Victoria and the museum theft, I don't know. Maybe Paladin is the connection. I think you should move to one of your other houses and take on a new identity."

"I'd think you would be more motivated than me to find the tattooed bastards given your former life as a Dragon Knight with Roland. Paladin didn't say anything. I know he didn't."

"I am, and I will, but your safety comes first."

There was more. There was always more, and right now, she was too tired to deal with him. "Tomorrow you're going to tell me everything."

He leaned over and kissed her forehead. Normally she would think it endearing, but not while she knew he was keeping secrets. "Go get some sleep. I will keep watch after the team is gone."

She eyed him for a long moment but eventually nodded. "I do need some sleep." She finished off the last of her drink and stood.

"Take the walking carpet with you tonight for an added layer of protection."

She knew he didn't want to deal with Munchkin without her around. The dog would probably bite him just for fun. She couldn't say he didn't deserve it. The man was a thief who stole her heart, and she was always a willing victim.

"Munchkin, come. Let's get you cleaned up." The dog lifted his head and then climbed to his feet. He followed her from the kitchen, and neither of them looked back at Damianos.

CHAPTER NINETEEN

Jo heard footsteps behind her and turned, expecting to see Alex, but it was Damianos. Even worse.

"What do you want?" Joanna said.

"Making sure you aren't about to do something ill advised."

"You mean like call the police or the newspapers?" she asked.

"Yes."

The simple word cut through her anger and brought reality back in a crash. Stavros, or Damianos or whatever he called himself, was big and scary and, by his own admission, willing and able to kill to protect his shadow world. Jo shoved her hands in her pockets and clenched them tightly to keep from shaking. "I'm not going to do that. I'm going to stomp upstairs, maybe throw my shoes around, and then go to bed like I was ordered to do. Happy?"

"Very."

She wasn't sure if he caught the sarcasm or was just ignoring it. She'd go with the latter. "Just what would you do if I talked?"

"I hope you never find out."

Jo swallowed past the lump in her throat. The man normally

radiated danger, but right now he was ablaze with it. She turned to go.

"One more thing," he said.

She stopped and pivoted on the balls of her feet. "What?"

"Before you nail Alex to a cross, know that she considers you one of hers and will do anything to protect you. Don't make her regret caring." It was more of a threat than words of advice. Scary man just got scarier. "Understand?" he asked when she didn't respond.

"I understand," she snapped. She turned and, as planned, stomped up the stairs.

Mike, Carrie, and Greg were waiting for her at the top of the stairs on the second floor. Jo joined them and motioned for them to move into the spare bedroom she would be sharing with Carrie.

"Why didn't you tell me?" Mike asked as they entered the spare room.

"It's not the easiest thing to tell people," Greg replied with a shrug. "It usually freaks them out. Of course, that's after getting them to believe me. There are six pups after me, so I don't even try. I have a family to protect."

"I would have believed you," Mike vowed. "You know I would have."

Greg gave Mike a look. "Really?"

"I think what Mike should have said is we would have eventually believed you," Carrie said. "It's incredible."

"Yeah, what she said," Mike said.

"Before anyone asks, I didn't get bitten. I was born this way."

"So the whole thing about being bitten by a werewolf and turning into one isn't true?" Mike asked.

Jo could hear the disappointment in her brother's voice, and she almost laughed.

"It's not." Greg sighed. "And it's stupid. People don't get to be werewolves if one bites them."

"What do they get?"

"Bloody. Sometimes dead."

Mike would not be stopped. "What about the full moon and silver bullets?"

"It's just a moon. I can be a wolf whenever I want. Silver will hurt us. It hurts to even touch it."

"Oh."

"Don't sound so disappointed," Greg said.

"I'm not," Mike assured him, but they all knew he was sorry his favorite monster movies from childhood weren't as accurate as he wanted them to be. "Just trying to process it all. Information overload night."

"Not for me," Carrie said. "I've learned a lot tonight, and I want to know more."

"You would," Jo teased.

"There's been a lot to process," Greg said. "Immortals were stories to us, myths really, and to meet two at once is a lot to take in."

"Why would they be stories?" Jo asked.

"They blend into the population better than any other species. They don't have any features or traits that are obvious or would attract notice. A person sitting next to you on the bus could be one, and you'd never know. No one I know has ever met one, but I don't think there's many out there. My parents won't believe me when I tell them she's been here all along."

"Is it okay to tell them?" Carrie asked. "I won't say anything about tonight. I swear."

Greg smiled at Carrie. Jo thought she sounded so earnest. "Thanks."

"Yeah, I guess you do have to say something," Mike said.

"I still have questions." Carrie looked thoughtful as she stared at a painting on the wall. Jo smiled. Carrie would have questions if the world was ending. "Alex said she was given to a temple of Artemis when she was little, and she was cursed. Do you think that means there might be gods? Are the gods really gods or just other another type of supernatural?"

"I don't know," Jo said.

"I don't know either," Greg said. "Immortals were myths until an hour or so ago. I have no idea about the gods."

"But they could be real, though, right?" Mike rubbed a hand over his head.

"This whole thing changes what we thought we knew about the world." Carrie moved to the small bookshelf in the corner of the room. She pulled a book out and turned it over in her hands. "Think about all the things that actually exist that we don't know about."

"I know very little," Greg confessed. "There's a lot out there I've never run into, and I wasn't looking to make contact."

"If magic is real, then what else is real?" She looked down at the book in her hands. "Oh my God. This is a first edition of *Jane Eyre*." She lifted the book to her face and sniffed. Then she colored when she saw they were watching.

"What do you think is going to happen now?" Mike sat down on the foot of the bed.

"I'm going to go home tomorrow and talk to my folks about the Inquisitor," Greg said as he leaned against a bookcase.

"No idea what will happen here," Jo said. "I imagine Alex is going to go after whoever is after her. I imagine she'll kill them. Agent Pain-in-the-Ass wants her to take us and disappear."

"Who do you think is after her?" Mike asked.

Greg shrugged. "No idea. If she's really over two thousand years old, she's had some time to make a few enemies."

"Maybe she pissed off another immortal," Mike suggested.

"That wouldn't be good," Carrie mused. She put the book carefully back on the shelf and wiped her hands on her pants.

"You think?" Jo snapped. "How do you stop another immortal?"

"Don't look at me. I'm just spitballing things. Maybe there's a way to get around the immortality. Maybe chopping their heads off does work."

"I'm willing to bet that works for just about anything," Mike said.

"Sorry. I know." Jo sighed. "I just want the craziness to stop." Unlike Mike and Carrie, she didn't see this as one big adventure. She saw it for the dangerous situation it was, where people could get hurt or killed. Except Alex and Damianos. Maybe Greg. This was probably normal for Greg. He did say something about having to leave North Carolina. She wondered if Claver had been responsible for that too. She wanted to ask him, but not now. Maybe someday she would.

"We won't be able to tell anyone about this crazy adventure," Mike complained.

"The only people we would tell are here, so it doesn't suck," Greg pointed out.

"I guess, but I'd love to tell my sisters and brother and rub it in." Carrie laughed a little. "Nothing exciting ever happens here, and when it does, it's overkill."

"You can help us rub it in with Ben," Jo said.

"Ben will get back at us. He's creative that way." Mike's voice held a note of brotherly admiration.

"What I want to know is why didn't Alex tell us when she learned people were after her? Not that we could have done anything, but we could have been more alert," Jo said, crossing her arms over her chest.

"She probably didn't tell you because she thought she was keeping you safe," Greg said.

"I know." Alex had shown she cared, that she was willing to kill to protect them. "It doesn't make being lied to any easier. If she lied about who she is, what else is she lying about?"

Carrie held up a hand. "Don't look at us. We can't answer those questions. Normal people don't have such big secrets. You'll have to talk to Alex and ask her to tell you everything."

"Like that'll ever happen," Jo grumbled.

She was still trying to process that the woman, the aunt she had grown up knowing, was almost a stranger she knew nothing about. It was difficult to reconcile her aunt with the immortal woman in the kitchen.

"You never know. She could tell you a lot more than you know now, which, judging by how old she is, could be an awful lot. It's not just you wanting to know everything. You might not be ready to hear the things she has to say," Greg advised.

Did she really want to know everything? She certainly wanted to know more, but everything? A part of her wanted to know what was out there, but there was a part that was apprehensive of anything she couldn't explain.

"We should get some sleep," Carrie suggested.

"Yeah, we should," Joanna agreed.

Greg straightened up and wrapped his arms around Joanna. She closed her eyes at the feel of his arms around her. Jo unfolded her arms, and she soaked up the warmth and safety he offered. She'd have his arms around her all night if she could, but given the circumstances, she'd be bunking with Carrie in the house tonight. It wasn't the night to test Alex's patience.

Mike trudged out of the room, and his footsteps echoed up the stairs to the third floor.

Jo followed Greg out of the room and closed the door behind her. He turned and took her hand, pulling her toward him. Greg wrapped his arms around her again and kissed her deeply. Jo's toes curled, and she returned the kiss.

"Jo, I'm sorry. I know it must have been a shock seeing me transform."

"You should be. Why didn't you tell me?" She tried not to sound demanding, but it was hard.

"It's not the thing we just tell people.

Even as irritated as she was, she didn't have the slightest urge to pull away. It was Greg, after all.

"We have to be careful. It's life and death for us. You did see the crazy guy trying to kill me, right?"

If this had happened on a boring night, she would be so freaked she might not come out of her room for days. Even knowing Greg's family was one of the nicest she'd ever met, it would have been terrifying. Luckily for him the guy trying to kill them ranked higher on the terror scale by virtue of being the first to scare her. "Would you have ever said anything?"

"I wanted to. I hoped to tell you one day."

"When would that have been?"

Gregg shrugged. "Honestly, I don't know. People either don't believe you, or they freak out. Freaking out usually means trying to kill you or running away and telling the villagers. Then they grab the torches and pitchforks. I wanted to make sure you would handle it okay."

"I understand." And she did. Telling someone something like this was on a whole new level that she could barely comprehend.

"Good. I really like you, and I'd hate for this to become an issue between us. You're the first person I've considered telling."

"Well, I think it's the first time I've met a werewolf."

He laughed a little. "That you know of. I am sorry you got mixed up in all of this."

"It's not your fault."

"The Inquisitor was after me, not Ms. Thorne," Greg reminded her.

Jo nodded slowly. Greg was right. Two of the attacks so far were because of Greg, not Alex. Still, the armed men showing up at the house was because of Alex, not Greg. It didn't change Jo's feelings about being lied to, but she couldn't lay all the blame for the craziness at Alex's feet.

"She's keeping a secret for a reason, like I was. Please remember that. For the most part, we just try to blend in with normal folks and live our lives. Most in our world are like that."

"The blending in worked well. Your family seem so normal. I

wouldn't have known if it weren't for the crazy guy in black. What else is out there?" Jo asked.

"Vampires, shifters, demons, faeries, and a lot of other things."

Her brain raced a million miles an hour trying to process the information. Too much information had been dumped on her in a relatively short time. Only Carrie had the mental fortitude to process so much at once. Jo half expected her brain to start leaking out of her ears. She didn't want to believe it all, but Greg had no reason to lie, and Damianos and Alex had basically said the same thing. "You mean they're all real?"

He squeezed her hands. "Most, yes. Some are just imagination."

Jo returned the squeeze. She had watched him rip a guy's throat out not too long ago, yet she put her hand in his without hesitation. She wasn't the least bit scared of him. Just the opposite. Knowing made her feel safer. Damianos was still scarier in her book.

Greg gave her a smile and a quick kiss on her mouth. Jo squeezed Greg's hands again.

"I'm sorry you found out this way." He released her to rest his forehead against hers. "I hope you can forgive me."

"Give me a few days to absorb it all." She was still a little too shaken now to completely forgive either him or Alex for the fright.

"It's not a no, and I can live with that."

Jo sagged a bit under the relief. Her last boyfriend dumped her when she said something similar after he upset her. She would have forgiven him after a few days, but since it wasn't right away, he decided to call things off. Greg was already a hundred times better in her book. Jo yawned. The shock wearing off left exhaustion in its stead.

"Whatever happens, I promise I will never hurt you," Greg said. "Or let you get hurt." He smiled and then kissed her forehead.

Jo closed her eyes at the feel of his lips. The promise comforted her as images of Greg's werewolf form flashed through her mind. He was probably the second most lethal thing to cross her path, yet she didn't fear him or what he could do to a person.

"We should probably go get some sleep. I'm sure tomorrow's bound to be almost as exciting as tonight," he said.

"I could do with a little less excitement," Jo said. "But you're right."

Greg kissed her again. More of Jo's anger melted away in the warmth of the kiss. It ended much too soon for her liking.

"Good night," he said and released her.

"Good night."

He grinned. His white teeth did *not* look longer than before. She was not Little Red Riding Hood dating the Big Bad Wolf. She eyed him climbing the stairs to the third floor. She couldn't be too upset if she was interested in watching his butt move under the sweatpants.

Jo sighed and headed into the guest room she would be sharing with Carrie.

CHAPTER TWENTY

ALEX OPENED AN EYE JUST IN TIME TO SEE A LONG PINK tongue coming at her. Munchkin licked her face, and Alex scrunched up her face in response. It was way too early to be up after going to bed around 3:00 a.m. She didn't want to be awake, and she certainly wasn't thrilled about being woken up by Munchkin licking her face. Every one of her years pressed down on her more than usual.

"Ugh, Munchkin," she grumbled and turned away from the dog. "I'm awake." Alex yawned and threw back the covers. She climbed out of bed and grabbed her robe, wincing against the pain in her shoulder. She cursed the man who shot her as she slipped on her robe. Every time something remotely exciting happened, she got shot. Stabbing would be a nice change of pace. She tied the belt while Munchkin scratched at the bedroom door.

Shaking her head, she opened the door and let the dog go first. She followed him down the stairs and into the kitchen. She opened the back door, and Munchkin ran out. Alex yawned and ambled over to the counter. She prepped the coffee maker and turned it on. Unfortunately, it would take a few minutes. Maybe she should consider getting one of those single-cup coffee makers that Jo kept mentioning.

The coffee maker finished, and Alex filled the largest mug she could find. Today called for copious amounts of caffeine. Today started the hunt for Durendal. She couldn't let that sword be out there in the world. Especially in the hands of a group like the Dragon Knights.

Alex retrieved her tablet from her office and sat down at the table in the breakfast nook. Not much time passed before Mike walked into the kitchen, destroying the morning quiet. To be honest, she would have put her money on Damianos being the first one in the kitchen after her.

"Morning," Mike muttered as he trudged into the kitchen.

"Morning," Alex replied, keeping the grumbling to a minimum. She noticed the dark smudges under his eyes. He'd probably had as much sleep as Alex had. Maybe less. She knew how the four liked to talk. "How'd you sleep?"

Mike shrugged. "Good, when I finally fell asleep. My brain wouldn't shut off."

"Are you hungry?"

Mike grinned. "You know the answer to that. My brain needs food."

She chuckled. "You're right, I do. Scrambled eggs with bacon?"

"Sounds good, but I'll make them. I'm not totally helpless in the kitchen. Would you like some?" he asked.

"No, thank you."

"You sure?"

"I'm sure, Mike."

"Okay. Yell if you change your mind," he said, and moved to fetch the eggs and bacon from the refrigerator.

Alex nodded and went back to reading. A few moments later, Alex looked up at the sound of approaching footsteps. Carrie entered the kitchen. She hadn't bothered to try to brush the bed head out of her hair.

"Mornin'," Carrie mumbled.

"Morning," Mike said. "Guess you slept as much as the rest of us."

"Hungry?" Alex asked her. "Mike's making scrambled eggs and bacon. Now's the time to put in your order."

Carrie paused to raise a hand to her hair. Her eyes closed in what appeared to be a moment of embarrassment before she shrugged it off. "I'll have some. Is there coffee made? Please tell me there is."

Alex smiled and noticed that Carrie also sported dark circles under her eyes. Most likely everyone would.

"Coffee is made," Mike assured her.

Carrie zombie walked to it. Alex was barely past the zombie stage herself. Mike fetched a mug for Carrie from the cupboard and handed it to her. Carrie smiled her thanks and poured a cup.

"Where's Jo?" Mike asked.

"She hasn't come down yet," Alex replied over the rim of her mug.

"Oh," Carrie said. "I thought she was down here. She wasn't in bed when I woke up."

"Is she in the bathroom?"

Carrie shook her head. "I was just in there."

"Which one?" Alex asked. The night passed without any disturbances. Munchkin would have woken her up if something had happened. Or she hoped. The bad feeling that hadn't totally disappeared flared back to life.

"I was in the one on the second floor," Carrie answered before taking a sip of her coffee. A smile crossed her face, and Alex recognized the pleasure that came with the first sip of a good cup of coffee.

Alex rose and walked to the first-floor bathroom, pushing down the dread building inside her. She knocked on the bathroom door, and when she didn't receive an answer, she opened it. An empty room greeted her. Alex closed the door and walked back to the kitchen.

Mike and Carrie looked at her when she stepped into the kitchen. "She's not in the downstairs bathroom," Alex said. "Maybe she went out to her apartment." Alex grabbed her cell phone off the table and sent a text to Jo. Seconds ticked by, and no reply came. She dialed the number and put the phone to her ear. She thought she heard it from the second floor, but she couldn't be sure. After a few rings, it went to voicemail. She disconnected the call, and her stomach sank.

"Where's Greg?" Alex asked Mike.

"Still sleeping."

Alex nodded and tried not to run into the living room. Somehow, she managed to walk. Mike and Carrie followed her. The last thing she wanted to do was to panic Mike and Carrie. She pushed down her own panic, and the anger seeped in.

"Alex?"

Alex snatched the paper lying on the couch and read it. Anger erupted and came out in a stream of curses. She switched languages and continued to swear. "Piss and blood," she swore and clenched her jaw. That bastard. She'd trusted him, and he'd betrayed that trust. Fury roiled inside her, white-hot and ready to be unleashed on Damianos the next time she saw him.

"What happened?"

Alex turned around to look at Mike. "Damianos took Jo."

"What?" Mike's jaw dropped. "That doesn't make sense."

Carrie's expression mirrored Mike's. "Why would he do that?"

"He was paid to do it," Alex growled, struggling to keep the anger in check. How could she have been so stupid as to let that man into the house?

"What?" Mike and Carrie exclaimed in unison.

"But why? He helped us last night," Carrie asked.

"Damianos has a long history of hiring himself out as a mercenary. The rumors were true. Someone is after me and hired him to do it. I let him in the door." Another flood of curses flowed from her mouth. She should have known better. Damianos always had ulterior motives, and she had let her feelings for him blind her. Never again.

"But he's an agent for the SPD," Carrie protested. "He's supposed to be protecting people like you and Greg."

"He is, first and foremost, Damianos. His self-interest will always be his number one priority."

Carrie was slow to grasp the idea. "But why take Jo? Why not take you? You were hurt, and we were all exhausted. He could have kidnapped you, and we wouldn't know where to start looking."

"Because he knows I'll follow to get her back, and he knew Munchkin was in my room. There was no way he could get me, and with Munchkin with me, I wouldn't have worried about any noises I might have heard through the night. Whoever is paying him wants me in person." Alex focused her sharp gaze on Carrie. "You and I will have a talk when I get back. I'm concerned about the way your mind works."

"What's going on?" Greg entered the living room, rubbing his eyes. He yawned. "I smell coffee."

"Damianos took Jo," Mike answered tightly.

"What? When?" Greg's voice held a razor-sharp edge. Alex looked carefully for signs of him shifting into his other form. Dealing with a werewolf was something she didn't need this morning.

"During the night," she answered.

"Are you going after her?"

"Yes. Greg, I'm going to call your parents. Do you think they would be willing to have Mike and Ben stay with you and your family?" At least the boys would be safe until she returned.

"I want to go," Mike said instantly.

"Me too," Greg added. "I can be useful."

"Me too," Carrie chimed in. "I can... Well, I can keep the truck running for a fast getaway." She offered Alex a weak smile.

Alex wasn't going to let any of them get in the middle of this. She would never forgive herself if something happened to any one of them. She shook her head. "None of you are going. It's far too dangerous. For any of you, even the werewolves," she added before Greg could protest. "I am not exposing your family to this danger."

"But—" Mike began and stopped at Alex's glare. He shook his head defiantly. "No. I'm going with you. Jo's my sister."

"We're going too," Greg said for himself and Carrie. "Jo's important to us. I'll protect Mike and Carrie, and I can get my dad. He's really good in a fight. If you want vicious, I'll get my mom."

Alex glared at all of them. No one relented. She took a deep breath. She didn't need them arguing with her on this. She had failed to keep Jo safe; she didn't want to add any more names to the list.

"No. I can't protect you all and go after Jo at the same time. Damianos is an immortal. Only another immortal stands a chance against him. Carrie, you're going to your parents' house. Mike and Greg, I've changed my mind. You two and Ben will come with me. Call him and tell him we'll be picking him up soon. Do not mention why, only that it's important. Pack a bag with enough clothes for several days for both of you."

"I'll call my parents and tell them I'm going," Greg said. "And I can borrow some of Ben's clothes."

"Go get dressed and get your things."

None of the three moved.

"Now!" she barked.

They jumped at the yell and sprang into motion. Anger replaced tiredness, and Alex stormed up the stairs to her room after the others. She pulled on a pair of jeans and a T-shirt. She grabbed a black duffel bag from the back of the closet and threw in two pairs of jeans and two shirts. She retrieved a box from the top shelf in her closet and opened it. She removed the two Sig Sauer pistols and tossed them in the bag, along with two ammo clips for each weapon. She fetched a pair of military-style black boots from the shoe rack and closed the door.

She pulled undergarments out of a dresser and stuffed them in the duffel bag. Sitting on the bench at the end of the bed, she slipped her feet into the boots, laced them up, grabbed the duffel, and hurried down the stairs. She dropped the bag near the front door and headed for the back door. She opened the door, and Munchkin pushed his way in. Ignoring the dog, she went straight to the apartment.

Alex packed clothes for Joanna and went to her office in the store. She removed an extra pistol with ammo and two bowie knives from the safe. The guns were for whoever was after her, and the knives were for Damianos. She'd never skinned a person alive before, but she was willing to give it a try.

She returned to the house and tucked the items into her bag with everything else. Mike, Greg, and Carrie descended the stairs. Munchkin bumped against her legs.

"Carrie, use my truck and go home." She dropped the keys in Carrie's hand. "Stay indoors as much as possible. Do not wander off alone. If Damianos happens to contact you, do not respond. Greg, check in with your family. I'm sure they're considering their next move. Your family might be safe now that Claver's dead. Until decisions are made, if your family would also watch over Carrie's family, I would consider it a boon."

"Yes, Ms. Thorne. You know about us now. We can help with this."

"No," Alex said firmly. "Take care of yourselves first. You don't want to end up on the wrong side of SPD."

"I hope you get Jo back safe and sound," Carrie said. "I know you will."

"Thank you," Alex said. "Let's go." She opened the front door and waited for them and the dog to exit the house. Carrie went first, followed by Greg and then Mike. Munchkin padded out ahead of Alex. Alex locked the door behind her and turned to see Mike watching. The old soul looking out at her was distinctly different from the fun-loving young man he was every day. Mike had depths that would bear watching in the future.

"We'll be back before you know it," she assured him.

Mike nodded. "I know."

Alex and Munchkin descended the porch, giving the three some privacy for goodbyes.

She tossed the duffel in the back of the replacement Jeep Grand Cherokee she had purchased a few days prior. She'd thought to have Ben learn to drive in the truck and let him use the old Jeep when school started in the autumn. The old Wrangler had sustained too much damage to warrant spending money on the repairs. The extra room in the new Jeep came in handy for Munchkin. She opened the door behind the driver's seat, and Munchkin jumped in. Alex closed the door and climbed into the driver's seat. She should have put some coffee in a travel mug before leaving the house. Thankfully there were places to get more caffeine on the way.

Mike opened the passenger side door and took his seat after saying goodbye to Carrie. Greg climbed into the back seat behind Mike and next to Munchkin. The dog promptly licked the side of Greg's face.

"I guess calling shotgun is a little useless," Grege said, giving Munchkin a friendly neck scratch. "I talked to Mom. She'll take care of everything. Carrie's family will be safe. One of my sisters is going over to hang out with Carrie's sisters."

"I did some time riding as a shotgun messenger," Alex said as she waited for Carrie to pull out first. She waved at the small face peering over the steering wheel.

"A what?" Mike fastened his seat belt and wiped off the dog slobber after Munchkin licked the side of his face. No face within reach ever went unlicked if the dog had his way.

"Shotgun messenger. In the Old West, stagecoaches carrying valuables had a driver and a guard. The driver sat on the right and the guard on the left. The guard carried a shotgun, usually loaded with buckshot, or a rifle. I did a few turns as a guard. It was dangerous, but fun." She started the Jeep and pulled out after Carrie.

"Were you ever attacked?" Greg asked.

"A few times. Bandits would sit along the route and attack coaches as they went by."

"Was anyone killed?" Mike asked.

"On occasion. Bandits, drivers, and even passengers sometimes. It was a rough time in history."

"Did you know any famous people?" Greg asked.

"A few here and there."

"Such as?" he prompted.

"I was in Athens during the time of Socrates," she said. "I didn't know him, but I did see him. The same with Aristotle. I knew Scipio Africanus the Younger." She frowned. She didn't like thinking of that man now. There would be a reckoning when she saw him. She steered the Jeep down the drive and pulled out onto the road.

"Who?"

Alex glanced over at Mike. "The Roman general who sacked Carthage during the Third Punic Wars. Considered one of the finest generals of all time." Someone she was going to skin alive when she saw him.

"I mean famous people I might have heard about."

"I'll give you some books to read about Socrates and Aristotle."

Mike groaned, and Greg laughed at him. "I bet you could fill books with all that you've seen and done," Greg said.

"Probably, but the goal is to stay unnoticed."

"Right. Don't want too many questions asked," Mike said. "Where are we going?"

"I'm taking you to a friend's house, and then I'm going after Jo."

"But—"

"I said I would take you and Ben with me, but I never said I'd take you with me to get Jo."

She glanced over at Mike, and his mouth dropped open as he stared at her. "Okay, you have a point," he relented. "What about Greg?"

Alex looked into the rearview mirror at Greg. "He's coming with me."

"Is it because he's a werewolf?"

"Yes," Alex answered firmly. "Did you reach Ben?"

"I did. He was grumpy about being woken up, but he said he'll be ready."

"Good."

"Did Mom and Dad know? About you being immortal, I mean?"

"Yes." A heavy sigh escaped her. "My history with your family goes back to your great-grandfather. I met him during World War II, and I kept in touch with your family through the years. Your father met me when he was a young boy, and we crossed paths again when he was in college. He recognized me when he saw me and realized that I hadn't aged. Jo is a lot like your father, but there's a lot of your mother in her too. Your father asked me direct questions and wasn't satisfied until he heard my story. We stayed in touch. I was there when he married your mother and right after each one of you were born."

"That's why you were appointed as Ben's guardian," Mike stated rather than asked.

Alex nodded. "I was yours and Jo's as well until you reached eighteen. Your parents and I were close for a long time. I was devastated when I heard about the accident. It's hard to make good friends that you don't have to pretend with, and losing them hurt that much more."

The mood in the Jeep took on a somber feel. The deaths of others composed a large part of an immortal's life. Some hit harder than others. She would mourn a long time for Thomas and Claire.

"You know what this means, right?" Mike asked after a few moments. "This means that there's real magic. Not mouse magic in cartoons, but real Harry Potter magic. What else is real that people think is made up?"

Alex glanced at Mike. "Who's Harry Potter?"

Mike gasped. "Are you kidding?"

"Why would I kid?"

"It's a series of books and movies about this kid who becomes a wizard. They were good movies."

"You didn't read the books?"

"Nope. Wasn't interested in reading them. So if magic is real, what else is real?"

"There are a lot of things out there that are thought to be myths and legends. Magic, in some fashion, does exist, but it's not as strong as it once was, and finding someone who can wield it is rare. Immortals exist. So do vampires, werewolves, witches, gargoyles, and other things used to scare children. Most aren't evil or harmful, but they tend to be very shy."

"Have you ever run into any vampires or werewolves? Besides Greg's family. Have you killed any? What were they like?"

"Yes, I've run across beings that would be classified as supernatural. Most of the time, they blend in with the rest of humanity and live their lives. I didn't know about Greg and his family, but they're very good at hiding in plain sight. It's rare to have to kill unless you're an SPD agent. We usually don't want to stand out and draw attention to ourselves."

"Did you really date Damianos, or is that a cover story?" Greg asked.

Alex didn't immediately respond. She didn't want to talk about Damianos, but she owed them some answers after the man had caused so many issues for them all. "It wasn't dating like the current definition of dating. We lived together for some time in Athens."

"What happened?" he asked. "I'm sorry if I overstepped."

"There's no reason to be sorry. Damianos left me for another woman."

"That bastard," Mike said. "I'm totally Team Alex."

"Me too."

Alex could only laugh. "I was a different person two thousand years ago. So was he."

"Do they let normal humans join SPD?"

Mike was full of questions, and Alex didn't have all the answers. "They do. Or I should say, I think they still do. It's been a while since I've had any dealings with them."

"Cool."

Alex glanced over at him. "What are you thinking?"

"I may check it out."

Alex wasn't sure how she felt about Mike wanting to join the SPD. She had limited dealing with the SPD, some tense moments, but never anything bad. First, they all had to get through the current crisis.

CHAPTER TWENTY-ONE

JOANNA STRUGGLED TO OPEN HER EYES, AND IT TOOK A few attempts to get them to stay open. She blinked to try and ease the grainy feeling behind her eyelids. A numbing sensation lingered in her whole body, along with the sick feeling in her stomach.

She had been asleep when someone entered the room, and at first, she thought it was Alex coming to check on her and Carrie, but the dark shadow was too big. It had to be Damianos. Jo had been about to say his name when he loomed over her bed, and something pinched her in the neck. Everything went fuzzy, then black. It was so quick that Carrie hadn't noticed anything.

Jo shook her head to clear the cobwebs and pulled herself up to a sitting position. The world shifted a bit, and she put her hands on the cot to steady it, or at least herself. She shook her head again, slowly this time, and the world cleared a bit. Enough that she could risk a look around.

Dampness hung in the air of the room, and Joanna assumed the room was partially underground. Dim light filtered in through a casement window with a dirty pane set high in the concrete wall. It looked to be too small for her to crawl through. A bare bulb provided the light. Empty steel shelving units lined one side of the room. Nothing in the room could be used to help her escape.

Jo took a deep breath and pushed herself to her feet. She wobbled a bit but remained in a more or less upright position. Small victories were still victories. The cold floor sent a chill through her. At least she wore jeans and a T-shirt and not her pajamas. Thank goodness for tiny favors.

She crossed the room and tried the door. The heavy steel door was locked, and it reminded her of the door that led to Alex's vault. She yanked on the doorknob in frustration before releasing it.

She startled at the sound of a key being pushed into the lock and the click of the release. The door moved, and she backed away. The door protested with the sound of metal scraping against metal, high and loud enough that it almost hurt. There would be no sneaking out of that door. Jo took a few more steps backward as the door opened wider, and Damianos filled the space.

"You!" Jo snarled.

"Hello, Joanna," Damianos said pleasantly. He was even close to perky. She wanted to shoot his eyes out. "I'm glad to see you're awake."

"Go to hell. I hope Alex catches up to you and cuts you into a million pieces."

His loud laughter echoed in the room and added fuel to her anger. She wanted to see something bad happen to him and hoped that bitch Karma had a lot in store for Damianos. She took two steps forward and aimed a punch at his jaw. It was stupid, she knew it the second she swung, but she couldn't have stopped herself for anything.

A hand came up fast and caught the punch. The laughter ceased just as suddenly, but the smirk remained. He held Jo's fist and squeezed.

"Let go!" The intense pain caused her to fold in against him. His hard fingers manipulated the bones in her hand, grinding them until she whimpered. He didn't let up, and the agony didn't lessen. Her voice turned pleading against her will. "Please."

Damianos walked her backward before releasing her hand. He shut the door behind him. "Don't try that again."

She didn't often experience fear, but she felt it now for all the times she should have been scared. "Why are you doing this?"

"Many reasons, but I won't go into any of them. Alex was warned twice, and she didn't listen."

"What did she ever do to you?" Nothing Alex ever did would merit drugging and kidnapping someone. Now she understood why Alex didn't like the man.

His mouth quivered, threatening to turn into a smile. "My dear little girl, she's done plenty to me over the centuries, but I'm not the one calling the shots here. I'm doing my job."

"You mean what you're paid to do," Jo sneered.

"I've done it a very long time, and I'm very good at it. I worked for the Pinkertons when they were starting out."

"Do you deny being an ass?" Jo shot back. She felt like she should know who the Pinkertons were, but right now, her mind couldn't process any other thoughts outside wanting to hurt him. Carrie would know. She knew just about everything. Fear slowly drained away, and anger took over. It felt good. "How could you do this to Alex? She still has feelings for you."

Damianos shrugged. "Feelings are convenient at times, but a job is a job."

"You're a bastard!" she yelled.

"I won't deny that either. Your insults are weak." He reached into his black tactical vest and pulled out a small vial of white liquid. He held it up. "Drink this."

"Go to hell."

"Look, we can do this the easy way, which is you drinking it voluntarily, or the hard way, which is me forcing you to drink it. Pick one."

Jo glared daggers at him and didn't speak.

"I see it will be the hard way." He closed the distance between them, and Jo backed away.

She moved backward until her body was flush with the wall. The solid concrete didn't budge. Panic seized her. "I won't drink it."

"You should do what you're told. You'll live longer if you do."

"You're going to kill me, so you might as well do it now."

"Do what you're told, and that may not happen."

Before she could react or process his words, his hand gripped her face, forcing her on tiptoe. He thrust his fingers into her mouth to pry open her jaw and poured the white liquid into her mouth. She gagged. A hand went to her chin and shoved her mouth closed. It was quick and painful enough that she didn't have time to think about biting him.

"Swallow, girl," Damianos ordered, glaring down at her. "I will not leave this room until you do."

She finally got it down, gagging at the bitter taste. He let her go. Coughing, she fell to her knees on the cold floor.

He tucked the empty vial into a pocket and strolled to the door. "Don't be stupid. You will play your part, and it will be over. I suggest you try to sleep."

"Go to hell," Jo gasped, unable to think of anything else to say. She wanted to cry but was too angry to let tears go. "What did you give me?"

"If you live long enough, Jo, you will find hell as comfortable as I do." He smiled, but there was no warmth behind it. "Insurance."

Insurance? Could that mean it was poison, and he would only give her the antidote if Alex cooperated? "You poisoned me!"

"Believe what you want." He opened the door and glanced back over his shoulder. "I'd get some rest if I were you. It's going to take Alex a while to get here." With that, he left the room. The metal door closed with a loud clang, sounding like a death sentence. The lock shooting home was overkill.

Jo glared at the door for a few moments, fantasizing about

hurting the man who'd just closed it. Alex couldn't get here fast enough and kick his ass before getting Jo out. She'd give anything to be back in the tiny apartment and even fighting Munchkin for space in bed during the nights he stayed with her and Carrie.

For a moment, she regretted finding the underground passage and the vault, but then she realized that the attacks would have come even if she hadn't nosed around in Alex's business. What she really regretted was returning home to Maine. If only that drunk driver hadn't run a red light and hit her parents' car. If only he hadn't been going excessively fast. There were a lot of if-onlys.

She couldn't change the past, and it was time to admit her failures. She couldn't control the present. Maybe if she did rest, she would figure a way to control the future.

CHAPTER TWENTY-TWO

It was close to 4:00 p.m. when Alex turned off the road onto Victoria's drive. The Jeep came to a stop before a three-car garage. Seven hours trapped in a vehicle with a teenager and two young adults was enough for Alex. Alex could have let Mike or Greg drive, but she would have gone crazy sitting in the passenger's seat with nothing to do. They stopped only long enough for bathroom breaks and to grab some food. Alex hated fast food, but it was the quickest and easiest option while on the road. The other three were satisfied with the options when they weren't arguing with each other. The stress was beginning to wear on all of them.

They picked Ben up twenty minutes after leaving the house. He was confused at first, and then Alex explained what had happened and where they were going. As expected, Ben had been upset and angry about Jo being abducted. He absorbed Alex's story of immortality a lot easier than Mike had. Like Mike, he wanted to help rescue his sister, but Alex once again refused help. They spent the good portion of the drive trying to convince her, but she remained steadfast in her decision.

Alex killed the engine and opened the door. She climbed out

and opened the rear door. Munchkin leaped over Ben and from the vehicle, bounding over to the house's side entrance. Mike, Greg, and Ben exited the SUV and stretched.

Victoria emerged from the house, and Alex smiled. Alex had helped the petite brunette adjust to immortal life back in the nineteenth century when Victoria had been Marie Viard, and the two became fast friends. They had kept in regular contact with each other since then.

Munchkin jumped up and immediately greeted Victoria with paws on her shoulder. The petite woman looked even smaller next to the dog on his hind legs. He licked her a few times, accepted her ear scratches, and wandered off into the yard.

"What brings you here?" Victoria asked.

"This is Mike and Ben Shepard, and Greg Sullivan," Alex said, gesturing to each.

"Hello," Mike, Greg, and Ben said as they approached the woman.

"Hello," Victoria said with a nod to each of them. She turned to Alex. "What's happened?"

"Before we talk about that, I need you to focus and not lecture," Alex said. "I'm short of time."

"No good conversation starts that way."

"I know. Damianos made an appearance. He took Mike and Ben's sister, Joanna. He wants me at a specific location, and he's using her to make sure I appear."

Victoria hissed out an angry breath and put her hands on her hips. "You shouldn't have trusted him! You always do, and it does nothing but get you into trouble!"

"I don't need a lecture about Damianos right now."

"Are you insane?" Victoria demanded. "The answer is yes. Yes, you are insane to let that man anywhere near you, never mind the children! And yes, you need a lecture about him because you never seem to listen. You've always had a soft spot when it comes to him. Right in the head. Come inside." She gestured them through the side door.

"We're not children," Mike protested. "Stop acting like we are."

"I know, Mike," Alex assured him. She turned back toward Victoria. "And I don't need to be reminded of who he is. Is Paladin here?"

"Yes, you do." Victoria paused at the door. "He's on the West Coast where you sent him, but I can get him back here tomorrow. If you can't wait, I'll go with you. You need someone to watch your back."

Alex shook her head. "No. What I need is a favor. Would you watch over Mike and Ben?" They were all adults, even Ben, but Alex didn't need them following her. She wanted them where she knew they would be safe, and right now Victoria's was one of the safest places she knew.

"I want to go," Mike insisted.

"So do I," Ben added. "Our sister, our fight."

Alex lost her temper. "Do you think I don't know that? That's all you say, and I still say no! It's too dangerous. After last night, do you seriously think this is one of your movies?"

"Don't leave us here to imagine the worst things happening to her," Mike said quietly. "That would be worse."

"I know how it is, Mike." Alex put a hand on his shoulder. "I will get her back." She understood their need to help, but it was far too risky. To say otherwise was a costly understatement. Especially for an untrained mortal. She didn't expect to come out of it unscathed, but she would live.

She was taking a huge risk bringing Greg along, but a werewolf was an unexpected wild card in her favor. Damianos only had hours on her, not enough time to gather silver weapons even with his considerable resources, even if he believed she would bring help.

"But—"

Alex cut him off. "This is no video game! This is real life, and people are dead! I will not add you to the death count."

"Of course I'll watch over them," Victoria interjected before they could respond. "Do you need anything?"

"I think I'm good," Alex answered as she entered the service porch. Like her house, Victoria's was filled with priceless antiques. She hoped Mike and Ben were careful. With their current agitation, they were little more than young bulls in an expensive crystal shop. "I was able to pack before I left home, but maybe the use of your truck. Damianos knows what I'm driving."

"Take it, my friend. The key is in the usual place. I'll add that to the other ones you owe me. I think we're up into double digits now. You have guns, right? You will not take a sword to a gun fight. This is the twenty-first century."

"I do, and I have them," Alex acknowledged. "But you know I hate guns."

"You didn't seem to mind them when you were behind enemy lines during both world wars."

"Yes, I did, but they were a necessity."

"Shouldn't you call the cops?" Mike asked in a desperate voice. "The FBI? Somebody?"

"It would just get them killed," Alex said. "They're not equipped to handle immortals. Damianos won't hesitate to cut down anyone who gets in the way, including the police, but he won't kill me. I will get Jo back."

"Bastard," Victoria muttered. "You should drag the spear out of storage and run him through."

"I am not bringing the spear into this even if I still had it. I never want to see that thing again." She shuddered inside at the mere mention of the Spear of Destiny.

"Can't that SPD group help you?" Ben asked.

"Damianos is an agent, so how do I know whoever they send won't help him?"

Mike looked at her for a long moment, his face an agonized

mask that struggled to deal with the situation. Then his shoulders sagged a little, and he reluctantly nodded. "You have a point. Fine. I'll stay here."

"Ben?"

Ben sighed. "Fine, I'll stay here with Mike and Victoria, but I won't like it."

"Thank you. Until I know what he's up to, I need you two here and safe. We'll be back with Jo."

Mike nodded. "Be careful." He hugged her, and Alex returned the hug. Mike looked much younger than his twenty-three years.

"Be careful," Ben echoed. He too wrapped his arms around Alex and hugged her tightly. She remembered all the hugs the kids had given her throughout the years. She had to save them, from herself if need be.

She released him and gathered her gear. "I will," she promised.

"No one will hold it against you if you separate his head from his neck," Victoria reminded her. "I know a place we can put it so he'll never bother anyone else again. Watch yourself around him."

"Keep talking like that, and it'll be premeditation." Alex looked around for Greg. He'd managed to fade into the background while they talked. "We'll be back as soon as we can. Don't call anyone."

She pulled open the front door. "Munchkin, come." With a last warning look at the boys, she and Greg followed Munchkin's bound out the door.

CHAPTER TWENTY-THREE

JO PACED IN THE UNDERGROUND ROOM WITH CLENCHED fists. She wanted to hit something or someone and needed a target. The thought of Damianos as that target brought a savage smile to her face. Her first try had failed spectacularly. Maybe the next time, if she caught him unaware, she'd have a chance of actually hurting him.

She stopped and looked at the window for the thousandth time. Maybe she'd been locked in long enough that it didn't seem as small as she had initially thought. She might be able to slip through it. It wasn't out of the realm of possibility, and it was certainly more likely than overpowering Damianos.

She had always been described as small-boned, and she certainly didn't have to worry about her boobs getting in the way, seeing that she barely had any. She had to try. It was better than sitting around like a damsel in distress waiting for a rescue.

A more thorough search of the room hadn't turned up anything outside the cot that could be used for a step to reach the window. Setting her mind to the task at hand, she went over to the cot and started sliding it toward the window. The metal legs sliding across the concrete floor sounded like nails on a chalkboard, and she hoped the walls were thick enough to muffle the sound. She didn't want Damianos coming in. She never wanted to see that man again for as long as she lived, which was probably not much longer. She lifted the end of the cot a little as she moved it. Her end quieted, but the other end made up for it.

She centered the cot under the window and stepped up, just being able to reach the latch on the window. It was painted shut and wouldn't move, but she wasn't about to give up. She scratched at the paint until she got the latch to wiggle. Hope pushed aside some of the despair, and she continued to work the latch, using as much force as she could. It eventually moved, turning just enough to allow her to push the window.

The window didn't budge an inch when Joanna pushed on it. "Dammit," she growled and pushed harder. The window gave way a tiny bit. Encouraged, she kept shoving at it until it opened. She took a deep breath and jumped, grabbing onto the small ledge in order to pull herself up. Her toes pushed against the concrete wall to get a foothold. With a lot of muffled groaning and effort, Jo managed to inch her way up to the window. The fresh outside air rushed in, and Jo gratefully breathed it in.

Jo exhaled as much of the air in her lungs as she could and pushed herself through the small window. She put one arm through the opening and then a shoulder, grabbing at the grass to pull herself through. Her head followed and then her other shoulder and arm. Halfway through, she inhaled two deep breaths of air. She prayed she wouldn't get stuck. Humiliation wouldn't even begin to describe it if she was discovered hanging halfway out a window.

She sucked in another lungful of cool air and let out as much as she could. The fresh air gave her new strength, and she used her elbows to lever herself the rest of the way out of the window and onto wet grass.

She rested a moment in the dark. The grass tickled her face, and the smell of damp dirt filled her nose. Nothing had ever smelled better. The dampness clinging to the grass seeped into her clothing, making her more uncomfortable. Joanna knew she couldn't delay and pushed herself up off the ground and to her feet. Her now damp clothes sent a shiver through her.

Light from windows above illuminated some of the ground below, while large trees along the border of the property created deep shadows, making the night darker and scarier. The tiny pinpricks of light from streetlamps beckoned her through the thick canopy of leaves. The safety the light offered seemed miles away. Taking a deep breath, she started toward the beacons of light. The wet grass of the manicured lawn would mark a clear path for anyone following, but she couldn't worry about leaving footprints in the grass now. Getting out was the top priority. She crossed the twenty feet of lawn and entered the shadows of the trees. Her toe stubbed against something hard and caused Jo to trip. She managed to get her feet under her and looked back to see part of a gnarly root poking out of the dirt.

Not wanting to twist an ankle or break a leg, Jo slowed. Even with the light from the streetlamps filtering in through the trees, she had to put her hands out to help her find her way. Skeletal branches reached for her and clawed at her face and arms. She wanted to cry out in frustration but gritted her teeth against to keep from making any sounds before they escaped her.

Movement in the corner of her eye made her pause and cringe back into the bushes. Two men appeared from around the corner of the house and the breath froze in Jo's chest. They continued to walk along the house, and Jo realized they were a guard patrol making their rounds. She prayed she was far enough in the shadows to not be seen if they turned to look her way. A nearby tree trunk offered better protection from being discovered, but if she moved toward it, the motion might attract the guards' attention. Fear kept her rooted in place. Panic grew as the two men stopped. Had they seen the opened window? Why didn't she take three seconds to close it behind her?

She watched the two men stand there only a few feet from the window she had crawled through with all the silent curses she could think up. Time seemed to stop, and each second lasted an eternity. Her heart pounded in her chest, and blood roared in her ears. Sweat beaded on her forehead, and she wiped her palms on her jeans. The men lingered there, and Jo wondered what they could possibly be doing. Then a small light flared to life and highlighted one man's face. He brought the flame up and lit a cigarette. The light extinguished, and Jo breathed a sigh of relief.

Time moved on as the two men resumed walking. Jo watched them turn the far corner of the house and disappear. She allowed herself to start breathing again.

She picked her way through the trees and bushes until she came to a stone wall. The rough stone reached at least seven feet high, and a black wrought-iron railing ran along the top. The light from the streetlamps continued to beckon to her. Jo put a hand to the wall and ran it lightly over the stone. There were enough protrusions to allow her to get hand and footholds to climb it. The top could pose a problem, but she'd manage it and get out of here. There were other houses nearby, and she could go to one of them to call the police. She just had to be fast.

Taking a deep breath, she reached up to find a handhold, then a toehold. She found another toehold and started to climb.

Three feet off the ground, someone grabbed the back of her shirt and yanked. She fell backward and slammed onto the ground, her ass making contact before the rest of her.

Silence wasn't necessary now. "Ow!" she yelled, her voice loud in the relative quiet of the night.

A dark shadow loomed over her. She looked up to see Damianos frowning down at her. Even in the dim light, his irritation was visible. It made her feel a little better.

"Where do you think you're going?"

"Out of here and away from you," Jo spat.

He laughed, and Jo glared at him, wishing he would

spontaneously burst into flame. "Can't have you doing that, now can we?"

"Go to hell."

He laughed more. "Come on, girl. With experience, you will find better curses. Maybe I'll teach you some." He reached down and grabbed her arm above the elbow and pulled. When Jo didn't move right away, he started to pull her across the ground. His grip was strong, and for a moment, Jo thought his hands and fingers were made of steel. She would bruise if she lived that long.

She stumbled to her feet, hoping he would stop hauling her. "Now I know why Alex hates you."

He didn't verbally respond as he shoved her through the back door and into a kitchen.

The surprised looks on the faces of the men in the kitchen were almost worth the bruises. She glared back at them, daring each one to say something as she was dragged through the room. "I hope she comes and kicks all your asses."

"I'm counting on her joining the party." He opened the door to the basement and pushed her toward the opening.

"Are you counting on her kicking your ass?" She gave the word a lot of relish as she stepped down on the top step.

"You don't know Alex as well as you think you do. Keep quiet and do as you're told. You'll survive this if you do."

"I know she'll kick your ass." The desire to keep repeating it was perverse, and she gave in. She wanted to punch or kick him, but she knew doing so would have no effect. She was no more than a gnat to the big bad traitor. "Kick your ass. I hope she shoots you so many times that it takes you decades to recover." Her words dripped with venom, but they didn't come close to expressing the anger simmering inside her. She moved down the stairs. His hand was still on her arm. Even if she could break free from his grasp, there was nowhere to run. She put her head up and walked down the stairs.

If her words had any effect on him, it didn't show. His

expression remained amused, but his dark eyes were hard. Jo mentally kicked herself for once thinking he was hot. "Don't try that again," he warned her as he opened the door to the room she had escaped from. "I can make your stay a lot less pleasant. There will be a guard outside the window now."

Jo knew he'd follow through with that threat. He seemed the type to take pleasure in making people miserable. "Maybe they'll order me a pizza," she muttered.

"Stay put," he ordered and shoved her in the room. "Alex will be here soon. Then you can go home." He slammed the door shut, and Jo collapsed on the cot.

Tears welled up in her eyes, and she hastily wiped them away. She wasn't going to cry. He was probably watching, and she wouldn't give him the satisfaction of seeing her cry. Jo wrapped her arms around herself. She wanted this nightmare to be over.

CHAPTER TWENTY-FOUR

ALEX LOOKED AT THE SLIP OF PAPER DAMIANOS HAD left and then at the house in front of her as she and Greg stood hidden by some bushes. It was exactly the type of place she imagined it to be. Large, stately, almost intimidating. It probably cost a small fortune. A high stone wall encircled the property, and a wrought-iron gate stretched across the wide driveway. Whoever was pulling Damianos's strings certainly had cash, and that meant a lot of power.

She originally thought they would try to sneak in but then realized the futility. Whoever was in charge knew she would eventually come for Jo, and Damianos would be ready. But they wouldn't expect Greg to be with her. Ringing the intercom at the gate was probably the best and least painful way—unless, of course, he decided to shoot her on sight.

She motioned Greg to follow her back down the road to where they parked the truck.

"So how are we going to do this?" Greg asked.

Alex looked over at him. "I'm going to walk up to the gate and get their attention. You are going to follow the fence around back to see if you can get in. Find Jo and get out of there. I don't care if you shred your way through everyone you run into. Here," she said, placing the keys in Greg's hand. "Get her back to Victoria's."

Greg nodded. It was a relief not to argue about her instructions. Her opinion of his control over the werewolf side was going up.

Munchkin nudged her hand, and she affectionately scratched behind an ear. "You know I have to go in there," she told the dog.

Munchkin woofed.

"Yes, I know. I'll make him pay for this."

Greg chuckled and scratched behind the dog's other ear. Munchkin rewarded him with a large pink tongue across his hand. Alex laughed.

Alex took a deep breath, summoned her courage, and climbed out of the truck. Munchkin jumped out after her. "You should stay here, but I know I can't make you." Munchkin looked up at her, his tail wagging. She knew logically the dog didn't understand her, but he had always been good at interpreting her moods. "Let's go then."

Alex looked over at Greg. "Ready?"

"Yeah," Greg said.

"It'll be okay," Alex said. "We'll get Jo out. Trust me."

Greg flexed his hands and rolled his shoulders. "I'm ready."

Together Alex and Munchkin walked toward the gate. Greg split off and disappeared through the landscape growth. Alex felt a stirring of the old anticipation of a righteous battle. She hadn't felt it in so long, she almost didn't recognize it. When she did, she welcomed it. It would let her do what needed to be done.

Munchkin suddenly whirled around. Alex drew a gun and spun, ready to fire. It would be just like Damianos to wait beyond the gate and waylay her before she could get inside.

"Don't shoot!" Mike held up his hands in surrender. "It's me!"

She grabbed his wrist and dragged him back to the truck. Greg reappeared, and she motioned for him to stop and come back.

"What are you doing here?" Alex demanded. She should have

expected Mike and or Ben to do this. She was slipping in her old age.

"I followed you in the Jeep." Mike glared back defiantly.

"I told you this isn't some movie or video game. This is real, and people will die. You being here could mean we get hurt."

"I don't believe that. I have to help."

Alex shook her head. "No. I can't trust you to follow directions. I can't believe you're putting Jo's life in danger like this. Greg is here because of what he is. You are very mortal, and I will not have your death on my hands. You are going to get in the Jeep and stay there until I return. Understand?"

"But—"

"No. You will not leave Ben and Jo with the loss of another family member."

Mike stared at her, and then his whole body slumped. Alex understood his need to do something to help Joanna, but he wouldn't die on her watch. Especially since she didn't know what she was about to walk into.

"I'll stay here."

Alex put a hand on his shoulder and pulled him in. She hugged him hard. "Thank you," she said before releasing him. "If anyone comes near the Jeep, pretend you're waiting for a friend to sneak out for a ride. Do not get noticed if you can help it. If they tell you to move along, drive somewhere else. If Damianos shows up, you're going to be in every bit as much danger as Jo."

Mike pulled back. "How many times have you done something like this?"

"Enough to know what I'm doing."

"We'll get Jo and be back before you know it," Greg assured him.

Alex opened the Jeep door and gestured for him to get in. She walked around to the other side and opened the passenger door. "Munchkin," she said. The dog hesitated before jumping in. He whined and licked Alex's face before she closed the door. She walked around back to the driver's side.

"We'll be back soon with Jo. My word. Don't make me break my word. Stay here."

Mike nodded and pulled the door shut. She looked at Greg. "Ready?"

Greg nodded and set off at a lope. Alex took a deep breath and headed toward the gate. She reached up to press the button on a speaker box near the gate, but the gate opened before she could touch it. They really were expecting her. Deep inside, she had hoped she would keep the element of surprise on her end. Greg would be that unexpected advantage she needed.

She stepped through the opening gate. It stopped and reversed course to close behind her. She walked with confidence and purpose up the drive. Despite her bravado, she didn't have a clue what she was going to do once inside. Like most things, she went with the situation, and adapted as she went along.

She walked up the four brick steps to the front door, and as she reached to ring the doorbell, the door opened. Damianos stepped out. She set her jaw and made the effort to unclench her fists.

"Akantha." He stepped to allow her entry.

She glared at him, not giving him the satisfaction of pleasantries or acknowledging his greeting. She entered the house, and he closed the door behind her. Two men armed with semiautomatic rifles stood in the foyer.

Damianos moved to stand directly in front of her. "You know the drill," he said silkily. "Assume the position."

That earned him another glare. She gave a brief thought of starting the violence now and just as quickly let that thought go. She held out her arms and stood with her feet apart. His hands patting her down did not stir any feelings inside other than fury. He lingered over it, stroking her arms and legs like a lover to the leering amusement of the guards. One by one, he removed her weapons. She knew he would be thorough, so she hadn't bothered to try to hide any in peculiar places. He even searched her boots and extracted the knives she had stashed in them.

If he had been playing mercenary to catch a bigger fish, he would have left the knives for her. She was utterly unarmed now. Only her combat skills were left.

"This way." Damianos gestured to the hallway stretching out in front of them. One guard led the way while the other followed. Alex had her own personal armed escort with Damianos bringing up the rear.

She was taken through a large, spacious kitchen, reminding her of the one in her house. The walls and countertops were white, and modern stainless-steel appliances filled the room. She had a sudden irrational craving for a cup of tea. The guard in front opened a door, revealing stairs stretching down into darkness. He flipped a light switch and descended the stairs. Alex followed him.

They turned right when they reached the bottom of the stairs and entered a hallway where two metal doors sat across from each other. The guard opened the door on the left, and Alex stepped inside the room without so much as a word. Damianos followed her inside the room, and the door shut behind him.

The concrete walls captured a dampness that hung in the air. A cot sat in one corner and a bare bulb provided the only source of light. A window sat on the far wall but looked too small to climb through.

"I'm honestly surprised you walked right up to the front door," Damianos commented to her back.

Alex ignored him. Simmering anger and rage threatened to bubble over, and she needed to keep her wits about her. There would come a time to unleash it and until then, she'd keep a tight rein on her temper.

"It won't be too long now. Then you and the girl can get out of here."

Alex whipped around and gave him a look that promised pain. "Where is she? Is she all right?"

"Of course she's all right. I'm not a monster. The two of you will be out of here shortly."

"Why did you take her? All of this could have been avoided had you just given me this address."

Damianos ran a hand over his head. "This all could have been avoided if you had assumed new identities."

She clenched her fists. "Damn you! You could have given me this address, and I could have taken care of it alone."

"You would have been riddled with bullets before getting to the front door, and the problem would have remained."

"Bullshit! There's always another way. You just want things done the way you want them," she shot back. "You could have told me, and we could have worked out a plan." Sometimes the truth hurt more than lies. He did this, meddled in her life again, with less consideration than he'd give a stranger. Had he told her, they could have taken care of whoever was behind this without getting Jo involved.

"And you are too damn stubborn. You could have just taken the kids to another one of your houses and given them new IDs."

Alex threw her hands up in the air. "Me? You're playing god with my life because you think you have the right? You have no rights. This is the last time. When this is over, I never want to see you again."

"I am doing what's best for everyone. Once you think it through, once you see what's here, you will know it too." With that, he left the room. The metal door closed, the sound echoing in the room.

Damn that man and the mess he had dragged her into. There was going to be a reckoning after all of this was done. A reckoning twenty-four hundred years in the making.

Not long after Damianos left the room, the door opened again. Greg stumbled through the door, followed by

Damianos and two guards with weapons aimed at Greg. The insufferable man led Greg over to a wall and fastened manacles on his wrists. Heavy chains connected the manacles to the wall. Greg tugged on them, testing them. Smart kid, Alex thought, but she knew Damianos would make sure even Greg couldn't break them.

Alex met Greg's eyes, and she slightly shook her head, telling him not doing anything. The time to unleash Greg would come. They just had to wait for the moment that would do the most damage.

Damianos and the guards left, and Alex focused her attention on Greg.

"What happened?" she asked urgently.

"He was expecting me. There weren't enough guards around for me to change and take as many as I could. I thought I'd wait for a better time to let the wolf out."

"That was smart of you."

"I might be able to break these chains," he said speculatively with a close look at the manacles. "I'm much stronger in my other form."

Alex considered it for a split second before shaking her head. "Not yet. I need to know who's behind this and what we're facing. I will let you know when it's time for action. Understand?"

Greg didn't seem accepting of it. Alex recognized the signs of a change arrested. His face had a wolfish look around the edges. Alex sensed the anger lurking below the surface and ready to be unleashed. The one thing they couldn't afford to be was reckless. If they were going to act, she had to make sure that everyone involved in abducting Jo would pay for it. Including Damianos.

"Fine," he finally agreed.

The door opened, and Damianos reentered the room with the two guards. "Your presence is requested."

"You mean demanded," she corrected and glared at him. "Seeing as how I don't have a choice in the matter."

He smirked. "Semantics. The sooner you do this, the sooner this will all be over."

"The sooner I kill you," she hissed.

Gods above and below, she hated that smirk. To think she allowed him back in her bed. As usual, she regretted it. Never again. No matter how long she lived.

"Let's go." He motioned to the door.

"I suppose I must." She straightened her back and assumed a haughty expression. Damianos gestured her through the door into the hall. She stepped through and the guards followed.

Damianos moved toward Greg. She couldn't see what he was doing, but the chains rattled, and she closed her eyes to send a prayer up that Greg would keep his composure as she asked. To distract herself, she eyed the door directly across the hall. Jo had to be in there. At least she knew where the girl was likely to be. When she returned, if she returned, that would be her priority.

Damianos came back to where she waited, his trademark smirk in full force. He jerked his head for her to follow him.

Alex calmly walked behind him upstairs and through the house to a large study.

The room, desk, and built-in shelves were of the same dark wood. Old leather-bound books filled the shelves. An Oriental rug covered most of the hardwood floor. A fireplace took up space along one wall. It was dark and screened. Leather chairs sat in front of the desk and behind the desk a figure sat in a large office chair. She might have enjoyed such a room if it hadn't been for the occupant.

The man was old. He had to be in his late nineties, maybe even past a hundred. Thin, pale, brown-spotted skin stretched over a bare head with a few wisps of white hair. His eyes looked like they were once blue but were now faded and rheumy. Clear tubing attached to an oxygen tank looped over his ears and under his nose. Two men with weapons flanked him and looked eager to shoot her.

The old man waved a hand toward one of the chairs in front of the desk. Light reflected off the large gold ring he wore. Alex glared at him for a moment and then sat in the chair. She perched on the edge, leaning forward, and kept her eyes on him.

"I'm glad you have joined us," the man wheezed in a weak voice.

"I can't say I'm glad to be here," Alex commented lightly. "What do you want?"

"You will soon find out," he said. "We are waiting for others to join us."

More? Alex narrowed her eyes and wondered who else they could bring in. Alex couldn't think of anyone else who needed to be here. The old man wanted her here, and Damianos hadn't mentioned anyone else. Who else had he pulled into this scheme?

CHAPTER TWENTY-FIVE

THE LOCK CLICKED AND GRABBED JO'S ATTENTION. SHE sat up and swung her legs over the edge of the cot. Exhaustion had caught up to her, and she had slept a little. How long, she didn't know. The door creaked open, and Mike appeared in the doorway.

Someone shoved him into the room before slamming the door shut. He fell to the hard floor, wincing. She jumped to her feet and rushed over to help him up. Mike wrapped his arms around her in a bear hug, and Jo returned the hug just as tightly.

"Jo!"

"Mike! What are you doing here? Is Ben here?"

"Alex is here. Greg too. I followed them and got caught." He squeezed her hard before letting her go. "Ben is with Alex's friend Victoria. I'm supposed to be there too, but I had to help."

She couldn't blame him. She would have felt the same way if their positions had been reversed. "Alex is here? Greg? Where are they?"

"Yeah, but I'm not sure where. I didn't see them when they brought me in."

"I haven't seen them either. I have no idea what's going on."

"That makes all of us. What do you think is going to happen next? Have you heard anything?"

She shrugged. "I don't know. Damianos isn't calling the shots. Someone else is in charge, and they had a real hard-on about getting Alex here. I'm glad Ben's not here. You shouldn't be here either. This is bad." Though she wished Greg wasn't here, a part of her was relieved. A werewolf in your corner had to be a game changer. Mike lived on past video game glory and a big heart that wanted to help. And she understood something Mike didn't. The more people they had to be hostages, the greater risk they had of not living through this.

"Did you see them?"

She shook her head. "No. The only person I've seen is Damianos. He came down here and made me drink something. Then he caught me while I was trying to escape."

"What did he make you drink? Do you think it was poison?" Mike grabbed her shoulders and peered into her eyes. Despite wanting to tell him she was okay, she let him do it. Mike needed reassurance as much as she did.

Jo shook him off after a moment. "I don't know. It was white and not a lot of it."

"How do you feel?"

"I feel fine." Annoyance rang out in her voice. "I'm ready to kill someone."

"This has been crazy from the beginning. And you thought Good Harbor was boring. Now you know it has at least one werewolf family and two immortals. Are you sure you feel okay? Maybe you should sit down." Mike motioned to the cot.

"Crazy is an understatement. I don't think there's a word for how insane all of this is." She waved Mike off. "I'm fine. I don't need to sit."

"I really think you should," he said. "I'm sure Alex has one of her weird words that would fit this situation. I wonder where they're keeping her. I haven't seen any sign of her so far."

"I'm fine and don't need to sit!" She glared at him. "I haven't heard or seen anything. I tried to escape once, but the bastard caught me and brought me back down here."

The sound of the door opening interrupted the impromptu reunion, and they turned to see a guard in the doorway.

"You're wanted upstairs."

Mike looked at Jo. She shrugged. "What other choice do we have?"

CHAPTER TWENTY-SIX

"WHAT'S GOING ON?" JO WHISPERED TO MIKE AS THEY stood outside a door on the first floor, with two guards flanking them. Thoughts of trying to escape briefly crossed Joanna's mind, but the guards and their guns made her dismiss those thoughts as quickly as they had come.

"No idea," he whispered back. "Maybe this is where we get to make a dramatic entrance."

"Shut up," growled one of the guards.

They waited for what seemed like an eternity until the guard in front opened the door. "Go in," ordered the guard behind them.

Jo stepped into the room ahead of Mike. The room reminded her of Alex's office in the house with the bookshelves and dark wood. Alex sat in one of the leather chairs in front of the desk. Damianos stood behind her. He held a gun to her head. Alex was cool, calm, and collected. An old man sat behind the desk.

"Come in," the old man invited in a wheezing voice.

"Alex!" Seeing Alex made Joanna felt a little less afraid, until she saw Damianos standing behind the woman and the gun in his hand. Alex looked calm, like she was having tea with someone. Not one dark hair was out of place, and the look on her face was serene. Jo wished she could be so composed in such a situation. She assumed it wasn't the first time someone had pointed a gun at Alex or the first time Damianos had stood in the execution position behind someone.

"Now, Ms. Thorne, as you can see, your incentive to cooperate has arrived. Allow me to introduce myself. My name is Max Woodville."

"Can't say it's a pleasure to meet you," Jo said.

"You're overestimating my attachment to them, Woodville," Alex countered, her voice cold, her face void of expression. "They're nothing to me."

Joanna stared at Alex. How could Alex say something like that? She had to be saying it for the old man's benefit. Right?

The guard next to her punching her in the gut would have had less of an impact than Alex's words. The woman who had been in Jo's entire life and who had been an aunt to them had just said that she didn't care. Jo's brain couldn't process what she had heard.

Anger raged up and out of her.

"You bitch!" she screamed at Alex and lunged. One of the guards grabbed the back of her shirt and hauled her back. She rammed an elbow into the guy's stomach, but she might have well elbowed a wall. There wasn't even a satisfying grunt.

"We trusted you!" she yelled. "I loved you!"

Alex didn't respond. Didn't even blink. She sat quietly and kept her eyes on Woodville.

"You were family!" Jo tried to pull away from her guard. She kicked at the man's leg and was shaken for the attempt. Rage consumed her, and she wanted to lash out at everyone.

"Clearly the girl is hysterical," Alex said to Max with a dismissive gesture of a hand. "They're nothing to me."

"Do you really expect me to believe you?" Woodville asked. "Had you cared so little for this girl and boy as you say, you wouldn't have risked coming here. You would have left her and gone about your business. Your actions betray your words, Ms. Thorne."

Anger burned inside Jo. Alex would be a pile of ash if looks could kill. She wanted to see bad things happen to the woman. Maybe Woodville would shoot Alex, and while it wouldn't kill her, it would hurt, and Jo could live with Alex in pain. A lot of pain.

"And wait for you to do something else to get my attention? I'm a busy woman. Stop wasting my time, Woodville. I'm here. What do you want?" Alex demanded.

"What I want is quite simple. I want your secret. When I met you, your name was Alexis Rowland, and it was 1941. You were Heinrich Himmler's secretary and mistress, but you were an Allied spy." His face twitched as if he was going to smile. "Himmler was quite upset when he discovered he'd let a spy into the Reich and more so when you stole the Spear of Destiny from his hands. He lost face with the Führer."

"Surely that couldn't have been me," Alex answered. "I'm far too young to have been alive in 1941. I don't even have a gray hair. Maybe it was a great-aunt on my mother's side. We all resemble each other."

"I do not forget a face. I remember seeing you when Gebhardt attended Himmler. You were always at Himmler's elbow, ready to do whatever he instructed. Imagine my surprise when I saw the same woman six decades later at a New York antiques auction and she hadn't aged a single day. Her name was no longer Alexis Rowland, but Alex Thorne. I even spoke to you, and you didn't know me. It was so intriguing that I had some of my people do a little digging, and it seems that Alexis Rowland vanished in 1975. No one knows what happened to her. It was almost as if she dropped off the face of the Earth. Then there's the other amazing thing they discovered. There was no record of Alex Thorne existing before 1975."

"Coincidence. Happens all the time."

"I'm not finished," he said. "Alex Thorne died hours after her birth in 1975, and now she is a grown woman sitting in front of me."

"People can have the same name," she pointed out. "It's not that uncommon."

"True, but having the same social security number is not common. How is it that a grown woman has the same name and social security number of a child who died a few hours after birth? Just more evidence to support my theory. I've built quite a file on you. I have even purchased items from your shop online through third-party buyers. You have very good taste."

A dark brow rose. "Is this where I'm supposed to thank you for the compliment?"

Jo watched the exchange with angry fascination. Her breath heaved in and out of her as she considered what she was hearing. Was this guy really an honest-to-God Nazi from World War II? If so, he had to be pushing a hundred. At least. Alex could easily kill this guy, yet she did nothing.

"Alexis Rowland and Alex Thorne are the same woman," he said harshly. "A woman who hasn't aged a day in nearly seven decades. During the war, we worked on finding the secret to immortality, and the answer was right in front of our eyes the whole time. I ask you this, Ms. Rowland, or Ms. Thorne, how did you manage this miracle?"

"So if I am this Rowland woman with the secret to immortal youth, I hand over the secret that I don't have, and you'll just let us go? We'll walk away unharmed, and you will forget we were ever here? If I am everything you say I am?"

Woodville smiled. It was the closest thing Jo had ever seen to a living jack-o'-lantern. "Yes."

She knew the man lied. The man would never let them go. He would kill them, and as for Alex, she wasn't sure what the old bastard would do to Alex. Right now, she didn't care what happened to the woman. He could toss her in a dark room and brick it shut, and Jo wouldn't waste one thought on her. Alex,

Damianos, and this old Nazi guy could burn in hell for all she cared. She was going to be dead along with Mike and Greg.

"And if I don't?"

"Then I shoot one of them. If you still refuse to cooperate, I shoot the other one. It's as simple as that. No one has to die or get hurt, Ms. Thorne. It's up to you."

"What's your real name?"

The old man seemed derailed at the question. "My real name?"

"Do you need me to speak louder? I know the elderly have trouble hearing. Yes, your real name. I can't imagine the U.S. would knowingly let a Nazi come into the country. Clearly you don't have the skills they looked for after the war was over, and they transported German scientists here to work for them. Not a paper pusher? A Nazi lackey who kissed Hitler's ass for sport?"

Joanna held her breath while they waited for him to speak again. Alex was provoking him, but why? The man clearly held all the power here, and the woman was intentionally antagonizing him.

A few moments later, he spoke. "I'll be generous and give you some time to think about your situation and make a decision. One hour. That's more than fair."

"I don't even get a name?"

Woodville motioned to the guards. The guard yanked Mike and Jo from the office and herded them at gunpoint down the hall in the direction of the cellar door. The guards didn't shove them down the cellar steps, though Joanna assumed the thought crossed their minds.

Damianos escorted Alex and followed behind them. Mike and Jo were locked in the room where Jo had been held while Damianos and Alex remained in the hall just outside. Jo watched the two immortals through the open door.

"I hope you'll be comfortable in there," Damianos said mockingly to Alex as he nodded to a door across the hall. "Perhaps this will dredge up some memories from other places you spent time in. You have an hour to make your decision. I'd use the time wisely if I were you."

The metal door to Jo and Mike's room closed with an air of finality, sounding like it had sealed their fate. Joanna collapsed on the cot and didn't bother to look to see what Mike would do. They each stared into the distance, listening to footsteps retreating.

"Jo! Mike!" she heard Alex call out.

"Alex!" Mike called back. He pressed his ear to the door.

Joanna turned away from the door, not that Alex could see her. There was no way she was going to give Alex the satisfaction of responding. The sting of betrayal hurt too much to listen to the woman she now hated.

"Are you both okay? Have you been hurt?"

"We're okay."

"Joanna? Did he hurt you?"

She knew who *he* was, but she wasn't going to answer.

"Jo, answer her," Mike pleaded. "She came to get you the second we found out you were gone."

Jo didn't turn to look at her brother. How dare he believe Alex's lies? Those lies had put all of them in danger and had almost gotten them killed.

Alex's voice came again. "Jo, at least tell me if you're all right. Did anybody hurt you? Can you make a run for it with Mike if I get can you out of here?"

Jo turned and glared at the door, imagining that Alex could feel the weight of that glare. The searing pain of Alex's betrayal was all she felt. It didn't matter how she tried to explain it, the look on the woman's face said it all. She, Ben, and Mike were a duty. Alex didn't really care. Decades of lies. Jo walked across the room and sat down on the cot.

"Jo, I need you to answer me," Alex called. "I will find a way to get you out of here."

"We'll make a run for it if we get the chance," Mike said for the both of them.

Jo knew Mike still believed in Alex. Mike could be so gullible and trusting. She would never be those things.

"Just be ready."

"We will. Promise."

"Stay strong," Alex told them. "Don't let them see any weakness. I know this is a scary situation, but you need to show them you're not afraid."

"We won't."

Mike turned an angry face to his sister. "Jo, you know Alex had to say those things. Woodville would have shot us on the spot if she hadn't."

Jo didn't say anything. She crossed her arms over her chest, and she scowled, hoping it would deter her brother from talking.

"Jo." Mike crossed the room to sit next to her on the cot. He put a hand on her shoulder. "Alex will get us out of here."

Jo pulled away from his touch. "No, she won't. She doesn't care about us. You heard her."

"That was for Old Crazy Guy's benefit," he insisted.

"Stop sticking up for her!" Her stomach twisted up in a knot, and she felt like she was going to be sick. Her parents were dead, and the one person other than her brothers she thought cared about her didn't. Now her twin was defending the woman.

"I don't believe for a second that Alex doesn't care. She has always been in our lives. All the time we've spent with her. All the things she did with our family. All the time we spent at her house. All the vacations she took us all on. She's our godmother. She cared about all of us. She took a bullet trying to protect us. What did you do besides get mad because you didn't know everything about everything before it happened?"

Jo didn't say a word or move a muscle. She wasn't going to respond if he kept defending the woman and her actions.

"She'll get us out of here," Mike said confidently. "I know she will."

Jo wasn't sure if he was trying to convince her or himself. It was probably a toss-up. She couldn't keep quiet any longer. "She lies. All she does is lie, and you're a fool for believing her." She unfolded her arms and wiped angry tears away with the back of her hand. She wasn't going to cry because of Alex. "She lied about who she was, what she was, and for all we know, she could be lying about everything else."

A heavy sigh escaped Mike, and Jo felt as well as heard it. "When this is over, you'll see she said all of that for Crazy Old Guy. Alex will explain everything."

"She'll do nothing but lie," Jo countered. "It's all she's done all our lives."

"Promise me that when we get out of this, you will at least listen to Alex's side of things. You need to do it. Listen to her. That's all I'm asking. You don't have to believe it. She took a bullet for us, and she killed people to protect us. You at least owe it to her to listen."

"Shut up!" Jo yelled. "She lies! She's a liar! Don't defend her!"

"She may have lied about who she really was, but she didn't lie about caring about us or Mom and Dad. She wouldn't have taken Ben in if she didn't care."

"You don't want to see it," Jo told him. "That's always been your problem. You always want to see the good in people."

"You always want to see the bad except when you're wrong, and you're wrong this time. You're acting like a spoiled brat who didn't get her way when this is real world danger. Don't tell me that I only see the good side of people. I see more than you think. Grow up."

"You're an idiot," Jo growled. The more he talked, the angrier she became. He was supposed to take her side. His betrayal cut deep to her soul. She pushed him off the cot and curled up into a ball. "Leave me alone."

Mike shook his head and went to the door. He sat down and leaned his back against it. Jo closed her eyes against the pain inside her and wished she was anywhere else but here.

CHAPTER TWENTY-SEVEN

DAMIANOS ESCORTED ALEX BACK TO MAX'S STUDY after an hour in the cell. She assumed that they were being monitored, and she didn't talk to Greg except to tell him to be patient. The opportunity to escape would present itself. They just had to be patient.

However, this time he handcuffed her to the chair in the office. She examined his expression, trying to discern the reasoning behind handcuffing her. Did he act under orders? His face gave away nothing.

The door opened, and Alex looked over. A guard escorted Mike and Jo into the room and stood near the door with them. She hoped the two would remain quiet and stay out of the way while she handled the situation.

"You've had time to consider my proposal. I hope you have come to your senses and made the correct decision."

Alex remained silent and glared at Woodville. If looks could kill, Woodville would be a pile of gore on the floor in under a second. The old man would not live to see the sunrise. Alex would make sure of it.

Movement caught her eye, and she turned to see Jo stomp on the guard's foot. The girl struggled to get out of the man's grasp. The guard grunted and tightened his grip. "Don't even try it," he warned. Jo went still.

"Do not think I am doing this for my own pleasure, Ms. Thorne," Woodville explained. "As you can see, we do not play games. Tell me your secret, or I will kill one of them."

Alex refocused her attention on Woodville. The bastard was lying. Mike and Jo would not get out of here alive, even if Alex told him the secret to immortality.

"I will ask you again, Ms. Thorne. What's the secret to your long life?"

Alex glanced over at the twins, and Mike met her eyes. Alex nodded ever so slightly. He nudged Jo's foot with his own. Jo stopped struggling and looked at her brother. He inclined his head in Alex's direction, and Joanna looked at Alex. Alex and Joanna stared at each other for a few long moments, and Alex dropped her gaze to the floor. Mike reached over and took Jo's hand.

Woodville coughed, and Alex returned her attention to him.

"I'm going to kill you before this night is over," Alex said in a conversational tone to Woodville. "I'm going to watch you gasp your last breath. I don't normally enjoy killing, but for you, I'll make an exception."

Alex didn't know if Woodville believed her or not, but she would kill him before the night was over. It dawned on her that Woodville only mentioned Mike and Jo. Did he not know about Greg? If he didn't, it was a weapon Alex could use at the right time.

"Very well." He gave the impression of a shrug. "The girl. Shoot her," he instructed Damianos.

"No! Alex isn't the only immortal!" Mike blurted out. He released Jo's hand.

Alex's stomach sank. What was the fool boy doing?

Woodville held up a hand to stop Damianos from shooting Joanna. "Speak, boy."

"Mike!" Alex snapped.

Mike looked at Woodville and then at Alex. "Alex isn't the only immortal," he repeated. "There's another one. Let us go, and I'll tell you who it is."

"The boy's stalling for time," Damianos said dismissively. "He doesn't know what he's talking about. He's desperate."

"I swear I know another immortal!" Mike insisted. "Him!" He pointed at Damianos.

Damianos laughed. "The boy is delusional."

Woodville regarded Damianos for a few long heartbeats. "Stavros is correct," he wheezed. "People will do and say anything when their life is at stake. I saw it at Ravensbrück and Auschwitz. Many pleaded for their lives. They offered false information just for the privilege of breathing for another day. Shoot the girl."

Alex turned to look up at Damianos. Would he really kill Jo? Alex had to believe he wouldn't. His jaw was set, and his eyes fixed. He glanced down at her, and she stared at him. He would not kill Jo. Deep in her heart, she knew he wouldn't kill her. He could be brutal and ruthless at times, but he never hurt innocents.

He looked away from her and focused on Jo and Mike. Damianos raised his arm, the gun pointed directly at Jo. The guard holding her stepped to the side, his hand on her arm, and the shot rang out. Above the din, she heard Mike scream. The guard's hold kept her body from dropping immediately. Crimson stained her shirt and spread out from the right side of her chest. The guard released his grip on her arm, and Jo fell lifeless to the floor.

"You bastard!" Alex yelled at the man standing behind her.

"No!" Mike screamed and lunged toward Woodville. The guard holding him yanked Mike backward, and Mike stumbled into the guard, nearly knocking him down.

Rage erupted inside her, and Alex pulled against the handcuffs.

As her rage grew, she struggled even harder, and the metal bit into her wrists and drew blood.

Damianos left Alex and walked over and stared down at Jo. He knelt and placed two fingers on her neck, checking her pulse. "She's dead."

"By the gods above and below, I will kill you," Alex snarled at Woodville.

Mike lunged again, and the guard's grip on him relaxed. Mike slipped out of the hold and charged straight for Damianos. He started pounding his fists against the man, but Alex knew the impact of Mike's blows weren't much more than a mosquito bite to Damianos.

"I will kill you!" Mike yelled. Alex recognized the grief and rage filling Mike's voice. The guard grabbed Mike and pulled him back. Tears streamed down his face. He didn't bother to wipe them away.

Damianos ignored Mike and picked up Jo's body, carrying it out of the room. She looked so small in the man's arms. Her limbs dangled, swinging with each step. Alex would mourn the death of the girl for some time, but not now. She didn't have time for mourning right now. She would grieve later, but now it was time to embrace the rage consuming her.

Alex turned toward Woodville. "Your death is going to be slow and very painful. You'll be begging me to put you out of your misery."

"I assure you, Ms. Thorne, that I am not moved by your idle threats. I hold all the cards here, and you'll do as I want."

"Like hell I will. You lost whatever bargaining chip you thought you had."

"Now, Ms. Thorne, we both know I have another opportunity to convince you. I'll allow you one more hour to change your mind. The boy will be next. Perhaps you'll use that hour to imagine what I can do to the boy that would be worse than death. After all, my people were very creative with their captives. I know there is another boy you may have tried to hide from me. He will die if you still refuse me."

He motioned to the guards. The guard uncuffed Alex from the chair with care and then cuffed her hands together. The guards weren't about to take any chances with her. She and Mike were dragged from the room and down to the holding cells.

CHAPTER TWENTY-EIGHT

Jo CLAWED HER WAY TO CONSCIOUSNESS AND GROANED
against the pain in her shoulder. She winced against the white-hot
pain and forced her eyes to open. The ceiling of the room where
she had been held greeted her.

She brought a hand up to touch her shoulder and instantly
regretted it. Pain spiked again, and blackness tried to rise. *Mental
note, never do that again.*

The lock on the door clicked, and Jo lowered her hand and
went still. They thought she was dead, and she wanted them to
keep believing it.

Footsteps stumbled into the room, and then the door slammed
closed. The footsteps continued and came toward the cot.

"Oh God, Jo," Mike sniffled between sobs. "I'm sorry. It was
me. I did this. She said people were going to die, and I wouldn't
listen." He took her hand and gave it a squeeze.

"For what?" she asked. "You never listen. I don't think you got
me killed, though. That was all Crazy Old Nazi."

Mike fell back and landed on his ass. He stared wide-eyed at
Joanna. "Jo? You're supposed to be dead!"

Joanna opened her eyes and struggled to push herself up to a sitting position. Her shoulder protested the movement with searing bolts of pain. "Yes, you big dork. Who else are you expecting?"

He lunged forward, threw his arms around her, and pulled her in for a bear hug. "I thought you were dead!" He hugged her tighter, and the pain level increased. "I promise I will always listen when someone tells me to not do something."

Jo gasped and tried to push him away. "Ow! Ow! I'm alive, but I've been shot," she protested. She hugged him back for a second or two. "Well, I'm supposed to be dead. Now keep quiet, or the guards will know I'm not. Let me go. You're hurting me."

"Sorry." He released her and wiped his face on his shirt tail. "How are you alive? I saw you get shot. There was blood."

Jo looked down at her shirt. Blood soaked her shirt from the wound outward. Bright red circled the wound, but darker, almost brownish, blood lined the edges of the stain.

"I was shot," she said slowly as the reality sank in. "I felt the bullet go in me. I've never felt anything like it. I think I must've blacked out. I woke up in here."

"But—" Mike wiped his eyes on his sleeve and then his nose. "Damianos said you were dead. He checked for a pulse and everything. Alex went nuts."

"I think Damianos did it. Whatever he gave me to drink did this. He shot me, and then he lied to Woodville."

Mike's eyes widened. "He made you immortal! That's why you're not dead."

"Shhhh! Keep your voice down!" she hissed. "Yes, that's what I think too. He knew something was going to happen and took steps to make sure it didn't. He even packed the wound to keep me from bleeding too much." She pulled her collar open enough for Mike to see the bloodstained bandage.

The situation created a unique dichotomy of being grateful that Damianos had made her immortal yet pissed off that he had shot her. She'd figure out how she felt about him later when they were out of this mess. If they got out of this.

"I'm just glad you're alive." Mike hugged her again.

"That makes two of us." Jo was about to tell him that all this hugging hurt, but the sound of the door opening cut her off.

Mike turned to see what she was looking at.

"You bastard!" Jo growled.

"Come with me," Damianos said. "Quiet now."

Mike stood and moved in front of Jo sitting on the cot. "Why should we?"

"Do you want to get out of here?" Damianos asked. "If you do, come with me."

"Did you make me immortal?" Jo demanded. She stood up and wobbled a bit. Mike put a steadying hand on the small of her back.

"Yes, I did. I could have let you die. I should have, but I knew the moment I walked into that house that Alex would never give the three of you up. Since I couldn't do what was necessary, I gave you the Elixir of Life so you wouldn't die. You can thank me when you're safe. The guards will be back soon, so I suggest you hurry." He turned and took a few steps out of the doorway.

Mike looked at Jo. Jo nodded. "Let's go," she said.

"You're really okay?" he asked.

"It hurts," she admitted.

"You said that already."

Damianos stuck his head in the doorway. "Of course she's alive. I know what I'm doing. I've shot many people over the centuries."

"Shut up," Mike said to the man. "Jo, as soon as we get out of here, we'll get you some painkillers and stitched up. I'll do it myself if I have to."

"No, you won't. I don't want to live through this just to have you cut something off I might need." No way was she letting her twin near her with any sort of knife.

"Come on," Mike urged. He moved Jo along a little faster. They exited the room into the hallway. They watched Damianos open the door across the hall.

"Get in," he ordered.

"Moving us from one room to another isn't getting us out of here," Jo snarled.

"Get in there so she can see you're alive and still bitching as you always do."

Jo looked around Mike to see Alex standing in the middle of the room. If she were relieved to see them, it didn't show. Jo thought her face looked like a mask of murderous rage, and she knew who it was directed at. She watched Alex's eyes narrow and her hands curl up into fists.

Movement against the wall caught her eye, and she sighed with relief when she saw Greg. Relief washed through her. He was alive and okay except for being chained to the wall.

Damianos became a blur as he moved toward Alex. He grabbed her wrists and maneuvered her to the side wall, pressing her against it with his body. Alex struggled to escape. Even Jo could see that Alex didn't have the strength to push Damianos away from her.

"I'M GOING TO KILL YOU!" ALEX PROMISED AS DAMIANOS forced her to the wall.

Damianos chuckled, and it only fueled Alex's anger. "You can do that later," Damianos said. "We need to get them out of here."

Alex looked at Greg, Mike, and...Jo. The girl should be dead. Realization set in, and she knew what had happened. She tore her eyes away from Jo and looked at Damianos, narrowing her eyes and glaring at him. The expression on his face didn't change.

"Start talking. From the beginning."

"Akantha, now is not the time. We need to get out of here."

"Talk," she demanded.

He sighed heavily. He could be dramatic at times. "I got word that someone was after you. I know, someone's always after you, but this time it was different. Usually, I can find out quickly and take care of it before it reaches you, but this took a lot of legwork, and I had to call in favors. They kept their tracks well hidden. I found out who it was and leaked a rumor that Stavros Nicademos's services were available. I still have a reputation in the underworld market. Morrow agrees that it doesn't hurt to take an occasional job outside SPD to keep it alive for those times it would help gain information. Woodville was thrilled to hire someone like me. I believed I could find out why he was after you if I was on the inside. I didn't count on you having three other people in the house." He nodded at Jo and Mike. "They were an unexpected complication. Because of them, I came to warn you. But no, you were too damned stubborn to listen, so damned sure you knew better. Your stubbornness is a major pain in my ass."

"Pot. Kettle. Black," she grumbled. "Keep talking."

"I didn't know Woodville had ordered a strike against the house. I would have tried to stop it had I known. Claver was the wild card after the werewolves. I was hoping that after the attack you'd disappear, but that stubbornness got in the way. I decided that it may be easier to bring you here than risk Woodville ordering another strike and having to hide more deaths from the mundanes. There was less risk of the children getting hurt if you came here. I intended to let Jo go as soon as we had you. I didn't plan on him using her as leverage against you, let alone ordering her death. I thought I'd have an opportunity to release her and fake her escape."

Alex looked past Damianos and at Jo again. The bloodstains were stark against the dirty white shirt. "How?" she asked, her gaze not leaving Jo. She didn't have to expand on the question. He knew what she meant.

"I took precautions."

"How?" she repeated.

He slowly released one of her wrists, wary of any attempt on her part to hit him, reached inside the vest of his body armor, and pulled out a small, sealed vial. There was a milky-white liquid inside it. "I made her drink this right after I grabbed her. Just in case."

"Is that—" Her stomach sank. The Elixir of Life. She'd recognize it anywhere.

"Yes."

"What have you done?" Alex whispered. She looked at him and then at Jo. Her shoulders slumped, and her heart ached for the girl. Any chance Jo had for a normal life ended at the hands of Damianos. Now she had more to deal with than just helping them move on with their lives.

"What did I do? I saved her life. Would you rather I have let her die?"

"No," Alex said immediately. She sighed and closed her eyes for a moment. She couldn't bear the thought of something happening to any of the kids. "It just complicates things a great deal." Complicated didn't even begin to describe it.

"Better a complication you can deal with than a death you will mourn."

That was debatable, but she would take the win. A live, immortal Jo was better than putting another body in the ground. "Thank you for saving her life."

He released her other hand and backed away. "You're welcome. I told you I wouldn't let anything happen to you or them, and I meant it."

She didn't want to believe him, but she knew he wasn't lying this time.

"What's going to happen to us now?" Jo stepped closer to Alex and Damianos.

"We're getting out of here," Damianos answered. "He will order Mike's death next, and he will not survive. I have people coming to shut this place down." He crossed the room and unlocked the shackles around Greg's wrists. Greg rushed past Damianos and clasped Jo in his arms. She clung to him as he held her, whispering into her hair.

Alex let Jo and Greg have a few moments. It was the most they'd get until they all got out of here. Alex moved around Damianos, approaching the three of them. "Damianos will get you all out of here. I'm going to stay and take care of this bastard. I'll sleep better when I put a bullet in his head and know he won't survive. God, I hate Nazis. I thought we got the last of them after the war in South America."

"They're cockroaches," Damianos said. "I think you should take them and go. I'll handle this."

Alex shook her head. "No. He'll just come after us again if I don't take care of this now."

"I knew you'd say that. You don't trust me to do what's necessary?"

"I don't trust cockroaches not to come back to life."

"We don't want to go," Jo said. "I want to see that bastard die."

"Me too," Mike added. "He needs to be punished for kidnapping Jo and ordering her shot."

"You just promised you would listen the next time someone told you to do something," Jo said, whacking Mike across the shoulder. "Are you trying to get yourself killed?!"

"Me three," Greg said. He let Jo go and took off his shirt. He handed it to her. "I can help. Their weapons won't do much to me, unless Agent Nicademos got them silver bullets."

Damianos looked insulted. "I did not. You earn silver weapons, and they haven't earned them." His expression turned placatory when Alex glared at him. "And I knew you were likely to bring one or more of the werewolves with you. They have not earned a death."

Alex wanted to get this over. Their babbling was going to break that one last nerve before she could kill Woodville. "Absolutely not. Mike, you and Jo are going with Damianos." Alex hated the thought of asking Greg to help her kill all the men upstairs, but after Damianos and her, he was the only one who could get out of it alive. Provided Damianos was truthful about the silver bullets.

"But—" Mike started.

"No buts," Alex said. Her voice was firm and didn't encourage arguments.

"Here comes the fun." Greg's voice deepened with a growl at the edge of his words. He sounded as if the change was already in motion.

Alex peered at Greg to check his status. He appeared in control of his werewolf side, but the werewolf seemed to like to party a little. She would use that to her advantage this once and never again. "Take them to Victoria's," she told Damianos. "She's expecting us. She'll have a contingency plan, if I know her. Mike drove the Jeep here. There's a kit under the driver's seat with the usual emergency items. Jo needs that bullet out of her before we have to reopen a healed wound." She paused. "Victoria mentioned something about a box and separating your head from your shoulders, so be very nice. You know she'll do it. Paladin isn't there to talk her out of it."

He nodded. "Yes, she would try. I rather like my head where it is right now and not in the collection of that society of hers. Ready?"

He looked at Jo and Mike when he said it. "Yes," they said in unison.

Damianos turned back to Alex. "You?"

"Wait," Mike said. "Munchkin was in the Jeep with me. He's on the grounds. I think."

"He's looking for me," she replied. "He won't leave without me. He'll be safer with me. I'm ready as I'll ever be. Greg, start outside and make your way around the grounds before coming back into the house. I'm hoping that will draw out most of the guards to you and away from Woodville. Take out anyone you come across who's armed. When you've gotten them all, meet me in the library on the first floor. That's where Woodville will be. I think he needs a little real-world scare."

Greg grinned, canines gleaming in the low light, and shifted fully into his werewolf form. Even knowing what to expect, the hairs on the back of Alex's neck and on her arms stood on end. Immortality was not immune to the presence of an apex predator. Mike and Jo both took a step away from Greg.

"The two guards outside should be back now," Damianos warned.

"How did you get them to leave?" Alex asked and shook her head. "Never mind. I don't think I want to know."

Damianos laughed and pulled her in to plant a firm kiss on her mouth. Alex slipped out of his arms and slapped him across the cheek. Bastard, and he had the nerve to laugh again.

"Enough foreplay, let's go," Damianos said and went to the door. He grabbed the handle and yanked it open.

CHAPTER TWENTY-NINE

THE GUARDS LOOKED AROUND WHEN THE DOOR OPENED, but they didn't go for their weapons when Damianos appeared. He grabbed one guard by the arm and yanked him inside, shoving him toward Alex. He stepped out into the hallway and reached the second guard, who was slower to react. He pulled him in and spun him around, putting the man's back to his chest and wrapped his arms around the man's head. The man's neck proved too fragile to withstand the quick, powerful twist he gave it. The body slumped to the floor. A shiver raced down Jo's spine.

Alex caught the guard Damianos shoved into the room. She spun him around and then snapped his neck with a quick twist of his head. Jo and Mike's jaws dropped in surprise. She'd expected Alex to disable the man, not kill him. It was scary and impressive at the same time.

Greg charged out of the room. A howl echoed out in the hallway, and Jo shuddered. A large part of her was thankful she didn't have to see Greg tearing through bodies again. Once more than enough for her.

"Come on," Damianos urged them.

Alex snatched up the guard's gun and joined Damianos out in

the hallway. Damianos disarmed the other corpse. For a moment, Jo thought he was going to give it to her or Mike. Instead, he tucked it into the waistband at the small of his back.

Alex didn't wait for them. She took off down the hall and ran up the stairs in the direction Greg had gone.

Damianos turned to them. "Okay, this is what we're going to do. I'm going to lead you two upstairs and to the back door. You're going to run out straight to whatever Mike drove here. I'm going to follow Alex and the wolf. We'll meet you back at Victoria's. Got it?"

"Alex said you had to take us," Joanna countered.

"And I'm changing the plans."

"She isn't going to like this," Mike pointed out.

"Get used to it. She never likes anything. Do as you're told."

"I hope Victoria does take your head off," Jo practically snarled. Despite the rescue, she wanted something very bad to happen to him. A good maiming would suffice.

"Do as you're told," Damianos repeated. "Victoria will be expecting you. Do not speed. You do not want to be pulled over. Understand?" He looked directly at Joanna.. She returned his look with a glare.

"We don't have any guns," Jo pointed out. She didn't expect Damianos to give either of them a weapon, but it never hurt to ask. The worst he could do was say no.

He seemed to consider it for a moment before he reached behind his back and brought out the pistol. He checked the safety before handing it to her.

"Hey. Where's mine?" Mike asked.

"She asked first," Damianos said. "And I only have the one extra. You need to get out of here with your sister."

Despite the situation, Jo couldn't help but smirk at Mike. Mike scowled and made it even better.

"We'll go to the Jeep and wait there for you. You might need us," Mike said.

Damianos shook his head. "Boy, we don't need your help with something we've done for centuries. Go to Victoria's. Jo needs medical attention now. The pistol is for insurance. Don't use it unless your life is at stake. Once you're out the door, don't stop running until you get to the Jeep."

Mike and Jo nodded, but Mike looked disgruntled at the curt dismissal.

"The gods be with you," Damianos said.

He led them out of the room and up the stairs. They emerged into the kitchen and found a guard lying on the floor in a pool of blood. There were huge gashes in his black uniform and skin. He blankly stared up at the ceiling, his throat ripped out and blood everywhere.

"He's effective for a young one," Damianos muttered with satisfaction as he stepped around the prone body.

Jo didn't have to ask who. She knew Greg had been through here. Screams and gunfire came from other parts of the house. Jo didn't want to know what carnage Greg and Alex were creating. She was better off not knowing.

"There's the door. Go!"

Jo and Mike ran. Mike grabbed the doorknob and threw open the door. Jo rushed past him, gun in her hand, and he followed her out into the darkness. They sprinted across the lawn toward the front gate, but Jo stopped dead in her tracks. Munchkin's bark echoed over the lawn. They watched the huge dog shadow race toward them.

Mike turned around. "Jo? C'mon. We have to get out of here. You heard Damianos."

Jo shook her head. "I'm going back. I have to know that bastard Woodville is dead. I'll have nightmares if I don't see it with my own eyes." She wasn't going to run away and hide. That asshole ordered her to be shot, and she was going to make sure he got what he deserved. She didn't care if Alex and Damianos would be mad. A part of her had to do this. She needed closure on this whole episode to get her life back on track.

"You heard him. They'll be right out. It's stupid to go back in there."

"I'm not going to explain it to you," she said. She turned around and ran back to the house. Munchkin veered toward the house with her. Mike followed.

Once inside, Jo noticed an eerie silence settled on the house. The screams and gunshots were gone. The coppery odor of blood was heavy in the air. Jo and Mike ran straight for the office. They made sure to step over the blood pooling on the floors and around the bodies Greg and the two immortals left in their wake. Munchkin gave them perfunctory sniffs but didn't linger either. They reached the office and paused in the doorway to find Alex holding a gun on Woodville.

Damianos was nowhere to be seen. Neither was Greg. Alex aimed a gun at the old man, and Jo's gaze met Alex's. Jo knew by the look in Alex's eyes that the woman was going to shoot the old man. Even though she knew it was morally wrong, she wouldn't deny wanting to see the son of a bitch pay for putting all of them through this. They had been through so much. Someone had to pay.

Max turned and saw the twins standing in the doorway. His face paled when he saw Jo.

"What do you think, Max? Should I kill you quickly, or should I kill you in the most painful way I can come up with? You ordered the death of a girl who did nothing to deserve her fate. That alone guarantees you will not live out this night." An unholy smile crossed Alex's face. "Do you know what scaphism, or the boats, is?"

Max slowly shook his head.

"Let me explain it to you. The Persians devised it, and it's perhaps the most horrific way to die. In all of history, I've never seen anything as cruel. First, the victim was laid across a boat and tied down. Then the person was forced to consume milk and honey until they suffered from diarrhea. Then milk and honey were slathered over the body, special attention paid to eyes, ears, face, genitals, and the anus. Another boat is fastened on the first boat and the victim's hands, feet, and head are sticking out. The boats are left out in the sun on a stagnant pond with the victim covered in milk, honey, and their own feces. Then the insects come. They feed and breed in the feces, in the person's orifices, and under the skin. Each day, the victim is fed more milk, honey, and water, preventing them from dying from starvation and dehydration. So while you're languishing for days waiting to die, you experience the agonizing nightmare of thousands of crawling insects on your skin, burrowing into your eyes, ears, and nose, filling your mouth, while parasites breed in the filth at the bottom of the boat. They crawl up into your bowels, and this all continues until you finally die. Plutarch wrote an account where the victim survived for seventeen days. I'd make sure you last longer."

Jo's stomach turned at the graphic description. Just hearing it made her want to puke.

"Remind me to never piss her off," Mike whispered to Jo.

Jo agreed with her brother but would never admit it. She made a motion to silence him. In those moments, Alex had become more terrifying than even Damianos or Greg in werewolf form.

"I have money," Woodville wheezed.

"I have money as well," she said, walking slowly toward the desk. The gun never wavered. "Quite a few centuries' worth. Your life has no value to me."

"I have power. Influence." Max put an unsteady hand around the hilt of a sword lying across the large desk.

"No value to me." She repeated each word slowly and deliberately. "The Nazis had power, money, and influence. Look what happened to them. I know the location of the Spear of Destiny. Imagine what I could do with that, or with Durendal." Max's eyes widened at the mention of Durendal, and he looked at the sword lying across the desk. "I could be the most powerful person in the world. What do I need with your power and influence?"

"Even if you kill me, you won't be safe. You will be hunted. We will find you," Max wheezed. "We will have what is ours."

Jo wondered who *we* was. More Nazis? God, she hoped not.

Alex shrugged. "It won't be the first time. I have more experience dealing with hunters than you could ever imagine."

"They won't be safe." He nodded at Mike and Jo.

"I will kill every single person anyone sends after them," Alex said, though it was more of a snarl.

The fierceness behind the words surprised Jo. Especially after all that Alex had told the old man how she felt about them. Jo didn't doubt Alex now. She knew the hurtful words Alex had said were for the old man, not for Jo or Mike.

"I have the time for it. You're clutching at straws."

The fear faded from his face as he gazed beyond her shoulder. A wavering smile appeared. "I'm afraid you're mistaken, Ms. Thorne. Now lower your gun."

Joanna looked to see Damianos behind them. Joanna grabbed Mike's arm to pull him out of the way. Damianos approached Alex with his weapon drawn and pointed it at her head.

Alex glanced back and shrugged. "Am I supposed to be afraid of him?" she asked and nodded in Damianos's direction. "Stavros and I go way back."

"She's right," Damianos answered and lowered his weapon. "I'd say a long time."

Alex turned her attention back to Max. "You were so focused on me you didn't do a sufficient job checking out who you were hiring."

Woodville stared at Damianos. "You're...you're one of them?"

"I'm not one of you," Damianos said in disgust.

Jo was hurt and tired, and she only wanted to leave. Glancing down, she remembered she still held the borrowed gun. She had fired a gun a few times back home when her dad had taken them to a shooting range, but it was for fun, and she missed the targets more than she hit them. She clicked the safety off and brought it up. She aimed it at the old man.

The motion drew the old man's attention away from Alex. "What are you going to do, little girl? Shoot me?" he challenged.

"Joanna, don't do this." Alex looked back at her. "Walk away." Their eyes met, but Jo had no intention of listening to the older woman.

Never in her life would she have thought she'd be capable of taking another life, but this man had been responsible for most of the recent bad things that had happened to her. This man had stolen her humanity, and everything came to a head. All the emotions of the past few months that had been a constant storm inside her faded to a dull roar, and her focus sharpened to a point, centered on the old man in front of her. She couldn't do anything about her parents' deaths, but right now, right here, she could do something about this.

She squeezed the trigger. The gun went off, the recoil more than Jo expected. It jerked back, but she hit her target. A look of surprise crossed Woodville's face. The desk chair rocked with the impact as the bullet slammed into his chest.

Jo didn't move as she stared at the body slumped in the chair. Anger drained out of her the longer she stared. A man was dead by her hand. Relief filled the void. She knew she should be horrified that she killed someone, but she wasn't. It was, well, good.

Damianos took the pistol from Jo. She looked up at him and blinked. He smiled reassuringly at her and put a careful hand on her arm to direct her toward Alex. "Get them out of here," he told Alex. "My people will be here shortly. We'll clean it up."

"Joanna?" Alex put a hand on her shoulder.

Jo nodded dumbly.

Alex took her arm and walked her over to Woodville's body.

"Your first lesson. You never, ever, walk away from a body without making sure they're dead. If it had to be done, make sure it was done right."

Jo looked at Alex and blinked. Alex's words filtered their way into her brain, and after a second, she slowly nodded.

"Get her out of here!" Damianos ordered "She doesn't need this now."

"In a moment. You made her immortal, but I must teach her how to live with it. If the gods are kind, this will be the only time she needs this lesson."

"Alex—" Mike began.

Alex held up a hand, cutting Mike off. "Jo, check for a pulse."

Jo stared at the woman for a moment before the words sank in. Her eyes flickered at Woodville's body. He looked dead, and she wasn't sure she wanted to touch the corpse. She felt a hand on her back, and she knew Alex wouldn't let her leave until she did this.

"It's only a body," Alex said quietly.

Jo sucked in a deep breath and placed two fingers on the side of Woodville's neck.

The skin was wrinkled and paperlike. Old people skin. It brought back memories of holding her grandmother's hand in the hospital. It dawned on her that her skin would never get like this. It would never be wrinkled, thin, or have age spots. "I don't feel anything."

"That's not long enough. Count off ten seconds in your head."

Jo did as she was told. She felt nothing against her fingers. After the ten count, she removed her hand and hastily wiped her fingers on her jeans. "No pulse."

"Now we can go. We'll talk about this later."

Jo turned to Mike and noticed Greg standing in the doorway. His bloodstained clothes hung in tatters on him. Their eyes met. Now they were both killers and had to live with what they had done. She tore her eyes away from Greg and looked at Mike. The worried look on his face was comforting. He put an arm around her shoulders and hugged her to his side. She didn't object.

Alex grabbed the sword lying across the desk and nodded at the door. Mike nodded and steered Jo toward the door. They reached Greg and Munchkin waiting outside the library door. They were both blood-streaked, Munchkin's coat tangled and Greg's hair sticking up in all directions. She handed Greg his shirt, and he used it to wipe his face and hands. The dog moved forward when Alex appeared. Damianos's voice from the library called for Greg to stay when he turned to follow the small group. Joanna glanced back at him, and he smiled reassuringly at her.

"I'll be right behind you," she heard Damianos say as they left.

CHAPTER THIRTY

VICTORIA'S HOUSE WAS A WELCOME SIGHT. RELIEF flooded through Alex when she spotted the lights on in the windows as they pulled into the long drive. The security lights flicked on, and Munchkin barked. Mike opened his door before they came to a full stop and jumped out to rush to the rear door to help Jo out. Munchkin had allowed Jo to lean against him during the ride, but now he forced his bulk over the front seat to follow Mike. The dog bounded for the side door to shove his weight at it, the shepherd's special knock.

Alex climbed out and walked around the Jeep. Alex nudged Mike aside and put a hand on Jo's arm. "Joanna?" No response.

"Is she okay?" Mike asked. "Why isn't she awake?"

Alex sighed. She could hear the panic rising in Mike's voice, and it was the last thing she needed to deal with right now. At least Greg would be coming back with Damianos, so she wouldn't have to deal with a protective werewolf.

"Jo, wake up!" Mike urged loudly.

Alex put a hand on Mike's arm. "She's passed out. It's her body's way of dealing with the trauma. She won't die." Alex gently eased Jo out of the back seat and cradled her like a large baby. Jo's weight made her stagger a bit, seeing how the two were similar in size.

"I can get her." He held out his arms to take his unconscious sister. "Let me."

"You get the door," Alex instructed.

"Munchkin got the door," another voice said.

Alex turned to see Jack waiting patiently. He was so good at that. A tired smile crossed her face. Ben hovered at Jack's shoulder.

"I'll take her, Boss," the man said. He didn't wait for a response but lifted the girl from Alex.

She tensed but released Jo in weary agreement. "Thank you. What are you doing here?"

"Victoria called, but I was already on my way back," he said over his shoulder on his way to the side door.

Alex followed, grumbling under her breath. Ben and Mike fell into step on each side of her.

Even in the shadows, Ben's face looked pale and scared. "Is she...I mean...Jo..."

"She'll be okay," Alex said, trying to reassure all of them.

"You sure?" Ben asked.

"Yeah. I'll tell you everything as soon as she's taken care of."

Ben nodded.

Victoria met them at the door. Her hands were on her hips. "What happened?"

"Jo was shot. We have to remove the slug," Alex said. "We need a workspace."

"I told you not to trust that bastard!"

"Marie, she's hurt!" Alex snapped. Victoria's birth name escaped her in frustration. She would apologize later. Right now, they had a patient to care for.

"And she's not getting any better," Jack said. "The two of you can have that argument after you save the girl's life."

At the mention of saving Jo's life, Alex straightened her

shoulders. "That's no longer an issue. You can thank or curse the bastard for it."

A sad look appeared on Victoria's face, and Alex knew she understood. "Take her to the first bedroom on the left at the top of the stairs. There's a first aid chest in the closet. Ben, run ahead and turn the lights on for them. Mike, come with me. We'll need a few things."

Ben dashed off while Mike followed Victoria. Alex followed Jack into the house. Hopefully Damianos would bring Greg to the house soon. She assumed the boy was okay, but she had to be sure.

Alex followed Jack up the stairs to a guest room. He laid Jo on the bed, and Alex moved to the side. Ben moved around the room, turning on lights before hovering near the wall, out from underfoot.

Alex settled Jo in, and Victoria and Mike appeared with extra towels. The decanter of liquor and glasses Victoria carried didn't go unnoticed. Alex would need a drink after this. Maybe three or four drinks.

Mike joined Ben near the wall while Jack opened the huge first aid kit from the closet. It was more like a huge toolbox. The top opened into multitiered compartments that held everything a person could need. The bottom center space had crisp, white, paper-wrapped bandages, packaged syringes, and swabs.

"Painkiller?" Jack asked Victoria.

Victoria put the pliers down on the bedside table, along with a decanter of whiskey and two glasses. "Hidden space," she said as she pulled out an insert from one of the tiered compartments to reveal several small glass vials. "Don't need the police after me for possession."

"Who are you?" Mike asked.

"Call me Jack. I'm a friend." Jack took a vial and packaged syringe over to the bed. Alex had prepped Jo and placed a folded towel over her chest for modesty.

The wound area was exposed, and Alex doused it with a squeeze bottle of fluid she'd taken from the chest. She pulled on latex gloves and used bandages to blot the wound before picking up a paper-wrapped scalpel. She waited expectantly.

"You have the better touch with needles. Would you?" Alex asked Victoria. She nodded to the items Jack held.

"Of course." Victoria took a seat on the bed at Jo's side.

"What is it?" Mike asked. "What are you giving my sister?"

Alex answered him. "Morphine. This isn't exactly painless, and I need her as still as possible." She removed the makeshift bandage Damianos had put on the wound.

"What's the booze for?" Ben asked.

"Later." Victoria tucked Jo's arm under hers to stretch a length of rubber around Jo's upper arm. She extended the elbow and lightly tapped the vein. Jack handed her a rubbing alcohol–soaked cotton ball, and Victoria rubbed the inside of Jo's elbow. "This will be quicker than a deep tissue injection," she told Mike. "I have tablets as well, but those will take time, and she's not awake enough for it."

"The faster, the better," Jack said quietly. He stood back to allow the women to take the limited space around the bed. "Is there anything else you need?"

"Jack, please take Mike and Ben downstairs," Alex instructed.

"No!" Mike and Ben both said loudly. Jo twitched on the bed in reaction to the noise. Her eyes fluttered as the needle was inserted into the vein.

"Mike! Ben!" Alex glared at them.

"I'm sorry, but I'm not going anywhere. I have to make sure she's okay," Ben said.

"I'm not going anywhere either," Mike added.

Jo turned her head in Victoria's direction as the woman removed the needle and briskly rubbed the site. She removed the rubber tubing and replaced the arm against Jo's side.

"What's going on?" Jo asked, her voice wavering. "Are we out?"

Both Alex and Mike began to explain, but Mike quieted at the glare from Alex.

"We're at Victoria's house," Alex said in a low, reassuring tone as she unwrapped the scalpel. "It was the closest place to go for help. We need to remove the bullet. I won't lie to you. This isn't going to be easy. You just had a shot of morphine. It'll take the edge off, but you'll still feel what we do. I need you to be as still and quiet as possible. If you yell, you'll tense up and make it harder for us."

"Okay, just make it stop," Jo said weakly. "Where's Mike? Is he okay?"

Mike moved to Jo's uninjured side and took her hand. "I'm right here, Jo."

Ben appeared next to Mike's side. "I'm here too."

Jo looked at them through slitted eyes and smiled. "We're all okay," she said. "Shoot Damianos for me."

Jack laughed.

"No more talking," Alex said. She placed the scalpel against the angry reddish wound and pressed down. A thin line of blood appeared, and Jo let out a scream.

Victoria moved past Mike to sit by Jo's head to hold her shoulders down. "Do as Alex says, and hold still. It will hurt more if you don't."

"It hurts a lot now," Jo said.

"I know," Victoria commiserated. "I've been shot before. Alex has to widen the wound to be able to get to the bullet. Jack would, but take it from me, he's heavy-handed."

Jack shrugged. "I leave it to the experts."

"I need more light," Alex instructed.

Ben and Mike both moved from where they stood near the wall and pulled out cell phones. They turned on the light and shined them both on Alex's hands.

"Thank you," Alex said as she made one last incision. She set the down the scalpel and tentatively probed the wound with a finger.

"Still hurts," Jo moaned.

"I'm sorry, but I have to find the bullet." Alex moved her finger around and then withdrew it. Blood dripped from the tip, and Jack offered her a towel. Alex wiped it off and grabbed the needle-nosed pliers. Victoria handed her another alcohol-soaked cotton ball, and Alex took it, wiped down the pliers and handed the cotton ball back to Victoria.

Alex slowly put the pliers into the wound tract. "Mike, bring the light in closer." Mike moved the phone closer to Jo.

Silence settled over the room. The only sound was Jo's grunts against the pain each time Alex moved the pliers a bit. After a while, Alex pulled the pliers out of Jo and plopped the slug on a towel Victoria held out.

"Small caliber," Jack commented.

"Which is why it wasn't a through and through." Alex set the pliers down next to the slug. "Thankfully it didn't hit bone and fragment." Jack handed Alex a threaded hook and what seemed to be a pair of scissors. "Thank you."

"I know what I'm doing," Damianos said from behind Mike. Mike turned to see him in the doorway with Greg behind him. Munchkin lifted his head from where he sat by the window and growled softly at the man.

"I should call the police and have you arrested for breaking and entering," Victoria said, giving him a glare like the ones Alex gave the man. "Or at least trespassing. I think I'll settle on decapitation."

Damianos smiled. "It's nice to see you too. How are the Masseys these days? Reports say they're enjoying their retirement in Florida."

Victoria shot him a death glare, but she didn't utter a word.

"I knew they were coming here," Damianos continued. "I wanted to make sure everything was fine."

Greg appeared at Jo's side, now dressed in what Alex assumed were some of Mike's clothes. He was mostly clean and back to looking like the polite young man she knew.

"How is she?" he asked.

"She'll live. There will be a scar." Alex refocused her attention on Jo, who winced every time Alex put the needle in. Alex tied off the sutures, stitching the muscle together.

"Were you a doctor in a past life?" Mike asked Alex as she worked.

"No, but I did some work as a resurrection man for a while, and in exchange for my work, I was allowed to observe doctors teaching their students."

"What's a resurrection man, and does it involve zombies?" Ben asked.

Damianos moved to the bureau and picked up the decanter. He poured some of the amber liquid into a glass. "She dug up fresh bodies for doctors." He took a drink and watched Alex work. Jo groaned loudly. "It could be pretty lucrative."

"That's so gross and so awesome!" Ben enthused. "Will you tell me more about it later?"

"I will. It was the only way I could learn. Women weren't allowed to study medicine then. Almost done," Alex said to Jo as she started to suture skin together. "Just a little bit more. You're doing great."

"I don't feel like it," Jo grumbled. She turned her head and looked at Greg. "Are you okay?"

"Im fine," he said.

"If you can complain, you're doing well," Victoria assured her.

"Too many people in here," Jo protested. "You're all watching me."

"You might do some tricks," Mike said and squeezed her hand.

"First gunshot wounds are a rite of passage." Damianos

drained his glass and poured more. "The second one is your own damned fault."

"I could have skipped this one."

"Where's the fun in that?" Alex asked with a ghost of a smile on her face. "Hang in there for a few more minutes."

"You shot her?" Jack asked Damianos.

"Somebody had to do it."

The answer didn't seem to satisfy Jack. "What happened, and do we need to be concerned about backlash?"

"Crazy, old Nazi guy is what happened," Mike answered.

"Say that again?" Jack looked at Mike and then at Alex.

"What Mike meant to say to say is that someone who knew me during World War II while I was spying inside the Reich wanted my secret of immortality and Durendal," Alex said. She tied off the last suture, and Victoria handed her a paper-wrapped bandage. "He's dead."

"I'm glad," Ben said quietly.

"And Durendal?" Victoria queried.

"There's nothing to be concerned about. He's burning in hell with the rest of the Nazis, and Durendal is safe. Anybody who looks for backlash is welcome to try me. I'm taking no prisoners," Alex said. She set a bandage over the wound. Victoria handed her a roll of medical tape. "There shouldn't be too much of a scar." She placed two strips of tape on the bandage to hold it in place. "All done."

"Good," Jo said as she slowly sat up with help from Victoria.

Damianos refilled his glass but didn't drink any of it. Instead, he offered the glass to Alex. She removed the bloody latex gloves, dropped them in a nearby wastebasket, and accepted the glass with a faint smile. She took a tentative sip and then downed it.

The tightness in her neck and shoulders lessened as the alcohol burned its way through her. "Thank you. Everything cleaned up?" Alex asked Damianos.

"It's being scrubbed as we speak. There will be a fire. It will be both devastating and contained to just the property," he answered as he poured whiskey into the other glass. He offered it to Victoria with a smirk.

She scowled but took the glass anyway. "Okay, the show is over. Everyone out. Joanna needs to rest. I'll settle her in. Alex, the room next door is ready for company if you'd like to freshen up."

"Thanks. A shower and a change of clothes will be welcomed." Alex looked at Jo and took her hand. She gave it an affectionate squeeze and smiled reassuringly. "Get some rest. You'll heal faster."

"Can I stay with her awhile?" Greg asked.

"Yes, but not long."

Victoria helped Jo relax back into a reclining position with the extra pillows. "The morphine should help you rest. I'll bring you some water and make sure no one bothers you."

"That would be wonderful," Jo said.

"I'll be back later," Mike told his sister.

"Me too," Ben said. "Get some beauty sleep. You need it now."

"Okay." Jo tried to smile at Ben's teasing but grimaced instead. "Get out."

"I'll see you later," Alex said, leaving the room.

GREG SAT ON THE EDGE OF THE BED ONCE EVERYONE left the room. He clasped Jo's hand and gave it a squeeze. Then he lifted her hand and kissed her knuckles. She smiled faintly. Her perceptions were all fuzzy with the morphine, but he was a good fuzzy.

"Are you okay?" he asked.

"I will be, seeing that I can't die now. How are you? How many times were you shot?"

Greg shrugged. "I didn't count, but I'm fine. None of the bullets were silver, so I'm already healed."

"Fancy trick. Wish I could heal that fast."

"I wish you could too, but it sounds like you'll heal faster than normal." He squeezed her hand, and Jo smiled.

"Not fast enough. I'm so sore." Her chest throbbed with dull pain, and she hated to think about how it would feel once the morphine wore off.

"I know. It'll go away soon."

"Thank you."

Greg tilted his head. "For what?"

"For helping to save me. You're my own personal knight in fur."

Greg chuckled and kissed her knuckles again. Jo smiled. "It's the least I could do," he said. "I didn't want anything to happen to you."

"I don't want anything to happen to you," she said.

"So what's next?" he asked.

"Probably going back to Maine tomorrow or the next day."

He nodded. "And then?"

"I don't know," Jo replied honestly. She thought she didn't have her life planned out before, but now since the crazy events of the past few days, she really didn't have a clue. "A lot has happened the past week, and it's going to take some time to process it all. Not to mention I have no idea what it means to be an immortal. I'm considering staying for a while to figure things out. At least for the summer."

"I like the idea of that," Greg admitted. "It means I get to see more of you."

Jo smiled. "I like that idea too."

"I have a confession," Greg said.

"Oh?"

"I know we've only been seeing each other for a short time, but I think we have something worth considering."

"I think you're right. A little more exploration is a good thing." She yawned, ruining the sultry effect she was trying to show while bloody and injured.

He leaned in and kissed her forehead. "Get some rest. You'll heal faster."

"Will you stay with me for a little?" Not that she was scared, she just liked having someone in the room. That it was Greg made it even better.

"Of course," he said and stood. He carefully climbed onto the bed and stretched out next to her, leaning against the pillows. "They'll kick me out soon."

"A little while is enough for now." Jo rested her face against his arm with a sigh and closed her eyes.

CHAPTER THIRTY-ONE

ALEX POURED WHISKEY INTO THE GLASS AS DAMIANOS closed the door to the guest bedroom. She took a long drink and closed her eyes. The liquid burned a trail down through her. Warmth settled in her stomach and spread outward even as the shakes began. She opened her eyes and finished off the rest of the liquid in a single gulp.

Damianos crossed the room and eased the glass out of her trembling hand. He sat it on the nightstand. He wrapped his arms around Alex and brought her in against his body. Her mind told her to resist, but she needed the warmth and strength he offered. She slipped her arms around his waist and sighed deeply.

Emotions, wild and swirling inside her, calmed and slowly drained away. The world slowed and disappeared, leaving only the two of them. Something she expected when his arms encircled her, and something she could never find elsewhere. He kissed the top of her head, and she closed her eyes.

She laid her head against his chest, listening to the steady rhythm of his heart. It grounded her and shifted the world back to normal. His love was solid ground when she needed it the most. Jo and Mike were both safe, Jo was now immortal, and the old man was dead. It wasn't exactly the best possible outcome, but she'd take it. Now she just had a newly made immortal to deal with.

Damianos pulled back and put a hand on her cheek. She opened her eyes and pressed her cheek into his hand. He used the palm of his hand to tilt her face up. "They're all okay," he said in a low, reassuring voice.

"I know."

"Tomorrow we'll go home if the girl is up to it," he said, kissing her on the forehead.

Alex sighed heavily. "We'll see." After all that she had just been through, she didn't know if she could handle Damianos being around on top of trying to help Jo adjusting to her new life as an immortal.

"Things will work out."

"I know they will, but don't think I'm not angry with you."

"What did I do now?"

Alex glared up at him but remained in his arms. "You could have prevented this whole thing, and you didn't. Now I have to deal with a new immortal."

"It was the most logical thing to do," he protested. "It got you in without being riddled with bullets. You know that's what would have happened if you had tried getting in on your own."

Damn him. He was right, but she would never tell him that. He would just hold it over her head for the foreseeable future. "There were options other than involving Jo."

"I did what I thought best."

"That's exactly the problem. What you thought best. Had you told me what was going on, we could have formulated a plan and kept Mike and Jo out of it. We could have kept all the kids out of it. You endangered them. You endangered our blood."

"What do you want me to say?" he asked, dropping his arms to his sides.

"How about I'm sorry to start?"

"I have nothing to be sorry for."

Alex threw her hands up in the air. "You're insufferable!"

"And you're being overly dramatic," he accused.

Alex ignored him and picked up her glass. She poured more whiskey into the glass. He took the glass while she replaced the stopper on the decanter. He smiled and drank some of it, ignoring the glares she gave him.

"I am not."

Damianos laughed. "Yes, you are," he said, setting the glass on the nightstand.

A soft knock on the door paused the conversation. "Enter," she said.

The door opened, and Jack poked his head inside. "Sorry to interrupt."

"You're not interrupting," Alex assured him. "What is it?"

"Bob Wharton," he said, his face grim.

Alex's chest tightened at the sound of her agent's name, and her stomach twisted. Tears welled up in her eyes as Jack shook his head. Bob had been in her employment for ten years. He was a valuable researcher and managed to find items, both for the store and the vault, that no one else could. Max might have ordered the death, but someone else had to have done it. Alex vowed she'd find them and make them pay.

"I'm sorry," Jack said.

Alex struggled to keep the grief at bay. She wanted to thank him for investigating and for his sympathies, but she couldn't form the words. She numbly nodded as Jack disappeared from the doorway, quietly shutting the door behind him.

Tears spilled from her eyes and ran down her cheeks. Damianos wiped them away and wrapped his arms around her. He held her while she cried against his chest.

.   .   .

Time flowed by. How much, she didn't know. She didn't care. She absorbed all the comfort Damianos offered. Eventually, the tears stopped, and she sniffled. She pulled away and looked at him.

"I'm sorry," he said quietly.

Anger dulled the grief. "I'd kill Woodville again if I could."

"I'd resurrect him if I could so you could do just that." He tightly hugged her and then released her.

He reached into a pocket and held out a heavy gold ring. "Max wore this."

Alex picked it up and examined it. The signet ring bore a dragon on the Oxford oval. In addition to being a Nazi, Max had been a Dragon Knight as well. When it rained, it poured.

"Yes, it's what you think," Damianos said. "I believe we are reaching a point where something permanent must be done about them."

"Maybe," Alex mused.

"Maybe? This is the second time they've come after an immortal. The old man is dead, but how many more are out there?"

"I don't know. I need to focus on getting them home and helping Jo adjust to the immortality you gave her. I don't have time to go hunting."

"Akantha, this is serious."

"I know, which is why you should start looking for them," she countered. "Or talk to Morrow."

"Morrow won't assign any resources to this. They're not a threat to the supernatural world yet."

"Oh, so we're not a part of that world unless it's convenient?" she challenged.

"You know we are."

"Then Morrow should agree to look into this."

Damianos shrugged, his heavy shoulders rolling with ease. "I'll talk to him."

"If he says no, then you can hunt for them. If you need help, take Rufus with you."

"Gods, no," he said.

Despite the grief inside her, Alex laughed. Rufus was...well, Rufus. Alex had never met another immortal like him and hoped she never would again. She could only take Rufus in very small doses every few centuries. Most of the other immortals she knew were the same.

Damianos reached out and pulled Alex into his arms. Before she could protest, he drowned her in a kiss so deep that she was able to forget for a moment all that had happened. Alex returned the kiss for a long moment but then ended it. She slipped out of Damianos's arms. He could distract her later when they were home. After she put Durendal in a new location. The attack on her house had covered the theft from her vault. New security measures would be implemented. How good of Woodville to have it on his desk in plain sight for her to grab on the way out. Victoria would have a meltdown if she knew it was currently under the cargo area carpet in the Jeep.

"I'm going to take a shower," she said, picking up her glass. She finished the rest of the whiskey and returned the glass to the nightstand. "Could you please make some tea for me?"

She didn't wait for an answer. She left him standing there with a surprised look on his face. She entered the adjoining bathroom, shut the door behind her, and locked it.

CHAPTER THIRTY-TWO

Jo woke to pain a second time, and she opened her eyes and looked around. It took a moment to remember she was at Victoria's and not in Maine. Sunlight filtered in through the sheer curtains. Greg was gone. A small clock on the nightstand read 2:00 p.m. She sat up with a groan and then realized she wasn't alone. Damianos stood near a window. He turned and looked at her.

Her first instinct was to scream at him, but she managed to choke it back. That would get her nothing but more people to watch her overreact. She gripped the edge of the sheets and blankets with a death grip. "What are you doing here?" she snapped.

"Just checking on you." His voice was low with a soft tone to it. It was like concern but from a crazy uncle who didn't deal with kids often and overcompensated the friendly voice.

"Why?" she challenged.

"Do I need a reason?" He turned toward the window for a moment. It was almost as if he was keeping an eye out for someone.

"Considering you drugged me, kidnapped me, and shot me,

yes." Not to mention scared the hell out of her. The man was the most terrifying person she had ever met in her life, crazy old man included.

"I had my reasons."

"I don't give a shit what your reasons are. You drugged me. You kidnapped me. You shot me!"

He turned back toward her. "I did those things to bring an end to all of this. Alex would have never backed down, moved, or changed your identities. That old man would have kept coming after her, and you three are targets. Bringing her to him was the best plan, and I couldn't do that unless I had something she cared about."

"He would have died soon," Joanna said. "He was ancient."

"Maybe you weren't paying attention during his grandstanding speech, but he said *we*. That means there are more players involved. Even if the old man died on his own, there would be others coming after Alex. He was the one we could deal with."

"Only the old man is out of the picture."

"Yes, but we now have some clues about who he's working with. We're already hunting the others down."

Now that he mentioned it and the excitement of the situation had passed, she did recall the old man suggesting there were others. Who else was after Alex, her immortality, and Durendal? And she realized now that people would come after her if they knew what she was.

"Good," she said as she crossed her arms over her chest, immediately regretting the pain it caused. She unfolded her arms and let them fall to her sides.

"I'm glad you approve."

He didn't sound glad at all. Joanna knew sarcasm when she heard it, and she let the comment go. "When am I going home?"

"We're probably going home tomorrow. It's up to Alex."

She scowled when he said *we*. That meant he was planning to go with them, and every day she would have to look at the man who hurt her. Maybe Alex would let her shoot him as payback. Sure, it wouldn't kill him, but it would cause him pain and possibly give her some satisfaction.

"Get some rest," he advised. "We heal fast, but rest helps."

"I wouldn't have to heal if you hadn't shot me," she complained.

He walked over to the bed and looked down at her. She sank deeper into the pillows, trying to pull away from his gaze. "One day you'll learn that sometimes you must make the hard choice to save those you care about. I knew you wouldn't die, and I shot you in a place that would be the easiest to treat. I know what I'm doing. I'm sorry I had to do it, but it was necessary. You are strong enough to survive immortality and a paltry wound."

The apology was a surprise. His words sank in, but she wasn't going to let go of the anger anytime soon. The anger kept the fear at bay. She settled for glaring at him.

"You'll understand when you get a few centuries under your belt." His forehead furled, and his mouth twisted up. He seemed to be thinking about something. His mouth straightened, and his face smoothed out. "I'll check on you later."

With that, he left the room.

Jo glared at the door for a moment and then sighed, restlessly trying to get the pillows into a better position. She stared at the ceiling, and her mind replayed the events of the past few days. Looking back on it, it all seemed completely insane. The things they went through only happened in the movies, but it was all real. Now she was young, immortal, and healing from a bullet wound. A soft knock on the door interrupted her reverie.

"Come in."

The door opened, and Alex entered with a tray of food. "I thought you could use something to eat," she said as she placed the tray on the empty side of the bed next to Jo.

"I'm not hungry." Her rumbling stomach told a different story. She glanced over at the plate and inwardly groaned. It was a full brother-type breakfast—omelet, bacon, home fries, toast with butter, orange juice, and a cup of tea. There was no way she could eat all of it.

"Your body is. Healing takes a lot of energy. If you don't, it'll take longer, and if we're going to keep your cover and get you back to normal life without anyone commenting on your injuries, you'll finish it." She smiled a little. "I can eat as much as a teenage boy when I'm healing. Ben reminds me of it every day."

Joanna didn't reply. She wouldn't give Alex the satisfaction of replying. Instead, she looked over at the clock on the nightstand. It now read 3:00 p.m. An hour had passed as she stewed in her rage at Damianos. Losing time only made it worse.

"We'll be going home tomorrow," Alex said. "If you feel up to the drive."

Jo didn't comment, but she looked at Alex. Their eyes met, and Jo managed a nod.

"I'll be back later to collect the tray. Get some more rest." She put a hand on Jo's uninjured shoulder in a motherly manner for a moment and then left the room.

Jo eyed the tray and couldn't resist a slice of bacon. She devoured it in two bites and then dived into the rest of the food.

CHAPTER THIRTY-THREE

ALEX SAT ON A LARGE ROCK ON THE SMALL BEACH ON her property and watched the waves crash on the shore. The wild, turbulent sea was the perfect remedy for the jumble of emotions inside her. Anger and grief lessened the more the water smashed into the shore. She imagined her emotions ebbing away with the surf.

A part of her missed the warm waters of the Mediterranean, but the tempestuous cold waters of the North Atlantic were well-suited to her current mood. White foam floated near rocks, and the slate-blue water churned. Dark clouds lined the horizon, moving fast. They promised a summer storm. Moisture hung heavily in the air.

She took a deep breath and slowly released it. Munchkin nudged her right arm, and Alex brought her hand up and scratched him behind an ear. He licked her cheek. She smiled despite the layer of slobber on her face.

Munchkin turned his head away, and a deep growl rumbled from him. Alex listened and recognized the pattern of footsteps. The dog growled again, and Alex put a steadying hand on his head.

"It's okay," she assured the dog. This moment was a long time coming, and there was no more avoiding it. She turned around. A peal of thunder accompanied Damianos's arrival. He flashed her a small smile and held out his hands.

Alex eyed the offered hands for a moment and then put hers in his. He pulled, and she rose to her feet. He tugged her in against his body and kissed her as the first droplets of rain fell. The kiss ended, and he slipped an arm around her waist. He turned her toward the house.

"Come inside," he urged as the clouds broke open and heavy rain fell from above.

Alex nodded and walked with him toward the house. Wind whipped the rain, driving it into their faces. There was no need to hurry—it was just rain. They both had been through worse in their long lives. Munchkin ran ahead of them.

They were thoroughly soaked through by the time they entered the mudroom. Munchkin, who had entered in front of them, took the opportunity to shake the water from his heavy coat. It went everywhere, soaking them even more. He walked out of the mudroom, leaving the two humans.

Alex laughed and shook her head. The dog had a habit of drenching her after their nightly walk of the grounds in the rain. Alex closed the door separating the mudroom and the kitchen, and she looked at Damianos.

"Strip," she ordered. A smirk appeared on his face, and a twinkle in his dark eyes. Alex rolled hers. "I don't want you dripping water through the house."

"Uh-huh." His grin widened.

Alex sighed and reached for a towel from a shelf over the washer and threw it at him. It hit him square in the face, and she smiled. She peeled off her wet clothes and took another towel for herself.

"How's the girl?"

"Good, I suppose. She hasn't come out of her apartment for the past two days." She paused in drying her arms. "I'm concerned."

"Have you gone in there?"

Alex shook her head. "No. I'm giving her some space. She has a lot to process. I'll check on her tomorrow if she doesn't show her face."

He nodded. "Now, we're going to talk."

Once dried off, Alex grabbed a robe from a hook and slipped it on, tying it at the waist. She looked at him. He finished drying off and stood there in all his naked glory. His long past was written in the scars marring his skin. Alex looked at the one running horizontal across his stomach. It was the largest and most prominent. Her throat tightened at how she almost lost him to the Spear of Destiny.

Not that she didn't appreciate the view, she really did, but dry clothing was a floor away, and she didn't need him parading through the house bare-assed. She tilted her head toward him and waited. He grinned and wrapped the towel around his waist, tucking it in at the top.

Satisfied, Alex opened the door to the kitchen and led him out of the mudroom. The conversation they were about to have required privacy. As long as there were others living in the house, the only privacy she could count on was in her room.

They made their way up to Alex's room on the second floor without seeing Mike or Ben. The boys only showed their faces when it was time to eat. They had both gone out with friends a few times, but most of their time they spent on the third floor playing video games. Their brush with mortality seemed to draw the brothers closer together.

Damianos closed the door behind him. Alex turned to face him, her arms crossed over her chest, and waited. He took two steps toward her, and she took two away from him. If he touched her, they wouldn't get any talking done. He wanted to talk, so they were going to talk.

"Talk," she commanded. He sighed, and it brought a slight smile to her face. She loved frustrating him as much as he did her. "You wanted to talk, so talk."

"Fine. I want you to give us an honest chance. I've been waiting for seventy-five years." She didn't respond, letting him continue talking. "I'm tired of being on the road. I want to come in from the cold to you. I want you to be the first thing I see in the morning and the last thing I see before I go to sleep."

Alex bit back a comment about how a picture would fulfill the requirement. Humor or snark wasn't exactly called for in this situation.

"I love you. I always have. Can we call a truce in this battle for a little while?"

"Yes."

He blinked and pulled back a bit. "Yes?"

"Yes. I know you're never going to drop this subject if I don't say yes. I'm tired of fighting with you. And no matter how much I deny it, I do love you. I always have." And at times she hated herself for it, but she could never stop. "But this doesn't mean I'm done being mad at you for what you did. Forgiveness won't come easily."

He closed the distance between them and wrapped his arms around her. "I love you."

The last pieces of resistance faded away in the warmth of his love, and Alex unfolded her arms, wrapping them around his waist. He'd ruined her for others. No one affected her like he did, and no one ever would.

He lowered his head and lightly kissed her. She smiled against his mouth.

"I love you," she whispered in their native tongue, the Ionic dialect of Ancient Greek. She looked into his eyes and drowned in the dark depths.

He smiled and captured her mouth with his. Alex returned the kiss. He would break her heart again in the future, but tonight was theirs, and she would take advantage of it.

CHAPTER THIRTY-FOUR

JO WAS STRETCHED OUT ON THE COUCH, MINDLESSLY watching TV, when someone knocked at the door. She knew it wasn't Mike. He'd left hours ago talking about meeting Greg to hang out. Besides, Mike only knocked the one time to see if she was okay, and promptly forgot he knew how. Ben always knocked. She wished he could train Mike to do it. Carrie was still with her family and would have called Jo to let her know she was coming home. Greg would have called first. It had to be Alex. She knew Alex wouldn't stay away forever, and she was surprised it had taken three days for her to show up. Jo had expected her much earlier.

"Come in," she called.

She sat up as the door opened, and Alex entered. Now that everything was over, Alex had discarded jeans and a blouse for the long flowing dresses she favored. No matter what Alex wore, she always looked elegant. Maybe Jo could master that talent in a century or two.

"Thought I'd come check on you." Alex looked her over, trying not to be obvious about it, but Jo knew better. "We haven't seen you in the house yet."

"I'm fine. I just needed some time alone. I can change my own bandages."

"I know, and I understand. Do you need anything?"

"No. I'm good."

"Okay. If you need anything, all you have to do is ask."

"I know."

Alex lingered in the doorway, and Joanna thought she was going to say something about what happened, but she didn't. She turned to leave.

"Alex?"

The woman stopped. "Yes?"

"Why did Damianos give the serum to me and not Mike?" Jo reached for the remote and clickedoff the television. Serious talks didn't need background noise.

Alex paused before answering. "I don't know for certain, but he probably counted on Woodville believing that I had more of an emotional attachment to you because you were a girl. Maybe Damianos thought I would as well. I don't think he counted on Mike following and getting involved. He had you and wanted to make sure nothing happened to you. As much of a pain in the ass that man can be, he does try."

"Oh." Joanna was quiet before she asked her next question. "Can a person become mortal again? If I wanted to think about it." Immortality was a daunting thought, something she wasn't sure she was ready to take on.

Alex sat down on the couch next to Jo and placed her hands on her lap. "Honestly, I don't know if yours can. In theory, I suppose it could. I'm not certain how the elixir works on the body, but some chemical processes can be reversed."

"Oh." She slumped. "You know Mike will want to become immortal too. Maybe even Ben." Jo had to point it out. They both knew her brothers well enough. Them asking to be made immortal was just a matter of time.

"I know. I'll have to cross that bridge when we get to it. Which brings up a very important point. I cannot stress this enough. Never tell anyone, including other immortals, how you became this way. If it can be reversed, someone will use it against you."

Jo tilted her head. "Not a big happy family, huh?"

Alex grimaced. "Not at all."

"That's why you wouldn't say what it was that you stole to get cursed."

"Exactly. We don't tell, and we don't ask other immortals."

"So it's one of those things you shouldn't bring up in conversation, like religion or politics?"

"Something like that. A person's state of being is highly personal, and it's considered rude to ask. Everyone has a right to privacy. Also, don't tell anyone outside your brothers, Carrie, and Greg about your immortality. They are already a risk to you, not because they would tell, but because they might give it away by mistake. Do you remember how Mike revealed Damianos's immortality to Woodville?"

"Yes."

"Anyone who knows your secret is a liability," Alex said. "If Damianos had been as evil as he was trying to appear, Mike's life would be in danger now. People will do anything to be immortal and will use you to gain an advantage if they can. Some will kill to protect their secret. Trust very few people."

Jo nodded. She had the nightmares to prove it. She had yet to sleep without recent events playing through her dreams like a movie stuck on repeat. She assumed the nightmares would fade away. She just wanted it to be sooner rather than later.

"I will have a talk with the others," Alex assured her. "They will need to know the importance of keeping your secret and how doing so protects them. Greg, I don't worry about. He knows firsthand what happens when secrets get out."

Alex's words slowly sank into her brain. Alex had trusted her parents with her secret, and they had never uttered a word to them. Alex placed her trust in them along with Greg and Carrie when she revealed her immortality to them the night of the attack. It spoke volumes about Alex and what she did, and what she might do if someone became a liability. Mike had shown himself to be a liability, even if he thought it was for the best reasons.

"Can we be killed?" Jo asked. She had a million questions racing through her brain but decided to get the big ones out of the way first. "The word immortal kind of suggests we can't."

"That's wordplay. Left alone, we can literally live forever. We won't get sick, but we'll age a little. A powerful weapon can kill an immortal. Some injuries will prevent our ability to regenerate. And before you ask, I've never tested decapitation or know someone who did."

"You mean like a nuclear bomb?" Joa didn't want to ask for specifics on injuries. Knowing Alex, she would go into graphic details. The description of scaphism and the images conjured up still lingered in her head.

"I suspect your clever friend Carrie has been asking questions and making you think. Jo, not everything in the vault are just pretty things I've collected through the years. There are objects and weapons that hold power, and some are even powerful enough to kill an immortal. Durendal, the Spear of Destiny, and a few others. There are other items that, while they can't kill an immortal, can cause a lot of harm. That's why they're in the vault and locked away."

"Which is why you didn't want us down there."

A faraway look settled in Alex's gray eyes, and she nodded. "If some of those things fall into the wrong hands, our world would be at risk."

"Alex?"

Alex's attention came back to Jo. Those gray eyes were now rimmed with sadness. "Sorry. I drifted off there for a moment. I've seen what powerful weapons can do to us and to others. I watched an immortal die by the Spear, and it's something I can't ever forget."

Jo wasn't as smart as Carrie, but even she had heard of the Spear of Destiny before Woodville talked about it. It was probably during one of the fantasy movies Mike liked to watch. "Damianos mentioned the Spear when he—well, it was mentioned. Did he kill them?"

"No. I did."

Jo blinked, surprised at the admission. She hadn't been expecting that answer or the truth for that matter. "Who were they?"

"He was someone I loved for a very long time."

Jo now knew how difficult it was to take another life, but she couldn't imagine taking the life of someone she loved, like her brothers or possibly Greg. Although she wouldn't say she was in love with Greg. At least not this soon. "Is the Spear in the vault?"

"No. When the war was over, I gave it to someone who can protect it. I did not want to be trusted with such a powerful weapon."

"You said you didn't care." The elephant lurked in the room, and it had to be acknowledged. "Back when Woodville had us. You lied."

"Yes, I lied. He was not going to let any of us walk out of there, but I had to try to convince him you and Mike weren't going to be the leverage he'd hoped. Tell me, what would you do or say if Mike or Ben's life were in danger?"

"Anything," Jo answered without hesitation.

"Why?"

"Because they are all I have left, and I would do anything to protect them."

"I am sorry I had to do it, and I'm sorry it upset you. It was a horrific situation, and you had been through the worst, but protecting the three of you is my top priority right now. I love all of you as if you were my own blood. Your parents were family to me, and I will mourn their deaths for a long time. Taking care of you is the least I can do to honor their memories." She tenderly moved a lock of hair from Jo's eyes.

Jo didn't respond.

"As for the lying, everyone lies, but immortals more so. Our lives are all lies. We lie about our age, where we're from, and even our names. It's a part of who we are, so you had better get very good at it. You will lie so much that sometimes it's hard to tell the truth from the lies. Finding people you don't have to lie to is priceless, and you treasure them. Like I did with your parents. Your family was the first I've gotten close to in decades."

Jo nodded, understanding the weight of Alex's words. "I'm sorry for what I said to you."

Alex patted her arm. "It's okay. It was a horrible situation, and your feelings at the time were valid. You thought I betrayed you and didn't care."

Jo remembered all the anger and hatred she held for Alex in those moments. Now she realized that it had been a foolish endeavor. She should have had more faith in the Alex she had known since her birth.

"How often do we have to change our names?"

"I usually assume a new identity every twenty years or so. In these times, we can go a little longer and blame cosmetic surgery. Long ago, it was every ten to twenty years, and it only required moving to the other side of a very large city. People physically aged quickly and died so young."

"How does one even change an identity?"

"It's complicated and expensive, but if you know the right people, it can be done. It was much easier in the past." Alex waved her hand in a little gesture, as if changing an identity wasn't a big thing. "I will help you when it's time for you to assume a new one."

"Thanks." Jo couldn't imagine being anyone else. How did one just drop a life and assume another? She hardly knew who she was now. Maybe that would make it easier. "Is it hard being immortal?"

"It can be," Alex admitted. "It can be very hard at times. The hardest part is watching everyone around you grow old and die. You'll fall in love and then watch them age before your eyes. Your heart will break, but you'll do it all again because the alternative is much worse. You'll have so many names and identities that eventually you barely recognize your birth name, and sometimes you wonder who you really are. It's not all bad, though. You'll get to see and do so much, the bad becomes bearable. Sometimes I look around me and I'm truly amazed at the things I see."

Jo remained quiet while Alex's words sank in. The realization of what the woman had lived through for thousands of years made Jo feel sorry for her. Before talking to Alex, Jo wouldn't have thought of living forever as a curse. Everyone dreamed of living forever at some point in their lives, Jo being no exception. Now she had a glimpse of the other side. Alex's sad expression when Damianos told her what he had done for Jo made sense. "Is there a chance for a normal life?"

"No, but you can have periods of normalcy. Work. Fall in love, get married, have children. You don't have to live alone or become a hermit."

"Have you—" Jo stopped, unsure how to ask.

"Yes. I've been married several times and I've had children. Even one with Damianos during the 1700s." A slight smile appeared on her face. "Not recently though. Don't believe those movies Mike and Ben are so fond of. They didn't inherit my curse."

"They'll be crushed nothing in the movies is accurate." Jo grinned. She had to be the one to tell them.

"Most likely."

Silence settled over the room for a moment. The events of the past few days played out in Jo's head like a movie, but one part always stood out more than the rest. She had to address it, but she wasn't sure she really wanted to. "I killed someone," she said quietly.

"Yes, and you shouldn't regret it. He would have spent the remainder of his life coming after us. It was self-defense. You did the right thing." Alex patted Jo's thigh.

"I killed him in anger."

"You saved Mike's life. I didn't want you and Mike there, but you were both too stubborn. You wouldn't have to live with this had you listened to instructions. Once you take a life, things are never the same."

Jo nodded. At the time, she thought the old man deserved to be killed. But now, since she had time to think about it, she knew they could have walked out of there. Alex had even told her to walk away before she pulled the trigger. She didn't like the person she had been at that moment, and she promised herself she would never be that person again.

"There are some roads you walk down that you can't come back from," Alex said in a low voice.

Jo nodded, understanding what Alex meant. She would have to live with what she had done forever. "Have you killed many people?"

"I kill only when it's necessary, but the numbers add up in twenty-four hundred years."

"Who was Woodville?"

Alex remained silent for a long moment. Almost to the point of being uncomfortable. "He was an assistant to Karl Gebhardt, Heinrich Himmler's personal physician. I don't remember Woodville well, but there were a lot of people around Himmler. He probably changed his name to blend in, and age changes a person enough that you don't recognize them from their younger selves. With a lot of thought, I could probably remember his real name, but I try not to think too much of my time with the Nazis and the war."

"That's when you were a spy, right?" Jo had learned of World

War II in history classes and couldn't imagine what it would have been like to be behind enemy lines and to be around evil people like Himmler. Woodville mentioned Alex being Himmler's mistress. Joanna also couldn't imagine having to sleep with someone so evil.

"Yes, one of the few times I was a spy. A good number of us were. Immortality doesn't take our humanity and sense of right and wrong if we already had it. If anything, history told us what would follow, so we did what we could do to stop the spread of Hitler and his armies."

"Mike thought you were a spy." Looking back, it was funny then, not so funny now. "I told him he was an idiot."

"He was probably thinking of something a little more modern. I haven't done anything like that since 1945."

"How many of us are out there?"

Alex smiled slightly when Jo said *us*. "I know twelve immortals, including Damianos. There are more out there. I just haven't met them all. We tend to keep to ourselves, and we don't go around announcing our status."

"What happened between you and Damianos?"

"He was the reason I stole from the temple and ran away at seventeen. Two years later, he left me. I was nineteen, a woman, and left all alone in a world that treated females like property." Alex shrugged as if it wasn't a big deal, but judging by the way her face tightened when she said it, Jo knew Damianos had hurt her deeply. "The temple was my entire world, but he represented freedom to me. He was my first love. Because of what I did, I was cursed to live until I returned what I had stolen. He was cursed to live as long as I do."

It sounded like a plot from one of the romance novels her mother used to read. It explained so much, but it created a million more questions. "Do you still love him?"

Alex was quiet for a few long moments before she answered. "It's not as easy as a yes or no answer."

"But you still have feelings for him," Jo pointed out. A blind person could see Alex still loved him but just didn't want to say it.

"Yes," Alex admitted. "There are times when I feel like that foolish seventeen-year-old girl, and there are other times when I want to see if it's possible to kill him."

"So, in other words, it's complicated."

Alex smiled. "Very."

"Victoria doesn't seem to like him much."

"The first time they met, he was stealing something of hers and he shot her. He couldn't have known what she was, and that set the whole tone of their relationship. Victoria holds a grudge for a very long time."

"He would say he did know."

"He would. We will never know the truth. She chooses to believe he didn't. Even if she weren't immortal, the shot wouldn't have killed her. Damianos knows how to injure and not kill. It was probably the first time her immortal life was called into question, and that can be a hard thing to reconcile. The two of them aren't always hostile to one another, but when they are, it's at the moment she needs something else to focus on."

Just like he shot Jo. They were a club of two. "But still, I can't imagine liking someone who shot you."

"It happens on occasion. You get so angry with someone that you just shoot them. You know they won't die, but you're so mad that you can't help it. Damianos and I have shot each other many times over the long centuries." Alex shrugged. "It's nothing for us."

"Don't tell Mike or Ben. I don't need them shooting me when I make them mad."

"I won't, but it's a different world for them. It wouldn't be their first impulse if they're mad at you." Alex smiled, but the smile didn't last. It faded as quickly as it had appeared. "Joanna, I am sorry for all that has happened. I never wanted any of you to be hurt or get caught up in anything related to my complicated life. Now you're twenty-three and immortal. It's a lot of weight to carry."

"I'm okay, Alex," Jo assured her. "I can handle this. What did Woodville mean when he said *we*?"

"An investigation is in progress. We believe he was part of a group of people that shouldn't still exist. I don't want you or your brothers to worry about it. It would have been safer for you all if your parents had chosen a better guardian."

"I've been thinking about that too. I can see why they did it now. Life is dangerous, and they wanted somebody who knew how to fight back and survive."

"I've spent a long time fighting back. You have a lot to learn, and that is only one lesson."

"Good." Jo's voice hardened. "I am never going to be helpless because someone decided to use me for their own reasons."

Alex smiled. "That's the perfect attitude to have. I can't always protect you, but I can teach you to protect yourself. I will also teach you when it's time to do a strategic retreat."

"So run away?"

"Strategic retreat sounds better than running away."

"Mike and Ben too," Jo added.

Alex nodded. "Of course. They need to learn how to protect themselves as well. We cannot allow another incident like this to happen."

"Speaking of learning to protect myself, what does it take to join the SPD?"

A brief frown appeared on Alex's face but disappeared quickly. "Damianos would be able to answer that question. Were you thinking about it?"

Jo nodded. "Me and Mike." Though to even talk to Damianos, she'd have to work through the fact he drugged and kidnapped her. Not to mention being a complete ass while she was being held.

"What about going back to Boulder?"

Jo realized she hadn't thought about Boulder in days. It was another lifetime ago. "I don't know. I'm not sure if it's for me anymore. It seems like there's so much more out there than a normal life, and Boulder seems as small as Good Harbor now."

"I understand. I can help you adjust to being an immortal, if you want. You always have a place to live here."

Jo took a deep breath and nodded. Weight disappeared from her shoulders. She really did feel better about the future. "I know. What else should I know about being an immortal? What's the secret to life?"

Alex was silent for a long moment before answering. "There's quite a bit, but we have time. I've helped a few adjust to their new lives, and I can help you. As for the secret to life, it's different for everyone. For me, there are three important things. Let yourself love. Laugh when you can. Otherwise you'll go insane. And learn as much as you can."

"Learn? I just left college."

"College is good, but it doesn't give you the experiences you'll need now. Never stop learning. People, places, and events all have something to teach you. Being old doesn't mean you know everything there is to know. Languages are a good place to start."

"That's amazing. How many do you know?" Joanna asked.

Alex had to think about it. "I've lost count. Some are no longer spoken, and I'm sure there are some emerging dialects I could study. But right now, you can focus on figuring out what you want to do. We have plenty of time for everything else."

"Is Damianos going to stay with us?"

A deep sigh escaped Alex. "For a little while. Just to make sure no one else is coming after us or the Sullivans."

"Better to be safe than sorry." They could be in for a good show. There was always entertainment when Alex and Damianos were involved.

"Something like that."

"Do you think he'll answer questions about the SPD?"

"I can't say for certain, but I think he will. He can be unpredictable."

"I bet he says the same about you."

Alex smiled. Unpredictable was never a word he threw at her during their arguments. Stubbornness was his go-to accusation. "Any more questions for me?"

Jo suspected they would have many more talks in the future. "A lot, but I need some time to process all of this before asking more." And continue letting go of the anger she still held. It was hard. She could win an Olympic event in angry grudges, although it seemed that compared to Victoria, Jo was an amateur. Perhaps Victoria would give a master class in the subject.

Alex smiled and pulled Jo in for a hug. Jo wrapped her arms around Alex and squeezed. The tight hug was exactly what Jo needed. Alex released Jo and kissed her forehead before making her way to the door.

"Alex?"

She paused in the doorway. "Yes?"

"Tell me you don't have a nuclear bomb in the vault?"

Alex gave her a smile but didn't answer the question. "I was thinking we'd go out to dinner tonight. Would you like to go with us? If not, we can bring something back for you."

Jo thought about it for a moment. Three days inside the apartment, and she'd have to admit that it was starting to feel like the walls were closing in on her. And she didn't want to cook. All the small kitchen had left was a box of microwave popcorn and the meals Alex had provided over the last couple of days in the fridge. Being cooped up got old fast. Life getting back to normal might help chase the nightmares away. If she got bored at dinner, she could always glare at Damianos across the table. She might come up with some useful ideas for revenge when she finally took it. At least she would learn some new curses as he suggested.

"I'll go," she said.

"We're going to leave at five thirty." Alex slipped out the door and closed it behind her.

Jo sat back on the sofa, processing the conversation and the realities of her new life as she listened to Alex's footsteps on the stairs. There could be some advantages to immortality.

CHAPTER THIRTY-FIVE

JOANNA PAUSED AT THE BACK DOOR WITH HER HAND ON the doorknob. Was she ready for this? Was she ready for life to resume? She was positive about it all the way down the stairs and across the deck. Now she had second thoughts. It would start the moment she opened the door and stepped into the main house. She still had the opportunity to retreat to the apartment and delay her new life for another day. Maybe two. She knew Alex wouldn't let her hide in the apartment for much longer, but did she want it to begin right now? That was the million-dollar question.

The old Jo would charge in headfirst, complaining all the way, but the old Jo was gone, and she wasn't missed. The new Jo had survived a drugged kidnapping, being made immortal, and getting shot. Her next challenge was forgiveness, but Damianos may be damned forever. At least for a century or two. She liked Victoria's attitude and name for him. She was going to use it until the next time he scared the crap out of her.

How weird it was to think in terms of centuries rather than years.

Voices drifted through the door. There were more voices than normal. She smiled when she recognized them and peeked in the window. Mike, Ben, Alex, Damianos, Greg, and Carrie were gathered in the kitchen. Despite plans to go out for dinner, Mike and Ben were eating sandwiches, of course, because they wouldn't last the ride to a restaurant. Even Greg was eating something.

She turned the knob, opened the door, and stepped inside. Warmth spilled over her. The feeling of home welled up inside. It was exactly what she needed. It was in that moment she knew she wouldn't be returning to Boulder. Her family and her life for the foreseeable future existed here in Good Harbor.

The conversation stopped as their faces turned toward her.

She gave them a little wave. "Um, hi."

Carrie moved first, rushing over to throw her arms around Jo for a hug. Greg was right behind her.

"I missed you!" Carrie said. "I'm so glad you're okay. Mike told us what happened, and I can't believe you're a, um, one of them now."

"I'm okay," Jo assured them all. As much as she thought she didn't want to be around people, seeing Carrie and Greg changed her mind. They made things seem more normal than they had been in the past few days. "Alex says getting shot is a rite of passage."

"I said that," Damianos grumbled. Jo ignored him.

"No more rites, no matter what they are," Carrie told her firmly.

"What she said," Greg told her. "Otherwise, we'll have to lock you in your apartment.

Jo returned the hug and felt better with each passing moment. She was home and surrounded by the people she cared about. Well, except for Damianos. She might care about him in the future, but she wasn't going to hold her breath. "I'm surprised to see you here," she said to Greg.

"I invited Greg and Carrie to dinner with us," Alex said.

Damianos stood behind her. Their eyes met and hers narrowed. He gave her a curt nod.

"You have to tell us everything," Carrie said, cheerfully breaking the brief tense moment. "Leaving nothing out."

Greg slipped an arm around her waist. Jo nodded. "Of course."

"And every little detail," Carrie added.

Jo glanced at Damianos and then looked back at Carrie. She wasn't going to repeat every detail. Not for a long time. "Okay."

Carrie seemed to realize she sounded bossy. "Sorry," she said apologetically, "but I have to live vicariously through you. I've already started a new notebook on it!"

"It's okay," Jo assured her. She leaned into Greg. "Where are we going for dinner?"

"I was going to leave that to you," Alex said. "Anywhere in Freeport or Brunswick you want to go."

"Can we go to that Tuscan place in Freeport?" Jo asked. It was an Italian restaurant they had been to many times before and had enough food choices for everyone.

"Yes, we can," Alex said.

Carrie beamed. "I love that place!"

Joa knew Carrie loved the restaurant. It was part of the reason she chose it. A new life also gave her perspective on the people she loved. She wanted to do something nice for her friend, and this was the perfect opportunity. Now that she knew Alex really didn't have to worry about money, she didn't feel bad for opting for a pricey place. Alex could afford to take all of them out and then some.

Mike walked over to her, wrapped his arms around her, and lifted her off her feet.

She hit his shoulder when he didn't release her before hugging him back. "Let me go, dork," she grumbled.

Mike laughed and set her back down on her feet.

She had her brothers with her, a potential serious boyfriend, and a best friend. It was a good ending to a terrible episode. She wasn't sure she wanted to see what was next in her life. At least right now. Maybe she'd be ready in a few months.

"Are we ready to go?" Alex asked.

"I hope so. I'm hungry," Mike moaned as he clutched his middle in mock pain. Jo rolled her eyes.

"I'm starving," Ben complained. "Do I have time to make another sandwich to eat on the way?"

Jo just shook her head. "I think we're ready. They might waste away to nothing if they don't stuff themselves with carbs soon."

"Good!" Mike said and headed for the front door. Carrie was on his heels, followed by Ben, Alex, and Damianos.

Greg guided her toward the door with his arm still around her waist. A whole new, very strange world awaited her, and she was eager to embrace it, later. For now, she just had to pretend to be normal. That might be the hardest part, but she'd give it a try.

Thank you for reading! Did you enjoy? Please add your review because nothing helps an author more and encourages readers to take a chance on a book than a review.

And don't miss more from Sydney Ashcroft and Dani Nichols with CHASING DESTINY available now! Turn the page for a sneak peek!

Also be sure to sign up for the City Owl Press newsletter to receive notice of all book releases!

SNEAK PEEK OF CHASING DESTINY

Berlin, Germany 1941

Sometimes, the call of angels demanded sacrifice, and this was the second time Akantha was deep within the heart of Germany during a world war. Akantha, now known as Alexis Rowland, had many jobs in the past twenty-four hundred years, but this was by far the worst and her least favorite. Two years as a spy in Nazi Germany wasn't glamorous, but it was necessary if the Allies had a chance of winning the war.

Voices drifted in from the open windows near the ceiling, and Akantha paused in photographing documents containing sensitive information. Other people in the offices at this time of the night was not an uncommon thing, but she recognized both voices and continued to listen. Himmler spoke freely when he thought no one else was around. Not everything was on the classified papers she looked at daily, and every bit of information helped.

"We have a spy problem," Karl Wolff, adjutant to Himmler, said. Thoughts of watching the life pour out of both men always brought a small smile to her face. "Our couriers carrying orders for the commanders for Operation Barbarossa were ambushed. We assume the information is now in the hands of the enemy. "

"Enemy spies are a hazard of war," Himmler responded. What would he think if he knew one sat in the next room listening? She allowed herself the briefest of smiles.

"Yes, but this one is quite concerning. The mission was top

secret and very few individuals were aware of the couriers' missions. The whole eastern operation could be in jeopardy."

Akantha's heart raced in her chest and blood thundered in her ears, drowning out the soft whoosh of the fan overhead. As Himmler's secretary, she was allowed access to the most sensitive information, and she passed it along to the resistance and Allied forces. Did they suspect her? The fear of being discovered sat in her stomach like a rock—cold, hard, and immovable.

"This is serious," Himmler agreed. "We need to find this person immediately. This is something that will reach the Führer, and I must answer to him. Who had access to this information?"

"You, me, your secretary, and three others."

Panic welled up, creating a lump in her throat, but she forced herself to remain calm. Panicking never solved anything and usually produced disastrous results. She'd stay calm and find a way to cast suspicion off her. It wouldn't take them long to find out she passed the information on to the Special Operations Executive if she didn't keep it together.

"I want you to ferret out this spy and bring him to me. I will deal with him personally."

"Of course, sir. Will this impact our plans for Russia?"

"I do not believe so."

Akantha looked at the papers and folders on the desk in front of her. She brought the camera up but stopped when she heard them continue.

"Our troops continue to move through Italy," Wolff reported. "A spear is rumored to be in the Vatican. Mussolini is cooperating with our search, though he is not aware of what we are searching for."

"Good. Acquiring the spear is our number one priority at the moment," Himmler replied. "Legends say it holds unimaginable power and can shape the fate of the world. I am confident the *Ahnenerbe* will find it. It's imperative we have it, even if we have to bring every spear we find back to Germany."

She sat down in the wooden chair and gripped the armrests, her knuckles turning white. The last thing the world needed was the Nazis getting their hands on the Spear of Destiny. They couldn't be talking about anything else. Himmler was obsessed with the occult and had sent teams all over the world searching for legendary, even mythical, objects. Others would have to pass information on to the SOE. Akantha had a new mission.

"Understood, sir," Wolff replied. "What about the one from Vienna?"

"I don't believe it's the true spear. Something so powerful, so important, would not be kept in such an obvious place."

"The Führer thinks it is the true spear."

Silence roared and each tick of the clock on the wall lasted an eternity.

"It is not." A chill froze her spine and her stomach twisted into a Gordian knot. Did he know more than he let on?

"Herr Holtz believes it is elsewhere."

Her heart pounded as she waited for Himmler to respond. "Herr Holtz will take as many troops as he needs. I want any rumored to be the true spear brought to Wewelsburg. With the Spear of Destiny in our hands, we will be unstoppable."

"It shall be done."

"How goes the search for the other items?" Himmler asked.

Other items? Fear wrapped icy hands around her heart. A myriad of weapons rumored to have power existed, and the Nazis getting their hands on any of them was unimaginable. It was bad enough bullets, bombs and tanks caused death on a scale unprecedented in history, but now the Nazis were looking for items that could alter the world in unfathomable ways. Millions would die. Tens of millions. Her own immortal existence was threatened as well, along with the existence of people she had known for centuries.

"The search continues, but so far we haven't been able to find any of the other items."

"I had hoped the news would be better. The summer solstice approaches and I would like to have all the items in our possession by then."

"We will have them."

"Good."

Silence settled over the two rooms and she wondered if they had left. The door to the office opened and Himmler's form filled the doorway. His head tilted to the side when he spotted her sitting at his desk. "Alexis? It's late. What are you doing in here?"

She slid her hands into the pockets of her jacket as casually as she could, slipping the small Minox Riga in. "It's only nine. I was going over your schedule for tomorrow and organizing all the paperwork for you to review." Despite the pounding in her chest and thundering in her ears, she kept a calm outward appearance. She placed her hands on the desk, hoping he didn't take notice of how they shook. This wasn't the first time he had walked in on her going through papers, looking for information. The prepared response slipped past her lips as natural as breathing.

Akantha took the position of Himmler's secretary when Hedwig Potthast left. A few months passed before she could get into his bed, but the invaluable information she collected made her personal sacrifices worth something. She played the good little Nazi and was paid in valuable information she then passed along to SOE contacts. Even in the heart of Berlin, people resisted Nazi rule.

"You work too much, my dear." He moved around the desk to stand next to her. Her eyes rose to meet his smiling face.

"Your schedule is complex and takes time to organize. Working odd hours isn't unheard of for either of us."

He nodded. "Yes, we do tend to work around the clock."

"You're too important to the cause for me to allow you to fail." The bitter words came out seamlessly across her tongue. Boosting his ego always worked to take his mind off what she was doing.

The last thing she needed was him questioning why she was going through papers containing sensitive information.

"Everyone must contribute to the cause as they can," he said. "I do what I can." Himmler smiled benevolently.

"I left a copy of tomorrow's schedule on your desk."

"Did you put in a few hours in the afternoon tomorrow for me to visit my family?"

"Of course," she answered. His plans presented her with the opportunity to sneak out of Berlin and start looking for the spear. Akantha usually used the time when he went to visit his wife, or his other mistress, to meet her contact in Berlin and pass information along to the Allies. It was dangerous, but she enjoyed the thrill.

He held out a hand to her.

Breathing deeply, she gathered her courage. Tyranny, like hell, was not easily conquered. She remembered reading Thomas Paine's words back in 1776 during the dawn of the American Revolution. A long time had passed, but the words still rang true. Hitler, with the backing of the juggernaut of the German army, was a tyrant and needed to be stopped. Placing her hand in his, she rose from the chair. She forced a smile as he stepped closer. His head lowered and his mouth covered hers.

Her stomach churned from the false intimacy and she fought to keep from pulling away. Revulsion welled up every time he touched her. Screwing her courage to the sticking place, she returned the kiss.

A slight sigh slipped past her lips when the kiss ended. Every moment around him was a test of self-control and every time he touched her she wanted to take a long bath and scrub her skin raw. "It's time we should be out of here and in bed," he whispered. Sex was a useful tool to get information and one she didn't mind using even if it meant cozying up with the enemy. She may regret sleeping with him for a century or two, but if it helped stop the Nazis it would be worth the burden of regret.

"Yes, it is," she agreed while thinking of interesting ways to kill him. One day he would die a slow and painful death by her hand and she would enjoy every second of it.

"Then come," he said as he brought her hand up and placed a kiss on her knuckles.

The door squeaked behind them and hope welled up. With luck he would be pulled away for the evening and she would be able to slip away earlier than planned.

He turned on his heel and faced the source. Akantha looked around Himmler, spotting a low-ranking officer. "I apologize for the interruption. Herr Holtz is downstairs."

"Very well," Himmler said. "I will go down and see him now."

The officer saluted and disappeared from the doorway. Himmler turned back to face her. "It seems our immediate plans are to be postponed."

She feigned disappointment. "Duties always come first."

"Yes, but I would rather keep our plans."

A genuine smile appeared on her face. Let him think it was for their 'plans', but it was more relief. She wouldn't have to tolerate his vile touch tonight. "As would I."

"I must see to Herr Holtz." He turned toward the door, took one step, and stopped. He turned back to her. "Come with me," he said and held out his hand.

"Is there something you require?" She straightened her uniform, looking every inch the loyal Nazi she was supposed to be.

"No, but I would like you by my side."

She regarded him for a long moment and nodded. Did he suspect something? He never had qualms about leaving her alone in his office. Nervously she wiped the palms of her hands on her skirt. She followed him out of the office.

The spacious building in the heart of Berlin functioned as the headquarters of the SS and it housed some of the top officers. Although Himmler had a private house in the suburbs for his family, he rarely stayed there. Instead, he stayed as close to Hitler and the center of power as he could. Despite the late hour, bright lights reflected off the polished marble of the floor. Plush carpet ran down the middle of the hall and stolen works of art adorned the walls. The looted paintings spoke to the art lover in her, and her fingers itched to tear them off the walls and return them to their rightful owners. The thought of the Nazis looting museums and stealing from people was another thing to hold against them. She clenched her hands into fists as she imagined reaching out and strangling the man walking in front of her.

She followed him through the building and ignored the few people they passed. They all gave Himmler a wide berth and looked past her. She preferred it that way. It allowed her to move more freely and gather much-needed information. She followed him and froze in the doorway when she saw the individual standing in the center of the room.

Six hundred years ago, when she had a different life and name, she first saw his face, but it cut through the present and let the past rush back in a torrent. "Matheus," she whispered as her heart skipped a beat.

Don't stop now. Keep reading with your copy of CHASING DESTINY.

And sign up for the latest news, giveaways, and more from Sydney Ashcroft and Dani Nichols at www.nicholsandashcroft.com

Don't miss more from Sydney Ashcroft and Dani Nichols
with CHASING DESTINY available now

If there was anything Akantha hated more than the Nazis, it was Damianos.

For twenty-four hundred years, Akantha has dedicated her life to defending mortals from destruction, yet the Nazis are determined not just to rule the world but destroy it. Working as a spy for one of Hitler's highest ranking officers, she learns that the Nazis are set to get their hands on the ultimate weapon, the Spear of Destiny. She will need the help of the one man she hoped she'd never see again to stop them.

Loving Damianos was never a problem. Trusting him is another story. Forgiving him is impossible.

Akantha is the Nazis' most wanted as she races them through Europe to locate the spear. The road is lined with bullets, betrayal, soldiers, and heartbreak. She must navigate it all, along with her past with Damianos, if she is to find the spear. Her life and the fate of the world hang on her success...or failure.

Fans of Indiana Jones and Wonder Woman are sure to love this fast-paced adventure about a new form of immortal hero. Not quite a goddess, not a mere mortal. A woman with a curse and a destiny she isn't sure she is ready to face.

win special subscriber-only contests and giveaways as well as receiving information on upcoming releases and special excerpts.

All reviews are **welcome** and **appreciated**. Please consider leaving one on your favorite social media and book buying sites.

For books in the world of romance and speculative fiction that embody Innovation, Creativity, and Affordability, check out City Owl Press at www.cityowlpress.com.

ACKNOWLEDGMENTS

We'd would like to thank Ellis Paul, Mark Erelli, Lori McKenna, and many other amazing musicians for providing background music used during writing. The playlist for this book can be found on Spotify.

We'd also like to thank all of our beta readers who read this and provided feedback. And we'd like to thank all of the folks who kept asking when the next book is coming out.

ABOUT THE AUTHORS

SYDNEY ASHCROFT originally hails from Pennsylvania and is a die-hard Penn State fan, but moved to New England over twenty years ago and has never looked back. She currently resides in Maine along with her daughter, a beagle, a cane corso, and a foster beagle. During the day she works full time in the information technology field and writes by night. Tea, chocolate, and folk music fuel her through the day and writing sessions. When she's not writing or working, she enjoys spending time with her daughter and dogs, going to see live music, and plotting shenanigans with her co-author.

DANI NICHOLS is a first time author living in the California Central Valley, happily ensconced between the wine trails and the foothills. She's a career public servant who frequently bribes the cat off the laptop so she can write the kinds of stories she loves to read. Dani stocks up with travel experiences, coffee, Ben and Jerry's Peanut Butter Cup ice cream, and the occasional bottle of wine to fuel her literary escapes.

www.nicholsandashcroft.com

ABOUT THE PUBLISHER

City Owl Press is a cutting edge indie publishing company, bringing the world of romance and speculative fiction to discerning readers.

Escape Your World. Get Lost in Ours!

www.cityowlpress.com

facebook.com/YourCityOwlPress

x.com/cityowlpress

instagram.com/cityowlbooks

pinterest.com/cityowlpress